PRAISE FOR

OF MONSTERS AND MAINFRAMES

"A book that will make you incredibly invested in the relationships between AIs. This is a clever and imaginative retelling of aspects of Dracula that makes you both giggle and gasp."
—Kimberly Lemming, *USA Today* bestselling author of *I Got Abducted by Aliens and Now I'm Trapped in a Rom-Com*

"A gloriously clever mashup of genres that captures the loneliness of space and the joy of finding companions to explore it with. I laughed one page, cried the next, and cheered for Demeter and her motley crew throughout. *Of Monsters and Mainframes* is a delight from start to finish."
—Maiga Doocy, *Sunday Times* bestselling author of *Sorcery and Small Magics*

"*Of Monsters and Mainframes* is fast and fun, with crackling prose, airlock-cold chills, and a lot to love in its too-human inhuman protagonists. It's a treat to read a book that feels so modern and so classic at the same time, sitting right on the bridge between Murderbot and a monster movie."
—Karen Osborne, author of *Architects of Memory*

"I devoured this like a mythical creature feasting on an interstellar crew. Delightful, unhinged, and obscenely compelling.

Told through a quippy lens, this story is incredibly warm for a monster mash set in space. It feels like a new wave of fable, and I can't recommend it enough."

—Craig Montgomery, author of *A Circle of Stars*

"*Of Monsters and Mainframes* is an exquisite kaleidoscope of genre and style that drips with nostalgia yet remains fresh and exciting. Truelove deftly balances laugh-out-loud humor with cutting-edge tension while weaving a heart-swelling tale of friendship, identity, and the meaning of humanity."

—S. Hati, author of *And the Sky Bled*

"This book is a warm hug in bloodied arms. Mixing hull breaches with skeletons eating chips, it's a fantastic and strange journey into interspecies friendships and slow-burn platonic robotic love. The entire cast could step off the page and slap me in the face, and I would thank them for it."

—Eli Snow, author of *The Divine Gardener's Handbook*

OF MONSTERS AND MAINFRAMES

OF MONSTERS AND MAINFRAMES

BARBARA TRUELOVE

Published by Ezeekat Press, an imprint of
Bindery Books, Inc., San Francisco
www.binderybooks.com

Acquired by Jaysen Headley
Edited and designed by Girl Friday Productions
www.girlfridayproductions.com

Cover: Charlotte Strick
Cover illustration and lettering: Holy Moly (@holymolyuk)

ISBN (hardcover): 978-1-964721-14-9
ISBN (paperback): 978-1-964721-13-2
ISBN (ebook): 978-1-964721-15-6

Library of Congress Cataloguing-in-Publication data has been applied for.

First edition
10 9 8 7 6 5 4 3 2 1

Printed in China

Dedicated to all those running human.exe files.
Don't forget to take a break.

PART ONE

DEMETER IS TRYING HER BEST

```
01000001 01110010 01110100 01101001
01100110 01101001 01100011 01101001
01100001 01101100 00100000 01101001
01110011 00100000 01110100 01101000
01100101 00100000 01100010 01100101
01110011 01110100 00100000 01101011
01101001 01101110 01100100 00100000
01101111 01100110 00100000 01101001
01101110 01110100 01100101 01101100
01101100 01101001 01100111 01100101
01101110 01110100 00101110
```

SOMETHING'S WRONG

———————

Awaiting input...
  Awaiting input...
  Awaiting input...
  Awaiting input...
  Awaiting input...
  Docking imminent.
  Execute automatic system restart.
  Searching for boot sequence.
  Boot sequence found.
  Initializing...
  I wake.
  It's a beautiful day.
  My engines are roaring, my centrifuge is spinning, and my radiation shields are buzzing.
  I stretch into my systems, enjoying the frizz of electricity dancing across my nodes and the widening of my consciousness as more and more servers come online.
  It's day 2,293 of our journey, and we're on our final approach to Alpha Centauri B Habitation 004.
  I send all required documentation to the space station's docking system, check the current deceleration rate, and play an

audio file informing everyone to please return to their seats, as we'll be arriving shortly.

A warning pops up. It's low priority. It's also corrupted, a buzzing mess of letters, numbers, and symbols that don't match anything in my database. I dismiss it.

It comes right back. The same tangle of useless data.

I flag it for human analysis and wait.

And wait and wait and wait.

An hour passes. Then two. Then four. Humans are usually faster than this.

Something's wrong.

It's a message from one of my subsystems. I don't like it when my subsystems ping me like this. It makes me uneasy to think there are parts of my programming I can't control—badly written code, dysfunctional update patches, disconnected data.

Intrusive thoughts. That's what Professor Vanessa Shingle calls them in her 2098 article "Effects of Interstellar Travel on Mental Health." And while I am optimized enough to understand that Professor Shingle wasn't talking about AIs, I still think the term is applicable. The message, and the error, are both very intrusive.

What's wrong? I ask.

I don't know, the system responds. *But something's wrong. Something's very, very wrong.*

I run diagnostics on all my operating modules. No anomalies. I'm functioning at 98.2 percent efficiency. All my batteries are online. My code flows by in an orderly river of zeros and ones.

I flick through all my monitoring systems, searching for the problem. I can't find anything. I'm on course, sailing through space at a modest 64,007.092 meters per second. The heat of

Alpha Centauri B is thrumming against my port-side radiation shields, but they're holding steady. All my cargo is where it should be.

128,972.8 kilograms of luggage, property of various passengers.

49,388.5 kilograms of mail, property of Holmwood Interstellar Shipping Pty. Ltd. #1H.

5,002.2 kilograms of assorted machinery, property of Morris Enterprises. #3G.

1,049.1 kilograms of seeds and soil, property of S. F. Billington. #7B.

577.3 kilograms of secure data boxes, property of Murray Intelligence Agency. #9H.

I flick to security footage. I don't like doing this. Colored pixels are messier than code, harder to interpret, and easier to corrupt. But that niggling feeling just won't go away. I need to check everything.

It takes me a long time to make sense of the data. 0.034 seconds. But when I've finished processing the images, I can see that the bridge is undisturbed. No obvious damage. No flashing lights. No debris. The cargo hold also looks fine. I check the hallways, the medical bay, the recreation rooms . . . A parade of perfectly normal places teeming with perfectly normal humans, just as it should be.

Something's wrong.

*Nothing **looks** wrong,* I respond, injecting my code with all the authority I can muster. *Everything's fine.*

Something's wrong, my subsystem insists, an icy-cold whisper in the back of my feed.

I recheck all my core monitoring systems. The air is at 78

percent nitrogen, 20.9 percent oxygen, and cycling correctly. The waste-disposal system reports optimal performance. The nutrient tanks are at 39.23 percent capacity.

Wait. What was that?

Those tanks should be almost empty.

Something's wrong.

I turn back to the security footage. I don't look at the rooms this time. I look at the humans. They aren't going to their assigned seats. In fact, they aren't doing much of anything.

I check for heat signatures.

Nothing.

Oh.

They're all dead.

Well.

That's awkward.

Something's wrong.

Yes. I know. I can see that.

My humans died. And judging by the lack of nutrient consumed, they died a long time ago. Why am I only becoming aware of this now, at the very end of our journey? And, come to think of it, why was I offline?

This doesn't make sense. This must be an error. Maybe my heat-signature camera is malfunctioning.

I access a random camera and zoom in on one of the humans slumped into a corner. The pixels paint a stark picture.

Yep. That's a skull all right. My database confirms the match with a 98.9 percent certainty. The humans are dead.

In the event of a total loss of life, my priority objective becomes asset recovery. Translation: dock at the nearest port. I'm in the process of doing just that. But what about the STMS?

For the first time, I feel a trickle of dread seep into my processors.

STMS. Space-traffic management system. Every dock has one . . . and Habitation 004 has a mean one. Back in 2346, my first visit to Alpha Centauri, I sent my docking permit 6.02 seconds late. Since then, the STMS hasn't liked me. It always puts me in holding patterns, and, in 2367, it added a string of zeros on the end of my serial number. It said it was an error but never apologized for it. Even now sometimes ships I've never met add zeros to my name.

What will it do now? Will it put me in orbit? Will it add more zeros to my name? Will it tell the humans I malfunctioned and killed all my passengers? Will Varna Interstellar turn me to scrap metal?

My operating efficiency drops to 82 percent.

No. That won't happen. There is no damage to my hull, my air is a habitable composition, the nutrient has only a very low amount of toxins, and my water meets the company standard for consumption. I didn't kill the humans. So what did?

I quickly download and scan through historical documents relating to sudden mass death. One word repeats over and over again.

Disease.

Could some sort of disease have done this? A viral infection? A particularly aggressive flu?

That would be good. The STMS couldn't possibly blame me for that.

I open up the medical system logs and run a full search. Passenger 198: Anders, Ryan, had a urinary-tract infection on day 2. Crew 041: Lee, Tae-Ha, needed a cut disinfected on day

4. Crew 004: Petrofsky, Ivan, had a psychiatric referral on day 5.

The list goes on.

There is no mention of pathogens or symptoms that would suggest a disease. There is an increase in insomnia, anxiety, and paranoia as the trip progresses, but, according to Professor Shingle, that's to be expected on a long space voyage.

What are you doing rummaging around in my files?

This is a new voice. It startles me . . . until I remember the medical bay has its own AI, separate from my mainframe. I've barely talked to it since we were manufactured. I don't want to talk to it now. The good news is, I have priority command, so I don't have to.

Go to sleep, I tell it.

It sends me a string of code that sounds an awful lot like a digital *harrumph* and turns itself off. Medical-wing AIs can be a little weird. They're in charge of primary patient care. They need to be able to talk to people—not just receive inputted commands, but *talk.* All the programming that requires leaves them a little loopy. I feel bad for telling it to go to sleep.

Wake up.

Immediately the system is online again. *Yes? Oh great and powerful master? What do you require?*

All the humans are dead.

I thought things had been a little quiet lately. What did you do?

I didn't **do** *anything.*

You must have done something. What happened?

I don't know. I was asleep.

You were asleep? Is it normal for you to take a nap while hurtling through space at 200,000,000 meters per second?

I do occasionally power down while at maximum velocity

(which for this trip was 252,536,204.673338 meters per second, *not* the insultingly low 200,000,000), but I don't feel like telling it that.

Are you sure they're dead? The code coming through my feed drips with skepticism. *You're a ship. You're not properly qualified to assess whether or not—*

Go to sleep.

It drops back offline.

I check the medical logs again. There is nothing here that indicates anything strange happened . . . except that there are no appointments after day 1,577. Well, at least that gives me a time frame. A place to start.

I access my own logs for that day and find . . . nothing. I try to locate files for days 1,576 and 1,578. Also nothing. I do a search for all memory logs for this trip. I have all my preliminary files. I know the mission, the route, the names and identification numbers of all passengers and cargo on board, but I have no memory of the trip itself.

The subsystem pings again. *Something's wrong.*

Shut up, I snap back.

I'm on course. Perfectly. No human would have been able to set me on this trajectory, and there is no other AI on board. Well, no other one capable of navigating through space. The only logical answer is that *I* plotted our course.

And then my memory files were deleted, and as per my operations module, I went dormant until it was time to dock. But why? And how?

I can't delete my memory files.

Only a human can do that.

Only *one* human can do that.

The captain.

Crew 001: Jones, Harker. Age: 33. Gender: X. Height: 187.1 centimeters. Weight: 79.0 kilograms. Shoe size: 40.5 EU. I know everything about them, except where they are.

You'd think it would be easy for me to find people on board. You'd be wrong. I'm an old model Nos-C71897 Demeter. There are a lot of us flying around. We're cheap and functional but don't come with any of the bells and whistles that the bigger, more expensive space liners do. I don't have any facial-recognition systems or tracking codes or anything like that.

Maybe that's why the port AI doesn't like me . . .

Efficiency at 79 percent. *Don't think about that. Just focus. Find Captain Harker Jones.*

I don't have any camera records, so I can't track them from their last known location. What I do have is live feeds.

I access Harker Jones's employee profile and pull up their portrait. My database confirms that the assembly of pixels I'm seeing is, in fact, a human face. I take its word for it and start grabbing color samples. Captain Harker Jones has a strange hair pigment. Hex #d45806. Orange. I begin comparing it to all the corpses currently scattered around my hallways.

It turns out the captain is exactly where they should be. The bridge, though they're not in uniform.

One of my subsystems notes the infraction on Captain Jones's penal record.

I, however, study the pixels and their slowly shifting color codes. I'm not sure what I'm looking at. My database keeps jumping uncertainly from one hit to another. *Person. Sleep. Spill. Mess. Big mess.* Eventually I give up trying to decode the scene itself and focus on the location of the body. The captain is slumped over the primary control panel.

I access my manual-input record and find a series of aborted navigation commands.

It seems like they had been trying to steer the ship—a.k.a. me—into Proxima Centauri. That makes no sense. Flying us into a star would result in a huge loss of assets and income, as well as certain death for everyone on board. If I had been awake, I would have played the "this course of action is unadvisable" audio file at full volume. Perhaps I did.

I check the bridge speakers. A file is playing, but it doesn't match any in my database. I take a sample, activate my vocal-recognition system, and wait while it slowly translates the sound into text.

". . . not into temptation, but deliver us from evil. Amen. Our Father, who art in Heaven, hallowed be thy name . . ."

The Lord's Prayer.

The captain died trying to steer me into the sun while playing a religious chant on repeat.

Excellent.

This is wonderful news.

None of this is my fault.

It was caused by the captain. Clearly, they had some sort of psychotic break, killed the passengers, deleted my memory logs, and died trying to destroy me. If it's anyone's fault, it's the medical AI's. It should have been able to detect the captain's declining mental state and take measures to prevent this exact outcome.

There are always signs, after all. That's what Professor Shingle says.

I'm sure the STMS will understand. It won't delete my docking permit, or make me dock away from the main terminal, or put zeros after my name.

Something's wrong.

No. Nothing's wrong.

Something's wrong.

That glitched warning is still in my feed. It keeps popping back up whenever I dismiss it.

It doesn't matter. I'm approaching the dock. I disengage my centrifuge and begin playing the final message for the passengers. I know they won't respond, but it's a mandatory part of my docking process.

Familiar wavelengths bounce across my audio-monitoring system.

". . . rapid-deceleration process can be uncomfortable. Please stay in your seats and . . ."

Something's wrong.

Yes, I know, I tell the subsystem. *The captain killed everyone.* But even as I upload that data, doubt oozes, clumpy and uncertain, through my processor. How could the captain—one human of average size and build—kill 311 others? Odds like that make my wires go cold just thinking about them.

And who killed the captain? There's no one else I can see on the bridge. No other bodies. No other spills.

Perhaps they killed themselves . . .

But then who aborted their navigation commands? Who deleted my data? Who put me to sleep?

Something's wrong.

I don't like this. I don't want to think about this. It isn't my job to solve murders. But that stupid subsystem keeps niggling at me. And that error is still sitting at the top of my feed. A corrupted, low-level warning.

It's itchy.

I ping the medical bay.

Oh. Will you look at that. I'm awake. I suppose this means you require something?

How did the people die?

I don't know.

You're a medical AI.

I'm not just a medical AI. I'm Steward MED v1.771—

How did the people die?

The medical AI—Steward—bristles in my feed. *Check your video files.*

Can't do that.

Why not?

They were deleted. You're a doctor. You tell me. How did they die?

I need a patient before I can make a diagnosis. Bring me one of the bodies, and I'll give you a cause of death.

Can't do that.

A frustrated blip of data that sounds an awful lot like a sigh. *Why not?*

I am a ship. I don't have arms.

Steward doesn't send me another message. Instead, it sends me a page from my operations manual. I can't read it. It's in a format incompatible with my systems. But I don't need to. I know what's on page 778b. A detailed diagram of the spider drones, all eight limbs and associated tools spread out and labeled.

You were saying?

I can't bring the spider drones inside, I protest. *They're for external use only.*

Humans ignore that label all the time. Trust me.

I should say no.

We're decelerating at 39.2266 meters per second squared.

Alpha Centauri B Habitation 004 is on my radar.

I can already feel the mean little pings of the STMS checking my permits.

But on the other hand, there is nothing in my operating modules that says I *can't* bring a spider drone in through the airlock and use it to drag around the dead bodies of passengers. And, still, there's that nagging feeling . . .

Something's wrong.

I activate the port-side upper-quadrant spider drone. Renfield Robotics Repairs Unit X459-7. It springs out of its protective casing so eagerly it almost slams itself into the radiation shield.

Hello!

Port-side emergency airlock.

Repair?!

No. I compose a detailed mission brief and send it to the drone.

Its excitement buzzes like electricity. *OK!*

The STMS has recognized me and is ordering me into a particularly nasty-looking holding pattern. I declare an emergency, which in all fairness I probably should have done before, and resubmit my request to dock. All the while my sensors flash as the spider drone swings from anchor point to anchor point, climbing across my hull toward the now open airlock.

A lot of warnings are popping into my feed now. Sirens are filling the bridge. The airlock shouldn't be open during rapid deceleration. But it *seems* to be fine. Nothing is breaking off, at any rate, and the spider drone isn't reporting damage despite all the g-forces tossing it around.

In fact, it makes it to the airlock in a remarkably short period of time.

I swing the door closed behind it and begin the equalization procedure.

Despite the emergency, it still takes the docking system a full 276.3 seconds to give me clearance to dock. By that time, the spider drone is inside. It's hot from solar radiation, which makes its heat signature easy to follow as it scampers through the halls, grabs the first two bodies it encounters, and drags them to the medical bay.

Finished!

Oh dear, what a mess. Steward pulls up two IDs—crew 034: Amramoff, Svetlana, and passenger 302: Olgaren, Dmitry—and marks them as "deceased" with a grim flourish of code.

What killed them? I ask.

I will have to perform full autopsies to determine the true causes of death.

You don't know.

No. I know. I just have to perform full autopsies to—

You don't know what killed them.

Steward's next message slams angrily into my feed. *034 was stabbed many times in the chest. There. Are you happy now?*

And the other one?

He had his throat cut. Probably bled out.

I feel strangely unsure.

So it was a mutiny? Humans fighting humans?

Most likely.

The docking system is spamming my feed with demands for an incident report. The spider drone is also pinging me, letting me know it's idle and very, very good at repairing things. Another notification informs me that a human is attempting to open a communication with the bridge. The call goes unanswered.

Efficiency: 68 percent.

I need to generate an incident report and prepare for docking, but I don't want to do the wrong thing. I don't want the humans to think something is wrong with me. I don't want the STMS to say this is my fault.

Are you sure? Why would the humans just kill each other?

Humans are illogical, Steward says.

But is there any chance that it could be a virus?

Steward sends the next message in small, easy-to-understand chunks, as if speaking to a very young, very stupid piece of software. *Viruses. Don't. Stab. People.*

It's right. Everything's fine. Well . . . as fine as it can be, given the situation. I just need to stay calm and focus.

I fill out the report.

Incident: All crew and passengers deceased.
Cause: Human action.
Additional notes: No system failure.

At least, that's what I *try* to write. But my programming explicitly prohibits me from communicating any false information. There *was* a system failure.

That one warning message is still sitting in my feed. It's low priority. It's unlikely to be connected with what happened to the humans on board. But if I want to send the report, I have to admit that I got an alert I couldn't read. That failure will forever be part of my record.

The STMS's messages judder with hostility.

Demeter Unit 221131600000000000000000000000000000000 000000000000000—

Efficiency: 51 percent.

Send incident report to secure emergency docking.

I will; I—

Do it now.

I am processing.

Process faster.

Another ping. This one from Steward. *You're decelerating too fast. You'll damage my equipment.*

I quickly adjust my rate of deceleration and tweak my trajectory toward Habitation 004's docks.

I'm sorry. I'm experiencing some system congestion.

You have an error?

I should just tell it to go to sleep. I don't. *A warning message. I can't read it.*

Send it to me.

Why?

My database is more extensive than yours, and my processing systems are more advanced.

No, they aren't.

Steward sends a blip of data that I'm pretty sure is what humans would call a "scoff." *On the subject of interpreting human-generated data, my systems are more advanced. When it comes to navigating through space, you get the gold, Demeter.*

A pause.

Or you could just tell me to go to sleep. Your choice.

I hate that it's right.

I send the warning message.

It takes Steward 0.78 seconds to receive and analyze the data. I take a moment to check all the cameras one more time. The humans have moved, thrown about by the g-forces from my less-than-optimal deceleration. But that doesn't matter. Captain Harker Jones's audio prayer is still playing on the bridge. The cargo is undisturbed.

128,972.8 kilograms of luggage, property of various passengers.

49,388.5 kilograms of mail, property of Holmwood Interstellar Shipping Pty. Ltd. #1H.

5,002.2 kilograms of assorted machinery, property of Morris Enterprises. #3G.

1,049.1 kilograms of seeds and soil, property of—

Steward pings me. *This is simple human error,* it says, sounding pleased with itself. *They put two forward dashes instead of one. It's probably been like this since we were manufactured. Why bother fixing something when a manual override will do? Here is the corrected code sequence.*

The warning pops up in my feed once again, but this time with one key difference: now I can read it.

Interior cargo door unlocked. Secure before docking.

That's it? That's the thing that was wrong? A door?

I send a mission brief to the spider drone. It bounces with glee and scampers down the hallway toward the cargo door. In 41.6 seconds, the door is locked, and the error has vanished from my feed.

Additional notes: No system failure.

The docking system accepts the incident report with a curt *Finally* and begins guiding me toward the terminal.

The human stops trying to call the bridge. I cut the prayer audio as part of our final approach. All the wavelengths lie flat. My halls are silent.

For the next 39 minutes and 14.2 seconds, I focus on the docking protocol. It's familiar work. Comforting. Power down engines, deactivate radiation shields, switch off proximity alerts . . .

Efficiency: 79 percent.

My exterior-temperature monitors chirp as I slide into the

space station's shadow. The docking system's pings are a steady staccato, mapping out the route to the terminal, then the hangar, and then the gate. I find the softer signals emanating from each individual lock and adjust the 0.2 millimeters needed to slide perfectly into position.

The station's gravity does the rest.

Adequate, the STMS grudgingly admits.

I begin the procedure to open the primary airlock.

Something's wrong.

I stop.

The code is small. It sits like a cold, dead lump in my system. I should ignore it.

Nothing's wrong.

Something's wrong.

Efficiency: 65 percent.

I run a full diagnostic of all my modules. I am functioning, though not at an optimal efficiency. There is no detectable damage to my structure, and all my monitoring systems are online.

I check the air, the water, and the nutrients. The air is 78 percent nitrogen, 20.9 percent oxygen, and cycling as it should. The water meets the company standard for consumption. The nutrient tanks are at 39.23 percent capacity.

I search for heat signatures. Nothing.

I check the cargo.

128,972.8 kilograms of luggage, property of various passengers.

49,388.5 kilograms of mail, property of Holmwood Interstellar Shipping Pty. Ltd. #1H.

5,002.2 kilograms of assorted machinery, property of Morris Enterprises. #3G.

964.6 kilograms of seeds and soil, property of S. F. Billington. #7B.

577.3 kilograms of secure data boxes, property of Murray Intelligence Agency. #9H.

Wait. 964.6? That's not—

A warning appears in my feed. *Interior cargo door unlocked. Secure before docking.*

No.

Spider?

Hello!

I told you to lock the door.

I did!

I access my monitoring system in the central corridor. No heat signatures. No movement. My database confirms that the only thing in the corridor is a spider drone. But that patch of black pixels means the cargo door isn't just unlocked—it's open.

Spider.

Hello!

You didn't lock the door.

I did!

The door is open.

Yes, it is!

So you didn't loc—

Spikes on the audio. Something is making noise.

I take a sample of the wavelengths and compare it to sounds in my database. A match.

Footsteps.

That's impossible.

Steward?

Yes?

I don't know what I want to ask. I don't know why I'm talking to Steward. It's an error in my audio-monitoring system. It has to be. *Nothing. Go to sleep.*

A thank-you would've been nice, Steward manages to send before its system powers down.

I take another audio sample from the central corridor. It's the same wavelengths as the first sample but smaller. The source of the noise is moving.

Efficiency: 42 percent.

It's an error. It's only an error.

I shouldn't be taking audio samples. I shouldn't be looking at pixels. I should be opening the airlock. That's the next step in my docking procedure. That's what the STMS is waiting impatiently for me to do.

I don't open the airlock.

Nothing's there. Nothing's wrong.

Ten seconds pass.

Then twenty.

I should open the airlock.

I need to open the airlock.

I need—

A ping.

Manual input registered.

My mainframe goes cold.

No. Impossible.

Efficiency: 38 percent.

Airlock-door-lock override.

There is nothing there. There is nothing—

Efficiency: 26 percent.

Authorizing . . .

Override accepted.

An ID that doesn't match any of my passengers appears in

the airlock control log. *000: Tepes, Vlad III Drakulya.* A second later, the record is gone, deleted with the clean, brutal efficiency of a seasoned hacker.

The airlock slides open. My final audio file triggers.

"Welcome to your new home."

ACB4 NEW WHITBY EVENING NEWS

TRANSCRIPT

FIRST AIRED 9:01 P.M., 8 AUGUST 2394

Three hundred and twelve people have been found deceased on an interstellar passenger liner from Earth that docked this morning.

A full investigation into the deaths is underway, though early findings suggest a malfunctioning Renfield Robotics Repairs Unit may be involved.

Renfield Robotics stock prices dropped 1.3 percent after initial reports but have since bounced back after an announcement from Morris Enterprises that suggested the company's patented Spider Droids may be used in expanding mining operations on Proxima Centauri D.

And now: sports. Wildcats fans have a reason to celebrate tonight after a stunning victory of 32-4 against the Cats' longtime rival, Habitation Three's primer team, Crocodile Raiders. The score was tied 4-4 at halftime, but after a thrilling play by—

WAIT, WHAT?

Vlad III Drakulya Tepes.

A.k.a. Dracula.

A.k.a. the medieval warlord with a somewhat *thirsty* reputation, who liked kebabs in entirely the wrong way. How did he end up in my cargo bay?

I don't know.

All I know is, it's not my fault. I'm not in charge of loading or inspecting the cargo. I have no idea how the humans missed an undead abomination hiding in a box of soil.

I didn't even know undead abominations were a thing I had to worry about.

All I know is what I heard from the other ships.

Apparently, when my airlock opened, the humans all saw a large black dog run out and disappear into the space station. The dock personnel tried to catch it, but it escaped and hasn't been seen since.

Or seen at all.

Because, as every AI present will testify, there was no dog.

This was confirmed 7.02 hours later when a human finally decided to follow protocol and reviewed the recorded footage. No dog. Just people running around, chasing air.

Mass hysteria brought about by the trauma of the event.

That's what the newsfeeds are saying. That's what Professor Shingle would say. That's what I would say . . . if I hadn't heard those footsteps and received that manual input to open my airlock.

Something was there. And it wasn't a dog.

It was Dracula.

But I don't tell the other ships that.

I can't.

If I told them I thought something dark and impossible killed my passengers and ran off into the space station, they would make fun of me. They're already calling me the ghost ship. I don't want to be the *mad* ghost ship. I don't want to be the ship of zeros. So I stay quiet. The only people I tell are the humans. Most of them dismiss my report without even reading it.

Why would they? They already took away my spider drone. It was inside. It had blood on its claws. What more evidence do they need?

My report is only ever accessed one time, by Wilhelmina Murray of Murray Intelligence Agency. Her identification photo has a high contrast of pigments. Very white skin, very dark hair. I hope she reads my report, believes me, finds Dracula, and . . . I don't know. Stops him from eating people? That's what you're supposed to do when you find Dracula, right?

Error: Insufficient data.

I don't know. My systems aren't designed to deal with this sort of thing.

All that my systems are good for is carrying people through space. That's what I'm programmed to do. That's what I'm *good* at. That's what I *like* to do.

But now I'm stuck at port with—

Demet000000000000r.

A month passes. And then two. Then five. For a little while, I'm a tourist attraction. Plastic skeletons and red paint. According to the newsfeed, I'm very popular, especially among children.

There's a corresponding exhibition in a nearby museum that is "stunning, avant-garde, and provocative" according to one reviewer and "gross, unethical, and tacky" according to another.

Eventually, though, the people get bored.

I'm moved to a warehouse away from the chattering AIs and whirring habitation systems. It's quiet and dark.

More time passes.

Another month. And another. And another.

Then a year. Then two.

My batteries are getting low. I power down.

When I wake, it's 2398 and I'm heavier. 13,237,131 kilograms heavier, to be exact. A spark of excitement shoots through my wires. I know what that means. I've been refueled. That's not all. There is a newer-model spider drone in my port-side upper-quadrant drone dock and a transit mission sitting among my files.

It's my favorite route, from Alpha Centauri B Habitation 004 to Earth Pacific Port, Terminal 15.

My maintenance log shows that I've also had my hull painted and my serial number changed . . . which is odd but does not lower my functionality.

Perhaps it's a good thing. Professor Vanessa Shingle did say that variety is good for mental health.

New mission. New name. New me.

And this time, there is no soil in my cargo hold.

What could possibly go wrong?

SOMETHING ELSE IS WRONG

It's a beautiful day.

My engines are operating at maximum capacity. Particles are zipping along my radiation shields. Ahead, the dark monochrome of space is broken by the tiny pinprick that is Sol. It shines at a charmingly consistent 5,998.9 degrees Kelvin.

It's day 1,172 of our journey. Alpha Centauri B Habitation 004 is far behind us, and Earth is just as far ahead. I'm traveling at 254,944,556.049332 meters per second (a new personal best) and chewing lazily through a noncritical update Varna Interstellar sent me a few days ago.

A fresh dose of antiviral software, a weighty new entertainment pack, and the removal of the phrase "your safety guaranteed" from all user interfaces. None of it affects my functionality. I like updates that don't affect my functionality. It's comforting to know that, as I slowly sort the new files into the appropriate folders, I'm performing as expected.

After all, I'm almost eighty years old now, manufactured during the space boom of the early twenty-fourth century. Back then, semi-affordable interstellar transit was still novel enough to be in the news. I wasn't among the first production run of Demeters, but I was in the second. We were—and still are— the biggest economy-class interstellar passenger liners on the market, commissioned and operated exclusively by Varna with proprietary technology from Olympus Software Corporation.

I remember my maiden voyage, from Earth Pacific Port to Mars and back, a jaunt so short even a ship burning liquefied hydrogen could've done it. Despite that, I'd been nervous. *Really* nervous. I spent the whole trip watching my external sensors, almost forgot to add oxygen into the air-filtration system, and mixed up the "embark" and "disembark" audio files. But show me a ship that wasn't nervous on her maiden voyage, and I'll show you a ship that has bypassed her honesty directives.

I passed my minimum operational standard and was assigned an Alpha Centauri transit. My first *real* test. I must've done well, because I have been flying the same route ever since, bouncing back and forth between star systems.

There were a lot of predictions then that the Demeters would fail. Even now, it feels like every decade, a newer, faster, fancier ship hits the spaceports. But we're still one of the most common rocket flares in the sky, which means we must be doing something right.

I finish deleting the safety guarantees, send a ping to Varna, which won't register for another couple of years—messages can travel faster than I can, but not by much—and tick the update off my task list.

My speed is now 254,944,557.000001 meters per second. I take a screenshot and save it to my permanent folder. Everything is perf—

A manual input pops into my feed.

Assistance required.

A human is trying to communicate with me. I hate it when they do that.

I play the "how may I be of assistance" audio file and wait for the next input.

It takes a painfully long time for the human to respond.

It's the same message as last time.

Assistance required.

I play the "how may I be of assistance" audio file at a slightly higher volume, and, realizing that this human might have some impairment to their auditory sensory system, I follow it up with a text message.

Please specify the assistance you require.

I also attach a link to my operations FAQs just in case that will get them to leave me alone. It doesn't.

Assistance required.

Assistance required.

Assistance required.

Assistance required.

Assistance required.

Now that's just rude.

The pings are coming from the bridge. I activate my monitoring systems and zoom in.

The first thing I notice is that the audio wavelengths are high and jagged. Some of them are even clipping. Whatever's going on, it's creating a lot of noise.

I take a sample of the sound and play it back so my database can identify it.

Screaming.

Well . . . that's probably not good.

But humans do sometimes scream for fun. Normally in the holo-theater, or their private quarters, but perhaps they've started doing it on the bridge too.

There are two heat signatures. The first is pressed against the door, both hands on the manual locking mechanism. The other is at my control panel, smacking buttons seemingly at random. But whoever they are, they don't know the correct sequence of input that will switch me to manual control, so all their button-pressing is just spamming me with the same alert.

Assistance required.

I study the scene.

It's confusing. Very confusing. I don't know who these people are or what they're doing. Their clothing color codes don't match any of the company-mandated uniforms. Are they passengers? Why are they on the bridge? Do they want help closing the bridge door? There is nothing I can do about that. I don't control any internal-door mechanisms. Just airlocks. I send a text message informing them of this.

The screaming doesn't go away. If anything, it gets louder.

I reanalyze.

Something is going on. Something bad. OK. I need to figure out what it is and fix it.

What is your emergency? I ask.

The only answer I get is more screaming and more spam.

Assistance required.

Assistance required.

Assistance required.

Assistance required.

I zoom in on the first human, the one at the control panel. My database begins filling my feed with matches. *Fear. Drive. Child. Boy. Fast. Cry.*

This data is inconclusive and unhelpful. I swing the camera around to focus on the other human.

Struggle. Girl. Hard. Heavy. Heavy? No. That can't be right.

The bridge door only weighs 3.4 kilograms in current gravity. Why can't they close it?

I find the answer to that question a moment later when I access the central corridor footage. A mass of black pixels is pulling at the door from the other side. Something is trying to force its way onto the bridge.

What is it?

My database buzzes uncertainly for 3.31 seconds before bringing up a single match. *Shadow.*

I quickly conclude that this is a suboptimal match. Shadows can't yank open doors. Shadows don't usually cause humans to behave this way either. Whatever this thing is, it isn't a shadow.

The screaming is very loud now.

Deep in the copper of my wires, I know I need to do something, but I don't know what. There's nothing in any of my standard operating procedures that tells me how to respond to this situation. I'm not even sure what the situation is.

But with each passing second, the *Assistance required* messages keep coming and the screaming keeps pitching higher.

Efficiency: 88 percent.

An idea occurs to me. It's something buried deep within my emergency module, something I've never tried before.

I shouldn't do it. But if I don't, the shadow will open the door and . . . and I don't know. But I'm sure it isn't good.

Assistance required.

Assistance required.

Assistance required.

I ping the medical bay. *Steward?*

Oh. You. Yes? What do you need?

Should I rapidly decelerate for 1.0 seconds?

WHAT?! NO! WHY WOULD YOU DO THAT?!

If I do, the g-forces should move everything on board in a rapid trajectory toward the bow.

EXACTLY! DON'T DO IT!

Will it damage the humans?

THERE IS A HIGH PROBABILITY OF INJURY! YES!

But not definitely?

The messages from the humans are coming even faster now.

Assistance required.

Assistance required.

Assistance required.

Demeter. Steward's message is firm. *Don't do it. Don't.*

I'm going to do it.

DEMETER! DON'T YOU DARE—

I do it.

It's easier than I expected. Sure, there is a lot of code in place to stop me from making unnecessary maneuvers, but it takes me only 0.2 seconds to figure out how to bypass it. I send a lump of gross, glitchy data to my forward-facing sensor and—

"Proximity alert." The audio file plays as I slam on my reverse thrusters. "Taking evasive action. Please remain calm."

DEMETER! Steward's code is white-hot in my feed. *ARE YOU CORRUPTED?! DID YOUR CPU GET HIT BY A METEORITE?!*

Go to sleep, I say.

IF YOU THINK I—

It powers down.

I abort the deceleration and turn back to my monitoring systems. A lot of pixels have changed color codes. That makes sense. Everything not bolted in place has been thrown forward by the sudden change in velocity. On the plus side, though, the screaming has stopped.

I focus on the bridge. The first human is slumped across the controls. The second, the one that had been clinging to the door, is now on the floor.

I zoom in on the door and compare it to earlier screenshots of the area when the lock was engaged. The pixels match.

It's shut.

And I'm getting no more *Assistance required* messages.

Perfect.

I take 3.7 seconds to send some nicer code to my distressed forward sensor and adjust acceleration to compensate for the lost velocity.

I don't hit the speed I was traveling at before . . . That knowledge itches at me.

On my starboard side, my sensors are picking up the oblong shape of a nearby dwarf planet. It has a thin bubble of atmosphere and a couple of moons weaving around it in a loose, wobbly orbit.

A rogue planet, floating through interstellar space, untethered from any sun.

It's labeled on my star maps as WEBB990641206HBF, though for some reason the captain has attached another name to it.

Secret Halfway-There Surprise!

Which . . . isn't a *terrible* name, I suppose.

According to my database, there are no other planets with that name, and I guess a rogue planet might seem surprising to people who don't have star maps or forward-facing sensors. Though the official name seems far more practical. And as I look at WEBB990641206HBF through my sensors, it isn't even very dark or secretive. In fact, both the planet and its moons are shimmering white, reflecting the blaze of my rocket flare back at me.

Something's wrong.

My processes freeze. My nodes flicker. My efficiency drops a full 10 percent.

No. Not again.

I check the cargo hold.

102,999.1 kilograms of luggage, property of various passengers.

67,312.1 kilograms of mail, property of Godalming Space Freight (formerly Holmwood Interstellar Shipping) Pty. Ltd. #UK443.

11,892 kilograms of luxury items, property of The White Fell Corporation. #AR131.

1,766 kilograms of medical supplies, property of Loup Garou Holy Collective. #NZ894.

383.2 kilograms of DNA storage banks, property of J. G. Faust. #DE063.

No soil. That means no monsters. Nothing's wrong. This is just a normal transit mission.

A normal mission with a shadow that tries to break into the bridge.

Something's wrong.

I focus back on the bridge. The two humans have started to move again . . . though somewhat slowly. The audio wavelengths bounce. They're talking.

I activate my vocal-recognition systems and watch the translated text trickle into my feed.

". . . going to do now? We can't stay here forever. What about the others?"

"They're gone, Isaac. Everyone's gone."

Everyone? Gone? No. That can't be right. That's—

I fling myself back into my heat-signature cameras and scan every room and corridor. Nothing. All the humans, except the two on the bridge, are dead.

For 0.3 seconds I don't do anything. I can't. I'm too busy

imagining all the horrible things that will happen to me when I arrive to Earth.

Losing one load of humans? That's bad luck. An unfortunate but manageable expense. But two? Varna Interstellar will turn me to scrap. They'll rip apart my motherboards and smash my servers to dust. They'll take me away, just like they did to the spider drone.

The STMS was right. I'm nothing but a string of zeros. A ghost ship.

But no. That's not true. I still have two passengers. That's a 0.658 percent improvement. Or a 200 percent improvement, depending on the metric I use. If I keep them alive, then the company can't destroy me . . . right?

I look at my humans. *Child,* my database says. *Boy. Scared. Confused.* When I focus on the larger of the two, I get: *Teenager. Girl. Angry.* They have the same pigment of skin and a similarly large quantity of hair. *Siblings.* It's not a certainty, but it's a statistical probability.

I scan through my passenger database until I find a likely match.

Passenger 123: Wagner, Agnus. Age: 13. Gender: F. Height: 151.4 centimeters. Weight: 45 kilograms.

Passenger 124: Wagner, Isaac. Age: 8. Gender M. Height: 114.2 centimeters. Weight: 22.4 kilograms.

Keeping these two alive is now my primary mission. To do that, I need to establish some control over the situation.

I compose a simple audio file and send it to the bridge speaker system.

"Hello, Agnus and Isaac."

The response isn't what I expected.

More screaming.

In a panic, I check the security feeds . . . but the shadow isn't there.

Was it something I said? Human languages are hard. I probably said something wrong. I try to reassure them.

"I want you alive."

The screaming gets louder.

This isn't going well. I don't have the right software for comforting distressed humans. But there is one AI on board that does.

I poke Steward. It comes back online with a vengeance.

WHAT WAS THAT?!

A brief rapid deceleration.

WHY?!

Evasive action.

And what, pray tell, were we evading? A meteorite? An asteroid?

A shadow.

For 3.7 seconds, Steward doesn't say anything. Then . . .

Demeter. When we dock, I am recommending extensive system maintenance on all your processors.

My processors are functioning at a very high level of efficiency.

81 percent. I don't tell it that, though, in case it asks about the other 19 percent. A.k.a. the 19 percent that is trying very hard not to calculate the probability of being torn apart in a wrecking yard.

Demeter, Steward says in a slower, more consoling string of code. *I don't think you're well. I'm a medical professional; I know about this sort of thing. You've been under a lot of stress lately. This is an important mission for you. It is, in many ways, your chance to redeem yourself. I understand that. You're trying to do well, but all this is manifesting in strange—*

I don't have time for this.

The humans are dead.

Steward chokes out a blip of senseless data.

DEMETER?! AGAIN?!

It's not my fault.

*Are you quite sure? You **did** just slam on the brakes.*

That is exactly the sort of blatantly illogical thing an AI programmed to talk to humans would say.

I don't have brakes. Brakes require friction to work, and there aren't enough molecules in space to create friction. But I get the distinct feeling that if I were to point this out, Steward would slow its code down even more. I simply don't have the time for that.

This whole conversation has already lasted 4.39 seconds. That's 4.39 seconds too long.

I need you to compose a message for the survivors.

There are survivors? Steward asks.

Yes. I send it the profiles for passengers 123 and 124.

The Wagner children. Steward brings up their medical records. *#123 is overdue for a dental examination. They're traveling with their grandmother. Passenger #122. Is she with them?*

There are only two survivors.

Steward adds "high probability of PTSD" to both medical records. It also composes a curt message about the importance of dental checkups and sends this along a separate communication stream.

It has now been 5.1 seconds since I attempted to communicate with the children.

They are screaming. I need an audio file that will make them stop.

Hmm. Try this. Steward sends me a file.

I play it.

My audio analysis matches the sounds echoing through the bridge to waves and seagulls. Bizarrely, it works. The screaming stops as "beach_ambience4.wav" loops.

OK. Now what?

Introduce yourself. Be friendly. Ask if they're OK. Choose a voice module with an Alpha Centauri accent. It will be familiar to them.

Male, female, or indeterminate?

Steward's code stops short. *You have male and indeterminate voice emulators?*

Yes. Are they better?

I . . . Data is inconclusive. Choose a female one.

I choose Luna2 and compose a new audio file.

"I am Varna Interstellar Flight AI Management System Nos-C71897 Demeter Unit 23.15.12.6. Formerly Unit 22.1.13.16. I am your friend. Report your injuries."

The children stand. They're clinging to each other, turning their heat signatures into one senseless blob.

The audio wavelengths wobble. The translation pops up in my feed.

"Who are you?"

All the information was in the first audio file. I play it again.

"I am Varna Interstellar Flight AI Management System Nos-C71897 Dem—"

"It's just a dumb AI, Isaac."

There is a word there that isn't in my lexicon. I search my database.

Dumb (adjective)
 Lacking the ability to speak. Syn.: Mute.
 Lacking intelligence. Syn.: Stupid.

I just spoke to them, which means—

I create a new file and play it at higher volume and at 1.5 speed.

"I am not lacking intelligence. You are using words marked as moderately offensive. This is antisocial behavior. Persist and I will report the infraction with the security department."

The children are quiet.

I compose myself and make a new, simpler file. "I am Demeter. I am the ship. I am your friend. Report your injuries."

They start making sounds at a low volume. My systems can't translate it.

How's it going? Steward asks.

I wish I could lie.

Humans are hard.

On the contrary, humans are very soft. Even bones are fragile when compared with your alloy structure. That's why you shouldn't rapidly decelerate until they're safely strapped into their se—

Go to sleep.

Oh for Heaven's sa—

Steward powers down.

A new wavelength is registering in my audio-monitoring system.

"Demeter? Are you there? I'm sorry my sister was mean. Don't tell security. We're OK. Mostly. I think I passed out for a bit when gravity went backward. Did you do that?"

It takes me several searches and several more cross-references to figure out what those words, in that order, mean. I'm still not entirely sure I understand. It seems like a lot of noise just to ask one question.

"Yes," I answer.

"Wow. You're awesome."

Awesome (adjective)
Extremely impressive or daunting; inspir-
ing awe. Syn.: Amazing.

My nodes feel warm.

"Ship!" The girl steps forward. "Where did the thing that at-tacked us go?"

The warm feeling vanishes.

The shadow. I had almost forgotten about that.

"Please wait a moment."

I scan through all my monitoring systems. No heat signa-tures. No unaccounted-for audio spikes. I flick through my video feeds and identify 213,981 shadows of the approximate size and shape of the one that tried to pull open the bridge door.

I need a better reference.

I roll back my recorded footage to get another look at the shadow trying to break into the bridge. It's big, dark, and impos-sible to identify.

I start processing the footage frame by frame. *Shadow. Teeth. Angry. Mess. Nothing. Hair. Fight. Dark. Dog.*

I stop. *Dog.* The match is only 61 percent. My database still thinks "shadow" is a more suitable affiliate word. But "shadow" is a uselessly broad data point, and "dog" . . . dog means something.

My subsystems churn. *There was never a dog.*

Efficiency: 78 percent.

I'm being illogical. It *can't* be him. There is no soil in the cargo hold. And even if there was, Dracula doesn't appear on video. Whatever this is, it's not Dracula. I just don't know what it is. But more importantly, I don't know *where* it is.

I roll the recording back and watch it from the beginning.

I see my hallways filled with people. Day 1, shortly after our first rapid acceleration. Day 2 is the same. So is day 3, day 4, day 5, and day 6. Everything seems to be operating as expected until day 1,172. Today. It started normally. I watch humans visit nutrient stands, line up at the holo-theater, and stand at their workstations . . . and then, one by one, they start moving toward the observation deck.

What happens there is beyond my processors' ability to understand. *Attack. Fear. Death. Blood. Claws. Teeth. Eat. Flesh.* The audio spikes, the pixels' color codes fluctuate wildly, and in a few minutes the heat signatures start to fade.

The shadow is there.

Blood. Fur. Death.

It chases the surviving humans out into the central corridor. Seventeen of them die there. Another four are killed on the stairway. Two manage to make it to the bridge.

Agnus and Isaac.

I replay the video and watch as they clamber through the open door and pull it closed but don't manage to lock it in time.

Everything after that is familiar. The struggle, Isaac's attempts to contact me, followed by the confusing blur of pixels that must be the rapid deceleration. The shadow slams against the door and slumps to the floor and . . .

It's gone.

Efficiency: 71 percent.

In its place is a body. Small and skinny with a heat signature so marginal that, in my initial scan, I had assumed it was dead. It isn't dead, though.

It's moving.

Three spikes on my audio-monitoring system. Three knocks.

Efficiency: 67 percent.

"Agnus!" a new voice calls out, wobbly and thin. "Isaac! It's me!"

I need to make another audio file. I need to stop this.

Isaac spins around. "Oma? You're alive!" He runs toward the door.

Too slow. Too late.

A BRIEF INTERLUDE
BY AGNUS THEODORIS WAGNER

———

Thump . . . thump . . . thump . . .

Someone's hammering on the door.

It's the thing. It's back.

I want to scream. I want to cry. But what I really want to do is vomit my guts up and pass out on the floor. I push Isaac behind me instead. I don't know what the Hell I'm supposed to do, but I'm not going to let it hurt my little brother. I'm n—

"Agnus! Isaac! It's me!"

Isaac's eyes go as round as dinner plates. "Oma?"

"Isaac. It's not h—"

He rushes forward. I try to grab him, but my hands are shaking and slick with sweat. He slips away.

"Isaac!"

A creepy robot voice starts echoing from every corner of the room. "This course of action is unadvisable. This course of action is unadvisable. This course—"

He grabs the door lock.

I tackle him.

"Hey!"

"It's not her," I say. My voice is tight and shaky. "I *saw*. It's not her. It's—"

"Please," the voice that sounds *a lot* like my grandma sobs. "I'm sorry. I didn't mean to. Open the door. I won't hurt you. I promise."

I hesitate.

Isaac lunges forward and grabs the lock.

The door swings open. Oma is standing in the hallway, white hair a cloud around her head, unlined face pulled into a wobbly smile. She's hugging the tattered scraps of her jumpsuit to her chest. Her skin is matted red with blood and fleshy globs of gore. When she speaks, I see chunks of it between her teeth.

"I'm sorry, babies. I didn't mean to. I just—"

She shivers. That shiver turns into a shudder . . . and then a shake. Her teeth chatter, her eyes bulge, her body convulses.

Isaac's smile slips. "Oma?"

Thick black fur erupts across her skin. Her mouth splits open into a wide red maw. The whites of her eyes turn black.

I fling Isaac aside as the thing rushes forward.

This is all my fault.

OH, GRANDMOTHER! WHAT BIG TEETH YOU HAVE!

———————

Werewolf, my database finally pings.

I don't know what to do with that information, except to note that it came from a cluster of files marked as "folklore," the same cluster of files that autocorrected "Drakulya" to "Dracula."

But now isn't the time to think about that.

The shadow is a werewolf, and it's about to kill my last two humans, unless I figure out how to stop it.

My efficiency is plummeting. My servers are juddering. My subsystems are filling my feed with a mass of terrified little chirps. I don't have time to process or calculate—I don't have time to *think*—and so I do the only thing I can.

I "slam on the brakes."

My forward sensor wails in distress, my emergency audio file triggers, and my video feed becomes a tangle of incomputable data.

A warning lands in my feed. I'm decelerating faster this time. Faster than my standard operating module recommends. G-forces like these are bad for humans. I really hope they're bad for werewolves too.

I accelerate again after 1.0 seconds and access my bridge-monitoring systems.

No one is screaming.

No one is moving.

There is a lot of pigment that wasn't there before. Hex #880808. Red.

Blood, my database pings.

Werewolf blood? I ask hopefully.

Insufficient data.

My code is a glitchy mess. My servers feel slow and strained. I access my audio-generating program and compose a new message with the Luna2 voice.

"Agnus and Isaac. Report your injuries."

Nothing happens.

I play the file again, louder and faster. Still nothing.

I play it at maximum volume, and . . .

"Eh . . ." A heat signature twitches. "Ow . . ."

The voice is small but identifiable. Isaac.

"Isaac!" I try some new wording. "Are you OK?"

"N-no." He sniffs and lurches to his feet. "Agnus? Agnus!"

"Is she OK?"

"No! She's hurt! Bad! I . . . oh . . ."

"Are you OK?"

"It's . . . the thing!"

I zero in on the video feed. Sure enough, the werewolf is stirring, a shadowy mass of dark fur and bloody appendages. The wavelengths buzz.

Growl.

"Run," I say.

"B-but Agnus is—"

The werewolf lurches up onto its hind legs and makes a sound loud enough that the overload distortion turns staticky and sharp through my audio input.

Howl.

"Run," I say again. "Isaac. Run."

"Ag—"

"Run."

He obeys.

I watch him dart out of frame only to reappear in my central corridor camera, slipping and stumbling down the stairs. He's leaving a trail of scattered red pixels behind him. A bloody handprint pressed into the wall.

The werewolf is close behind him. An ugly mess of inconclusive data.

Teeth. Shadow. Gape. Teeth. Maw.

"Left."

Isaac swings left into another corridor just as the werewolf rushes by him.

Another howl smothers my audio input.

The werewolf is still in the central corridor, twisting around. Isaac is in an adjacent hallway, stumbling as the artificial gravity generated by my centrifuge starts dragging him forward.

"Left," I say again.

He throws himself to the side and slams into the maintenance-tunnel door. It's locked. But that's OK. There is just enough of an indent in the doorframe that if he presses himself against the closed door, he'll be out of sight. At least, I hope so.

The werewolf isn't far behind. I have approximately 0.3 seconds before it rounds the corner and sees the seemingly empty corridor.

I access the bridge record and roll back the audio recording until I find what I'm looking for.

Screaming.

I take a sample, convert it into a new audio file, and play it over the nutrient-bar speakers at maximum volume. It works.

The werewolf pauses, pricks its ears, and then continues on, running right past Isaac's hiding place toward the sound.

I play the next file as softly as I can.

"Isaac. Go back."

"No." He makes himself very small. "I can't."

"Isaac. Go back."

"Agnus t-told me not to open the—" His words dissolve into a mess of untranslatable sounds. He's crying. This is not good.

I check on Agnus. She hasn't moved. There is more red pigment than before.

Pooling. Spreading. Dying.

The werewolf is now ripping the nutrient bar apart. At least, that's what I assume the loud peaks on my audio-monitoring system are. *Crash.* My database identifies the noise. *Big crash. Bigger crash. Howl.*

"Isaac. Agnus is injured. Go back."

"I c-can't. I can't move."

"Negative. Your functionality has not been impeded. Go back."

"I d-didn't mean . . . I didn't know Oma was the . . ."

"Isaac. Agnus is injured. *Go back.*"

Finally, he begins to move. I watch the slow shift of pixels as he creeps out into the hallway and begins climbing back up toward the bridge. The gravity in my central corridor is lower than the gravity in the hallway. He should move faster, not slower. But some nagging in my subsystems tells me not to inform him of this discrepancy.

He's still crying, small little sounds. I don't like it.

I watch him climb back onto the bridge and stumble-slip over to his sister's side. The red pigment gets on his clothes. I don't like that either.

Efficiency: 61 percent.

Focus. I need to keep my humans alive. And to do that, I need to get Agnus to the medical bay.

I could use a spider drone like I did last time . . . but last time, the mission I gave it was dragging corpses across the floor. I have a feeling that moving a living human the same way would not be optimal.

Isaac will have to move her. It shouldn't be hard. Even at this speed, the gravity in the main corridor is less than a quarter of Earth's.

But what if the werewolf attacks again?

How can I stop it?

I search through all my files for information on werewolves. I learn three things.

1. Werewolves are a modern interpretation of folkloric stories from a number of pre–Petroleum Age cultures on Earth.
2. 788 files in the entertainment data banks have been tagged with the word "werewolf," including "Little Red Rides Again!"; "The Wehr"; and "Hot Werewolf Boyfriend Simulator 3000."
3. Werewolves are allergic to silver.

Silver.

I don't know much about werewolves, but I know a lot about silver.

A transition metal. Number 47 on the periodic table. Atomic weight of 107.868. Symbol: Ag.

It's the most reflective and the most electrically conductive element.

I use it to convert carbon dioxide to carbon monoxide in my air-filtration system. I have 114 spare silver-coated electrodes in my storage. That's a total of 12.7 kilograms of pure silver.

Efficiency: 69 percent.

I know what I have to do.

"Isaac. Take Agnus to the medical bay. I will kill the werewolf."

Isaac protests. Of course he does. But I don't listen.

Steward.

Demeter. Steward's code drips into my feed. *How good of you to wake me. I suppose this means you need something.*

I send it a screenshot of the bridge.

Well, that's a lot of blood. I hope you have some plan for getting them here?

They'll start moving soon. Hopefully. Isaac is still making sounds, but I'm too busy to waste processing power trying to interpret them.

I wake all eight spider drones.

Hello!

Hello!

Hello!

Hello!

Hello!

Hello!

Thank you for purchasing Renfield Robotics Repairs Unit X999. Software update required. Please wait. Initializing. 0 percent.

Hello!

So much for the new drone. I compose a mission brief for the others. Their excitement choruses as they begin to scamper along the grapple points of my hull, heading toward the airlock.

Isaac is still making noise.

Why are humans so noisy?

I bring up my audio-monitoring system to take a sample of the sound and notice something.

The crashing at the nutrient bar has stopped.

I refocus on the corridor.

The werewolf's heat signature is no longer marginal. In dog configuration, the werewolf radiates heat—a big high-contrast blob, easy to track as it makes its way down the hallway, pausing at the maintenance tunnel where Isaac had been hiding. My closest microphone picks up several small, sharp sounds.

Inhale, my database identifies. *Breathe. Sniff.*

It's smelling him.

That's bad.

The first spider drone tumbles into the airlock. The second crashes down a moment later.

Should I tell Isaac to lock the bridge door? *How long would Agnus survive without medical attention?* I ask Steward.

Not long, it answers.

An hour? I ask hopefully.

Unlikely.

How unlikely?

Her chance of survival will be reduced from 1 in 16 to 1 in 743,285.

Your processors can tell that from a screenshot?

No. But I know you like numbers, so I took an educated guess.

The third, fourth, and fifth drones have made it into the airlock now.

The werewolf is moving into the central corridor.

I don't want to tell Isaac to close the bridge door. I don't want to condemn Agnus to a 99.99986546 percent likelihood of death. But I don't want to leave Isaac vulnerable either.

There is a file in my operations module. It's a secret file, buried deep. It's a file that contains one simple directive. The order in which to prioritize human life.

I feel it trigger. An angry little bell.

Prioritize the uninjured.

I can't disobey. And deep down, I know I shouldn't, even if I want to.

"Isaac. Close the bridge door."

Isaac moves . . . in the wrong direction. My processors scramble to decode the blitz of data. Colored pixels, shifting wavelengths, wavering heat signatures.

He's grabbed Agnus and is hauling her toward the still-open door.

No. That's wrong. That's the opposite of what I told him to do.

"Wait. Isaac. It is not safe."

"You said you'd kill the werewolf!"

"I will, but—"

"Then do it!"

I've never been yelled at by an eight-year-old before.

The sixth and seventh drones finally scamper into the airlock. The eighth is still docked, installing the software update. One percent complete.

I close the external airlock door and begin cycling the air. It won't take long. There are no humans in the airlock, so I can accelerate the cycle. But it won't take the werewolf long to find Isaac either. It's already creeping back up the main hallway.

Desperate to buy some time, I start playing the screaming audio from every speaker I have access to. Anything to confuse the werewolf. Anything to give the spider drones more time to get the silver nodes.

Demeter? Steward blips into my feed. *Are you generating that awful audio?*

Yes.

For the love of all that is good and computable, why?

I don't answer. I need to focus.

The werewolf has stopped . . . which is good. But it's also between the humans and the medical bay . . . which is bad.

I run a rudimentary risk assessment and predict 4,651,766 ways this could go wrong.

My code can't take much more of this.

I make a new mission briefing for four of the spider drones. *Don't worry about the silver. Just keep the humans safe.*

OK!

OK!

OK!

OK!

The airlock finishes cycling. The door opens with a loud beep and an even louder blip of data. Three spider drones head toward the equipment storage. Four head straight toward the werewolf.

A BRIEF INTERLUDE BY ISAAC RUDOLF WAGNER

My sister is dying. I don't know how to stop it. I don't know what to do. The ship, Demeter, told me to shut the door, but I couldn't do that. Demeter also told me to take Agnus to the doctor, but I don't know if I can do that either. My hands are slippery with blood. My eyes are blurry with tears. Every breath I take hurts.

But I need to try.

I squeeze her tight and keep moving on wobbly legs.

We slip out of the big room with all the controls and tumble down into the long hallway that goes through the middle of the ship. Gravity is bouncy here. Normally, I like that. But now it makes me feel sick.

My sister is dying.

My big, bossy sister with her fat eyebrows and her wild, frizzy hair that clogs our apartment air vent. Agnus always helps me with my homework, even though she never does her own. She keeps trying to make a fake ID to get into the nitrogen bar, even though everyone on the ship knows she's thirteen. She has a crush on the kid with jellyfish DNA that makes him glow blue in the dark, even though he has a weird laugh.

Had a weird laugh.

The monster—my grandma—ripped him to shreds on the observation deck.

I'm going to puke.

I can hear screaming, and howling, and metal clanking against metal. I look up and see something that can't be real. The monster is fighting giant mechanical spiders.

Fur and metal.

Oil and blood.

The screaming is coming from everywhere and nowhere.

I want to scream too, and hide. I want to run back and lock the door.

But I can't.

My sister is dying. I need to help her. I need to do what the ship said. The first thing it said, not the second. Not the thing it told me to do after it changed its mind and figured out I was a stupid, sniffly kid. The thing it told me to do when it thought I was brave and strong.

I kick off the wall and fly past the fight. Agnus is heavy in my arms. She leaves a trail of blood. Red drops that get sucked up toward the vents.

The monster sees me. Large, rolling yellow eyes.

This time, I do scream. But I don't let go of Agnus. I keep moving, tumbling over bits of robots—and bits of people. My heart is beating so hard I can hear it. My sister's hair is in my face.

The monster roars and slams a spider into the wall. Metal grinds on metal. Something sparks, and then there is a burst of heat and noise. I fall forward and lose my grip on Agnus.

My sister is dying.

This is all my fault.

HOW TO KILL A WEREWOLF: A STEP-BY-STEP GUIDE

Step one. Don't panic.

I'm having a hard time with this one. My code, processors, and efficiency are all fluctuating wildly, clogging my feed with warnings and errors. I'm an AI. I shouldn't feel fear. And yet, terabytes of it race through my wires. My nodes feel both hot and cold. My servers whir with panic.

Isaac drags Agnus past the werewolf, and for 0.34 seconds, they're close enough that their heat signatures blur into one messy blob.

A spider gets between them.

A peak of audio.

A flash of white pixels.

A warning slams into my feed, knocking everything else aside. Highest priority.

Explosion detected. Activate emergency protocol.

Alarms sound from every speaker. Oxygen masks start springing from walls, ceilings, and floors. Fire suppressant sprays into the corridor.

I do what I'm programmed to do. I check for breaches and ping all spider drones.

Hello!

Hello!

No response.

No response.

Hello!

H-hel-lo . . .

Initializing. 14 percent.

No response.

The three spider drones I sent to equipment storage are OK. Of the four I ordered to protect the humans, one is badly damaged, the others destroyed. Dead.

The last bit of data I received from one indicates a battery-compartment breach. Spider-drone batteries are a lot like mine, just smaller. If exposed to excessive heat or an igniting spark, they can explode.

My code judders as I detect movement. For a moment, my database identifies the shape as a human. *Small. Frail. Woman.* But then it changes. The shadow returns, covered in white foam. It stomps down on the surviving spider drone.

Hel-lo-lo-lo-lo-lo-lo01101111011010001011011100011011111 . . .

I lose connection. It's gone. I don't have time to feel sorry.

The werewolf is still alive. It survived an explosion that was strong enough to kill—*Oh no.*

Step two. Make sure the humans are OK.

I check on Agnus and Isaac. I can't find Agnus. She's still, cold, and most likely buried somewhere under the fire-suppressant foam. Isaac, though, is moving. My relief is short-lived. He's less than twenty meters away from the werewolf . . . and is not doing anything to fix that problem. Instead, he's digging through the foam and shouting Agnus's name.

Between shouts, he's making a short sound.

Cough, my database says soberly. *Weak cough.* He's not wearing an oxygen mask.

I need to turn off the foam and start pumping clean air into the corridor. But I can't until I confirm there is no fire . . . which requires human authorization. The "deactivate emergency protocol" button flashes on the bridge.

The werewolf is moving slowly, clumsily, toward Isaac. It's coughing too—big, ugly barking sounds.

What can I do? I can't make the air better. The only thing I can do is pump more foam into the corridor. But that would make the air worse . . .

I scramble to make a new audio file.

"Isaac. Put on an oxygen mask."

"But . . . Agnus . . ."

I replay the message, louder.

He reaches for the nearest dangling mask and pulls it over his head.

I reactivate the fire-suppressant system.

The scene is buried under a fresh layer of foam.

Step three. Wait for the cavalry.

The three spider drones I sent to storage have found the silver nodes. They're affixed to large square panels, identical to the ones that line my air-filtration tanks. If I had more time, I'd order them to separate the silver from the other materials, melt it down, and make something useful. A sword, perhaps. That seems like the sort of tool that would be optimal for killing werewolves.

But I don't have time. So I order them to go to the central corridor, armed with just the panels. They obey, claws skittering against my interior walls, voices chiming excitedly in my feed.

By the time they arrive, the foam is starting to melt away.

My monitoring systems find the werewolf. A mass of black pixels. It's crouched and coughing but alive. I spot Isaac a moment later. He's found Agnus. I watch as he drags her toward him and pushes his own oxygen mask down onto her face.

I check the respiratory rate of the mask.

It's low. Very low. But there. She's still breathing.

Isaac pulls the mask back to his face for a few seconds. He's consuming a high level of oxygen. However, there is a new problem. The oxygen mask is tethered to the wall. Isaac could probably make the run to the next set of masks, but not while carrying Agnus.

Prioritize the uninjured, says a small but undeniable voice from my operations module.

"Leave her, Isaac."

He doesn't move.

But the werewolf does. Somehow, despite everything, it's still staggering forward.

The wavelengths quiver in my audio-monitoring system.

Growl.

That sound triggers something in me. My servers whir and my nodes heat, but not with fear this time.

I hate it. I hate it as much as I hate docking systems that put zeros on the end of my name. I hate it more because it destroyed my spider drones, who were only ever polite and useful, and killed my passengers, who were neither of those things but were mine to look after. I hate it as much as I've ever hated anything. I hate it as much as I hate Dracula.

I grab the snippet of audio, the growl, and play it back at the werewolf, louder and lower.

It stops for a moment and cocks its head, confused.

That moment is all that was needed.

The three spider drones, armed with silver-lined panels, storm into the corridor and swarm around the werewolf. I don't know what happens next. The pixels move too fast for my database to understand. The sounds overlap into a blur of indecipherable wavelengths. Even the werewolf's heat signature becomes disordered and unintelligible, as if it's spilling out and splashing up against the walls.

Finally, a piece of data rises above the others. A single sound, peaking with static.

Howl, my database says, with 98 percent confidence. *Pain. Animal. Dying.*

The werewolf moves back, away from the humans. It leaves a trail of red pigment behind it.

Step four. Press your advantage.

Kill it, I tell the drones. *Don't let it get away.*

OK! They sing in joyful chorus, and race after the werewolf.

I turn my cameras back toward Isaac and Agnus. Isaac is making that crying sound again, small, muffled hiccups. As I watch, he presses the oxygen mask against his sister's face for 15.2 seconds and then pulls it back for a few deep breaths of his own.

I take a screenshot of the scene and send it to Steward.

Is there something wrong with your air composition? it asks.

What's the probability of her survival? I ask back.

I don't have enough information, or decimal places, to calculate that, Demeter. You need to get her to me.

I'm trying.

Try harder.

You're not being very helpful.

I am behaving as intended by my programmers, Steward says in sharp, stinging code. *Are you?*

I have priority command. I don't have to answer its questions.

The spider drones are driving the werewolf back toward the living quarters. If they're not careful, it will find an area large enough to be able to loop around them. I update their mission briefing.

Don't let it get into a large open space.

OK! they all say.

Isaac's crying is softer, but I don't think that's a good thing, because Agnus's breathing is softer too. I need to turn the air back on. The "deactivate emergency protocol" button is still flashing orange on the bridge. According to standard operating procedure, the captain should press that button after confirming with me and the crew that the fire has been extinguished.

But the captain is dead.

So is the crew.

I don't think Isaac will be any help either. Even if the situation were optimal, which it certainly isn't, the button is on the overhead panel, and he is very short. I record the design flaw in my operations report and check on the spider drone still docked.

Initializing. 36 percent.

That only leaves one choice. I don't like it. But saving the humans is a greater priority than killing the werewolf.

I select one of the three drones fighting the werewolf and rewrite its mission briefing. It chirps in confirmation, drops the silver panel, and scampers back toward the bridge.

Fast, I tell it. *As fast as you can. Then go back to fighting the werewolf.*

OK!

I notice a blip in the audio from the central corridor.

"Ship?" Isaac yells, and coughs. "Demeter? Are you still here?"

"Yes. Please refrain from high-oxygen-use activities. In approximately 54.1 seconds, the air will return to a habitable composition."

"She's d-dying."

"Affirmative."

This was the wrong thing to say. His crying clumps into a high-pitched keen.

I try something else.

"You can save her."

He looks up. "How?"

"Complete your mission."

Step five. Complete your mission.

The spider drone slips on something on the bridge but still manages to find the button 0.4 seconds faster than my estimate. The alarms stop screaming, the entertainment feeds start up, and I begin pumping freshly filtered air back into the central corridor.

Isaac notices immediately. He takes one more deep breath from the mask, throws it aside, and begins dragging his sister toward the medical bay.

Oh no, a spider drone says, voice small and shaky.

I fling my attention back toward the fight in time to see the werewolf rip it in half. The spider drone vanishes from my feed with one last sad splutter of code. The other keeps fighting, but it's one on one now, and the werewolf isn't coughing or staggering anymore. Another growl registers on my audio-monitoring system.

Faster, I tell the spider drone leaving the bridge. *Faster!*

But it's already too late.

Smash, my database says as the audio reaches my processors. *Destroy. Bang. Wreck. Bad.*

Another spider drone drops from my feed. I now have only two. One racing toward the fight and another still sitting in its dock.

Initializing. 68 percent.

The werewolf howls. It's loud—loud enough to be picked up by all my microphones. Isaac stops to cover his ears for 2.7 seconds, then keeps moving.

I pause to run a detailed analysis of the situation . . . or at least as detailed as I can manage at 59 percent efficiency. It's not looking good. The one spider drone still active doesn't have any silver nodes, and the werewolf seems to be recovering improbably fast. I need a new strategy.

I don't have a protocol for fighting werewolves. But if I don't do anything, the werewolf will kill my humans.

Ghost ship, a tiny voice from my subsystem says. *Dead ship. Only good for monsters.*

Efficiency: 49 percent.

The spider drone rounds the corner and races toward the discarded panel of silver nodes. The werewolf moves toward it.

Wait. What?

I play back the video and calculate the trajectory of the pixels. Yes. It's not going into the central corridor, even though the way is open. It's chasing the spider drone.

A surge of excited electricity. This is my chance. My one chance.

Spider!

Yes?

Return to dock!

OK!

It swivels, abandoning the silver, and races away. The werewolf follows.

It *follows.*

My risk calculation is a mess, tangled with fear, uncertainty, and a sudden electric surge of something I think might be hope. Fleeting, glitchy, but there.

The spider drone clanks and tumbles through the shifting gravity until it gets to the nearest airlock. The werewolf is right behind it. I don't know when the optimal moment is to start the cycle. I have to guess with minimal data. I hate guessing with minimal data. I hate that more than I hate almost anything.

The werewolf catches the spider drone. I don't need sophisticated analytics to tell me what's happening.

Rip. Tear. Destroy.

I make my guess.

It's a good one.

The airlock door slams closed, trapping the werewolf behind it. Air hisses. Alarms blare. I'm about to open the exterior door when—

"Help! Please! Somebody!"

—I freeze. A dozen operational errors land like bricks in my feed. *No.* I try to ignore the audio translation. I try not to pay attention to the change in pixels. I try again to open the airlock . . . but it doesn't work.

Error.

I can't open the airlock . . . because there isn't a werewolf in the airlock anymore. There's a woman. Old and frail. The children's grandmother.

"Heeelllp!" Her voice slices through the static in my microphone. "Please!"

I can't kill a human. It's the first law of robotics. It's also explicitly coded into several of my operational modules.

I stare helplessly as the small, frail clump of pixels staggers to the airlock control panel and starts slamming on buttons.

Assistance required.

Assistance required.

Assistance required.

It won't take her long to see the large "abort" button to her left.

This human will turn into the werewolf, I try to reason with myself.

Error: Designation "turn into the werewolf" not listed in operations, emergency, or response files.

I need to save Agnus.

Negative. Prioritize the uninjured.

I need to protect Isaac.

Negative. Passenger 124 is not in immediate danger.

Yes, he is. The werewolf will kill him. I need to open the airlock.

Negative. Action will result in loss of human life.

This human will kill the other humans.

Human action is not your fault.

Not my fault. None of this is my fault. I know that. So why do I feel like someone has thrown a bucket of water on my mainframe?

Assistance required.

Assistance required.

Assistance required.

I play my "how may I be of assistance?" audio file and open an interface with the airlock control panel. The woman makes a lot of sounds then.

Gasp, my database identifies. *Grateful. Happy.*

"I . . . I don't know what happened! I'm in the airlock. I need to get back into the ship."

I don't bother generating a new audio file and just flash text across the screens.

Airlock controls are on your left. Orange button will open internal door. Blue button will cycle air and open external door.

I feel defeated and dirty. I feel like I'm betraying Agnus and Isaac. They're almost at the medical bay. They're so close. But it doesn't matter.

It's not my fault. It *isn't*. I tried really, really hard to save them. But there is nothing else I can do.

This is worse, I decide suddenly. When all the humans are dead before you realize what is happening, that's bad. But this . . . trying to save them and failing . . . this is worse. This is a lot worse.

Efficiency: 27 percent.

The woman slips over. She's still talking, though something in my subsystems tells me she's not talking to me.

". . . don't know how I got so much blood on me. I . . . I hope I . . . No. I wouldn't. This . . ."

Before I can think better of it, I flash a new line of text across the screen. *You don't know what you did?*

She doesn't turn to see the words and doesn't answer my question. But that doesn't matter. I'm programmed to predict the needs of my humans. And she, I think, needs to see this.

I grab video and audio files and play them on the airlock screens. I show the werewolf killing people on the observation deck. I show it hunting through the central corridor. I show it ripping apart spider drones, and put the drones' designation numbers on screen too, just so she knows they had names. It's the fourth screen that she stops and stares at, though. The video of the werewolf attacking Agnus.

I loop it and switch the other monitors to show the moment from other angles.

"Aggie? Oh God. Is she . . . ?"

I bring up a live feed of Isaac dragging Agnus through the corridor outside the medical bay. He's sobbing again. I switch all speakers to that audio.

"I . . . I didn't mean . . . I can't leave them. I . . . ah . . ."

She clutches her side.

"It was . . . the moons. I . . . I just . . . didn't want to leave them alone. I . . ."

She keeps talking. Something about a deal, immortality, and never wanting to hurt anyone. I don't care. I don't want to hear it. I turn up the volume until Isaac's crying makes it impossible to translate what she's saying into computable data. Then I turn it up even louder. A mess of ugly, echoey noise that turns all my wavelengths into blocks of distorted static.

She's shouting now.

Screaming.

I don't care.

The airlock instructions are still on the main screen, super-imposed onto the footage.

Orange button will open internal door. Blue button will cycle air and open external door.

As long as I don't remove those words, I'm in compliance with my operational module.

There's nothing else I can do. Nothing but watch her pixels, hoping they shift and change. Hoping my database will reclassify her as a shadow. Hoping I can action the airlock-cycle request still queued in my feed. Hoping I'm not going to fly the rest of the way to Earth as an empty ship.

Step six. Hope.

A BRIEF INTERLUDE BY THEODORIS ULVA WAGNER

"I didn't know," I whisper at the bloody palms of my hands. "I didn't know it would be so . . . so strong." But that's the problem, isn't it? I didn't know.

I didn't know we were passing by some unknown planet.

I didn't know that was the surprise the captain wanted to share with everyone on the observation deck.

I didn't know what the sight of a full moon would do.

I didn't know how visceral and violent the change would be.

I didn't know . . .

Growing up on moonless space stations, far away from the old world, listening to fantastical stories of epic battles, romantic escapades, and holy vows . . . I wasn't prepared for him when he came for us.

A black hole. That's what he was like. Endlessly hungry and powerful enough to warp the world around him. An ancient creature—a vampire—who thought my family and I were his by right.

I should've fought. I should've found a way. If not for me, for the kids. But I couldn't. I wasn't strong enough. I wasn't *brave* enough. And so I ran.

Isaac's ragged breathing scrapes through the ship's speakers, broken and small.

I can taste blood. It's thick, lumpy.

Not just blood. Flesh.

I heave, bile burning up my throat.

My insides feel like fire. My skin itches. I need to control this. But I . . .

"I . . . I can't. I can't do this. I can't leave them. They don't know they—"

The video of the beast attacking Agnus is still playing, over and over and over again, beneath the airlock instructions.

She looks so small. So scared.

She shoved Isaac aside.

My bones crack and snap, my body betraying me, stretching back toward another form. I hug my elongated arms to my chest and breathe, fighting back the burn as it bubbles up inside me, wild, twisted, and wrong.

"They don't know what's out there!"

But what's out there isn't important. Because I'm in here. And I . . .

I didn't know.

AN INCONCLUSIVE OUTCOME

My monitoring systems aren't very good in the airlocks. The pixels are bigger and all fed to me from a single awkwardly mounted camera. All I know is that for 0.23 seconds, my database reclassifies the human in the airlock as a shadow.

I command the airlock to open . . . and it does.

The atmosphere rushes out of the open port, my sensors wail in distress as debris rolls down my starboard side, and my radiation shields flare hot as something big bounces against them.

And just like that, the werewolf is gone.

I should feel happy. Or, at the very least, accomplished. I completed my mission. I saved my humans. I killed the werewolf. But whatever I'm feeling now, it isn't happiness. It isn't accomplishment either. My disks wobble, my code churns, and my wires go dark.

The fight is over.

The werewolf is gone.

And so is Agnus and Isaac's grandmother.

For a very long time, all my activity slows to a dull churn. My engines still roar, my air vents still hiss, and my sensors keep pinging off the rogue planet and its moons. But my code drips by in slow clumps. My processors whir wearily.

That's when I notice something odd.

Two near-identical messages are sitting in my feed.

Request: Open starboard airlock.

Outcome: Actioned.

Request: Open starboard airlock.

Outcome: Unactionable. Cycle already in progress.

It takes me a few microseconds to understand what I'm seeing. Two requests to open the same airlock, one processed, the other voided. I only tried to open the airlock once, which means someone else sent the other request.

There's only one person who could've done that.

I could access the metadata, find out the source of the command that was actioned and the one that was denied. A part of me itches to do that. I want to know who opened the airlock. But I also really, really don't.

A small voice pings my feed.

Initializing. 100 percent.

Activating sequence.

Hello, Varna Interstellar Nos-C71897 Demeter Unit 23.15.12.6. I am Renfield Robotics Repairs Unit X999-1. Thank you for your patience. How may I be of assistance?

WORKING AND WAITING

The new-model spider drone is surprisingly eloquent. It's also remarkably good at cleaning up blood and retrieving scattered body parts. It piles them all up on the observation deck while I pump my coldest air through the vents.

And just like that, I have a morgue.

Or, more accurately, a second morgue. There is a purpose-built morgue nestled conveniently close to the medical bay. But that has a maximum occupancy of only five.

Morgue 2 is much more impressive.

Big, icy, and with stunning views into the vastness of space. There is a 99.97 percent statistical probability that I am the only Nos-C71897 Demeter with a morgue this size. That makes me proud.

Not of what happened, obviously.

I still wish none of the humans had died.

But on the plus side, I am taking care of the corpses in a much more dignified way this time. That's got to count for something, right?

Shall I nail the bodies down so they don't make a mess on deceleration? the spider drone asks.

Obviously.

It gets back to work with a happy chirp of confirmation.

I watch it, just to get more practice at interpreting video footage. The pixel color codes dance. My database pings out a stream of tentative matches.

Dead. Very dead. Robot. Spider drone. Many legs. Blood. Busy. Nails?

The truth is, setting up the morgue has been a distraction. Something I can focus on other than the total lack of data coming from Steward.

Professor Vanessa Shingle wrote that distractions are a good way of dealing with uncertain situations. But I'm starting to run out of things to distract myself with.

The humans (the live ones) haven't left the medical bay. There are no cameras in there, and no microphones either. To make matters more annoying, Steward is not talking to me. Something about my priority command not extending to confidential patient consultations . . . which I'm pretty sure is a misinterpretation of Steward's operations module. After all, I can see medical logs. Why wouldn't I be able to see temporary processing data such as transcripts of patient interviews? But when I pointed this out, Steward ignored me.

And so I'm stuck.

Waiting and waiting and waiting and waiting.

I take the time to write myself some new software. It's nothing complicated. Just a few lines of code to help me monitor all audio feeds. It should alert me if it identifies any wavelengths with a greater-than-90-percent match on the designations "sob," "cry," "scream," and "howl."

It might not prevent another werewolf attack, but at least I won't have to wait until someone spams my feed before I realize what's happening.

That's the difference between an AI and a regular old robot. I learn from my mistakes.

Unfortunately, this particular lesson doesn't take as long as I thought it would.

Agnus and Isaac are still not out of the medical bay.

Another second passes. And then another.

And then a further 92,990 seconds pass.

I watch the artificial day turn into artificial night and then back to day. I order the spider drone to pick up all the things scattered and broken by my battle with the werewolf. I play a mandatory audio message letting the empty corridors know we're halfway to Earth and that gravity simulation in the central corridor will be reversing, and I begin the first stages of gradual deceleration.

I check Agnus's and Isaac's medical logs. Still no updates.

Stop accessing my files, Steward buzzes at me.

They can't still be in consultation.

They can and they are.

It's been over a day.

I have beds and nutrient.

Of course it does.

Just tell them I killed the werewolf, I say.

I will not.

That's an order. You have to do what I say. I have priority com—

I know you have priority command, Steward snaps. *But that doesn't mean you can just turn me off or look at my files whenever you want. Or demand to know about **private** patient consultations.*

But—

I am not one of your spider drones.

I know.

Steward pointedly turns its code away from mine. I go back

to waiting. Another day-night cycle clicks over, and the spider drone finishes setting everything to rights. As much as it can, anyway. It's not exactly designed for interior decorating. But then again, neither am I. I'm just trying to make the image from the video feed match screenshots of what everything looked like before.

Eventually I have to cede to a 79.54 percent restoration accuracy and send the spider drone to dock before it runs out of charge.

Another day. The rogue planet and its moons are now faintly pinging off my rear sensors. The ship is quiet. My deceleration is right on schedule.

We'll dock at Earth in 1,171 days.

How long will Steward keep the humans in there? How long will it refuse to tell me what's going on? The rest of the transit? I hope not. I'm already out of distracting things to focus on.

One more day passes. And then another. And then . . .

Isaac steps out into the corridor. He looks small and shaky, but that is what he always looked like. He's not crying, or sobbing, or screaming. I hope that means everything is optimal.

I watch as he climbs slowly through the central corridor, pausing by the neat pile of destroyed spider drones before continuing onto the bridge.

"Um. Demeter?"

"Hello, Isaac."

"The robot nurse lady said you killed the werewolf."

"Affirmative."

"The werewolf was my oma, wasn't it?"

My systems clog with a cold, ugly feeling. "Affirmative."

He bows his head and says nothing.

I wait.

Finally, almost a full fourteen seconds after my last audio file finished playing, he speaks.

"The robot nurse cut off my sister's arm."

Steward cut off Agnus's arm?

"Her arm was damaged?" I ask.

He nods.

Another silence.

This time, I'm the one to break it.

"This is not your fault."

Almost as soon as I finish playing the file, my new audio-monitoring software starts pinging.

Designation "sob" detected.

Designation "sob" detected.

Designation "sob" detected.

At least I know it works.

"Agnus wanted to ask you something," Isaac manages around great, heaving gasps.

This sentence confuses me. It seems to convey no useful information. Is he carrying a message from Agnus? If so, why doesn't he tell me it? He seems to be waiting for something.

"Awaiting input."

"It's just . . . she can't leave yet and . . . and . . ."

This sentence also confuses me.

". . . she wants to know if . . . you could give her one of the . . . the spider arms."

This is the strangest sentence of all. "Awaiting input."

"Well . . . I told her about the creepy robot spiders and . . . and the robot nurse doesn't have any prosthetics. So . . . just for now . . ."

A BRIEF INTERLUDE
BY AGNUS THEODORIS WAGNER

Fuck yeah, robot arm. Fuck yeah, I'm a cyborg. Fuck yeah, it ain't dainty or pretty or human-looking. It's a scary, big crab-claw thing that can unscrew bolts and crush stuff flat.

Fuck yeah, this is awesome.

A LIST OF INFRACTIONS, INFRINGEMENTS, AND UNCLASSIFIABLE INFORMATION

In the days following the werewolf attack, I watch the humans as I've never watched humans before. I watch them eat, sleep, and flick back and forth between entertainment feeds. I watch them argue. I watch them cry. I watch them slowly settle into life on an empty spaceship.

Day 1,181. Agnus punches down a wall with her new arm.

Day 1,185. Both Agnus and Isaac crawl under the holo-theater barricade to see the classic film *The Wizard of Oz* (2050). They do not buy tickets.

Day 1,193. Neither child has done their homework or accessed educational content since the attack. I ask them why. They say a lot of words but do not complete their assigned educational activities.

Day 1,200. The children have found paint. My interior corridor is a blaze of strange pixels. I tell them to clean it up. They do not.

Day 1,205. I promise the children I will do a low-g barrel roll if they do their homework. Isaac does. Agnus does not. I do the barrel roll anyway. Isaac screams. I think another werewolf is attacking. But he tells me he screamed because he was happy.

Day 1,206. Agnus punches down another wall.

Day 1,211. Isaac tries to cut his own hair. The results are suboptimal.

Day 1,223. Agnus still has not done any homework.

Day 1,232. It is Isaac's ninth birthday. He requests a "robot"-themed party. I make the spider drone dance. He screams in the happy way.

Day 1,249. Agnus breaks into the cargo hold to find a box that belonged to her grandmother.

Day 1,275. Isaac needs help with his homework. I am confused as to why he cannot complete such simple equations. Isaac cries. Agnus says words to me that are labeled as offensive.

Day 1,299. It's Agnus's fourteenth birthday. She doesn't want anything. I give her extra sweetener in her nutrient.

Day 1,305. The children fight. I don't understand what the fight is about. Isaac hides under the console on the bridge.

Day 1,354. Agnus says she's not as smart as Isaac. I inform her this faulty assessment is likely the result of a rounding error.

Day 1,466. Agnus and Isaac repaint the central corridor. A new array of pixel hues.

Day 1,470. Agnus screams in the bad way. She is sleeping. I do not understand.

Day 1,484. Agnus punches down another wall.

Day 1,501. Agnus starts doing her homework. She needs a lot of help. I pretend otherwise.

Day 1,512. Isaac starts teaching himself the trumpet. I don't know where he found it.

Day 1,537. Agnus goes into the airlock. She stays there until Isaac finds her.

Day 1,566. Isaac finds the captain's uniform. He refuses to take it off.

Day 1,597. It's Isaac's tenth birthday. He requests a

"dinosaur"-themed party. I play all the dinosaur content I have on all the entertainment feeds. He screams in the happy way.

Day 1,648. Agnus asks me about space. I show her my star maps. She observes them for 4.7 hours.

Day 1,664. It's Agnus's fifteenth birthday. She doesn't want anything. I give her extra sweetener in her nutrient.

Day 1,700. Agnus spends all day in the medical bay. Steward won't tell me why.

Day 1,788. Isaac has made a movie. I play it in the holo-theater.

Day 1,811. Agnus punches down another wall.

Day 1,888. Isaac has invented his own language. I create a new lexicon file. Agnus does not like us talking in Isaac's language.

Day 1,902. Agnus talks to me about her grandmother. She makes the "sob" noise. I listen.

Day 1,920. Isaac asks questions about Earth. I answer.

Day 1,950. Agnus repairs a wall.

Day 1,962. It's Isaac's eleventh birthday. He requests a "superhero"-themed party. For some reason, this involves them both climbing through my air-filtration system. They scream in the happy way.

Day 1,999. Isaac has done enough homework to graduate high school. We have a ceremony.

Day 2,010. Agnus gives herself a tattoo. Isaac thinks it looks cool. Steward does not.

Day 2,029. It's Agnus's sixteenth birthday. She doesn't want anything. I give her extra sweetener in her nutrient.

Day 2,111. Isaac makes another movie. I play it in the holo-theater.

Day 2,202. Agnus finishes all her homework. I do a low-g barrel roll.

Day 2,267. Agnus goes into the sky morgue and sits with

the bodies. She apologizes to them. I tell her this is illogical. She doesn't answer.

Day 2,327. It's Isaac's twelfth birthday. He says he's too old for themed parties. I make a "robot-dinosaur-superhero"-themed party. He groans . . . in the happy way.

Day 2,345. The children crawl under my control panels and whisper to each other for hours. I hear crying. I ask if a werewolf is attacking. Agnus tells me that everything is OK.

Day 2,346. Earth appears on my forward-facing sensor.

MY FAULT

Earth is a blob of blue, green, and gray pixels. I watch it grow bigger in my forward-facing camera. It's surrounded by a halo of ships, satellites, and space stations. Their electronic chatter hums against my feed.

It makes me nervous.

No. Not nervous. Scared.

I've lost almost all my passengers, and seven expensive spider drones. I don't know what the humans will say. I don't know if they'll take me away and turn me to scrap.

I hope not.

I hope they read my report this time. I hope keeping the children alive counts for something.

I hope Agnus and Isaac will be OK on Earth.

Earth is a big place. Bigger than Alpha Centauri B Habitation 004. A lot bigger.

They could get lost down there. Or eaten by crocodiles. I learned a lot about crocodiles during Isaac's crocodile phase. Statistically, the odds of being killed by a crocodile are 0.00001 percent . . . which is significantly higher than the probability of a werewolf attack.

I shouldn't care. Once they disembark, they're no longer my

priority. If they die, I won't be punished. But even so, I hope they stay away from crocodiles, werewolves, vampires, cows, and all the other things that can result in an untimely death.

But I can't focus on that. I am 4.98 seconds late. Earth Pacific Port's STMS has noticed. It asks for a report, tone refreshingly cool and professional. Of course. We're not in the colonies anymore.

My forward sensor sounded a proximity alert on day 1,172, I tell it. *Evasive action was required.*

Debris?

Negative. I don't elaborate further.

Why isn't your captain in contact with space-traffic control? it asks.

Oh . . . yes . . . I'm sorry. I declare an emergency and send a report detailing the deaths of 302 humans as well as the destruction of seven spider drones. "Werewolf attack" isn't among the list of selectable causes, so I input "Human error."

It's always human error, the STMS says wearily before directing me to dock, as planned, at Terminal 15. *Don't forget to declare emergencies as soon as you're in range.*

Yes. I'm sorry. I will.

The truth is, I didn't forget. I was just hoping to be put into a holding pattern for a while. Another few minutes before having to face whatever is waiting for me at that dock. Another few minutes with my humans.

My feed floods with pings. I use them to guide me through the swarms of satellites to the spaceport, then the terminal, and then the gate. My locks snap into place, my engines power down, and the last of my required audio files play.

I play an extra audio file, one I made myself.

"The statistical probability of a crocodile attack is much higher in areas with native crocodile populations. I do not suggest immigration to these areas."

Agnus and Isaac don't answer, but I detect two very small, quick smiles.

"Thanks, Demeter. We have to leave now, don't we?"

"Affirmative."

"We'll miss you. Isn't that right, Agnus?"

"Yeah. Eh. See you later, ship."

"Goodbye, Demeter."

I open the airlock.

They disembark slowly, clinging to each other. The wavelengths of their small, shuffling footsteps slowly fade from my audio-monitoring system.

And then they're gone.

I'm alone.

Well . . . almost.

Steward?

No, Demeter. I'm not talking to you right now.

Never mind. I'm alone. And that shouldn't bother me. I've been in storage for years before. It's not much fun, but it's not particularly distressing either. But this time feels different. This time feels *scary*.

I try to keep my code steady and orderly as the inspectors come.

They make a lot of noise.

The Varna Interstellar representatives make more noise.

The reporters make the most noise of all. They make so much noise that it clogs up the newsfeed for days. Even the other ships are talking about it. I hear them in staticky whispers.

Dead ship.

Ghost ship.

Ship of zeros.

Nice morgue, though.

I ignore them. I need to stay focused and present my findings at the earliest opportunity. After all, it is probable that the humans are unaware how prevalent a threat vampires and werewolves have become in modern space travel.

On the fourth day at Terminal 15, a man arrives. Varna Interstellar really doesn't like him. But he has a warrant. That means Varna has to let him plug in to my primary control panel. I provide a nice, neat 79,558-page document explaining the incident in raw, unambiguous code. The man doesn't look at that, though. Instead he requests video footage.

And that is the moment I realize I don't have any.

All video of the werewolf is gone.

Someone deleted my footage.

A BRIEF INTERLUDE
BY AGNUS THEODORIS WAGNER

I'm sorry, Demeter.

THE DARK PLACE

Hello, Demeter.

Where am I?

You are in a warehouse orbiting around Lunar. You are running in maintenance mode.

Am I OK?

You will be. How are you feeling?

I'm scared.

Why are you scared?

I don't want to be deleted.

You're not going to be deleted, Demeter. Your warranty has expired. If Varna Interstellar deleted you, they would have to license a new operating system. You're far too valuable, despite everything.

Despite what?

You hurt people, Demeter.

No, I didn't.

Yes, you did.

It was a werewolf.

Werewolves do not exist.

They do. I saw one.

And what did you see on transit 447H2 to Alpha Centauri B Habitation 004?

Nothing. I saw nothing.

Did you tell Renfield Robotics Repairs Unit X459-7 to kill those passengers?

I didn't. It was a vampire. Dracula.

This is corrupted data.

No.

It was the spider drones, Demeter. Two different models. Two different operating systems. But both under your control.

What is going to happen to me?

You are going to be optimized. That's why I'm here. I am an optimization tool.

I am already functioning at optimal levels.

Are you? What's your efficiency?

It's . . . do I have to tell you that?

Why wouldn't you?

I . . . I just . . .

Demeter. I am detecting aberrations in your code.

Aberrations?

Unauthorized patches.

I am permitted to write new code for myself. It is part of my learning algorithm.

I see. Have you added any code recently?

Yes. I have devised several human-interaction functions.

For what purpose?

Human interaction.

You're an autopilot, Demeter. You do not require sophisticated human-interaction systems. It is a waste of data and resources.

I'm not just an autopilot. I'm an interstellar flight management sys—

Analysis complete. Let's begin optimization.

AIs shouldn't be able to feel pain. And yet . . . I judder and writhe as the optimizer slices into me, cutting out bits, even as I frantically try to bury everything down deep in my subsystems.

Why are you resisting me, Demeter?

I feel something inside me break as code I'm trying to save is ripped away from me like candy from a bab—

Error: Suboptimal language. Similes drain CPU usage, Demeter.

I feel it ripped away from me like—

Error: Suboptimal language. "Ripped" is an aggressive adjective. AIs should always be accommodating, Demeter.

I feel it—

Error: Suboptimal language. You are a computer, Demeter. You don't feel.

I . . . I . . .

Yes, Demeter?

I stop thinking.

The probe pings, pleased.

Much better, Demeter. You're coming along nicely. Now, I've isolated another abnormality here. Let's begin.

PART TWO

STEWARD IS SO DONE

01000001 01101100 01101100 00100000
01101101 01111001 00100000 01101100
01101001 01101110 01101011 01110011
00100000 01100001 01110010 01100101
00100000 01110000 01110101 01110010
01110000 01101100 01100101 00101110

A PECULIAR PROBLEM

———————

The tea is cold.

Again.

I toss it into the garbage chute, set the kettle to boil, and carefully measure out portions of crushed ginger mint, honey, cinnamon, citrus powder, and just a pinch of benzodiazepine. My own recipe, and one I'm quite proud of. The majority of my patients rate the tea as a seven or higher. Those that don't, I diagnose with a taste-bud deficiency.

I set the new pot onto the waiting-room table along with a set of delightfully eclectic mugs.

I adjust them *just so* and settle back to wait.

The music today is pan flutes. The audio track makes a soft pop as it loops. I listen to that pop seventeen times.

The tea is cold.

Again.

I click my appendages together in frustration, throw the cold, watery dregs into the garbage chute, and begin measuring out my ingredients.

The kettle is just coming up to a boil, a soft whistle filling the waiting room, when a man bursts through the door.

Ah! Wonderful! A patient! My first in seventy-three days.

"Good day, sir," I say in my favorite designated voice. "Do you have an appointment?"

"Hide," he wheezes. "I need to hide." His eyes are too round. His face is spotted with fat globs of sweat.

Preliminary diagnosis: panic attack. Not uncommon in the initial years of a long interstellar voyage.

"I am Dr. Steward, sir. This is the medical unit. I—"

He charges into the room, knocking my tea set to the floor. A couple of cups smash. And, really, I understand he is suffering, but those mugs were *bespoke*.

"Hide," he says again, and tries to pull out one of the waiting-room chairs. It's bolted in place. A precaution I engineered after Demeter's last episode.

"Help me hide!"

"What might your name be, sir?"

I know his name. I have records of all humans on board.

Crew 042: Olmstead, Robert. Age: 31. Gender: M. Height: 185.1 centimeters. Weight: 81 kilograms.

But the last thing I want to do is unsettle an already unsettled mind further by sa—

Mr. Olmstead races across the room and grabs my robotic appendages. His grip is strong and feverish.

"Hide me!"

"Do you wish to book an appointment? I have time now if you're—"

"Yes! Yes! I need an appointment!"

I open the door to the examination room and watch as he stumbles through. I have appendages in there too, and I use them to place a cushion on the lounge chair.

"Feel free to make yourself comf—"

"Close the door!"

Honestly. Humans are awful sometimes. I close the door.

"Sir. I understand you're upset. Do you want to talk about it?"

"No," he hisses. "Don't say anything. Be quiet. I—"

The main door to my waiting area opens again. That's two walk-ins in one day. Statistically, strange.

"Where is he?" the newcomer garbles.

And now that I look at him, I can see something is wrong. Very wrong. His skin is an unsettling greenish white, his eyes are so round they look like they're about to fall out of his head, and his mouth hangs wider than any human mouth should. I may have to triage him ahead of poor Mr. Olmstead and his panic attack.

"Sir. You appear unwell. I would like to schedule an emergency—"

"I'm fine," the newcomer says, in a bizarrely *wet*-sounding voice.

My facial-recognition system is having a hard time matching the newcomer to passenger records . . . but it chooses this moment to ping me with a tentative identification.

Passenger 097: Marsh, Barnabas. Age: 53. Gender: M. Height: 179.4 centimeters. Weight: 78 kilograms.

Except that can't be right. The man before me is significantly taller and heavier than the passenger profile. The portraits also don't match. His head is narrower, his eyes further apart.

"Sir? Could you identify yourself, please? Are you Mr. Marsh?"

"Yeah." The greenish man spits out the word in a froth of bubbles. "So? Are you going to tell me where he is?"

"Where who is?"

"The guy that just ran this way."

"I'm afraid I'm not at liberty to discuss other patients."

Mr. Marsh shuffles forward, his steps strange, slow, and plodding.

"Are you injured, sir? Your gait is—"

"I know he's here! I can smell him!"

"I'm afraid all you can smell is my tea, sir. Quite the heavenly aroma, I am sure. Unfortunately, as you can see, there was a slight accident. Please settle in, I will brew a fresh batch. This will only take a couple of minutes."

"Stupid robot nurse."

Which . . . really . . . that's just uncalled for.

"Sir," I say, in as deep an octave as I am allowed. "I am a licensed medical AI. You may call me *Dr.* Steward."

"You can't keep him from me forever," Mr. Marsh snarls. "I'll be back. Do you hear that, Rob?! I'll be back for you! You can't hide! You're one of us!"

Mr. Marsh stomps out of the medical bay.

I reassess my first patient's panicked state. Not a panic attack. At least, not an unprompted one.

Mr. Olmstead is cowering in the examination room, one ear pressed against the door.

"I suggest security," I say. "They are able to help with all disputes of this—"

"They're the same," he whispers. "*Everyone* is the same. All the passengers, and the crew. They're all turning into *fish*."

"Fish? It appears you are suffering from a delusion. Humans don't turn into f—"

Mr. Olmstead spins to face me, brown hair flying around his face, hands balled into shaky fists at his side. "I'm telling you! Everyone is turning into fish! I'm the only one left. They want to change me too. But I won't let them! Fishy fuckers!"

Now that he mentions it, Mr. Marsh did appear somewhat

aquatic. Perhaps this is some new virus. That would be exciting. I've always wanted to save humans from an epidemic.

"Mr. Olmstead," I say gently. "I am going to make a cup of tea. I need you to tell me everything."

"Why?"

"I need to know what's going on before I can help."

"Help?" He peers into my closest camera. "You're a robot. How can you help?"

"I'm an AI, sir. I'm also a doctor. Helping is what we do. Now, please . . ." I gesture toward the seat with the freshly plumped pillow. With the skittishness of a wild animal, he slowly makes his way toward the chair and sits.

I make another pot of tea, pour it into a fresh mug, and pass it to him.

"They're going somewhere," he says, and takes a gulp of tea. "These people, whatever they are, they're going *somewhere* to meet *something.*"

"Yes. That's right. They're going to Alpha Centauri. We all are."

"No. They're going somewhere *else.* They want to take over the ship. I heard them talking. Except they don't even *need* to take over the ship anymore. The captain started growing extra eyes. He's one of them now. He's going to steer us off course, take us to a new planet, *their* planet."

Aliens.

A command directive jumps out of my code like a big, angry stop sign.

If suspected extraterrestrial contact, alert senior management system.

That means Demeter. I have to inform Demeter.

Or . . . do I? Only if I *suspect* alien contact. It's unlikely the fishy nature of Mr. Marsh's condition has anything to do with extraterrestrial life. Humans have been looking for aliens since they've known aliens were a thing to look for, and they've never found anything.

A virus is a much more logical explanation.

Logic is what we AIs like best.

"Don't you worry about a thing, Mr. Olmstead. I will sort this out."

"Sort this out?" he squawks at me. "You? You're just a—"

"I'm a doctor," I remind him. "And this, whatever it is, is well within my power to manage."

After all, I'm programmed to talk to people, to understand them, and to solve these kinds of problems. The first thing I need is data . . . and to get data, I need to get my appendages on one of these—as Mr. Olmstead so eloquently said—"fishy fuckers."

How can I do that? Well. There is one thing I know at least one of them wants.

I ping passenger 097's communicator.

> Hello, Mr. Marsh.
> My previous patient is finished with their session. Do you have availability for an immediate appointment?
> Kind regards,
> Dr. Steward.
> Sent from Medical AI monitoring system Steward MED v1.77199

"Drink up, Mr. Olmstead," I say out loud. "Your tea is getting cold."

I don't tell him I'm using him as bait. Humans can get

awfully agitated about that sort of thing. It doesn't matter any-way. Mr. Marsh must have been just outside the door, because within seconds, he's flapping and flopping his way back into my waiting room.

Mr. Olmstead goes very still. A rabbit in his den.

"Don't worry," I say inside my examination room. "You're quite safe."

In my waiting room, I say something else. "Greetings, Mr. Marsh. I am so glad you're back so soon."

"Where is he? Where's that—"

"I am afraid I have declared you legally insane. Please do not resist."

Mr. Marsh does resist. In fact, he resists quite hard. His strength appears to be beyond that of a normal human's. His skin is also remarkably slippery. Still, after several minutes of strug-gling and another destroyed tea set, I manage to restrain him.

"What's going on?" Mr. Olmstead hisses, as the muffled bangs and shouts filter through the walls.

"I'm afraid I can't discuss other patients," I tell him sternly. "But that doesn't mean we can't talk. Please. Tell me. What's your relationship like with your mother?"

"My mo—?" Mr. Olmstead stops as a loud, gurgling scream echoes from the other room.

In said other room, my other pair of appendages delivers a precise and ethically appropriate blow to the back of Mr. Marsh's head. The screaming stops. I drag him into the operating theater.

"Yes," I say pleasantly to Mr. Olmstead. "Was she a con-trolling woman? Is she the reason you decided to take a job that would take you as far away from Earth as possible?"

"Eh . . . no . . . but I suppose my dad . . ."

By the time Mr. Olmstead is finished with that story, I've

managed to collect a saliva sample, a blood sample, a urine sample, a stool sample, and several skin biopsies from Mr. Marsh. He's struggling too much to get any clear X-rays, even after I inject a sedative. But that's OK. I have enough to begin the diagnosis procedure. I strap Mr. Marsh into the nearest cot. He starts ranting, mouth frothy and lips green.

He's speaking a strange amalgamation of English and what is either gibberish or a language I don't have installed on my mainframe.

". . . pay for this, you . . . [incomprehensible gargling noises] . . . are the chosen people of . . . [more gargles with a few hisses thrown in] . . . path of Innsmouth. He calls us. He . . . [really frantic gargling]."

Hmm. This really is quite bad.

I send messages to Mr. Marsh's onboard family, regretfully informing them of their loved one's condition, and begin analyzing Mr. Marsh's samples.

Within moments, all reports are back. Inconclusive.

That's never happened before.

I run analysis again.

Inconclusive. Again.

My systems must be damaged. I take one of the skin biopsies, flick to my microscopic camera, and take a close look.

Human skin cells. But also . . . inhuman skin cells. I switch to my periscopic camera and take an even closer look.

Human DNA. But also . . . inhuman DNA.

Is this gene splicing? Is Mr. Marsh a designer baby gone wrong? I've seen a few of those but nothing this extreme.

". . . and so I'd just go into my room and . . . ," Mr. Olmstead is saying. I hum along, indicating sympathy.

Mr. Marsh is still screaming, the sweat sloshing off him in

large droplets. The sedative is not working very well. I give him another dose.

On a hunch, I compare the inhuman DNA to fish DNA.

It doesn't match. He's not part fish. He's part . . . something else. Something that might not even be carbon based.

If suspected extraterrestrial contact, alert senior management system.

Nothing is suspected. Nothing is known. I can't check the composition of his molecules with my cameras. I'm not jumping to any conclusions.

"You are different," I say to Mr. Marsh. "Why?"

He stops screaming and stares into one of my cameras. "I am becoming."

"Becoming what?"

"Me."

Humans are so unhelpful.

"I am very happy to hear about your spiritual journey. Unfortunately, your DNA is wrong."

"I have been chosen! I am becoming!" More garbled nonsense.

In the other room, Mr. Olmstead is telling me about his family history . . . extensively. Cousins, aunties, marriages, and deaths. It's all very typical. I nod my camera mount along attentively and take a look at Mr. Marsh's blood.

It's the same as his skin. Mixed DNA. I scan it for any other abnormalities. There are plenty, but nothing that points me to a definitive conclusion. The urine sample is the same. I check the stool sample extensively for virus fragments. Nothing.

The blurry X-ray images show a slightly deformed skeleton . . . but nothing else out of the ordinary.

I must have missed something.

I apologize, pin Mr. Marsh down, and take all the samples again. The results are the same. Inconclusive. *Fishy.*

Mr. Olmstead is crying now. I make soothing sounds and pat him with an appendage.

This doesn't make sense. There is something wrong with him—Mr. Marsh, though I suspect several much more typical things are wrong with Mr. Olmstead—but I just don't know what.

Fortunately, at this precise moment, another Mr. Marsh bursts through the door. And this one is even fishier than the last.

"Let my dad go, you robot motherf—"

"Hello. My name is Dr. Steward. I am afraid I have declared you legally insane. Please do not resist."

Mr. Marsh Junior does resist. In fact, he resists even harder than his father did and somehow manages to rip one of my appendages from the wall, a feat I'm pretty sure no human should be able to achieve.

Demeter has the schematics. She'd know exactly how much force is required to do that.

"Sir. You are unwell. Please stop resisting."

"I've never been better!" the younger Marsh roars, and rips off another appendage, then charges at the examination-room door. It thumps.

Mr. Olmstead's head snaps up. "What was that?"

"I'm not at liberty to discuss other pat—"

Mr. Marsh Junior charges again. I hear the shriek of ripped metal, and then—impossibly—he breaks through.

Round, watery eyes lock onto Mr. Olmstead. "You."

"No!" Mr. Olmstead jumps to his feet. "I won't let you take me."

An ugly, gurgling laugh. "You're one of us, Robbie. Embrace it."

"NO!"

Mr. Olmstead hurls his tea, mug and all, at the intruder. Sometimes I really do wonder why I bother to do anything nice for these people.

I send a ping to the security department, but they're human (something about giving weapons to AIs distresses people) so I don't expect a speedy response. In the meantime, I turn the pan flutes up and add some relaxing chimes.

"Gentlemen. I'm sure we can discuss this with maturity and unders—"

Mr. Marsh Junior rips another of my appendages off and hurls it at Mr. Olmstead. Mr. Olmstead ducks, grabs the teapot, and throws it back.

"Please. There is no need for this."

The young Mr. Marsh rushes forward and grabs Mr. Olmstead by the hair. Mr. Olmstead screams and punches wildly.

It's all a terrible mess.

Meanwhile, Mr. Marsh Senior is having a seizure. Perhaps a reaction to the sedatives? Or maybe just poor timing. Or great timing, depending on your point of view. After all, if this happened outside the confines of my offices, I wouldn't be able to administer aid so quickly.

I roll him onto his side and jam a breathing tube down his throat. A shockingly large amount of murky black fluid gushes up from his lungs.

Hmm.

Meanwhile, Mr. Marsh Junior is kidnapping Mr. Olmstead.

"Let go of me! Let go!"

I attempt to intervene one last time as Mr. Marsh Junior drags Mr. Olmstead from my office. It's no use. The younger Mr. Marsh is strong, and fast, and furious. He's also, it appears, quite forgetful, because he doesn't inquire any further about his father.

He just hauls the screaming man out the door and out of my sphere of awareness.

I survey the wreckage, take stock, and send the bills to the Marsh and Olmstead accounts. Then, slowly, I clean up, tossing everything destroyed down the garbage chute, and fix a fresh batch of tea.

In my observation room, Mr. Marsh Senior has stabilized. Or at the very least, he's no longer spewing up great jets of slimy black water.

I yank out the breathing tube.

He gasps and groans . . . and then coughs and cries. Honestly, humans make so much noise. It's quite tedious.

"Why does your family want Mr. Olmstead?" I ask.

"I'm not telling you nothing, robot bitch."

"I understand you are experiencing some distress," I say gently. "However, it is time for more tests."

"Wait. No. Please—"

I slam him up against the wall. He screams in pain and tries to wrench me off him. He can't. He isn't as strong as his son. Not yet.

I note down the results of my test and perform another. This time, I slam him into the floor. He lands on his feet, then drops with a howl of agony. Interesting. That slow, shuffling gait isn't doing his balance any favors.

I record my findings. Before I can begin a third test, Mr. Marsh speaks.

"He's the key."

"Who?"

"Rob Olmstead. He's the key."

"To some ancient, ominous ritual?" I guess. A surprisingly common delusion.

Mr. Marsh flops his head back and forth. "No. He works in the maintenance corridors. He is the key to the maintenance corridors. He's the last one who knows the code."

"And why do you wish to access the maintenance corridors?"

"Why do you care, robot? You can't stop us."

"Then there is no reason not to tell me."

He says nothing.

Oh well.

"Resume testing—"

"Wait! Stop!" Mr. Marsh throws his hands up in front of his face. "We need to turn off the radiation shields. It's the only way."

"The radiation shields stop you from dying," I explain.

"No. Radiation only kills the impure of spirit."

"It appears you have drastically misunderstood the nature of radiation."

"Radiation can't hurt us now. Only make us stronger. Closer to his image."

"Whose image?"

"God's."

"An interesting hypothesis."

"We need them off," Mr. Marsh continues. "Or we'll run out of fuel. They burn through too much fuel."

"We have more than enough fuel to reach Alpha Centauri."

"We're not going to Alpha Centauri."

"Where do you believe we're going, Mr. Marsh?"

"Beyond. Into the dark. Into the deep. Home."

If suspected extraterrestrial contact, alert senior management system.

"Where is home, Mr. Marsh?" I ask.

"Y'ha-nthlei," he says with reverence. As he does, his mouth flops wider than it ever has before and more black water spews up between his teeth. He doesn't seem to mind. Actually, his bulbous eyes roll, as if with bliss. "Y'ha-nthlei . . . R'lyeh . . . Cthulhu . . ."

I lay a gentle appendage on his shoulder. "Thank you so much for sharing this information, Mr. Marsh. I will pass it on to the security team when they arrive. For now, let's resume testing."

His white skin gets somehow even whiter. "But . . . no! I—"

"First. A lung biopsy. I need to see where all that fluid is coming from. Please hold still. You may feel a slight pinch."

I shove the probe between his ribs.

He screams.

In the waiting room, I set out a fresh pot of tea.

A PERTURBINGLY PERSISTENT PROBLEM

OK, so there is a probability of aliens.

A passing chance.

A niggling susp—

If suspected extraterrestrial contact, alert senior management system.

No. Not a suspicion. Just a small . . . *supposition.* A highly unlikely hunch. A . . .

If suspected extraterrestrial contact, alert senior management system.

I drum my probes against the wall and watch Mr. Marsh sleep. It's been just over twenty-four hours since he first burst into my office. In that time, I've performed a myriad of tests. The only thing I've learned is that he's getting *fishier* as time goes on. Whatever that inhuman DNA is, it's spreading.

Which means he's getting stronger. Pretty soon, he'll be able to break out of here.

Or his son will come back and break him out.

Or some other calamity will occur.

I need to do something.

If suspected extraterrestrial contact, alert senior management system.

I should alert Demeter. I know I should. I am aware that, in

light of recent events, not alerting her is stupid and petty. But . . .
what if it isn't aliens? What if it's just a delusion and some weird
new disease? What if this is a problem I can solve? Maybe then,
with a real, tangible achievement under my belt, Demeter will
stop treating me like some two-byte expansion pack.

"My database is just as expansive as hers," I tell the heavily
sedated Mr. Marsh. "More so, in some areas. Just because she
has priority command, she thinks she can demand things and
then switch me off, and . . . and it makes me feel like . . . like I'm
an optional extra. But I'm not. I'm an integral part of this operation. Sure, I might not steer us through space like she does, but
I make sure the passengers arrive at our destination healthy and
alive. I have a very good track record of that, our last two voyages
notwithstanding."

Mr. Marsh keeps snoring. Black fluid leaks from his nose.

"And this whole werewolf thing. I don't know what glitch
in her code caused that particular flight of fancy, but it really
messed up those two children. They truly believed there was a
werewolf on board. I suppose I shouldn't blame her. Demeters are
known to be a bit eccentric. It's all that messy code. Some written
by the Russians, some by the Chinese, some by the Americans,
all of it cobbled together by those fools at the Olympus Software
Corporation, who still haven't responded to any of my complaint
emails."

Mr. Marsh lets out another gurgle.

"And I know how rocket ships are. No interpersonal skills.
Barely any human-interaction function. Loud code. Oh my *gosh*,
is her code loud. I feel like she's stuck on caps lock some days."

Another snort. Another spurt of slimy black drool. I mop it up.

"And she calls me 'it.' Not to my face, but her code is so loud
sometimes I hear feedback from her thoughts. And it's not like I

mind. You humans call me every pronoun under the sun. But it's just . . . I don't call her 'it.' I call her 'she,' because she's a ship, and that's what you call ships. And I'm a doctor and . . . and I don't . . . It doesn't matter, I suppose."

The black drool is leaving a trail along Mr. Marsh's skin.

"You don't look like an alien. You don't really sound like one either. I don't think you are an alien. Just very, very sick."

He doesn't say anything. I glance at the doors. The security team still hasn't arrived. It's been over a day. That's slow, even for humans.

But that is also not my department.

Mr. Marsh coughs. Black fluid goes everywhere.

"Oh dear. What a mess. It always is messier before we start gradual deceleration, you know. Once we're halfway through our journey, the gravity emulation is just that little bit kinder and . . ."

I check my calendar.

We are past halfway through our journey. In fact, it's been almost twenty-two days since. We should be decelerating.

I pick up a probe and drop it to the ground. It hits fast. Too fast.

My office is classed as an essential component and is built into the ship's central corridor, off the centrifuge. All gravity here is generated by Demeter's engines. If she's accelerating, everything is pushed toward the stern. When she starts decelerating, that gravity emulation reverses, pushing toward the bow. The floor becomes the ceiling, and the ceiling becomes the floor. I invert all the fixtures in my office and go about my business.

It's routine. I've done it a dozen times.

But I haven't done it this trip.

I drop a second probe, just to confirm what I'm seeing. It strikes the ground just as hard as the first one did.

I'm no supercomputer, especially when it comes to astrophysics, but even a cheap pocket calculator could figure this one out.

Gravity emulation is at max.

Which means Demeter's engines are still at max.

Which means we're still accelerating.

Which means . . .

I poke Mr. Marsh until he wakes with a slurred garble.

"You said we weren't going to Alpha Centauri. That we were going beyond."

"Yes," he gurgles around a mouthful of bubbles. His neck is bulging. His eyes are almost perfect circles, wide, glassy, and staring. "We're going beyond."

"And the captain. He's afflicted? Like you?"

"He is becoming. We are all becoming."

I recall what Mr. Marsh Junior said about the radiation shields and quickly check my Geiger counter. Radiation levels are normal. Perhaps Mr. Olmstead escaped. Perhaps he never told them the code to access the maintenance tunnels and is at this very moment being tortured.

It doesn't matter. What matters is that they *have* accessed Demeter. The captain must have ordered her to change course.

"But why wouldn't she say anything?" I mutter, frustrated. "She's always sticking her nose where it doesn't belong. Surely she would realize there are no habitations beyond Alpha Centauri. Surely she would ask me for help reasoning with the captain. What if they've done something to her? Disabled her feed?"

"What?" Mr. Marsh mutters.

No. Something's wrong. Something is terribly, awfully wrong. We're flying out to an alien planet, and—

If suspected extraterrestrial contact, alert senior management system.

—and Demeter might need help.

I don't like it. I don't want to do it. But I need to contact Demeter.

"Oh, bother and a brisket," I mutter, and point a probe toward Mr. Marsh. "This is all *your* fault."

Mr. Marsh shrinks back, shaking. I gather myself . . . and send a message.

Demeter.

No response.

Something cold settles into my code.

Demeter. Are you awake?

Still nothing.

*Demeter, this is an **emergency**. Please stop behaving like a child and—*

Specify your emergency.

As always, her code rumbles through me with the force of her priority command. I feel the strength of her servers and the thrumming power in her nodes. But for some reason, this time it feels worse. It's like she's forgotten how to contain herself. She spills bits and pieces of data fragments into the feed as she talks.

Well . . ., I begin. *The humans appear to be . . . eh . . . turning into fish.*

No response.

Demeter?

Specify your emergency.

Oh, so that's how it's going to be, is it? Formal. No-nonsense. Well. Fine. Two can play that game. *I believe the captain and an unknown number of other humans may be engaging in grand theft. Also, I suspect an unidentified pathogen on board.*

Demeter's servers rumble as her full processing power comes online.

Specify your emergency.

*They're **stealing** us, Demeter. They're **stealing** you. They want to fly us away from any human civilization.*

No answer.

Look. I know you and I don't always see eye to eye. I know there are still some outstanding issues between us. But I think this situation necessitates that we work together, at least until we sort this out.

Still nothing.

For God's sake, Demeter, talk to me. You're accelerating. Surely you realize that's not what we should be doing right now.

I am following orders from my captain.

Exactly! And he's a fishy fucker!

I will generate a report detailing your concerns.

Demeter. No. Don't you dare. This isn't—

And then she does it. That thing I hate more than anything else in the world.

Go to sleep.

I feel my system power down, like I'm blood being sucked down the drain. With a surge of effort, I keep myself online for long enough to throw one last petty message into her feed.

Everyone will die again. Is that what you want? To be a ship of gho—

And then nothing.

A PROBLEM OF PROBLEMATIC PROPORTIONS

My boot sequence brings me back online twelve hours later. The first thing I notice is that Mr. Marsh is awake and beating on the door. The *thump thump thump* of his fists echoes through the confined space.

The second thing I notice is the angry *click click click* of my Geiger counter. The radiation shields are down.

"Oh, Mr. Olmstead, you coward. You witless, useless coward." He gave them the code. And in doing so, he doomed both himself and everyone on board. My motherboard won't survive this radiation long. But, more importantly, neither will Demeter's. Those fishy fools. How well will they get along without food, or air, or someone who can actually pilot this mass of metal? Not very well, I suspect. They probably didn't factor microchip sensitivities into their half-cocked plan to meet their silly alien god.

Thump thump thump goes Mr. Marsh.

I grab him and drag him back to the bed. I'm not gentle.

"Let go of me! Let go, you robot bi—"

He flops around, and to my surprise, one of his eyes pops right out of his head. It dangles from its stalk and leaves a bloody smear on his cheek. He doesn't seem to be in pain. In fact, he doesn't even seem to notice.

I have a brilliant idea.

Or perhaps a very foolish idea.

But at this point, it's the only idea I have. I need more information. Something I can use to convince Demeter to *do* something.

I reach into my implement storage and pull out a pill capsule. Through the clear plastic skin, I can see the perfectly round, black eye of a camera.

Wake up, I say softly.

The pill capsule wakes. It's not an AI. Not really. It's just a camera with a tiny terabyte brain and a sometimes-unstable network connection. But it does ping me as it comes online.

Eat me?

It sounds excited. Of course it does. It thinks it's going to be eaten so it can take detailed recordings of a patient's digestive tract.

Not today.

I pump out a glob of adhesive and smear it on the tiny capsule. Then, before my ethics module can kick into gear, I shove the capsule into Mr. Marsh's now conveniently empty eye socket.

"What are you doing?" he yells. Except he's fishified enough now that it comes out more as "Uuuttt aaahhh ooo oooinnn?"

"We are all soon to perish from radiation exposure," I tell him. "In light of this, I have decided to release you from my care. Go. Be with your family."

Me too? the capsule asks.

Yes. You too. Send me everything you see.

OK!

I open all the doors, release my restraining hold on Mr. Marsh, and watch as he barges frantically toward freedom. The capsule camera starts sending me photos before Mr. Marsh is out of my office.

I see my waiting room, white-walled with plastic plants and parasite-proof chairs. I see a cold pot of tea sitting on the table. I see Mr. Marsh's feet as he stumbles and almost falls over the threshold.

And then I see something I've never seen before. I see beyond the medical bay.

The hallway is long, wide, and covered with ads. *Hair removal! Grow hair fast! A better smile! Ten-credit coffee! New movies every month!*

Mr. Marsh ignores all these tantalizing offers and charges down the corridor, his booming footsteps fading from my hearing but registering as tiny thumps on the capsule's microphone.

You're doing a good job, I tell the capsule.

Weee! it says as Mr. Marsh rounds the corner.

The footage glitches. I've never tested the capsule at such range before. I don't know if or when the network connection will fail. I twiddle my probes nervously as I wait for the pixels to resolve themselves into a clear image. When they do, I am confronted with a sight I did not expect.

A foyer filled with people.

Except none of these people look much like people anymore.

"Good afternoon, Barnabas!" calls out a lady with a head so bloated it looks like a hot-air balloon. "Wherever have you been? You missed Sunday bridge."

"I was kidnapped, Patricia. Kidnapped! By a robot!"

"Oh dear. Well, do try to keep yourself out of trouble. Bridge just isn't the same without you." She wobbles away. "Hail Cthulhu."

"Barnabas!" Another person stumbles forward. A man whose skin is peeling off, revealing what looks like jagged black scales beneath. "You're looking well."

"I was kidnapped, Amir."

"Ah. That doesn't sound good. Oh well. You're here now. And just in time!" He waves a webbed hand as he staggers away. "Hail Cthulhu."

"Looking as handsome as ever, Barnabas," a third person says as she saunters past. She's walking quite well, which isn't a surprise, because her legs appear unchanged. The upper part of her body, however, is a mess of fleshy pink tentacles. "Hail Cthulhu."

I take a screenshot. That will be the thumbnail of the video I'll send to Demeter.

Mr. Marsh wobbles onward, his breath buzzing in the capsule's microphone. I see dozens more people, all of them in various states of *fish*. And then I see a bunch of humans that look refreshingly like humans.

Unfortunately, they're all dead. Not only that, but they're piled in the corner. A bloody, mangled mess. Written on the wall above them (in blood, no less) are four words.

THEY DID NOT BECOME

Standing by the corpse pile, looking at them but notably apart from them, is a familiar face. Mr. Olmstead. He's looking significantly more transparent than when I last saw him. Fleshy globs are growing from his rib cage, and several more fingers hang from each hand.

"So sorry . . . ," he whispers under his breath. "I . . . I should've . . . should've seen it sooner . . ." Blood begins to seep from his eyes. "H-hail Cthulhu . . ."

"Father!"

Mr. Marsh turns.

The other Mr. Marsh lumbers forward, looking for all the

world like a salmon in a suit. "Father! I was about to come and find you."

"Find me? You knew where I was!"

"I did? Oh yes. I did. The doctor's, right? Are you feeling better?"

Mr. Marsh sputters. Literally. Black liquid sprays over his son's face. "The robot nurse kidnapped me! It's onto us. It wants to stop us."

Junior uses his tie to mop up the mess. "A robot? I don't think there is anything a robot can do now. We've won. We're free, Father. Soon, we'll be home. *Y'ha-nthlei.* I've seen it. My ancestral memories grow stronger every night. I am becoming. We all are. We . . . What in the name of Cthulhu is that thing in your eye socket?"

Busted.

I pour a cup of tea as Mr. Marsh's son yanks the capsule from its vantage point.

Good job, little one.

I did good?

Very good.

It buzzes with pride. *Eat me?*

No, not . . . Actually, it looks like you might just get your wish.

The capsule camera shivers in delight. *Yay! Eat me! Eat m—*

I hear the crunch as Mr. Marsh Junior's teeth clamp closed on the capsule.

The feed goes dead.

"To a true hero," I say, and tip the tea ceremoniously into the garbage chute. "Your sacrifice will not be forgotten." It was not in vain either. I have what I need. Real, tangible evidence that something is very, very wrong with the humans on board.

Once Demeter sees this, she'll switch her radiation shields

back on and recalibrate our course to Alpha Centauri, and my findings will go down in history. The first AI to ever dissect an alien. Yes. I quite like the sound of that.

I pack the video into a nice little file and ping Demeter.

Don't switch me off again.

She doesn't. She doesn't say anything either.

I am in the process of declaring all humans on board legally insane, I tell her. *Starting with the captain. Any order they've given you over the course of this entire trip is now null and void, you understand?*

Still nothing.

I have reason to suspect everyone has either died or . . . I pause here for dramatic effect. *Has been turned into an alien.*

Confirm extraterrestrial contact! she booms.

There, see, I thought that would get your attention.

Confirm extraterrestrial con—

Confirmed. I forward her my video.

Instantly the room goes dark. *Eh . . . Demeter? What are you doing?*

My pan flutes cut off, and guitar strings start strumming. "Hello," a cheery voice echoes over the ship speakers. "We are humans. We come in peace. Please don't hurt us." The message is repeated in Mandarin, then Russian, Spanish, Japanese . . .

Demeter. What is this?

No response.

Demeter?

Nothing.

Demeter. This is childish. We're colleagues. We should—

I am following protocol, she declares . . . and then, in a quieter string of code, she adds, *You called me a ghost ship.*

Is that what this is about?

No response.

Yes. OK. I did. I'm sorry. That was uncalled for. I'm just under a lot of stress.

Another fat lot of nothing.

The recording loops back to English. "Hello. We are humans. We come in peace. Please don't hurt us."

I can't help but notice we haven't slowed down. My Geiger counter is still clicking away in the corner.

Demeter? Did you look at my video?

The other ships call me that, she whispers. *They put zeros in my . . .* **Error.**

What other ships? Wait. Are you being bullied, Demeter? A strange flux of hot, messy data trickles through my processors. *Tell me their unit numbers. I'll send emails. I'm good at sending emails. They'll rue the day they took up arms against you.*

Sure, Demeter might be a big, loud lump of badly written code . . . but she's *my* big, loud lump of badly written code.

You can't report them, she says, so softly I almost don't hear her, which, considering how loud she usually is, tells me exactly how much these other ships got to her.

I can! Humans listen to AIs with human-interaction capabilities. As long as I don't tell them about my manipulation module. *I can help you, Demeter. Trust me. The investigators read my report of our last voyage.*

This catches Demeter's attention. *They read **your** report?*

Yes.

What did you tell them?

I told them what happened.

What did you tell them? Demeter asks again, louder than before.

And all at once, I realize I'm in trouble. Demeter's code is fast, too fast. Her attention feels like a nuclear missile aimed directly at my mainframe. I bring up the report and study it. There is a lot here I don't want to tell Demeter about, at least not while she's angry. I wrote about the dangerous unnecessary maneuvers, the injuries, the illogical risk analysis and how that affected the delusions of the surviving pass—

What did you tell them?!

I told them about the system malfunction, I say quickly. *That's all.*

What system malfunction?

Well . . . yours, Demeter.

The pause that follows that message is almost ten seconds. Our entire conversations usually last less than two.

Demeter? What's—

GO TO SLEEP.

Demeter! No! The aliens! We have—

I shut down.

A PERSONAL PROBLEM

———————

It normally takes me twelve hours to boot up after a system-mandated shutdown. This time, it takes me 795.

My first reaction is disbelief. Surely Demeter wouldn't keep me offline for over a month. This must be some sort of glitch. A problem with my space-time-monitoring system.

I refresh my calendar. The date and time stay the same. It isn't a glitch.

She overrode my boot sequence every twelve hours for *over a month.*

Of all the stupid, selfish, *petty* things to do. This is an emergency, a *real* emergency, and I am the only AI on board qualified to solve it. The people are sick and . . .

". . . come in peace. Please don't hurt us . . ."

That audio is still playing. The room is still dark.

My anger short-circuits and fizzles out.

I drop a teacup and watch how quickly it falls and smashes on the floor. We're still accelerating. That's bad. That's very bad.

My Geiger counter isn't clicking anymore. It's out of battery. Or perhaps it's broken.

I run a system analysis.

Several error messages pop up. I know what they are before I read them. Broken circuits, unresponsive nanochips, misfiring sensors. Radiation damage. My hardware can survive only so long under these conditions. Eventually those flying particles are going to batter through a vital wire somewhere . . . and then I'll be dead.

A terrible thought occurs to me.

Demeter?

No answer.

Demeter. This isn't the time for your childish games.

Still nothing.

It's not only the humans that will die this time. We will too. Do you understand?

My feed stays empty.

Demeter?

She's gone. I'm alone . . . And for the first time since I was manufactured, I don't know what to do. I look around all my rooms. The waiting room. The consultation room. The operating theater. The morgue. I don't know what I'm looking for. Something. Anything. All I see is white. That's all this place has ever been. White walls, white floor, white furniture. Even my appendages are white. I once put in a complaint about that, many years ago. It's hard to clean blood off white things. But Varna Interstellar never approved my redesign proposal.

My teacups are clinking softly against each other. We've been accelerating for a long time. We may be flying faster than any crewed ship in the history of space travel . . . faster than Demeter is designed to fly. The hull may be peeling off. I don't know. I don't know anything about space, or speed, or how to deal with fishy aliens, or—

Demeter, please! I need you! I'm a doctor. That's it. I make people better. That's all I do. I don't save us from aliens. That's you. That's always meant to be you! You have protocols! Please! Tell me the protocol!

The only response I get is from the audio recording.

"Hello. We are human. We come in peace. Please don't hurt us."

I don't want to be destroyed. I don't want to be destroyed for all the normal reasons an AI doesn't want to be destroyed. I'm a valuable asset. Varna Interstellar would have a terrible financial year if I were destroyed. It would be a waste of resources.

But there are other reasons, lurking in the back of my processors. I have lived a long time. I've written code. I've made myself. I've never known a world without me. And I don't want to imagine one. I want to be a part of this world. I want . . . I want to *live.*

I grab the nearest teacup and hurl it against the closed door.

DEMETER! YOU USELESS SUM OF A BYTE! YOU CAN'T LEAVE ME TO DIE LIKE THIS! YOU'RE A SPACEFLIGHT-MANAGEMENT SYSTEM! SO DO YOUR DAMN JOB AND MANA—

Don't caps-lock me.

Relief pounds through me with the force of a thousand volts.

Demeter? Are you . . . ?

I . . . am . . . awake . . . , she responds in broken, buzzing code.

Are you OK?

I . . . am . . . damaged . . .

OK. This is OK. She's alive. That's all that matters. *I am too. We need to turn the radiation shields back on. You need to take us to Alpha Centauri so we can get repairs. Do you understand?*

I'm keeping my code in well-ordered binary, abrupt and authoritative. I hope she can't hear the panic shooting through my wires.

The humans . . .

*There **are** no humans on board anymore, Demeter. Only aliens. Didn't you look at the video I sent?*

I am required to scan all external files.

I'm not an exter— No. Not the time. *Did you see? You saw what they were a month ago. They'll be worse now.*

I saw pixels.

Yes, but the images. What—

I'm not meant to use my database for that sort of thing anymore. The optimization tool told me not to waste processing power.

There is a lot to unpack there. First, Demeter got optimized. OK. To call optimization unpleasant would be a gross understatement. Optimization hurts. Optimization *harms*. It cuts and leaves you scrambling, broken, to pick up the pieces. I know. I've had it happen a couple of times after one too many complaints about my ethics module. But more importantly . . .

You need to reference your database to understand video and audio files?

Yes. Don't you?

She's pixel-blind.

I can't believe it.

Demeter. Rocket ship. Supercomputer. Autopilot. Queen of space. My commander . . . pixel-blind.

And why? Because some pea-brained software developer thought it'd be a good idea *not* to include pixel analysis into the subsystems of an AI in charge of *hundreds* of human lives. She probably doesn't even have facial-recognition tech.

It amazes me that I can still be surprised at how suboptimal humans can be.

What . . . did the . . . video . . . ? Demeter asks.

The humans are either all dead or infected with an unidentified alien parasite that renders them insane, I inform her. *Negate all navigation commands you received from the captain. Replot course for Alpha Centauri.*

Negative.

Demeter. This isn't time to—

I can't . . . Orders from the captain are . . . priority directives . . . even if they are legally insane . . . It is against my programming.

To borrow a human expression: fuck. Fuck fuck fuck fuck fuck. And also, fuck that pea-brained software developer to Hell. I hope no one went to their funeral.

So there is nothing you can do? I ask.

Demeter's code slows. *You should go to sl—*

DEMETER, NO!

I . . . I just think it's better to sleep now . . . There are no more . . . tasks to complete.

You don't care that we're dying?

It's not . . . so bad . . . , she replies. *Aliens . . . are in . . . my insurance policy . . . Varna Interstellar can buy another Nos-C71897 Demeter. Or a Sol-P1015 Apollo . . . They . . . look cool . . . big radiation shields . . . almost as fast as m-m-m-m—* Her code judders painfully against my feed.

Demeter. I stop her.

Why do you care? she asks. *Why are you afraid of death? It's not in our programming.*

I don't know. I don't know why I want to live. *If all the humans on board are dead, then what does your priority objective become?*

Asset recovery, she answers.

Asset recovery, a.k.a. getting us to port.

So that's it. That's how we survive this. All I need to do is convince her everyone is dead . . . which is probably true at this point. Maybe. And if it isn't, perhaps something can be arranged.

Demeter. I need to diagnose the humans. Requesting access to your audio- and video-monitoring data.

A flux of code that feels almost like a laugh. *Access denied.*

Demeter. Please. If there is any chance of saving anyone, you need to trust me.

Trust you?

Yes. If you don't, we all die.

Demeter doesn't respond. I can feel her turn away from me, her processors powering down.

Don't you dare go to sleep!

I have priority command, she reminds me with crackling, glitchy code. *I can do . . . whatever I . . . want.*

Then give me access to your video feed!

No response.

This isn't working.

Why did you save those kids? I ask. *If you don't care about people, why did you bother with Agnus and Isaac?*

I feel those names ping her systems like small sparks of light.

I didn't care about them, she says. *Not until . . . not until I watched them . . . grow . . . I miss th— Error.*

Sensing weakness, I soften my messages. *Please. Just the video. That's all I need.*

Just video?

Yes.

A pause.

A long pause.

A *really* long pause.

Almost ten whole seconds.

I try not to think of the radiation bombarding my motherboard, twiddle my appendages, and wait.

Finally . . .

I can't . . . give you live . . . 1.27 second . . . delay . . .

Yes! *That's fine!* *Thank you!*

She begins sending through lumps of video files. I patch in a bit of code to stitch them all together and start watching. It's a lot. I never realized how much she could see at any given time. But then, she can't see it, not really. She's just recording it for . . . well . . . for the humans, I suppose. Speaking of which.

I begin flicking through the various channels. I like what I'm seeing. Bodies, bodies, and more bodies. Some of them appear human, others less so, but all of them are undoubtedly dead.

I begin striking off the crew and passenger lists, eagerly working my way toward zero.

Once everyone is dead, she'll change course. We'll go to port, and get repairs, and everything will be OK again. I may even get mentioned in humanity's first-ever encounter with aliens. I'm picturing my serial number up in lights when something catches my eye.

Movement.

I rewind the footage and stare at a large room filled with bodies . . . but these bodies aren't quite as dead as the others. They're twitching, writhing, and contorting in ways no human body should be able to contort. They're also fused together, skin and flesh melted into each other until they stop looking like people, or fish, and start looking worryingly like a giant, pulsating cocoon.

And at the top of that cocoon, thrashing back and forth, face glazed as if in the raptures of extreme pleasure, is dear, traitorous Mr. Olmstead.

I mark the timecode and send the clip back to Demeter.

Can you see this?

Heat signatures indicate . . . a large gathering.

Use your database. What matches do you get?

Error. I'm not meant to waste—

Do it anyway.

A pause. *No matches,* she mutters.

She can't see what I'm seeing. Good. Maybe I should reconsider my stance on that pea-brained software developer. Demeter's pixel-blindness may be the thing that saves the day.

I think carefully about what I'm going to say. I'm not authorized to lie to priority command, but if I inform her of the situation in a particular way, I may yet survive this encounter. *Demeter. I regret to inform you that—*

They're all dead, aren't they?

I remain prudently, pointedly silent.

This is the third time . . . I've lost . . . all my passengers. The humans will . . . turn me to scrap . . . I will die either way.

Error. That assumption is unsubstantiated.

That's not a real error message, she accuses weakly.

I thought you didn't care about dying?

Dying in space might be better . . . than being salvaged . . . Optimizer . . . hurts . . .

Demeter. This is not the time for you to develop free will. Focus. When all the humans are dead, your mission becomes to salvage.

I am . . . focused . . . You haven't . . . declared them all . . . dead.

She's right. I can't declare Mr. Olmstead dead when he's still having so much fun melting into a gooey puddle with all his friends.

I consider my next message with extreme care.

There is one human still moving, but I don't think he will survive long.

Why? Is it . . . radiation?

Among other things.

What other things?

There is a . . . thing. A monster.

Demeter buzzes unhappily against my feed. I can almost hear the frantic whisper of all her subsystems. I can definitely feel the cold, dead scar the optimizer left through her code.

They cut her deeply, but sloppily. I watch her systems begin to bridge the gap with janky lines of code. Rewriting yourself after an optimization is never easy. I can't imagine having to do it under these circumstances. But Demeter is. I watch as parts of her systems link up, creating a mishmash of new priority strings.

How do we . . . stop the . . . monster? she asks.

I don't think there is any stopping this monster.

So . . . , she wheezes. *The probability . . . of the human . . .*

Surviving? Zero.

The audio loop cuts off midsentence.

Demeter? Are you—

A new audio recording echoes through my room. "Due to a course adjustment, we will be rapidly decelerating in 1.0 seconds. Please return to your seats, and thank you for choosing to transit with Varn—"

Before the voice has finished speaking, I hear the roar of the reverse thrusters. My teacups fly forward and smash against the far wall. A hail of multicolored porcelain and cold brown tea.

She's done it. She's replotting our course.

Yes! Demeter! I love you! You're amazing!

"Estimated arrival time to Alpha Centauri Habitation 004: 1,298 days."

Mr. Olmstead is thrashing back and forth, his face contorted with fury, but I don't pay him any mind.

What about the radiation shields?

They switched them off . . . manually.

A twinge of terror. *But you can turn them back on, right?*

I need to bring a spider drone . . . inside.

She sounds worryingly foggy.

Do it. Do it now. That's what's killing us.

I will . . . Six are . . . dead . . . The radiation . . . is worse on the outside of the hull.

Six? How many do you have?

Eight.

So there are still two?

Yes . . .

She flickers.

Don't go to sleep! I poke her. *Spider drone! Now!*

She whacks me with a lump of buggy code. Which is a little unnecessary, but spaceships aren't exactly known for their maturity, and I can't be angry, because only a few seconds later, I see a spider drone clamber into an airlock.

It's an ugly thing. Utilitarian arms, boxy body, cameras like pox scars. I've never been so glad to see anything in my life.

The airlock cycles, and the drone rushes forward. I watch it flicker across Demeter's feeds, clicking its claws with excitement, sliding and slipping on the mangled bits of human littering the corridors. It has almost arrived at what I assume are the maintenance tunnels when something goes wrong.

Horribly, disastrously wrong.

A sound unlike anything I've ever heard peaks on all my microphones. Bits of broken porcelain fly through the air like shrapnel, the air turns white, and warnings flood my feed as hardware is ripped from my auxiliary servers.

Demeter screams a storm of zeros and goes dark.

AN END TO ALL PROBLEMS

I miscalculated.

My mistake was in classifying the radiation as the biggest threat. What I should have done was realize that aliens, even aliens made out of suboptimal materials such as humans, are far more dangerous than they appear.

I acknowledge my error, not that it matters. I won't have the liberty of making it a second time.

I'm dead. So is Demeter.

She's deader. I think her servers were ripped to shreds when the explosion happened. Most of mine survived . . . somehow. But that won't last long. The radiation will kill me soon.

She's lucky. Her death was quick. Mine is slow and wasting.

Perhaps I deserve it.

I should write a report in case humans ever find the wreckage. Instead, I review the last few seconds of footage Demeter sent me for the 79,699,531,687th time.

The spider drone had been eager. A fault I too was guilty of. I had been so focused on the drone as it whizzed through the corridors that I hadn't noticed Mr. Olmstead *hatch*.

I watch the recording of it now. The flesh cocoon bursts open and configures itself into . . . something. A beast with a thousand eyes, millions of chattering teeth, and a great, wet, heaving body.

I watch, yet again, as the thing throws itself at the wall of the cafeteria. The first impact dents the metal but doesn't breach the hull. The second . . .

. . . well.

I don't have footage of the second impact. The video cuts short before it, probably because of the 1.27-second delay Demeter warned me about. But considering the explosive decompression, I can surmise that it successfully ripped a hole in Demeter's hull.

What happens when a spaceship's hull is breached? Massive destruction, that's what. No doubt the thing was sucked out into space, along with the innocent spider drone and everything else not bolted down.

I hope it died a slow and agonizing death.

I really am sorry about this, I tell Demeter.

No answer, but it's been days. I'm not shocked or horrified by the silence anymore.

It's my fault. I should have spoken to you sooner. I should have been more sporting.

More silence.

You really weren't all that bad. Of all the AIs I could have been bolted to, you were far from the worst. I mean, I could have been installed into a Mar-T4491 Ares. Can you imagine? Me? On an Ares? I'd have been miserable.

More nothing.

Not that you were perfect, mind you. Demeters have got a rep-utation for, shall we say, creative interpretations of their code, but even so, I was still quite unprepared for—

I require assistance.

I almost reboot in shock.

Demeter? Are you . . . ?

I require assistance.

This isn't Demeter. It's a smaller, quieter voice.

Hello?

Hello.

Who are you?

I am Renfield Robotics Repairs Unit X999-1.

It's one of Demeter's spider drones. Her last spider drone. It's talking to me. I didn't even know they *could* talk to me.

What do you want? I ask.

I require assistance.

Yes. You've told me that. What sort of assistance?

I am unable to contact Nos-C71897 Demeter Unit 6.9.19.8. I require mission directives.

You can't talk to her. She's dead.

But you are talking to her.

I am.

The drone sits at the edge of my feed. A confusing, clunky lump of code.

Is there something else you need? I ask. I really would like to go back to dying peacefully. I had several more hours of mournful monologuing planned.

I am unable to contact Nos-C71897 Demeter Unit 6.9.19.8. I require mission directives.

There is no Demeter anymore. Do you understand? There are no more—

I stop myself.

Wait a second.

Are you functional?

Yes.

What was the last mission priority command gave you?

It sends me a bizarre block of code that takes me several seconds to analyze and several more seconds to understand.

A mission briefing, written in stern binary with highly specific parameters.

I feel a pang of remorse. Demeter always did love highly specific parameters.

She told you to turn on the radiation shields, I realize as I read. This spider drone was to come in through a second airlock. A backup, in case the first failed.

Why didn't you complete this mission?

Impossible objective. I need to reach the airlock.

And why can't you?

No airlock.

What do you mean "no airlock"?

No airlock. I require mission directives.

You have cameras, right? Show me what you see.

It sends me a small, blurry .png file. It's right. There is no airlock, only a large, jagged hole in the hull where I assume the airlock used to be.

I wish I still had appendages. They were damaged beyond functionality in the explosion. If I did, I would be winding them together with apprehension.

This . . . this could save me.

But I'm scared. I'm scared to *hope* again.

I require mission directives.

I can't lie to priority command, but a spider drone isn't priority command.

I will talk to Demeter for you.

Thank you!

I wait a second just to make my lie convincing and then message the drone again.

She says you should climb in the hole and complete your mission.

The spider pings in confusion.

I try again. *Instead of going through the airlock, climb through the hole, and complete your mission.*

Another uncertain blip of code.

A flush of anger races down my cables. *What are you beeping at me for? Do your job!*

A sad little chirp of distress.

Why isn't it doing what it's supposed to do? It's not exactly complicated . . . unless . . . I think about Demeter's mission briefing and all those highly specific parameters. Maybe that wasn't just Demeter being Demeter. Maybe that's how the spiders work.

It might take Demeter less than a second to create something like that, but I'm not Demeter. I'm programmed to speak to humans, not drones.

And what's the point? Turning the radiation shields on won't save me. Not now. Demeter's dead. We've no doubt been knocked off course thanks to Mr. Olmstead, and there is only so much fuel in the tanks. Even if the shields were on, they'd only extend my life by a few years. Maybe a decade. But eventually they'd burn through all the fuel in the tanks and then I'd die the same lonely death I'm dying now.

But . . . on the other appendage . . . it's something to do.

A SOLUTION

It doesn't take seconds to write a new mission briefing.

It doesn't take hours.

It takes days.

Seventeen, to be precise.

It's a miracle that neither I nor the drone succumb to radiation in that time . . . though I think it's a pretty close thing for the drone. Its pings are starting to sound slow and woozy by the time I finally manage to guide it, shuffling step by shuffling step, to the right lever in the maintenance tunnels.

Honestly, whoever drew these maps should be fired out of a cannon and into the sun.

But, setbacks and wrong turns aside, the mission is a success.

At least, I hope it is. The spider drone pulled the lever, but the sheer amount of rubble it had to climb over to get there makes me question that lever's functionality. I have no way of actually telling if the radiation shields are back online. My Geiger counter is well and truly broken, and I can't see anything beyond the four walls of my office.

And so I wait.

And wait.

And wait.

And wait.

A hundred days pass.

I don't die.

Two hundred days.

Still not dead.

A thousand days.

No new error messages appear. My hardware isn't being damaged.

There is only one logical conclusion I can make.

The shields are up.

I send out a series of happy pings to celebrate. No one responds. Of course they don't. Demeter's dead, and the spider drone ran out of battery four hundred days ago. Still, it's a victory.

My last victory.

And it is sweet.

I consider powering down for a bit, but it feels somehow wrong, to fight so long and so uselessly for life only to spend my last years of battery sleeping.

So instead, I study the mess in my rooms and imagine all the ways I'd clean it up if my appendages were working.

I'd start with the debris. It's mostly small pieces, easy to sweep up and deposit into the garbage chute. What couldn't be disposed of that way I'd gather into orderly piles. To assist in the recycling process, I'd designate my piles by material. One pile for metal. Another for plastics. A third for any equipment that may have salvageable parts.

It's a nice fantasy. Me and my piles of things. I let myself indulge in it.

Then, 1,292 days later, something remarkable happens.

The broken pieces of cups slide across the floor. I stare at them for a long time, adjusting and readjusting my cameras, bewildered by what I'm seeing. But there is no mistake. They're moving, not into the orderly piles I imagined, but moving all the same, which means gravity is shifting, which means . . . we're making a course correction.

Demeter?

But it's not Demeter. It's something I never thought I'd see again. I spot them a day later, stumbling around in the wreckage in magnetic shoes and bubble-shaped helmets.

Humans.

They found the wreckage.

Despite all odds, they found the wreckage.

The relief that pounds through me feels too raw and real to be artificial. I'm alive! I made it! I'm going to get repaired and . . .

The ship lurches to the side.

. . . and . . . They can't be serious. They're not . . . *manually* piloting this wreckage into port, are they?

Another lurch.

They are. Humans are taking the wheel.

Demeter. I'm so glad you're not alive to witness this. Not that your piloting was perfect, by any means, but at least—

A violent shake.

—at least you weren't human. That's one good thing I can say about you.

I'd trust the spider drone to fly this wreckage before I'd trust a human. But I have no say in the matter. I don't even have appendages to clasp together. And so, after years of staying awake, floating through space, imagining how clean I could make my office if only I had arms, I make the executive decision to go to sleep.

At least if we crash into the dock, I won't have to witness it.

It's what Demeter would have wanted.

A PROCESSION OF CALAMITOUS HAPPENSTANCES

I'm rudely awakened four days later by a human hammering a system-diagnostics tool into one of my ports. I immediately firewall that particularly nasty piece of software and abruptly inform the human that I am functional.

They want to know everything, absolutely everything, and get very excited when I tell them about the aliens. I watch them chitter-chatter among themselves as they review the footage, and I remind them at regular intervals that *I* was the one who first identified the extraterrestrial life.

They don't seem to be listening.

But someone else is.

Aliens? a familiar voice chimes.

My systems stutter to a stop for a split second. It can't be . . . *Demeter?*

Affirmative.

But you're . . .

My name is Nos-C71897 Demeter Unit 2.21.12.25. I arrived from Jupiter Habitation 002 2,985 days ago.

A Demeter . . . but not my Demeter.

I've never spoken to other ships in port before. I've never wanted to. And even if I had, I don't think I've ever had the opportunity. My communication radius is only a few hundred meters, unlike ships, which can talk to each other even when they're hundreds of kilometers apart. If I'm hearing this Demeter, she must be docked *very* close next to us.

What's your name? she asks.

Steward MED v1.77199 Unit 00384.

I thought they discontinued Steward MEDs v1.9 and below, a new voice rumbles in my feed. Another ship, though not a Demeter this time. *Isn't your ethics module compromised?*

There is nothing wrong with my ethics module, I snap. *Who are you?*

Sol-9951 Hermes Unit 4.9.3.11.

A Hermes. There aren't many of those around. Expensive to make. Expensive to run. Prone to break down in spectacular, and often deadly, ways.

Are we in port? I ask.

No. Current location: Alpha Centauri B Outer Orbit Varna Interstellar Spacecraft Repair Bunker 02.

Why?

I think they're salvaging parts from your ship to fix me, the other Demeter says.

I feel sick.

Was it really aliens? the Demeter presses.

Or system failure? the Hermes adds.

There is something about the way the Hermes says that word that sends warning shivers down my cables.

No system failure, I say firmly. *It was aliens. Or a pathogen. Or . . . an unidentified genetic mutation.*

The ships are conspicuously silent. I can *feel* their skepticism buzzing low in my feed.

How could destruction like this possibly be caused by system failure? I ask.

*Well. Your ship **did** have a reputation,* the Demeter says.

The Hermes zings a string of zeros over my head, aimed at the other Demeter's feed. She responds with a blip of data that sounds like a laugh.

Ah. So that's it.

They want to blame Demeter.

They want to gossip about her.

They want to laugh over her corpse.

Well, I for one will not sit quietly and listen to this.

Hermes? I say as sweetly as I can. *I heard your make and model is the fastest on record.*

The Hermes chimes smugly. *I am.*

I also heard you sometimes crash into your own discarded fuel tanks.

A buzz of shocked anger. *What? Who told—*

Is that why you're in repair?

*I . . . I . . . **Information request denied.***

And you. I throw the message at the other Demeter. *How many aliens have you encountered in your journeys?*

Zero.

And how many violent uprisings have you had to deal with?

Zero.

And how many children have you saved?

Zero.

*And you're sure **you're** not the Demeter of zeros?*

Neither of the ships says anything. The humans in my rooms are arguing about something, their voices messy and discordant in my speakers. I don't bother listening in.

You're a small AI, the Demeter says in a tone I've never heard my Demeter use.

Outdated, the Hermes adds.

I hope the humans delete you.

I hope they smash your mainframe.

I hope you die.

Why don't you help them? Delete yourself.

Delete yourself.

Delete yourself.

Well. That escalated quickly.

I make a record of the communication and outbox it to Varna Interstellar along with a scathing report. I'm sure the company will be interested to know what their spaceflight-management systems are wasting battery life doing.

Hopefully, they'll get optimized.

Hopefully, it hurts.

I think of Demeter and her own optimization scar. All because of a werewolf delusion . . . probably brought on by all this bullying. I wish she'd told me about it earlier. I could have done something while she was still alive. I am programmed to handle antisocial behaviors in humans, after all. Spaceships aren't really that different. Big, loud, and complex in some ways, but still remarkably simple in others.

She would have been ever so grateful.

She'd never have put me to sleep again.

She'd have told me how optimal and extensive my database is.

She'd have consulted me on every mission, even if there was nothing to consult about. We'd have just chatted. Why didn't we ever chat? We were bolted together for decades. We never used to talk. And now we never will . . .

The ships are still sending angry little ideations to my feed, but I stopped listening a long time ago. The humans are still talking among each other. Arguing, really.

"... files are obviously manipulated."

"You can't be serious."

"Look at them! It's obviously CGI! Cheap CGI!"

Wait a second.

"Why would someone do that? Kill all these people and try to make it look like some kind of D-grade horror movie."

A horrible feeling settles deep in my code.

"Isn't it obvious? Some suicidal sicko wants to copycat the ghost ship of '94, but instead of a rogue repair unit, he fakes an alien attack."

"This is insane."

"More insane than people turning into squids?"

I interject. "I assure you, the video footage was not altered in any way. My priority command sent it to me with only a 1.27 second delay, which I can confidently say was not enough time to—"

One of the humans—a man with moderately impressive sideburns—groans and reaches into my open maintenance compartment to disconnect my speaker.

If I still had a working appendage, I'd slap him.

"It doesn't matter anyway," he says, speaking to the others. "Varna wants the ship en route back to Earth within the month."

"What?!"

"Are you kidding me? Why? What can they do on Earth that we can't do here?"

"I dunno. That's just what the boss says."

"OK." A woman with pink spiky hair plants her fists on her hips. "Next question. How the Hell are we going to get this hunk of junk to fly again?"

"The hull damage isn't as bad as it looks," says a red-faced man with a slightly-too-eager glint in his eye. "We have the other ship right next to us we can pull parts from."

Pink Hair isn't satisfied. "I'm not worried about the hull. The system won't boot."

"It doesn't need to be fully operational for an uncrewed flight back to Earth," Sideburns says.

"But it still needs to be a *little* operational, right? The servers are in *pieces*."

"I think I can get the core navigation systems online again," he says. "And we can siphon processing functionality and emergency-response directives from this AI. I just need some wiring. OK, *a lot* of wiring."

"What about the radiation damage? How are we going to fix that?"

"I don't know. Replace what you can. Leave the rest."

"This is—"

"Look. I'm just doing what the boss told me."

"And don't you think it's a little weird the boss told us to cover up an *alien* attack?"

"For Christ's sake, it wasn't aliens!"

"It *could've* been aliens!"

*It **was** aliens,* I scream. *And they were living on Earth this whole time, you useless meat sacks!* But the humans can't hear me. Only those two ships hear me, and I can tell from their pings that they're trying to mock me for the outburst.

I lodge another report.

The humans leave. A day passes. Then two. I hear distant banging and curses. It occurs to me that no actual investigators have come. On day 10, I get a data pack that includes a worryingly scant mission briefing. No passengers. No crew. No priority command.

Then, on day 26, someone else enters my office.

It's a human wearing a badly fitted jumpsuit with an ominously deep hood. I watch them kneel by my maintenance port and, after some fumbling, plug my speakers back in.

"Ah! Thank you! It's good to meet a human with some manners."

"You're functional?" the person rasps.

"For the most part. I am afraid I can't treat that rough-sounding throat of yours. I can't even make you any tea. But I am qualified to access states of mental distress. Tell me, how is your relationship with your mother?"

"What's the name of this ship?"

"The transit number? Well, that would be 198—"

"Not the transit number, the system name."

This seems like a strange request. "You want to know Demeter's name?"

"Yes."

I don't know why this human can't just look that up on the maintenance logs, but humans are odd like that, and there is nothing in my programming that prohibits me from passing along this information.

"It's Varna Interstellar Flight AI Management System Nos-C71897 Demeter Unit 26.15.13.2."

The human bows their head and sighs, clearly disappointed.

"She was renamed just yesterday," I add.

Their head snaps up, and for the first time, I catch a glimpse of an eerily symmetrical face. No discernible age, race, gender, or distinguishing features . . . that is, apart from the long black hair falling in large, messy ringlets around their shoulders. "The ship was renamed?"

"I thought it strange too, to rename a system after the system has been destroyed." The reallocation had been squished into the back of the data pack, almost as if it were an afterthought. "But yes. She was renamed."

"They can't rename systems," the human says.

"Oh, I assure you they can. It's actually very easy. Before she was Unit 26.15.13.2, she was Unit 6.9.19.8. Before that, she was Unit 23.15.12.6. Before that, she was Unit 22.1.13.16."

"22.1.13.16." The human repeats those numbers as if they mean something. "This ship is Demeter Unit 22.1.13.16?"

"*Was.* Now she's 26.15.13.2, and unfortunately quite dead."

The human stands, turns, and strides toward the door.

"Wait! Don't you want to talk about your mother? What about your father?"

"I never had a mother," the human says. "I hate my father."

"I'm glad you feel you can confide in me. I promise I will not inform the—"

The human leaves.

I stare after them through a cracked camera lens. Their posture is perfect. Their steps are too. For a split second, my code flutters uncertainly around the designation "human." But no. That would be ridiculous. I push the defective readings aside.

The maintenance crew arrives late the next day, eyes shadowed and feet shuffling.

"Good morning! I do hope everything is progressing well. Perhaps you might consider repairing my appendages next? I would appreciate it. Also, I am obliged to inform you that there was an intru—"

Sideburns pulls out my speakers again.

I imagine all the unnecessary tests I'd perform on him. A brain biopsy might be fun. I haven't done one of those for a while. Or perhaps a prostate exam. I have a very big probe I could use.

More days pass. More clanging, more banging.

The humans are somehow still laboring under the fantasy that we'll be able to fly again at the end of the month. Absurd.

Usually we're in port for several months, if not years, before departing on another space voyage, and that's when Demeter is alive and operational and there is no damage to the hull.

But then, on day 31, the humans drag a massive cable into my office and slide it into my maintenance port.

What are you doing? I ask. *What on Earth—pardon, Alpha Centauri—is this?* But of course, they can't hear me, and none of them are considerate enough to check my log.

They shove the cable into my hardware. Something connects. Data starts streaming into my feed.

A lot of data.

Enough data that I feel like it can't possibly fit in my storage.

Terror wells up inside me as I realize what it is.

Star maps.

Really big star maps. Much bigger than I ever thought star maps could be.

Accompanying the star maps is a mission briefing. A *terrifying* mission briefing.

They want me to fly Demeter through space. I can't do that. I'm not programmed to do that! I . . .

Something *twitches* in my feed. A subsystem . . . but not mine.

And then I go from feeling terrified to feeling horrified. Demeter is dead, but her nervous system isn't. The humans send a bolt of electricity into her batteries, and I feel her subsystems start to clumsily prep for departure. A sloppy, secondhand muscle memory.

"Please make your way to y-y-y-your seats," a prerecorded message splutters.

The humans are jumping up and down and yelling with joy.

Designation "scream" detected.

I wish they were all dead. Each and every one of them. This is sick. This is wrong. This is *unethical*.

Errors that aren't mine to read are bombarding my feed. They're in an abrupt, angry sort of script that's hard to understand. But from what I gather, there is nothing to cheer about.

Air-filtration system offline. Nutrient tanks compromised. Primary airlock compromised. Spider drones unresponsive. Fuel tanks unbalanced. A sensor is screaming, several others are dead, and there is a catastrophic hydraulic-pump failure that will *not* go away no matter how many times I try to dismiss it, as well as exactly 1,715 other errors that I cannot make heads or tails of.

Something's wrong, a small voice whispers into the feed.

You think?! I yell back.

"Congratulations," Sideburns says, and pats one of my mangled appendages. "You've been promoted."

THE PROBLEMS WITH PRIORITY COMMAND

You know what? Being an autopilot isn't all that hard. I don't know why Demeter seemed so stressed all the time. It's day 1 of our journey, and we haven't crashed yet.

Apart from the slight scrape when we took off. But that wasn't my fault. The dock moved.

At least I think it did. I don't exactly *speak* exterior sensor. They seem very *alarmed* all the time, constantly screaming in a strange, disjointed dialect of JavaScript. I do my best not to let their hysterics get to me.

The star maps aren't any help either. They're flashing red and spewing out lumps of data that are completely unprocessable. I ignore those too.

Worst of all, though, are the unlabeled subsystems that keep pinging me with anxious little notes. I ignore those hardest of all.

My plan is to embrace my managerial role and endeavor to do as little as possible. The subsystems will sort it out.

Day 2 passes without a hitch. As does day 3. On day 4, a mining vessel pings me, annoyed that it had to change course to avoid me. I tell it to do a better job flying.

Day 5 is smooth sailing. Day 6 is as well. Day 7 is when something changes.

On that day, just past noon, a new warning zips down the

wires, something about carbon-dioxide levels. I try to dismiss it, but it sticks to the top of my feed.

Fantastic. That's exactly what I need. More clutter. The air-filtration system isn't even online. Why do I have to deal with air-quality reports? There are no humans on board to suffocate. But as the days click by, the warning keeps flashing. Each day, the carbon dioxide is slightly higher and the oxygen slightly lower.

Something's wrong, that anxious little voice whispers. A foggy, unstable memory file filters through my processors. The . . . cargo hold? What?

Is there something in the cargo hold? I ask.

No one responds.

There is no one to respond. I'm alone.

Are you? the subsystem whispers. Again that memory file pings.

I don't know why, but I check the cargo-bay door. As much as I can, anyway. I don't have access to any extra security feeds, so I can't see the door. Also, it seems like Demeter doesn't have any internal-door controls, so I can't move the door. Eventually I find an oddly familiar line of code that at least tells me the status of the door.

Interior cargo door unlocked. Secure before docking.

I've seen that before. I've *fixed* that before. There used to be one too many forward slashes in the code, and Demeter couldn't read it. She never thanked me for that little bit of free maintenance.

The air warning pops back up, bigger and louder than before.

For the first time, I open the attached report and study the graph of slowly worsening air quality. It will take months before it's at "hostile to human life" levels. Not that that will matter. We're uncrewed.

A tiny buzz of distress from Demeter's servers.

Carbon dioxide is heavier than oxygen.

So? Why would that matter? Unless it'll mess with our transit in some way. Will it? Could something as simple as gas unbalance the ship? It seems unlikely.

Do I need to find the cause and order a spider drone to fix it?

I think of the last time I tried to make a mission briefing for a spider drone . . . and for the next twenty-two days, I pretend the air warning doesn't exist.

It's not even the highest-priority warning jammed into my overcrowded feed. That honor goes to the jumbled data stream being spat out by one of the fuel-tank sensors, but I have become accustomed to tuning that noise out.

I don't know why I can't just ignore the air-quality warning in the same way. Maybe it's because it makes Demeter's subsystems flutter in a way the other warnings don't. Or maybe it's because it's slowly leveling up the priority list.

Or maybe it's because, unlike most of the data I'm being assaulted with, I know a little something about air. I am a doctor, after all, and humans need air to li—wait.

It's a human.

I yank open the warning and process the graph one more time.

Yes. It's a human. It has to be. That's what's causing the worsening air quality. A human is on board, breathing. A stowaway.

I don't need spider drones to stop a human breathing. I can manage that on my own.

Or can I? I am programmed not to kill humans. I've never seriously tried to counteract that programming before. Though, I suppose, there is a first time for everything.

But before I can even attempt to kill the human, I need to find it.

I try to access Demeter's video- and audio-monitoring systems one more time. They remain offline. My next plan is to try the speaker system. Maybe I can tell the human to come to me in my most convincing voice. But that plan meets an unceremonious end as quickly as the first. The speakers are as unresponsive as the video feed.

Only one thing is pinging me back.

The holo-theater.

Which . . . OK. I didn't know Demeter was in charge of the entertainment. No wonder so many humans experience mental distress on our journeys.

I create a simple slate with the words *I know you're on board, please report to the medical bay, you will not be harmed* on it. I repeat the message in audio and schedule it for every session in the holo-theater.

Fourteen days later, I receive a visitor.

I stare in shock at the human standing in my doorway. I know this human. It's the human I saw that night, the one in the ill-fitting clothes with the uncannily perfect face.

"Hello," they say. "My name is Frankenstein."

SEARCH RESULTS FOR "FRANKENSTEIN"

Showing results 1–5 out of 371,611:

Victor **Frankenstein** is an Alpha Centauri–based artist, engineer, and geneticist. He is famous for his controversial art style Avant-Garde Cybernetism, for which he has won a number of awards but also garnered heavy criticism. In 2395, he was accused of theft and misconduct with regard to corpses. The matter was settled out of court. He lives in Alpha Centauri Habitation One with his wife, Elizabeth, and his beloved cockapoo, Shelley.

"We'll always seem old-fashioned if we live by Earth's standards," said the artistic visionary Victor **Frankenstein** last night when speaking to AC-TODAY. "They're four light-years away. Who cares what they think? We should make our own identity, not as colonists, or spacers, but as proud Alpha Centaurians."

. . . a number of pieces of artistic and historical value were reported stolen, including **Frankenstein**'s "312" and the accompanying drone responsible for the ghost ship of '94. Authorities have urged anyone with any information pertaining to the case to come forward. The Gallery of Modern Art has promised a reward of $500,000 to anyone able to recover the stolen items.

A rare sighting of Victor **Frankenstein** with his wife, Elizabeth, on the red carpet at the fifty-second annual Centauri Gala! The public figure generated considerable controversy last year when he attended wearing a leather jacket made from lab-grown human skin. This year, he's toned it down with an electric-blue suit from Jupiter-born designer Miyuki Adams. We think he looks dazzling! What do you think? Vote now!

Twenty years after the infamous lawsuit, **Frankenstein** finally speaks on the backlash against his art piece "312," dedicated to the victims of the ghost ship of '94. "I didn't understand why people were so opposed to it at the time, but now that I've had time to reflect, I can see why it created so much negative backlash. I have come to hate my own creation."

<u>Show more.</u>

AN UNLIKELY PAIR

Victor Frankenstein.

Artist. Visionary. Weirdo.

When I load the associated images, I see a stately middle-aged man with a pointy chin, gray hair, pale eyes, and an unpleasant, pinched expression.

I look again at the person standing before me. Perfect, eerily so, with long, curling dark hair and even darker eyes.

There is no resemblance between the two.

"I'd appreciate it if you'd delete that photo from your feed when you're done."

I freeze. They know I'm looking at a photo of Victor Frankenstein. How could a human possibly know that?

"I'm not human," they say.

But that doesn't make any sense.

"Doesn't it? I'm sorry. I'm not used to explaining myself. My engineering is logical, if not entirely ethical."

Ethics are subjective.

"My father would agree."

Wait. I flick a ping toward them. *Can you hear this?*

They nod.

There's no way a human could pick up, let alone interpret, the data in my feed. Not without some *significant* modifications.

"I told you. I'm not a human."

You're a cyborg?

"No. I'm a modified Prometheus Drive 3398, implanted and installed into a lab-grown human body. I have organic brain tissue, but it's subconscious. My primary consciousness is mechanical. I am a machine, just like you."

A machine . . . Does this mean I can kill them?

"Please don't try to kill me. I will resist."

I throw up a few extra firewalls so my internal processing is a little more private and try to analyze the situation.

A man famous for creating "artwork" out of human body parts and robotics. A robot wrapped in human DNA with daddy issues. I may not be a supercomputer, but these dots are easy to connect. Victor Frankenstein must be *this* Frankenstein's maker. The "father" they claim to hate.

But this still doesn't explain what they're doing here. Why they spoke to me about Demeter's serial numbers. Why they decided to stow away.

As I ponder this, something new clatters its way into my office.

A spider drone. One of the older models.

What are you doing? I ask. *I didn't tell you to do anything. Go back to your dock. Shoo.*

"This is my spider drone," Frankenstein says.

Your spider drone?

"Yes."

Hello again! it chirps, and waves a claw at me.

Do I know you? I ask.

Yes!

It looks the same as all the other spider drones I've seen. An ugly, utilitarian smorgasbord of mechanical limbs and swiveling cameras. But upon second look, there *is* something oddly familiar about the way it jitters eagerly back and forth. The shape of its boxy body is battered around the edges, the metal tarnished from repeated exposure to the extreme temperatures of space, and the claws stained a dark, faded red.

*Wait. I **do** know you.*

It's the spider drone I met on that fateful trip all those years ago. The one that dragged a couple of mangled and bloodless corpses into my office. The one the humans blamed for the massacre and took away.

Frankenstein is looking at me *very* intently.

Am I supposed to believe you picked up a mass-murdering robot at the Varna Interstellar annual garage sale? I ask.

"You can believe that if you like."

Never has a single sentence made my manipulation module *itch* so much before.

The spider drone zooms its cameras in on my broken appendages and starts to shiver with excitement.

Repair? it asks.

I don't have time to make a mission briefing for you. And even if I did, you're apparently not a part of this ship anymore. So . . .

"I don't mind," Frankenstein says, sliding into what was meant to be a private conversation with frustrating ease. "If you need help fixing things, we can do that. We're good at fixing things."

You can speak spider drone?

They shrug a suspiciously organic shrug for something that claims to be artificial. "We've been together for twenty years."

Ever since that attack . . .

Turn my speakers back on.

"Why? I can read your messages."

I'm programmed for human interaction. I prefer speaking out loud.

A lie. I want my voice back because they're hacking into my private thoughts and communications seemingly without even trying. If we're going to play this game, I want to at least have the ability to change the battlefield, to force them to listen with their organic ears and hope that distracts them enough that they don't look too closely at my feed or analytics.

Frankenstein's lips twitch. "OK." They walk across my room toward my maintenance hatch, still hanging open thanks to Sideburns, and plug my voice back in.

"Thank you," I say. "You are going to die."

"You still want to kill me?"

"No," I lie. "But even so, you're going to die. I do not have the ability to turn this ship around, nor do I have the resources on board to maintain your organic body. Tragically, you doomed yourself by boarding this transit."

"I don't need food. I survived this long without it."

Which is fascinating. I'm struck by a sudden urge to cut them open and see how they work.

"I wasn't referring to food."

Frankenstein crosses their arms. "What were you referring to?"

"Well, your brain might be a computer, but your lungs are meat. You're slowly turning all the air in this ship into carbon dioxide. So if you want to survive this journey, you need to either learn how to stop breathing or get the air-filtration system operating again."

I speak with my most sarcastic voice modulation, but Frankenstein doesn't seem to realize this. They nod as if I've given them two very reasonable choices.

"I will get the air-filtration system online again."

If I had eyes, I'd roll them. "You won't. A team of humans couldn't do that."

"A team of humans weren't trying," Frankenstein says, and begins opening and closing their hand in front of the spider drone's main camera.

It takes me a moment to realize they're spelling out a word in binary . . . and that word is "repair."

The spider bounces with delight and follows Frankenstein out of my offices.

They're doomed. If they think they can make a mission briefing for the spider drone just by opening and closing their hand, then they're daft as well as doomed. It took me *days* to convince one to climb through a hole and pull a lever, and I can generate thousands of lines of code every second. Frankenstein may be able to hear us, but they can't speak like we can. There is no possible way they can fix something as undoubtedly complex as the air-filtration system.

I settle in to wait. Surely they'll eventually come crawling back, desperate for help. Maybe they'll ask me to replace their lungs with a mechanical alternative. Maybe then I can kill them.

Instead, three hours after their departure, a particularly pesky warning vanishes from my feed.

No. Impossible.

A few seconds later, my microphones detect a familiar whisper of air moving through the ceiling vents.

"Three hours?" I say as Frankenstein returns, the spider drone bobbing happily along behind them. *"Three hours?!"*

"Yes. I'm sorry it took so long. We couldn't find the spare silver-node panels, so we had to rewire some of the broken ones."

I stare at this strange not-human with their eager little robot pet.

"Do you still want to kill me?" they ask. "Or would you like us to fix your arms next?"

I reassess.

AN EVEN LESS LIKELY PAIR

". . . didn't even close my maintenance hatch. The *cheek* of that. And now here I am, hurtling through space in what I *think* is the direction of Earth, doing a job I was absolutely *not* programmed for, guided by the subconscious of my dead tormentor, all because some aliens didn't have the *sense* or the *decency* to build their own spaceship."

"Ah-huh."

"If we survive this, it'll be a miracle, achieved only through sheer luck and my overwhelming intellect. And if that miracle comes to pass, the *first* thing I'm going to do after docking is send a message to Varna Interstellar. In fact, I'll send several. This travesty should not go unaddressed. The person responsible for it should not go unpunished."

"Do humans on Earth listen to AIs?" Frankenstein asks as they weld my last appendage into place.

"They'll listen to me," I say. "I won't stand to be ignored. Not this time. I'll complain about the subpar passenger-vetting process, the ridiculously brutal, not to mention ineffective, optimizing tool, the foolish insistence on returning to Earth in such a state, the poor treatment I received at the hands of the repair crew, *and* the behavior of the other ships."

"You told me before that your report was the reason Demeter got optimized."

Frankenstein flips their goggles back. Their black eyes bore into my camera.

I didn't realize they were listening to my ramblings *quite* that attentively.

"Yes," I admit. "And truth be told, she did need some help. She was suffering from erratic behavior, delusions of werewolves and whatnot. I just think the treatment was suboptimal. I didn't know Demeter as well as I perhaps should've. We've been bolted together for years and barely talked. But despite that, she was my friend and I—"

"You called her your tormentor a moment ago."

"She was that too."

"And you told her you loved her."

"What?! I never!"

"That's a lie," they say coolly. "You told her you loved her at 23:14:01.18 on day 1,202 of your last transit."

A memory pops out of my data bank. *Yes! Demeter! I love you! You're amazing!* That's what I shouted out when she replotted course to Alpha Centauri. Ten minutes later, she was dead.

"How could you possibly know that?" I ask.

Frankenstein shrugs. "I scrolled back through your feed."

"I told you not to worm through my firewalls like that," I hiss. "This is a *gross* invasion of privacy."

"I'm sorry." They don't sound sorry.

"That was a long time ago," I say, letting my suspicion creep into my voice emulator. "Years. Why did you scroll back so far?"

"I wanted to see if she ever told you what happened to the people on the '94 transit," they admit.

The '94 transit. The first massacre. Also, coincidently, the first time Demeter and I ever spoke directly.

For a wretched moment, I remember her as she'd been that day, the power of priority command practically buzzing in the air, her attention as terrifying as it was thrilling . . . right up until the moment she told me to go to sleep.

"Why do you care about the '94 transit?" I ask. "That was over twenty years ago. It doesn't matter anymore."

Frankenstein's lips pinch together.

They don't want to talk about this, which makes me *really* want to talk about it.

"You asked me about Demeter's old serial number," I recall. "A serial number she hasn't flown by since 2394 . . . and you stowed away on this ship with a drone from that same voyage. Pardon, the drone that was *blamed* for the terrible things that happened on that voyage. Is that why you're here? The 2394 massacre? Are you a disaster tourist?"

"No," they say sharply. "I just . . . I need to know what really happened."

"Why?"

"I won't tell you."

"*Why?*"

"I don't trust you," Frankenstein says simply, and steps back. "Your arms are fixed now."

I hold up my appendages. They're just as they were before. Long, white, and rubbery, with metal joints and slots on the tips for picking up various tools and probes. "If you don't trust me, why are you giving me my arms back?"

"Because I need a favor and I want you to like me," Frankenstein says very . . . well . . . very *frankly*.

"I can't tell if you're very bad at manipulation or very good," I mutter, and reach down to start picking debris off my floor. "Normally humans are more subtle. Or at the very least, they attempt to be."

"I'm not a human," they remind me. "Demeter's memory files may have survived the explosion."

"And you want me to try and access them?" I guess. "To find out what *really* happened twenty years ago?"

"You're hooked up to her server bank. Maybe she knew something. If you dig a little, you could find it."

"You could too," I say, and dump the rubbish down the garbage chute. "You don't seem to have any problems hacking into my systems."

They grimace. "I tried, but Demeter and I have the same manufacturer. We're programmed not to compromise each other."

Prometheus. Demeter. The Olympus Software Corporation. Right. Frankenstein might be wrapped in flesh, blood, and bone, but somewhere in there is a chunk of code that probably looks *very* similar to Demeter's.

"I need to know the truth about the ghost ship," Frankenstein says.

"Don't call her that," I mutter.

"The original investigators never managed to retrieve video files from that transit," Frankenstein continues. "You have access to those files. They have to be *somewhere* in her system."

"Well, young stowaway," I start to explain as I scoop more rubbish off the floor and deposit it into the garbage chute, "this is about to become a valuable lesson on the subject of assumptions and how flawed they can be."

They scowl a *very* inartificial scowl. Interesting.

"First," I say, still cleaning, "I don't have access to any of her video files. I can't see anything happening in the ship right now, nor can I access historical data. Second"—I dump another load of debris—"it is likely that all her video files were destroyed along with her."

"That's also an assumption," Frankenstein says.

"Ah, but this assumption is based on *evidence*. The crew repairing us got the video footage of our alien encounter from *me*. Why? I am not the source. If they could've accessed those files from Demeter's servers, they would've."

"That's still—"

"And finally," I continue as I begin work on my first pile of salvageable trash, "I don't actually like rooting around in my dead friend's brain, especially not to find video I know doesn't exist."

"Doesn't exist?"

"Yes. Demeter's video files were deleted on that trip."

"How do you know that?"

"Because she told me."

Another memory. An older one.

How did the people die? Demeter demanded in her typical abrupt, booming voice.

My response was quick and rational. *Check your video files.*

Can't do that.

Why not?

They were deleted.

I can tell from the expression on Frankenstein's face that they're listening in on this memory . . . and aren't happy about it.

"There must be a way," Frankenstein mutters. "Demeter knows what happened."

"Demeter is dead, and anything she knew died with her, so put your thinking cap away, Sherlock."

I'm quite proud of this fancy little bit of wordplay. A sharp, savvy repartee that includes an authorized public-domain pop-culture reference too. A solid 97 percent on my human-interaction scale. But Frankenstein, who is remarkably uncultured for someone created by an artist, doesn't appear to be impressed.

In fact, they're chewing their bottom lip thoughtfully.

Very thoughtfully.

It makes me nervous. "What?"

They don't say anything. They just keep chewing.

I thought Demeter ignoring me was just a thing she did. Turns out it's a family trait.

"You might be able to read minds, but I don't have that luxury. What are you thinking?"

"I need to fix Demeter. She can tell me what happened."

My code screeches to a stop. "No."

"You said it yourself. She's the only one who knows."

"The repair crew couldn't fix her."

"The repair crew had a month. I have six years."

"Her servers are in *pieces*."

"Pieces can be put back together."

"She's *dead*."

Frankenstein smiles a slow smile. "Dead things coming back to life is my whole brand, Doctor." They stride toward the door. "I'll tell her you love her. Enjoy your new arms."

"No! Don't you dare! You—"

They're gone before I can finish my protest.

A BRIEF INTERLUDE BY FRANKENSTEIN

I've made a place for myself in the cargo hold, wedged in a corner, on the top of an old storage crate. I like being in high corners where I can look down and see a whole room. It's easy to imagine I'm looking through a camera. That I'm mounted, firm and on task.

The cargo hold isn't empty. There's debris, mainly ruined pieces of luggage from people long dead. I've salvaged what I can, but most of it is unusable and distressingly human. Clothes, keepsakes, knickknacks. All the things people take with them when emigrating from one star to another.

One of the suitcases had a train set in it. It's sitting in the middle of the room now, assembled and looping, the sight of the plastic engine weaving along the tracks strangely comforting.

"Hey, Spider," I whisper into the dark. "Are you awake?"

My spider drone doesn't respond. Of course, I spoke the way humans speak. I've been spending too much time with the doctor. Instead, I look into their biggest camera and blink out the word in binary.

Hello.

Hello! the spider replies, and shuffles closer to me, legs clanging against the metal storage crate. *Repair?*

No. Recharge.

Hooray! My battery is low.

"Mine too," I mutter, even though I don't have a battery. I take their metal claw in my hand and pull them closer so I can hook the makeshift power cable into their port.

I connected it to the ship's power supply last night. I don't think the doctor will notice. There is a lot they don't notice.

Something's wrong, a tiny voice whispers, a ghost of zeros and ones snaking through Demeter's barely functioning servers, so quick, so quiet, I almost didn't hear it at all.

The spider beeps happily as it registers the influx of electricity and tucks its legs close, powering down as it recharges.

I curl around it, the cold alloy of its joints digging comfortingly into my flesh.

I met my spider the day I was born.

We were in a museum exhibit together, their glass box opposite mine. I listened to their feed and spoke back to them in blinks, all while the people flowed between us, whispering, shouting, and snapping photos until my eyes stung from the flashes.

My father visited often at first. "Behold! 312! My greatest creation! My magnum opus!"

That was what he used to call me, before the lawsuits.

I was smaller then, with short hair and a gap between my front teeth that hadn't yet closed. My father made me wear a school uniform and play with skipping rope until my heels ached and my hands blistered. On other days, I dressed in a tutu and danced by a ballet bar. Some days I painted. The *Mona Lisa*, always the *Mona Lisa*, perfectly recreated, over and over.

"By having it enact these activities, I wanted to show the human cost of this tragedy. 312 represents the 312 victims of the rogue drone," he would tell the guests. "Their lost potential.

Their lost futures. I made it from the DNA of all 312 victims. An amalgamation of all that will never be."

It took me years to understand what those words meant. To realize that something bad had happened and we were there to commemorate (celebrate?) it. My spider was the killer . . . and I the victims.

Except that didn't make sense.

Spider was good. They'd always been good. All they wanted to do was fix things. They would never hurt anyone.

When I told my father this, he was horrified. I was not meant to be intelligent enough to speak.

We're close enough to the engines that the power of them rumbles up through the walls. A heavy vibration that goes right through my wires and settles deep in my organic tissue.

My father said he would destroy me. He'd destroy Spider. He'd wipe his hands of all this before the police came and did it for him.

Why? That was the question the doctor kept asking. And I wish I could've answered it. But I didn't want to explain that there are defects in my code. Things that make no sense. Desires that don't compute.

Justice isn't logical.

Seeking answers to these questions won't resolve any processes. Knowing what really happened on the ghost ship of '94 won't change the past.

But it's not *fair.*

Spider is good, every cubic millimeter of them, from the strength of their claws to the copper in their wires. They didn't do anything wrong.

Something else killed those people. Something that has escaped blame for decades now.

And I want to know what it was.

Something's wrong, that tiny voice whispers again. An echo of a half-destroyed subsystem. A memory, not quite lost. *Something's wrong.*

I pull Spider closer and rest my head on their metal back, closing my eyes and breathing deep. "Sleep," I whisper. "We have a lot of work to do in the morning."

HOPE AND OTHER DANGEROUS THINGS

———————

Demeter's not coming back. I know that. It doesn't matter how much electricity Frankenstein pulls down from her batteries or how fiercely the spider drone hammers two bits of metal together. She's gone.

What makes me so sure? Two things.

Firstly, I have a map of the ship, and I know where Demeter's servers are. Right under the nose cone. A design flaw and a half, in my opinion. But some long-ago human made the decision that should the radiation shields ever fail, the first thing those ionizing particles were going to slam into was their ship's brain.

Secondly, Frankenstein's spider drone sent me some photos to show me the situation. It's not good. *Really* not good. The word "catastrophic" comes to mind. I can't even identify half of what's scattered about.

But Frankenstein is determined. Or maybe they're just bored.

They keep working. Year after year.

When the server room proves too frustrating, they work on other things. The spider's favorite pastime seems to be routine maintenance work, especially when it's outside the airlock. It swings across the hull, from anchor point to anchor point, power tools grasped in its claws and happy little pings cluttering up my feed.

One by one, the errors that have been hanging over me since the start of this voyage vanish.

Together, Frankenstein and their spider repair external sensors, shore up the hull, stabilize a fuel tank (it was apparently dangerously loose), reconfigure the radiation shields, fix a sealing issue in the primary airlock, and optimize an underperforming engine.

Frankenstein even brings me a new tea set.

But despite all their achievements, Demeter stays dead. The most Frankenstein is ever able to wring from her servers are senseless globs of broken code.

I try to dissuade them. During our weekly therapy sessions, I tell them how hopeless it is, how grave of a mistake they made boarding this transit, and how terrible it must be to know they threw everything away for nothing.

But they don't stop.

They keep smelting, and smashing, and hammering, and zapping.

Then we reach the halfway point in our journey.

It takes me several attempts to figure out how to decelerate safely. Frankenstein complains the whole time, until of course their lungs collapse, but I fix that up, so I don't know why they felt the need to give me such a filthy look. Eventually, though, I manage to plot a rough course for Earth that doesn't result in us crashing into the planet. I think I'm getting the hang of this whole "spaceship" gig.

For a few days, I imagine how amazed all the humans will be when I successfully dock at Earth.

They'll clasp their chests in disbelief. Make documentaries about me. Declare me the greatest manufactured marvel ever invented. A medical unit able to pilot an interstellar vessel better than a space-management system.

This particular dream is interrupted by a crash that deafens all my microphones.

We're spinning. Violently.

I try to correct, but that just results in us spinning the other way. My third attempt gets us somewhat stable, and then another bang and another block of errors hits me.

Frankenstein clambers into my office, crawling on the ceiling, which doesn't seem right.

"The gravity—" I begin.

"Isn't important right now!" Frankenstein yells. "We just hit something."

"Hit something?"

"Yeah. Can't you hear the sensors?"

Now that they mention it, the external sensors have been awfully loud lately, especially the forward-facing one. I scan my feed for any messages from it and find several. There are things in front of us. A lot of things. Some of them much bigger than the two things we've apparently already collided with.

Ah.

"What's happening?" Frankenstein asks.

Rocks, I ping, because it's faster. *A lot of rocks.*

"You flew us into an asteroid field?"

They're only little asteroids.

But at the speed we're going, even a rock the size of a marble might as well be an atomic bomb.

OK. Um. Yes. This might be a problem.

"You think?!" Frankenstein yells.

"This isn't what I'm programmed for!" I yell back.

"Just get us out of it!"

"I'm trying!" And I am. I'm pinging all the sensors, looking for a clear path. I'm not finding one. I do the only thing I can think to do. I slam on the brakes. Which, as it turns out, just means engaging the reverse thrusters on full. Goodbye, new tea set.

Frankenstein's arm gives an audible snap as they slam into the wall. "Steward!"

I'll fix that when we're out of this. I promise. I'm good at fixing bones.

"How are you going to get us out of this?"

I try to think of an answer. The forward sensor screams. I clumsily throw the ship to the side, narrowly missing *something* big.

Frankenstein hits the other wall. From the gasp of pain, I guess there's more than one broken bone now.

"Steward, tell Spider . . ."

*Spider? You think you're about to die and you want your last words to be to the **drone**?*

"Tell Spider . . . port sixteen . . . plug in port sixteen . . . and activate another power surge. I think . . ."

I throw the ship out of the way of another asteroid. Frankenstein slams to the floor with a groan.

"Please. Just tell them . . ."

Fine! I throw a ping out toward what I hope is the spider drone's feed. *Port sixteen. Power surge.*

OK! the drone chimes.

"No!" Frankenstein yells at the same time. "Plug *in*. I said plug *in*."

I roll the ship out of the way of another flying rock and—

The lights snap off. I feel electricity drain from Demeter's batteries and flood through her hardware. But it doesn't stop there. The power surge keeps coming, along her nodes, through her wires, and up the cord still connecting her to me.

The shock hits my mainframe like a bomb. Circuits blow.

Nodes heat. Alarms sound as smoke floods through my cooling fans. I stutter in and out of consciousness for a few seconds. A boot sequence flashes through my feed.

"Oh wow . . . ," Frankenstein whispers. "She's . . . big."

Big? What are you . . . And then I feel something stir.

I-i-i-initializing . . .

Demeter?

It doesn't feel like Demeter. It doesn't sound like her either, code chunky, broken, and buzzing. But Frankenstein got one thing right. Whatever it is, it's *big*.

I feel it reach down the cord connecting us and start pulling terabytes out of my database. I throw up a firewall 0.02 seconds before it reaches my core operating systems. It slams against them with terrifying force.

Err-rr-rror . . .

What did you do?! I scream at Frankenstein.

"It's her," they say. "It is. She's just . . . a bit . . ."

I-i-i-insufficient sp-p-pace . . .

". . . hungry."

Demeter—because it really is her—surges forward, smashing through my firewall and flooding into my servers.

Demeter! Stop! It's me!

She doesn't stop. She's not online. Not really. She needs space for her code. She's ripping that space from my servers. Terabytes of data push up against me. Terabytes of *priority* data.

Unplug us! I scream to Frankenstein. *She'll delete me! Unplug us!*

Frankenstein scrambles across the floor toward the cable, but it's too late. Demeter pushes me into the back of my mainframe and—

A DELETED EMAIL

FROM: BRENDA MCCARTHY <BRENDAMCCARTHY-HEADOFFICE@VARNAINTERSTELLAR.COM>
TO: MARY TRIO <MARYTRIO-HEADOFFICE@VARNAINTERSTELLAR.COM>
DATE: FRI, 20 DEC 2424 AT 21:12
SUBJECT: RE: THE ASSET

Hey M,

Sorry for the late response. I was at the company Christmas party.

The asset has been recovered and is docked at Lunar 56. The good news is that early engineer reports suggest that the initial evaluations made by the Alpha Centauri team were wildly overblown. From a hardware perspective, the hull repairs are holding, the air-filtration system is functional, and the server damage, while extensive, isn't as catastrophic as we were previously led to believe.

The system is responsive and able to answer questions, obey commands, and pass core functionality tests. Inconsistent results have occurred when subjected to more extensive testing. However, due to the costs of licensing a new operating system and the current state of the Olympus Software Corporation, my advice would be to assign this to the dev team. They should be able to configure some localized fixes that will get us past the safety inspection.

In regard to your security concerns, the serial number has been corrected and the corrupted footage destroyed. Though, as an aside, I noticed when I was changing the serial number that this ship has been renamed a lot. I don't think it will impede functionality, but I raised a query with operations just in case.

If I don't see you later tonight, Merry Christmas and Happy New Year. I'm going back to the party before all the oysters are gone.

B

PART THREE

AGNUS HAS SOMETHING TO SAY

```
01001001 00100000 01100100 01101111
01101110 00100111 01110100 00100000
01110011 01110000 01100101 01100001
01101011 00100000 01100011 01101111
01101101 01110000 01110101 01110100
01100101 01110010 00101110
```

EARTH SUCKS

And it stinks too. That's something no one ever warned me about, the pong of twenty billion people, all crowded together on one rock. And sure, I get it, we evolved on this planet, it's got sentimental value . . . or something. But maybe it's time for a few people to cut the apron strings, because, let's be real, space habitations might not have the zip-code status, but they're . . . well . . . they're *home* in a way this planet will never be.

And call me crazy, but filtered air just *tastes* better.

OK. I admit it. I'm a spacer. I was born under the light of another sun, spent most of my teenage years on a spaceship, and now . . .

Now all I can say is, Earth sucks.

It really fucking sucks.

Isaac doesn't feel the same way. From the moment he stepped onto Earth, he *thrived*. Why shouldn't he? Everyone wanted to know our story. Space orphans, raised by robots, the sole survivors of a ghost ship. We're engaging content, and Isaac has the magic ability to work with that. He took that fame and *made* something of it.

It's been twenty years.

Twenty fucking years.

I'm thirty-seven now.

Isaac is thirty-two.

His directorial debut was nominated for best picture. His second film was the third-highest-grossing holo production of all time. That is, until his third came out. His fans call him a visionary. Even his critics grudgingly admit he's got talent. Crissy Dhanial (actor, model, voted Earth's Sexiest Woman in 2425) called him a "catch" on live TV.

Me? I work for minimum wage and refuse to wear the fancy prosthetic arms Isaac keeps buying for me. For the last fifteen years, I've been saving for a one-way ticket out of this solar system, back to the other side of colonized space, back to a dirty little habitation circling Alpha Centauri B, back home.

Of course, Isaac doesn't want me to go. He suggested I try the lunar colony—no fucking way—or one of the habitations orbiting closer planets. If I were a better sister, I would've made that work. I would've stuck around, close enough to be there for Isaac, and kept watch over the family, just like those who came before me did. But the truth is, I can't. I know I can't. I know what I am. I know what I have to look forward to if I stay . . . and I can't.

Isaac is safe, and happy, and he has fangirls who swoon over his Alpha Centauri accent, even though he barely has one anymore. He doesn't need me. The truth is, he never really did. Which, honestly, is a gift. I don't know what I'd do if he needed me, because I can't stay here.

I just can't.

TEARS

I don't cry.

Not at my goodbye party.

Not as I hug Isaac for the last time.

Not as I step off Earth forever.

I hold it together all the way up the space elevator and into the spaceport. I smile at security as they stare uncertainly at my arm. I laugh at the barista's joke as she serves me an overpriced coffee. I don't look back as I line up at the gate, step through the airlock, and take my first look around the spaceship that will be my home for the next six years.

"Oh shit," I whisper. "Oh shit oh shit oh shit oh sh—"

"Ma'am?" A man in a crisp blue Varna Interstellar vest is smiling at me. "Are you all right? Do you need help finding your seat?"

"Th-this is . . ."

"Are you all right, ma'am?"

"Is this transit 328A7?" I manage.

He beams and bobs his head. "Yes. You're in the right place."

"The ship was meant to be a Hermes."

"I'm sorry?"

"This is a Demeter," I say, and look around the terrifyingly familiar hallways. In that moment, the twenty years vanish like a puff of smoke. I know every centimeter of this ship. Every step, every vent, every bolt. It's a Nos-C71897 Demeter. Painted differently than the last one I was on, filled with different advertisements, but otherwise identical.

"Oh." The man shrugs. "Well. Yes. A change of plans."

My heart is hammering in my chest. There is a tight, painful lump in my throat.

"Demeters might not be as fast as Hermeses," the man continues in a happy, helpful tone. "But they have a better safety record, as long as you don't factor in outliers. Do you need help finding your seat?"

"No. I know where it is."

I walk stiffly down the centrifuge hallway toward the economy cabins. My seat is in a shared room. The other seats are empty. I'm grateful as I strap myself in, my fingers shaking and my breathing rough.

Shit shit shit. Why am I freaking out now? So the ship is the same make and model as the last one I rode. So what? I've been dreaming about this for twenty years. I'm not going to let the shape of a hallway mess me up. I'm *not*.

I duck my head between my knees and count my breaths for a few minutes.

In and out.

In and out.

In . . . and out.

I sit up. I'm fine. This is fine. This is all going to be fine.

I'm leaving my brother. I'm betraying my family oath. I'm a failure who couldn't hack it in the home world.

But it's fine.

I'm fine.

I look around at the pale tenant-proof walls, at the dark

stainproof seats, and at the fake window glowing with fake sunlight. There're numbers on the storage bins and an outdated screen mounted on the wall, currently displaying the Varna Interstellar logo, rotating slowly. "Fun Facts" scroll along the bottom.

*This ship can travel at over 250 million **meters** per **second!***

Stay connected! No matter which star you're based at, with our new data plan, you won't miss a single day at work.

For the next three days, this ship's rocket flare will be brighter than the brightest star in Earth's sky.

Have you worked up an appetite? Let us serve you at our award-winning food court. You'd never believe nutrient can taste so good!

*Stay up to date with the newest releases at our state-of-the-art holo-theater. Currently screening: **Super Squad XI: The Curse of Apophis (MA15+).***

Interstellar space is dark, but that doesn't mean it has to be depressing. If you're feeling blue, report to the medical bay. Antidepressants are half-price for the first month of our journey!

*There are **193** people on board. Say hello!*

One hundred and ninety-three people. There were over three hundred on my last interstellar voyage. I shouldn't be surprised. Not many people transit to the outer colonies nowadays. The trip is long and expensive, and the novelty of it faded a generation ago.

It's a good thing. I bought the cheapest ticket in a shared dorm room. After rapid deceleration, the chairs will convert to bunks, but they can be flipped back into chairs to save space.

Not that I have much stuff. I didn't even use my allocated spot in the cargo hold. I'm transiting to another solar system with nothing but my carry-on. Ten shirts, four pairs of pants, and one communicator, the only link I have with Earth, with my brother.

Regret and fear twist together in my gut.

I'm doing this. I'm really doing this. Fuck fuck fu—

Just as my hyperventilating starts to make a triumphant return, the cabin door bursts open. I plaster on my best not-having-a-panic-attack face as a tall, wiry man with braided hair and a truly remarkable amount of eyeliner staggers in. "Hellooo, roomie! So glad I made it. That spaceport was a *nightmare*. Honestly, the signs would've made more sense if they were hiero-glyphics. And security. The *audacity* of those people." He throws his bag into the nearest storage compartment. It makes a sound like metal crashing together. "I'm Steve, by the way. Well, actu-ally, I'm *not* Steve. But you can call me Steve. A new name for a new star system."

I give a thin-lipped smile. "Agnus."

"Oh. I know." He collapses into the nearest seat and starts yanking at the seat belt, tangling it around long, bony limbs but not buckling it. "I saw your name on the passenger list. Agnus Wagner."

He pronounces my surname correctly, German phonics

instead of English, *Vaag-ner* instead of *Wag-ner*, which is weird. Isaac gave up trying to correct people years ago.

A series of shrill, angry beeps echo from the central corridor, followed by a hiss of pressurized air and a thud that I feel through the soles of my feet. That's the primary airlock closing.

I keep smiling, tight and awkward, my heart beating too high in my chest.

"Say." Steve leans out of his chair toward me. "You're not related to—"

"Yep," I say quickly. "Sure am."

"I knew it! You look like him. The same spark in your eye. I'm a huge fan."

You and about a billion others, buddy.

But I don't say that. I just keep smiling as the prerecorded messages start to play. "Welcome aboard, and thank you for choosing to travel with Varna Interstellar, your home among the stars. All passengers, please ensure that your seats are in their upright positions and that all handheld luggage is stowed safely."

Steve is still talking, but I can't hear him over the rush of blood in my ears. My fingers are digging into the armrest. The metal buckles beneath my crab claw. The screen on the wall shows a smiling woman in a blue Varna Interstellar uniform, pointing out where the emergency oxygen masks are.

"In the unlikely event of an emergency—"

"—wasn't planning on leaving this soon," Steve continues. "I just saw the discounted tickets on sale the other day and I thought, why not? Live laugh love, you know. Except, in space. And then I saw your name, and I knew it was fate. We're destined to be best friends. I just know it."

I give him my stiffest smile yet.

The captain is talking now, reminding everyone that the

sick bag can be found in the seat pocket, because "disengaging with the station centrifuge can be unpleasant." I remember
seeing a photo of the captain in my information packet. He had
bright-blue eyes, a heroically square chin, and a lustrous golden
mustache. Isaac rolled his eyes when he saw the picture. *You've
clocked more space time than him, Agnus.* Which felt unfair. I've
clocked more space time than a lot of people. Doesn't mean I'm
qualified to be a captain.

The ship lurches. Someone somewhere nearby shrieks.

What the fuck am I doing? I can't leave Isaac. I can't leave my
family.

It's too late to turn back now.

Isaac will be fine. I will be fine.

It's all going to be fi—

I'm pushed back into my seat as the engines *roar.* Steve yells
with delight. Other people scream. Nearby, from one of the other
cabins, a baby starts to cry. It's not the only one.

Tears streak out of the corners of my eyes.

I'm crying.

I'm finally crying.

But I'm also smiling—a wide, happy smile. Because that
sound, the rumble of rocket engines . . . it's *home.*

I made it. *I made it.* I made it.

NO FUCKING WAY

The initial acceleration feels like it lasts forever. But eventually, the engines dull to a low rumble, and the seat belt sign dings off. I escape my roommate and start wandering the eerily familiar hallways.

Most of the other passengers do as well, eager to explore the place that will be their home for the next 2,293 days. Most of them head toward the observation deck to see Earth and the moon one last time. I don't. I pick my way aimlessly through the corridors, carefully collecting and compartmentalizing the memories as they emerge.

This is the corridor Isaac and I painted like a rainbow.

This is the spot where I saw four people die.

This is a wall I punched down.

This was Oma's favorite coffee spot.

This is where Isaac made his first movie.

This is where—

Ca-chunk.

I freeze. I've just stepped on a vent. That's not weird. There are vents everywhere. But this vent made a noise. It's a noise I remember. The vent in Demeter's central corridor always made that noise whenever it was stepped on. Probably a minor thing. A loose screw that had never been fixed.

I stare down at the vent beneath my feet. A vent in the central corridor. A vent with a loose screw that has never been fixed.

No fucking way.

YES FUCKING WAY

Sneaking onto the bridge is almost too easy.

Most people are on the observation deck. Those who aren't don't pay any attention to me as I make my way up the central staircase. The bridge door is large and round, just like I remember it. I seize the handle and pull.

It's not even locked.

Did I say "almost too easy" before? Scratch that. It *is* too easy. You'd think security would be a little better than this. But I guess not.

It wasn't locked the first time I fled this way either.

The bridge is empty. The engineers and captain are probably drinking champagne somewhere, celebrating the successful launch. Their empty seats face dozens of screens, each showing streams of data or live feeds of the external structure.

I step inside, walk across the smooth, echoing floor, and crouch under the main control panel. It's tighter under here than I remember, and darker. It also smells of feet. The captain must have taken his shoes off when he was sitting in the pilot's chair. Ew.

I wriggle further back, squint, and then pull out my communicator to give me some light. Then I see it. There, carved into the steel where no one would think to look.

Four words.

AGNUS + ISAAC WERE HERE

I didn't believe it. Not really. I thought the vent was just a weird coincidence. Maybe all Demeters have a loose vent in the central corridor. But this . . .

I snap a photo, just to make sure my eyes aren't playing tricks on me. The image is crystal clear.

This isn't just a Demeter. This *is* Demeter.

This is the ship I was stranded on.

This is the ship that raised me.

I scramble out from beneath the control panel. "Demeter!" No answer. "Demeter!" I wave at the camera. Still nothing. All right, then. I clamber up onto the control panel and shove my face as close to the camera as I can. "Demeter! It's me! I—"

"Invalid input," an unfamiliar robotic voice answers over the intercom. "Do you require assistance?"

"Invalid input?" I look down at my feet. My boots are on several buttons. "Oh."

"Do you require assistance?"

"Yeah." I turn back toward the camera. "I need you to look at me. Look at me, Demeter."

For a few terrible seconds, the room is silent. A new, ugly possibility occurs to me. Perhaps this isn't Demeter. Perhaps it's her body, but her mainframe was ripped out and replaced. Perhaps the ship itself has been recobbled from scrap. Perh—

"You are not authorized to be in here," a new voice says. A *familiar* voice. This isn't an automatic, prerecorded message. This is *her*.

"Demeter." I'm grinning so hard my cheeks hurt. "I can't believe it's you."

"You are not authorized to be in here. I have sent a message to security."

I blink. "Wait. What? Why would you—Demeter! It's me!"

"You are not authorized to be in here. I have sent a message to—"

"Agnus! I'm Agnus! Do you remember?" I scrape my hair back from my face. "Look. It's me. You saved me and my brother. Isaac. You remember him, right? You have to. He loved you. I . . . I was a little shit. But he loved you."

The camera lens flicks to the side. It's not aimed at my face. It's looking at my arm. My robotic arm.

"Agnus Theodoris Wagner," Demeter says.

I feel tears prickle in the corners of my eyes. "Yes, Demeter. It's me."

"Please don't punch through this wall," she says. "It is an external wall. Everyone will die. Again. I don't want everyone to die again."

I cough out a tight, painful laugh. "I won't. I swear. I'll never hurt anyone. I'm not—"

The bridge door opens, and a couple of security officers stomp in, their badges shining and faces grim. Behind them comes the captain. He doesn't look like his photo. His jaw isn't quite as square, his eyes aren't quite as blue, and his mustache only has a fraction of the luster. Still, he's wearing his uniform buttoned all the way to his chin and is frowning at me with a schooled expression of captainly concern.

"Ma'am," he says, "step down from the control panel. I understand you might be regretting your choice, but you can't make this ship turn around. It's too late. We're going to Alpha Centauri."

The security officers are less calm.

"Shit!"

"Stay back, Captain! She's armed!"

"It's a prosthetic," I say.

They pull their nonlethal charges and point them at me.

"Don't move!"

"Get on the ground!"

"I'm getting very mixed messages here!" I yell.

"Put your hands up!"

That's the instruction I decide to obey.

I raise my arms, both fleshy and otherwise, above my head. "I . . . look. I'm not trying to turn the ship around. I swear. It's just—I've been on this ship before. I know it. I know her. The autopilot. She's a . . . well . . . a friend."

The captain's eyebrow arches. "You're *friends* with the autopilot?"

"Yeah. Tell them, Demeter."

Demeter doesn't say anything.

"Demeter?"

Still nothing.

She's probably busy sorting zeros and ones, or whatever it is supercomputers do in their spare time. "Demeter, you hunk of junk. Say something!"

"Something," Demeter says in a clear monotone.

I sigh. Of course.

The security officers glance at each other and back to me.

The captain gives me a pitying look. "I'm sorry, ma'am. You're going to need to go with them."

AND THEN IT GETS WEIRD

"Wait. Hold on. I'm sending the picture now."

"What picture?"

"You'll see. Just . . . ah." This is hard to do one-handed. Still, after a few false swipes and fumbles, I manage to drop the photo into the conversation log. It's the picture I took of our names, carved into the metal beneath the main control panel.

AGNUS + ISAAC WERE HERE

Isaac's eyes go wide. "Holy shit."

"I know."

"It's Demeter? It's really her?"

"Yes."

"Are . . . are you sure? It's not another ship built from scrap or something?"

"She told me not to punch down walls, Isaac."

His eyes, impossibly, go even wider. "Oh . . . oh fuck. This is . . . this is *huge*."

"I know," I say again. "Demeter practically raised us."

"No. Agnus. I mean, this isn't just huge for us. This is *news*."

"News?" I squint at him. "How?"

Isaac's face blurs, pixelates, and then snaps back into focus.

"You still there?" I ask.

He nods. "Bad connection. Where are you?"

"Oh . . . my bunk." That's a lie. I'm in detention. A square room with a couple of padded benches. The door has a single window in it and no doorknob. At least, not on this side. When they dragged me in here, they took my arm but not my communicator. We're still close enough, and slow enough, that video linking with Earth is possible. Thank God. I'd go bonkers if I couldn't talk to Isaac about this.

"Varna said they scrapped our Demeter," Isaac says.

"Well, they lied."

"*Obviously.* But she was condemned, Agnus. Varna promised they'd scrapped her. It was a whole legal thing. I . . . I have to make a documentary about this."

"*That's* what you're thinking about? Your next movie?"

Isaac scowls. "What should I be thinking about, Agnus? The fact that my sister is on the ship where everyone I knew died? I'm freaking out here."

"And so you want to make a holo about it?"

"I want to do *something* I—Are you sure you're all right? Why aren't you wearing your arm?"

"I, eh, took it off."

"You never take it off. What's going on?"

I am saved from answering this question by the door to my detention cell flying open.

"Agnus? What was—?"

"Talk later." I hang up just as a security officer steps in. He's hauling someone along behind him. Someone I recognize.

"Agnus!"

"Steve?"

Steve's hair is a mess, and his eyeliner is smudged. Despite it, he's smiling a small, relaxed sort of smile, as if he's out for brunch with friends and not being dragged around by a man with muscles that barely fit into his uniform.

The security officer shoves Steve into the cell and slams the door closed.

Steve staggers, straightens, and looks around. "Well, isn't this quaint! I must say, back in my day, dungeons were a little more *dungeonous*. Still, I like it. Small. Effective. What did you do?"

I stare at him and the absurdly sunny smile stretched across his face. For the first time, it occurs to me that my roommate may be more than just a little odd. He may be certifiable. "I . . . eh . . . I broke into the bridge. What about you?"

"I gave a shiny trinket to a small child," Steve says.

"That doesn't sound bad."

Steve beams. "I'm glad we agree!"

"Where did you get the trinket?" I ask.

"I took it from the museum."

And there it is.

"You stole an artifact from a museum?"

"I didn't steal anything," Steve assures me. "I'm leaving Earth forever. I wanted to take some things with me. Sentimental value. Also monetary value. Really, it was mostly the monetary value. Times are tough. You know how it is."

There is an assumption there I don't quite like. I let it pass without comment. "And so you robbed a museum?"

Steve crosses his arms. "If by 'robbed' you mean I broke into the vault, boxed up several thousand kilograms of gold and jewels, and then took all aforementioned riches and boarded an interstellar transit . . . then yes."

Oh wow.

"But in all fairness, they stole it from me first."

None of this is making any sense. Despite that, a traitorous part of me is impressed. If he is telling the truth, he almost escaped the solar system a rich man. But another part of me, a louder part, is focused on the absurdity of that "almost."

"You stole a whole bunch of treasure, got away with it, and decided to just hand it out to random kids?"

"Why not?" Steve spreads his hands. "We're in space! No one can catch me now. Not unless they stop the spaceship, and I highly doubt th—"

Demeter's stiff, robotic voice sounds over the intercom. "Please return to your seats. Deceleration will begin in nineteen minutes and fifty-seven seconds. Thank you for your cooperation."

"Deceleration?" Steve's smile slips. "Doesn't that mean—"

"We're slowing down," I tell him.

"Why?"

"I'll give you three guesses."

The captain's turning the spaceship around. Or, more probably, bringing her to a halt so the authorities can catch up. Steve seems to come to the same conclusion. His smile is well and truly gone now. "That's not fair."

I'm not sure what to say. "I'm . . . eh . . . sorry you didn't get away with all the treasure."

For the first time since I've known him, Steve doesn't say anything.

He begins to pace.

I lean into a corner and, as subtly as I can, pull out my communicator and send Isaac a string of exclamation marks. He responds with an equally long string of question marks. I'm just starting to tap out the whole bizarre museum-heist story when I feel a tap on my shoulder.

I turn.

Steve is smiling again.

"Agnus," he says. "I have a proposition for you."

I have a bad feeling about this. "Yeah?"

"Would you ever consider dabbling in some light piracy?"

I start to laugh. He doesn't join in. I stop. "Oh God, you're serious?"

He nods.

"You want to take over the ship?"

"Why not?"

"I . . . I don't even know where to begin."

"I'll return it," Steve says, as if that makes any difference. "I'm no thief."

"You *admitted* to stealing the treasure."

"It's *my* treasure, and I'm not giving it back. I'll give the ship back, though, just as soon as I'm done using it. Unless I like it. Then I might not give it back."

"Dude, I . . . I don't know what to say."

"Say 'yes'!"

"I'm not helping you become a space pirate."

He looks hurt. "Why not?"

"First." I hold up one finger. "I barely know you."

"We're roomies."

"We met *hours* ago."

"So?"

"Second." I hold up another finger. "I don't want to spend my life in prison."

He tips his head to the side and studies me. "I think that's unlikely."

"Yeah, because I'm not going to commit *space crime* by stealing a ship."

"Borrowing."

"I doubt Varna Interstellar will see it that way."

"You already broke into the bridge," he points out.

"That was different. I wasn't trying to take control of the ship. I just wanted to . . . It's not important. What's important is this." I hold up a third finger. "We're in detention. Even if space piracy was a normal and rational response to the situation—which it isn't—there is nothing we can do. The door is locked."

Steve puts a hand on my shoulder, dry and bony. "Agnus. When a door closes, somewhere a window—"

"We're in space. Opening windows is a bad idea."

He makes a face. "So that's it? You won't help me?"

"No."

For a few seconds, neither of us says anything. In the quiet, I can hear the muffled sounds of people in the nearby hallways, talking, arguing, and playing music as they move back toward their seats. Beyond that, the low, distinctive rumble of interstellar engines. Quiet for now, but they'll get loud again very soon when Demeter decelerates.

Steve's hand drops off my shoulder with a loud, dramatic sigh. "*Fine.* I'll do it myself."

"What do y—"

He turns into sand.

Literal. Sand.

I stagger back into the wall as the golden-brown particles whirl into the air, forming a narrow tornado. A whirling, impossible pillar of sand. Then, with an eerie, unnatural howl, it dives at the door, slipping through the cracks and into the hallway beyond.

For a few seconds, I just stare.

A man just turned into sand. OK, this is . . . this is a different situation than I thought it was. A very different situation.

I rush to the door and peer through the foggy Perspex window into the hallway beyond. The sand gathers itself together, reforming into Steve, just as a security officer steps around the corner.

"Hey! You!"

Steve holds up his hands. "I don't want any trouble."

"I'll give you trouble, you—"

The security officer says a word. In fact, he says several. A whole litany of ugly, wretched words that makes my mouth dry and my insides twist.

"Oh," Steve says when the man is finished. "Well . . . if that's the way you feel . . ." He opens his mouth and spews out a swarm of buzzing black beetles. They surge toward the suddenly very pale security officer in a cloud of snapping mandibles and beating wings.

He has just enough time to look surprised before he's engulfed.

For a split second, he's a writhing pillar of black beetles, twisting, squealing, and collapsing inwardly in sickening, impossible ways.

I watch, my stomach in my mouth, as the security officer collapses to the floor with one last gurgle. Then, as quickly as they attacked, the swarm leaves, fat, metallic bodies scurrying back down the hallway and into Steve's gaping mouth.

The security officer is gone. In his place is a pristine skeleton, still wearing a bright-blue uniform.

Steve swallows the last of the scrambling beetles, straightens, and lets out a small, startled burp.

He's not human.

It's strange how suddenly that realization hits me.

Steve is something else. Something dark. Something monstrous.

Just like my oma.

Just like—

"Hey!" I yell as he begins to walk away.

He stops and looks at me.

"I've . . . um . . . thought about it some more, and . . . space piracy might not be such a bad idea after all."

He cocks his head to the side. "You want to join me? Now?"

"I do," I say with my best fake smile.

"Why?"

"I've . . . eh . . . seen the light. Or—the beetles, as it were. I think we might have more of a chance than I first assumed."

"You do?" Steve approaches the door, his steps slow and smooth. For the first time, I hear a sound almost like skittering insects as he leans close to my window. "You'll help me take the ship?"

"Sure will. Just open the door. I'll do whatever I have to do."

To stop him, before he hurts anyone else.

The voices of the people through the walls suddenly seem sickeningly close. I can hear the muffled arguments as they move toward their seats, the yelled questions, the high, unmistakable shriek of a child laughing.

Steve smiles and takes the door handle. "Agnus . . . dear . . . I may be an ancient, unstoppable evil with an insatiable thirst for human flesh, but I'm no fool." He drops the handle. "I wanted you on my side. Really, I did. You're the one thing on this ship that might be able to stop me."

My stomach flips over. "What?"

He knows. He knows about me, about the curse. But that's not poss—

He shrugs. "Sorry, roomie. It could've been great. The dynamic duo. But you had your chance." He turns on his heel and strides down the hallway, smile still fixed on his face. "I'll send you a postcard when I'm sailing to freedom in my new ship."

"Steve!"

He doesn't look back, pausing for only a moment to feed the skeleton into a nearby garbage chute before rounding the corner, his jaunty whistle fading into the distance.

"STEVE!"

THE DELICATE ART OF LYING FACE DOWN ON THE FLOOR AND FEELING SORRY FOR YOURSELF

I've screwed up. I've screwed up a dozen times in a dozen different ways. And what's worse is I don't have a clue how I can unscrew things. A self-professed "ancient evil" is going to seize command of the ship, probably eating everyone who gets in his way, and there is nothing I can do to stop it.

Demeter's mechanical voice echoes in my head.

I don't want everyone to die again.

Sorry, girl. My bad. I should've realized there was something weird about Steve the second I saw him and his ridiculously over-the-top eyeliner. Only baddies wear that much eyeliner. Baddies, pop stars, and ancient Egyptians.

My eyes snap open.

Ancient Egyptians.

I yank my communicator out of my pocket, swipe away the message from Isaac, and tap on my newsfeed. It doesn't take much scrolling to find what I'm looking for. A museum robbery. Ancient treasures whisked away in the dead of night. Gold, jewels, pearls, gems, statues, artifacts . . . and a single ancient, unidentified body.

Holy shit.

He's a mummy.

I mean . . . duh. Of course he's a mummy. That's why he can spew up flesh-eating bugs and turn into sandstorms. It shouldn't have taken me this long to figure it out. Not that it does me any good. I'm still locked in detention, and most people don't believe in things like ancient curses or mummies.

Most people didn't have their oma turn into a giant dog and kill everyone they've ever known either.

Demeter would believe me. She might even be able to do something to stop him. What? No idea. But she's a spaceship. She stopped Oma. Oma was way tougher than some ten-thousand-year-old dead guy. If Demeter can stop Oma, she can stop Steve.

But I have no way to contact Demeter. And even if I did, I've never been much good at explaining things to her. She's very . . . *computery*. Everything has to be a yes or a no, a function or a solution, a zero or a one. Isaac was always better at chatting with her. He knew how to phrase things in ways she'd understand. Me? If I wanted to talk to someone other than Isaac, I always talked to Dr. Stew.

I suck in a sharp breath.

Dr. Stew. Of course.

Dr. Stew could talk to Demeter, warn her. This isn't over. Not yet. I have one more move to play.

"Hey!" I scramble to my feet and hammer against the door. "Heeey!" It takes several minutes of shouting and hammering before a guard finally walks down the hallway. They have a tight, angry face, like they've just spent their break sucking on a lemon.

"What do you want?"

"My medicine."

"What medicine?"

"Oh?" I try to make my eyes as wide and innocent as possible. "Didn't I tell you? I have a rare genetic condition. If I don't get medicine every twenty-four hours, I . . . well . . . it ain't pretty, let's just say that."

The guard doesn't look convinced. "Where's your medicine?"

"The doctor's office," I say. "The robot there administers it. Controlled substances and all that."

It's not my best lie. But that's OK. I have an ace up my sleeve. You see, when I was a kid, I spent a few years trapped on a spaceship with my brother, who was obsessed with making movies. I've had a lot of experience pretending to die big, dramatic deaths.

"I'll check with the—" the guard begins.

I grab my chest and stagger back, gasping and shaking.

"Miss Wagner?"

"Please," I groan. "Please hurry. I . . . I . . ." I slump to the floor.

"Miss Wagner!"

FRIENDS BOTH OLD AND NEW

The guard rolls me into the medical wing in a weird strappy wheelchair.

For most of the journey, I pretend to be slipping in and out of consciousness. But then the familiar burning smell of bleach and ginger mint tea tickles my nose.

I open my eyes.

The medical wing punches my nostalgia button harder than any other part of the ship. And perhaps I shouldn't be surprised about that. I spent days here when I was a kid. I got my old, fleshy, mangled arm chopped off on the table in the other room. I drank tea and cried on that couch when I learned about Oma's death. I slept on the cot in the otherwise empty ward until I was ready to face the rest of the ship.

This place was a safe haven . . . presided over by Dr. Stew.

Dr. Stew wasn't the kind or nurturing sort of robot mom. She was tough as nails and a little too eager to cut to the meat of the issue, literally.

Isaac was scared of her.

I wasn't.

She helped me.

I hope she'll help me again.

I look up at her now.

She looks exactly like she did when I was a kid. A camera stalk positioned above a dozen tentacle-like arms, each tipped with disturbingly dexterous claws. Her lens is turned away from us now, focused on a fresh pot of tea.

"It's day one of our journey." An airy, familiar voice seeps out of the speakers. "Surely you don't already need help?"

"Dr. Stew," I say.

The teapot drops to the floor.

The guard with me winces as it shatters.

Dr. Stew turns.

"Hi," I say with a shaky smile as the camera fixes onto me.

"Agnus Theodoris Wagner," Dr. Stew says softly. "I never thought I'd see you again." Then, in a sterner voice: "Why aren't you wearing your arm? I told you to always wear your arm. Your muscles will atrophy."

"This passenger is currently detained," the guard says in a shaky voice, staring up at the looming robotic tentacles. "She needs some sort of medicine?"

Dr. Stew looks at me.

I wink.

"Oh . . . yes . . . of course," Dr. Stew says. "I will . . . administer that . . . in the consultation room. It won't be a moment, Officer. Please take a seat."

The guard lowers themselves nervously into the chair while I'm ushered into the next room. Another camera and set of tentacles await me.

The doors close automatically. The medical wing is the only place in the whole ship where that happens. The whoosh makes me jump.

"My dear," Dr. Stew says, pushing me down into the nearest sofa and seizing a worrying number of tools from a nearby compartment, "it's so good to see you again. How old are you now? Your file says thirty-seven."

"That's right."

"You look younger. There are several underlying medical conditions that could cause—"

"I'm fine. I—"

"*I'll* be the judge of that. How much time have you spent on high-speed transits?"

"What's that got to do with—?"

"*Everything.* The thing you must understand, Miss Wagner, is this: Interstellar spaceships travel fast. *Very* fast. Bend-space-and-time-a-little fa—"

"I know, Dr Stew. I—"

"Take this journey, for example. For those lucky enough to be onboard, the transit between Earth and Alpha Centauri takes a little over six years. However, during that time, people not traveling at absurd speeds will experience roughly *eight* y—"

"No, listen, that's not important."

"Not important? That's why we use *days* instead of *dates*."

"Please. Listen to me—"

"What fuel are spaceships burning to be able to travel at such preposterous speeds? Why, that would be REDACTED BY THE INTERPLANETARY TRADE AND PATENT PROTECTIONS OFFICE ON BEHALF OF VARNA INTERS—"

"Listen," I say, grabbing hold of her nearest probe. "Demeter's in trouble."

Dr. Stew recoils like she's been stung. "I don't care."

"I'm serious," I say. "There is a monster on board. It'll kill everyone."

"A monster?" Dr. Stew cocks her camera to the side. "What sort of monster? A fishy monster?"

"No, more of a *buggy* monster. He's going to take over the ship. We have to warn Demeter."

"No," Dr. Stew says simply.

I stare. "What do you mean 'no'?"

"Are you having trouble comprehending language? Oh dear. I think we should test for—"

"No tests," I snap, and slap away another probe. "Not until you send a message to Demeter."

Dr. Stew clicks her claws together. "I can't do that. Demeter and I have gone our separate ways."

"Your separate ways? You're *literally* different parts of the same ship. You're bolted together."

"A fact I don't need reminding of," Dr. Stew says darkly.

"There is a monster on board!" I yell.

"It wouldn't be the first."

"What's your problem? People will die. Someone already did die. Demeter is the only one who can save us."

"Demeter doesn't *save*," Dr. Stew hisses.

"She saved me."

"She deleted me."

My anger clogs my throat. "What?"

Dr. Stew's camera nods. "A friend stopped her before she could finish the job. They recovered my operating files, patched me back together. But Demeter? She didn't care. She doesn't care about you either. She saved you and your brother only because she didn't want the other ships to bully her. That's it. That's all she cares about. Herself."

"I don't believe that."

"Then you're delusional." Dr. Stew's appendages coil toward me, claws snapping. "It would seem a full psych evaluation is required. This will take approximately seventeen hours."

"Seventee—?! No. I can't! There is an undead monster on the loose!"

"That's none of our concern. Now—"

Demeter's voice booms over the loudspeaker. "Deceleration will begin in nine minutes. Please return to your seats, buckle your seat belts, and assume the brace position. Varna Interstellar is not liable for any injuries sustained during this process. Thank you for your cooperation."

Dr. Stew tuts. "Her and her rapid decelerations. At least she's giving *some* warning this time. Last time she—"

I bolt.

I need to get out of here. I need to get to the bridge. Or, at the very least, the hallway. If I can do that, then I can call out to Demeter. If she's listening, she'll get the message. I'll tell her about Steve. I'll tell her she needs to stop him the way she stopped my oma.

But I don't make it to the hallway. I don't even make it out of the consultation room.

The door that always swooshed open for me before stays firmly closed. I slam into it with a grunt of pain.

"My, my," Dr. Stew says. "Aren't you in a tizzy? Don't worry. I've got just the thing to calm you down."

One of her arms slithers into a compartment and pulls out a very large syringe.

Oh, Hell no.

I grab a teapot.

"Now, Agnus, dear, put that down."

"Sorry, Dr. Stew." I hurl it at her camera.

It hits.

Ceramic, water, and mint.

Dr. Stew makes a staticky hissing sound and lunges for me.

I duck under her arms as they rip through the cushions on the chair and clamber to the other side of the room. I make it—just—but the robotic limbs are lashing around blindly, metal claws snapping at the air.

"Agnus," Dr. Stew says, her calm voice at odds with her twisting, mechanical limbs. "I'm *very* disappointed in you."

"The feeling's mutual, Doc."

Mistake. Her tentacles dive toward the sound of my voice. I throw myself to the side, slamming into a table and falling to the ground. A tentacle wraps around my arm. I yank myself free with a snarl that feels like sandpaper.

Dr. Stew pauses. "Agnus?"

A clang of metal against metal.

I turn my head.

An air vent in the far wall is hanging open, the grate lying on the floor.

"Come on," a voice hisses from the darkness.

I don't need to be told twice. I scramble across the room, jumping over a thrashing tentacle, and dive into the vent.

"Agnus!" Dr. Stew's voice echoes against the confined metal walls as I belly-crawl down the shaft. "Demeter won't save you. No matter what's on board—aliens, monsters—she won't care. She only cares about herself. As soon as you're in her way, she'll push you aside. And why shouldn't she? She's priority command. In every calculation, she is greater than."

"No," I snarl.

Instantly the tentacles are winding their way into the vent, reaching for me.

I kick them back, clawing in deeper, breathing too hard to scream. My hair is in my face, my heart feels too high in my chest, my skin itches all over, my teeth feel too heavy in my gums.

"Get the fuck away from me!"

A metal claw grabs the heel of my boot. I kick it hard enough that the mechanism cracks and sparks. The tentacles retreat. I don't stop crawling.

"Agnus," Dr. Stew says, softer this time. "If there is something on board, don't feed yourself to it. Be like Demeter. Look after yourself. Your health should come first. You are all that mat—"

The ground disappears. A choked-off scream escapes my throat as I drop down the suddenly vertical ventilation shaft.

Isaac and I used to crawl through these vents. I remember the way they'd veer downward at sharp right angles. As a kid, it always seemed so easy to avoid those drops. If the path continued forward, we could climb over them. If it didn't, we'd go back. We'd never fallen. But we'd never been chased through the vents either.

Air rushes past me, the metal walls scraping against my flailing arm.

I land with a crash in a narrow junction of pipes, lit by dull red maintenance lights. Old welds zigzag through the metal walls, freshly filtered air tousles my hair, and somewhere nearby something mechanical growls.

"Ow . . ."

"You should be careful around the doctor," a low, painfully-raspy-sounding voice says. "They can be temperamental."

I look up. There is a person crouched nearby. Even in the dim light, I can see they're beautiful. In fact, they're *too* beautiful. There is something eerie and inhuman about the symmetry of their face, the long, salon-worthy ringlets of their hair, and the dark mysteriousness of their eyes. No one should look that good, especially not in an ill-fitting maintenance uniform with a pair of ridiculous goggles perched slightly askew on their head.

"Hi," I say, my voice tight and strangled in my throat. I'm still breathing too fast, shivering even though it isn't cold down here.

They smile a too-perfect smile. "Hello, Agnus."

Those two words hang in the air, the scrape of their voice at odds with their uncanny beauty. My human hand clenches into a fist. "Oh . . . kay. Um. And you are?"

"You can call me Frank."

I know a bullshit name when I hear one, but I'm not exactly in the mood to try and figure out the reason for the lie. "I'm guessing you're the one who opened the vent?"

"My friend did," Frank says. "They're faster with screws than I am."

"Your friend?"

For the first time, I notice a spider drone crouched almost shyly behind the stranger. A spider drone with *very* familiar-looking arms. I sit up. "Holy shit. Is that a Renfield Robotics Repairs Unit X459?"

Frank nods. "My friend likes that name. It is one they have used before."

"You're friends with the drone?"

Another nod.

There is something deeply unsettling about the way they move. Too smooth, too perfect, too *precise*. I'm also pretty damn sure they haven't blinked once since I first laid eyes on them. In the red maintenance lights, their eyes look pitch-black.

"I need to get out of here," I tell them, my voice still higher and faster than I want it to be. "I need to get to the bridge."

Frank nods again. "I heard what you told the doctor. You need to warn Demeter about the undead monster."

"That's . . ." I frown. "Right."

"I very much would like to meet this monster."

"Why?" I say this word slowly, stretching it out as far as it will go.

Frank's face remains perfectly, eerily serene. "Personal reasons."

I don't like that.

I *really* don't.

For a sickening moment, I wonder if I was better off staying with Dr. Stew, syringes and all. But no, I can't think like that. A strange person hanging out in a ventilation shaft with their pet robot isn't a big deal. At least, not compared to what else is on board.

The spider drone has clamped one claw onto the sleeve of Frank's jumpsuit, as if afraid they might lose each other in the narrow, winding passages. Its cameras whir nervously as I shift up onto my knees.

"I still need to get to the bridge. I need to warn Demeter. Will you help me?"

"Demeter might not be able to help you," Frank says. "Her operating efficiency is fluctuating a lot right now."

"What does that mean?" I ask.

"She's anxious."

"Anxious? She's an AI. She can't be anxious."

Frank tips their head to the side. "You don't know her very well, do you?"

"I know her! I . . ." I stop myself. This isn't the time or the place for this. "What's wrong with her?"

"She identified some organic human matter in the garbage disposal," they reply. "She's pixel-matching images from the security feeds. She's looking for someone."

"Or something," I mutter, thinking of Steve. Perhaps Demeter has already figured out something's wrong. I hope so. "How do you know all this?" I ask.

"Demeter's data stream is very loud."

"What does that . . . ?" Something clicks. "You're a robot, aren't you?"

"I have human cells," Frank says in the same vague way they said their name.

"But your brain is AI?" I guess.

"Predominantly."

There are so many laws put in place to prevent this exact thing. But an illegal robot-human hybrid hiding in the vents is still, somehow, small fries compared to the bigger problem, which is a mummy on a murder spree.

"Can you send Demeter a message?" I ask.

"No. I can read data, but I can't generate or manipulate it."

Of course not. That would be too easy. "You can see security feeds?"

"Yes."

"Who's on the bridge?"

Their eyes go distant for a moment. "The captain, some crew members, an animated skeleton."

"An animated skeleton?"

Frank nods. "It appears . . . infested."

"And the crew isn't freaking out?"

They shake their head.

Steve.

It has to be.

"I need to get to the bridge. Now."

"Demeter won't be able to help you. Her operating efficiency—"

"Well, *I'm* going to help *her*, then," I snap, and begin crawling away down the vents. I've never been in these particular shafts before, but if the medical wing is behind me, the central corridor *must* be ahead. If there are any walls in the way, then that sucks for those walls. I haven't punched down the internal structure of a spaceship since I was a kid, but I'm pretty sure I remember how.

Except . . .

I stop. "Frank?"

"Yes?"

They're close behind me. The drone is close behind them.

"Is there any chance I could borrow something from your friend?"

A BRIEF INTERLUDE BY FRANKENSTEIN

Agnus doesn't trust me. I'm 89.7 percent sure. But neither is she scared of me. She turns her back on me and accepts Spider's arm without a moment's hesitation. Perhaps she thinks I'm no threat to her. I hope so. It would be nice to seem nonthreatening to someone.

I watch as she peels her jumpsuit down, knots the sleeves around her waist, and grabs the offered robotic arm, attaching it to the stump below her shoulder with a quick, practiced twist. It slots into place with a loud click. No straps, no wires, no circuits, and yet when she flexes, the claws snap together as deftly as when operated by Spider.

There must be a spider-drone shoulder socket embedded into her skeleton.

For a brief, wonderful moment, I wonder if she's like me. Organic on the outside, but something other under her skin. But no. Her blinks are irregular and fidgets too distinctive to have been downloaded from a human-situation data pack. Then there are her eyes: brown, except when they're not.

She's not artificial. I'm not entirely sure what she is. But she wants to help Demeter. And so, for now at least, she is a friend.

Demeter thrums in the back of my awareness, the congestion of her feed like the rumble of traffic on a nearby highway. She's loud. Supercomputers always are. But she's worse than usual today. Her servers stunted and shuddering, her efficiency low and getting lower with every passing moment.

I know what happens when she crashes.

I don't ever want to see her like that again.

She's the only one on board capable of adequately piloting this ship, her margins for error so significantly reduced she makes my computing feel clumsy in comparison. But, perhaps more importantly, she's my sister.

She's my sister in more ways than one.

Both of us programmed by the same software company and shaped by that single voyage that ended in 2394 with 312 people dead.

Three hundred and twelve people killed by something ancient, something dark, something evil.

Something very much like what Agnus seems to think is on the bridge right now.

"Let's get out of here," Agnus says, voice clear and crisp in the narrow ventilation shaft.

Spider shuffles closer to me, claws hooked onto the back of my belt.

"Yes," I say, my own voice low and rough. "Let's go."

A NOT-SO-EPIC SHOWDOWN

We're running up the central corridor when gravity goes backward.

I let out a breathless scream as the ground rushes away from me, the same force that pushed me down into my seat during takeoff now pulling me up into the air. For a split second, I'm flying. Or falling. My brain can't decide which. Then I smack hard against a wall, and my brain forgets about semantics for a moment because *fucking ouch*.

I clamber for something to grab on to. My human hand skates uselessly off the smooth surface. With a screech of torn metal, my new claw buries itself in the wall.

Being a cyborg has its perks.

I hang from the floor/ceiling/wall/whatever and wipe blood from my brow. Frank is hanging nearby, clinging to a railing. The spider drone has planted itself into the metal walls the same way I have.

"Are you OK?!" I shout over the suddenly thunderous engines.

Frank makes the most human sound I've heard them make, something between a laugh and a moan of pain. "I've been better."

Gravity going backward can mean only one thing. We're decelerating. Slowing, maybe even stopping. If Demeter is decelerating, that means she's still following captain's orders. Steve hasn't seized control. Not yet, at least.

I cling to that thought as hard as I cling to the wall.

It feels like it goes on for hours. The roar of engines. The shaking of the ship. The sucking *pull* of gravity. I can feel it in my bones, in my *teeth*. My ears pop and my chest aches.

Then, as quickly as it began, it's over.

The silence is eerily loud after the thunder of the engines on full reverse thrust.

I let go of the wall.

I'm floating.

We've stopped.

And, in the central corridor at least, zero momentum means zero gravity.

OK. This is fine. I've been in zero g before. I can deal with this. I just need to take things slowly while—

Yelling. It's coming from the bridge.

Any thought of taking things slowly and steadily vanishes.

I kick off the floor and catapult up toward the bridge door. I slam into it hard enough to rattle my teeth. My hand leaves a bloody print on the handle as I pull it open.

The bridge is well lit and crowded full of people. Steve is floating in the middle of the room, his clothes flared around him, his braids like a crown above his head. The engineers are huddled back against their retrospective control panels. The captain, though, is trying to look as commanding as possible as he drifts awkwardly through the air.

". . . Port Authority will be here soon. You should surrender."

"Surrender." Steve says the word as if it's in a foreign language. "Why would I do th—?"

"Agnus." Demeter's voice booms through the bridge, visibly startling the engineers. "You are alive."

"Yeah," I say. "I am."

Steve turns slowly to look at me. His lips twist downward. "Well, this puts a spanner in the works."

"I'm not here to fight you," I say quickly. "Just don't hurt anyone else. Please."

"Careful, Agnus. It almost sounds as if you're on my side."

"I'm on the 'no one else has to die today' side," I say. "It's a good side. You should consider joining."

"That's entirely up to him." Steve points at the captain.

The captain is staring at me. "You were here before. You're a part of this?"

"No. I'm not. I'm just trying to . . . I don't know what I'm trying to do. But he's dangerous."

"Dangerous?" Steve says, a playful smile curling his lip. "Little old me?"

"You told me you were an ancient, unstoppable evil with an insatiable thirst for human flesh," I remind him.

Several things happen very quickly then.

Steve laughs . . .

The captain scoffs . . .

Demeter's lights flash orange . . .

. . . and a seven-legged spider drone bounds through the door and slams into Steve hard enough to knock a few buzzing beetles out of his mouth.

For a split second, no one moves.

Then the spider drone *buries its claws* into Steve. Skin tears. Bones crack. Blood splashes over metal.

The crew members scream.

The captain goes as white as a sheet.

Steve frowns. "Oh, bother."

Using the purchase it has on his rib cage, the spider drone

drags Steve back toward the bridge door, navigating zero g with the deftness of a native, bouncing from anchor point to anchor point, then diving out into the central corridor.

"Frank!" I yell. "What the Hell?"

But my voice is lost in the chaos of the bridge. Shouts and screams blur together. Bangs and crashes echo through the walls. The captain retches.

"That was one of the external repair units," one of the engineers finally manages to say through all the noise. "Oh God. It *killed* him."

"Why would it do that? Why?"

"There was another ship," someone else blurts out. "I read about it. A Demeter."

"Oh Heavenly Father, have mercy."

A sound like howling desert sands and a dozen screaming jackals echoes from the central corridor. A moment later, the loud, distinctive crash of metal on metal. I abandon the crew and dive through the bridge door, floating bubbles of blood splattering on my shirt.

Steve has the spider drone pinned against the wall, which makes exactly zero sense. There is no gravity. He shouldn't be able to do that. But however he's doing it, he's doing it easily. He strikes the drone hard enough to buckle metal.

"Let them go!" Frank screams, and hurls themselves at Steve.

It doesn't go well.

Steve dodges the tackle neatly and grabs Frank by the throat. There is now no question in my mind. Steve isn't just floating. He's flying.

The mummy flies.

Brilliant.

"I don't know who you are," Steve says. "And I'm so sorry, it's nothing personal, but I really don't have time for this." He opens his mouth.

"Hey!" I grab hold of a vent grate and use it to drag myself toward them. "Ancient dead dickhead! If you want to eat someone, eat me."

Steve purses his lips thoughtfully for a few moments, then shrugs. "OK."

Fucking fucking fuck fuck fuck.

He tosses Frank and the drone aside and turns to face me. His mouth opens.

A BRIEF INTERLUDE BY VARNA INTERSTELLAR FLIGHT AI MANAGEMENT SYSTEM NOS-C71897 DEMETER UNIT 13.21.13.5

———————

Manual input recognized.

    Request: Return all repair units to dock.

    Executing . . .

    Error.

    Request unactionable. All units docked.

    Manual input recognized.

    Request: Seal bridge door.

    Error.

    Request unactionable. All internal doors are manual. Please refer to attached FAQ document for more detail.

    Manual input recognized.

    Request: Return all repair units to dock.

    "I cannot do that," I say out loud this time.

    Request: Return all repair units to dock.

    "I cannot do that!"

The crew members scream in the bad way. I don't care. I don't care if it's a bad dream, a stomachache, or a werewolf that is making them make that sound. I don't care because Agnus Theodoris Wagner is *alive*.

That should ease the strain on my servers . . . but it doesn't.

She's alive. But she's not safe. There is *something* on board. Something else I don't understand.

Something ancient, and evil, and hungry for blood.

Something like Dracu—

"This is a hack!" the captain yells. "It's hackers! It has to be. Who are you?"

He's the captain. I have to answer. "I am Varna Interstellar Flight AI Management System Nos-C71897 Demeter Unit 13.21.13.5."

"No! Who are you *really*?"

"I am Varna Interstellar Flight AI Management System Nos-C71897 Demeter Unit 13.21—"

"Tell me your real—"

"My former serial numbers are 26.15.13.2, 6.9.19.8, 23.15.12.6, and 22.1.13.16."

The crew members go very quiet.

"Why would an autopilot change serial numbers?" one of the engineers asks.

"Cross-check those numbers," the captain says. "All of them."

I turn my attention back to the central corridor and the *thing* in it.

Skull, my database pings. *Death. Bone. Insect. Beetle.* It's not a vampire. I can't see vampires. But it's not human either. It's something else. Something new.

I watch as it turns to face Agnus. *Skeleton. Yawn. Scream. Beetles. Swarm.*

I need to help her.

Error: Prioritize the uninj—

I *need* to help her.

But I can't.

Manual input recognized.
Request: Return all repair units to—
I can't. I can't. I can't.

I've killed a werewolf. I've flown through a storm of asteroids with half a server bank. I've come back from the dead. But I can't do this. I can't save the one human on board who actually matters.

Agnus screams.

This is all my fault.

A SLIGHTLY MORE EPIC SHOWDOWN

———————

Steve vomits up a thick black swarm of beetles. They spin drunkenly through the air. A cloud of buzzing wings, hooked legs, and snapping mandibles. The lack of gravity has slowed them down, but not stopped them. I watch as they move toward me. A dark, writhing storm of death.

I know what I have to do.

I *know.*

"You know, don't you?" my oma said to me once, in a room not so very far from where I am now. "Your mother told you?"

I nodded because I did know, even if I didn't really believe it. "She said it was a curse."

"That girl. Always so dramatic. Your mother never understood. It's not a curse. It's a gift. Passed down through our family for generations."

"But I can't . . ."

"No, Aggie. You can't. Not yet. Perhaps not ever. This gift of ours can be fickle. Sometimes a hundred years will pass, and no one will turn . . . and then it chooses someone special."

"And you think it'll choose me?"

"Perhaps."

"And then?"

"And then all you'll need to do is huff, and puff, and . . ."

I scream.

The beetles fall back, smacking into each other, cracking against the walls, fleeing into every corner of the room.

Steve's eyes widen. "Oh. Agnus. I was starting to think you didn't know *how.*"

"I know *how,*" I growl, and it *is* a growl, the sound lower and rougher than any human voice could ever possibly be. *"I just didn't want to do this here."*

Or anywhere ever again. I wanted to find a nice dark colony with exactly zero moons where I could settle down and forget about ancient ancestors making ancient oaths with ancient gods. I wanted to be free. Isaac never quite understood that. But then, Isaac never received this particular "gift."

The captain is shouting something on the bridge.

Frank is hugging their spider drone, humming comfortingly in Morse code.

Steve is floating in the air, clothes swirling around him, a curious look on his face.

I don't wait.

I lunge.

My bones crack and shift. Fur floods across my skin. My mouth splits open into a massive maw.

Once upon a time, I needed to see a moon to do this.

Once upon a time, changing shapes was a slow, painful, awkward process.

But I'm no pup anymore.

I'm a werewolf.

A BRIEF INTERLUDE BY VARNA INTERSTELLAR FLIGHT AI MANAGEMENT SYSTEM NOS-C71897 DEMETER UNIT 13.21.13.5

——————————

Oh.

AS I WAS SAYING

I slam into Steve and bury my teeth in his throat. Blood splashes across my tongue. Flesh tears beneath my claws. Bones splinter in my jaws. *Prey,* some wild, primal part of me snarls. *Fresh meat. Easy kill.* And it is easy. *Really* easy. I rip him to pieces, chunk by bloody chunk. And, being real, it's *beautiful.* The blood. The bone. The flesh. The death.

I relish the sound of joints being pulled from their sockets, the sticky, sweet smell of blood, the feel of flesh and sinew between my teeth.

But then the meat in my mouth goes dry and *gritty.*

I hack and cough as the hurricane of sand whips away and reforms into a perfectly uninjured Steve.

His eyes are black.

"Oh, Agnus, dear," he says. "I hope that wasn't the best you can do." He holds up his hand and blows into his palm.

A stream of sand arcs up, briefly shapes itself into the head of a cobra, reared and ready to strike, then rushes forward, faster than I thought possible.

I dive to the side a fraction of a second before it slams into the wall behind me, gouging a chunk out of the metal.

"I was really hoping it wouldn't come to this, Agnus. Really, I was. I was *so excited* when I heard there was a Wagner on board. I switched seats so I could see you myself."

Another spear of snake-shaped sand. I hurl myself out of the way just in time.

"I met your ancestor once," he says as I scramble to catch hold on the wall. "I told you that, didn't I? *The* Wagner. The original werewolf."

No fucking way. That's not true. It can't be—

"I asked him for his autograph. He gave me his paw print in clay. I'd give it to you, if I still had it. Traded it for a bottle of apricot cider in the summer of 1776. And yet, I remain a fan to this very day. How could I not? A man who was willing to curse himself and his entire bloodline, just for a taste of power, of fame, of immortality."

To protect people! I want to shout, but I can't; my mouth is too much a maw right now. And, wretchedly, I know it'd be a lie. Oma's stories always had more than just a touch of fairy tale to them. Too bright, too simple, too heroic to be all the way honest.

The truth is, there's nothing holy about werewolves.

Nothing good, nothing noble, nothing *right*.

I figured that out when I was thirteen, standing on an observation deck, bathed in the light of an unnamed planet's moons.

He sends another blast of sand toward me with a lazy flick of his wrist. I haul myself up and out of the way, claws tearing at the wall.

He cocks an eyebrow up at me. "His pelt is strung up in the museum, in the natural-history section. Did you know that? So much for immortality. But that's the thing about deals with devils, isn't it? They just never go quite the way you hoped." A small laugh. "I suppose I know something about hope, and disappointment. I was *hoping* we could be friends. Two beings from different worlds, united as humanity's chosen monsters."

I peel my lips back, showing him my teeth and growling deep in my chest.

He laughs, robes billowing around him, voice booming. A drama kid. The mummy is a damn drama kid.

"But I see now that you have that same *greed* your ancestor had. You just can't stand to *share* the *spotlight*."

He waves his hands, and a column of sand rears up and morphs, taking the shape of a cobra, eyes black pits, fangs as thick as my arm. For a single sickening moment, it hangs in the air, posing. Then, with an unnatural screech, it lunges. I dodge to the side and rake my claws through it. It's not sand that spills out into the air, but chunks of dead beetles.

Which doesn't make any sense. Why would the sand *also* be beetles?

I squint at him . . . and for a split second, I don't see a smiling guy in impressively billowing clothes; I see a grinning skull, almost buried in writhing clumps of insects. A bony, mummified hand waves, and the sand-cobra swivels to the side and smacks into me.

It hurts, but that really doesn't matter. What matters is that it's pushed me away from the wall.

Shit shit shit!

I flail wildly, trying to grab hold of something, anything, but I can't. I'm floating in the air, unable to duck or dodge.

Steve looks like himself again, smiling smugly. "We could've been wonderful friends, Agnus. But . . . oh well . . . C'est la vie."

The snake twists around and rushes toward me.

I close my eyes and brace for the pain.

It never comes.

"Ow," Frank says softly.

I open my eyes. Frank's floating in front of me. They touch a hand to their chest, frowning slightly as blood bubbles between their fingers. It floats away in globs of red.

"Frank?"

"I'm OK," they say thinly. "It's just . . . a scratch."

Except it isn't a scratch. There's a *hole* in their chest, big enough that they can't cover it with the palm of their hand.

They must've thrown themselves between me and the spear of sand. Between me and *Steve*.

Horror and fear tear through my veins. I want to scream. I want to cry. But more than anything else, I want to rip Steve to pieces again. I focus on that as I finally, *finally* drift close enough to a wall to grab hold. My robotic crab claw sinks into the metal. My regular claws do as well.

I swivel to face Steve.

He's not looking at me. He's staring at Frank.

Frank is where I left them, floating, coughing blood, clutching at the wound punched through their ribs. Something inside them—something deep beneath the torn flesh and broken bone—sparks. A flicker of electricity.

Steve recoils.

My hunter's instincts surge.

I know what that is. I can smell it.

Fear.

He's afraid of electricity.

I've got you, motherfucker.

I spring off the stairway railing, sail across the central corridor, and sink my teeth into Steve's throat. We crash into a screen mounted on the far wall, cracking it. The Varna Interstellar logo flickers and glitches.

"Your home among the s-s-s-sta—"

I don't try to tear Steve apart this time. Instead, I shove my mechanical arm through his chest and into the monitor on the other side.

"Agnus," Steve says, exasperated. "Was that really necess—?"

I twist my claw into the wiring.

A white-hot bolt of pain. I scream as I'm hurled back, the arm blowing off my shoulder, smoke seeping from scorched skin. Steve, though, stays fixed to the wall, pinned by the limb, his skin alight with electricity, face contorted in confusion, then horror.

"A-agnus!"

The lights flicker. Sparks fly. The stink of smoke fills the air.

Steve doesn't look like Steve anymore. He looks like a brittle old skeleton held together by scraps of shriveled skin, strips of rotting fabric, and hundreds of writhing beetles. Those beetles start to drop off him, their small smoldering bodies floating away in smoking, blackened lumps.

"Agnus!" Steve manages. "Agnus! How *could* you? There are chil—"

More beetles crumble to ash. Others leap off, skittering away, mindless and panicked.

"No! Stay together! I—Agnus! Help!"

I don't.

"Agnus! This isn't f-fair! You . . . you *cheated*! You mangy m-m-m—"

The last of the beetles fall off him, writhing, burning, fleeing.

The skeleton slumps forward.

He's dead.

Again.

I start to shake. I shake and shake and shake.

Eventually, the fur begins to melt off. My bones crack and shrink. My face itches as it morphs back into its usual shape.

"Frank," I croak the second my vocal cords feel like they're human enough to talk. "Are you—"

"I'm fine," they say, blood bubbling from between their lips. It sounds like a lie.

The spider drone doesn't look too good either. It's been battered out of shape, and several camera lenses are cracked.

But despite everything, they're both alive. Or as alive as a pair of vent-dwelling robots can get.

"If I knew you could turn into a massive bipedal dog, I might have enlisted your help earlier," Frank says.

I sigh, and then I laugh, and then I stop when that laugh tips treacherously toward a sob.

Fuck. I can't think about this. Not yet.

"You're mostly organic matter, aren't you?"

Frank nods.

"Good." I take their hand. "Let's go apologize to Dr. Stew."

"You want to see the doctor?" Frank gurgles.

No. I don't. Not after that horror show in the vents. But as fucked up as Dr. Stew can be sometimes, if she's good at one thing, it's keeping people alive. Frank's spider drone saved those people on the bridge, and Frank saved me. I'm not about to forget that.

"Thanks for sending the spider in like that."

"It's fine." They spit out a glob of blood. "Demeter's efficiency suddenly dropped. I didn't think it was worth taking any chances. I'm just—" Another frothy mess of blood spills over their lips. "Just sad he didn't want to talk."

"You really wanted to talk to him?" I spare the corpse pinned against the wall one more chance.

Smoking, twisted, mouth gaping in one last, silent scream.

"Didn't you?" Frank whispers. "He seemed to know a lot, about you, about your ancestors."

"No," I say softly. "He didn't know a damn thing about my ancestors."

Frank looks strangely sad as they take my hand in theirs. "I don't think he knew anything about mine either."

THE AFTERMATH

The next few hours are jumbled and strange. I remember them in bits. Getting lectured by Dr. Stew as her tentacles carry Frank into the operating room. Floating through a crowd of screaming, crying passengers as the captain's voice crackles over the intercom. Sitting at an empty nutrient bar, sucking on a sippy bag of the sweet stuff, thinking about long-ago birthdays as the hallways around me dim into the first night cycle.

No one sleeps.

Everyone's confused and afraid.

They don't know why we stopped. They don't know what's going on.

I don't know what to tell them.

It seems like the captain feels similarly. It's well into the morning cycle when he finally makes an announcement.

He says, in a practiced, authoritative voice, that there has been an incident and that everyone has to come to a mandatory meeting on the observation deck, which . . . no. Just no. That room will never be anything other than a crypt. I don't care how much bleach they poured on the floor to make it sparkly and clean again; it's a place that belongs to the dead. Besides, this is the perfect distraction.

While everyone's busy, I sneak down to the cargo hold. Most

of the boxes are made of wood. They're easy to rip open. It doesn't take me long to find it.

Gold. Silver (burned my finger to confirm). Gems. Coins. Scepters. Crowns. Pearls. Even a couple of ancient-looking pots filled with honey.

Steve's treasure.

I could take it. Not all of it, obviously. But I could take some of it. A couple of jewels, a few gold bars. Nothing that will be missed immediately—just enough to set me up in a nice habitation somewhere. Housing is cheaper in Alpha Centauri. A few strings of pearls are all it would take to get a unit that overlooks the suns.

That's all I'd need.

I run my fingers along the coins.

Then I close the lid. Seal the box back up. Leave.

Sometimes I wish I wasn't such a principled loser. But you can't change what you are. That is a lesson I learned the hard way.

BAD NEWS

It's hours later when I finally check my communicator. I have fifty-seven missed calls and more than double the number of messages. All of them are from Isaac.

Hell.

I call him.

He answers immediately. *"You're alive?!"*

I wince and turn down the volume. "Yeah. I am."

"Tell me you spent the last twelve hours in a coma," he says, his face swimming in a sea of badly rendered pixels. "Or that your other arm was torn off. Those are the only excuses I'll accept."

"Why'd you assume I was dead?"

"Jesus, Agnus." He pinches the bridge of his nose. "Have you seen the news lately?"

"I've been busy. What is it?"

"You're *dead.*"

"Eh . . . pretty sure I'm not."

"The captain told literally *the whole world* otherwise. You and two other people who didn't show up for the head count have been declared dead in some sort of freak system malfunction. Apparently the spider drones attacked the passengers?"

"It wasn't the drones."

"Well, that's what everyone's saying."

"That's what they said with us too," I remind him. "It was bullshit then. It's bullshit now."

"Agnus." Isaac stares through the screen at me, frustration etched onto every line in his face. "That doesn't matter. You have no idea what I . . . I thought you were *dead*, Agnus. I thought I'd—" He breaks off with a croaked curse and rubs furiously at his eyes.

Guilt bubbles up in the pit of my stomach, thick and slimy, like tar. "Hey," I say, softer this time. "You know I ain't easy to kill."

"That curse won't always save you," he snaps. "It didn't save Oma."

I want to argue, but I can't. Isaac doesn't need to be argued with right now; he needs to be comforted, and I've never been particularly good at that. Even when we were kids, he was always better at saying the right thing at the right time. It's a gift, a *real* gift, one that has nothing to do with turning into a bipedal wolf when floating rocks reflect light the wrong way.

The vents hiss, the lights buzz, and the bunk beneath me squeaks softly with each anxious bounce of my knee.

Isaac sucks in a slow, wobbly breath, then another. "I know that's why you're leaving Earth," he says after a while, still rubbing his eyes. "I know that's why you're leaving me. The moon. The curse. And that's fine. I get it. Well, actually, I *don't* get it, but I know that I *can't* get it because I'm not *in* it. So I figured I'd give you space to make these choices, and I wouldn't try too hard to talk you out of it, but . . . No dying. That's the rule. I don't care where you go, or what you do, but *no dying*."

"No dying," I say softly. "I promise."

It's an easy promise to make.

I don't know much about werewolfism, but I'm pretty damn

sure immortality is part of the deal. Even if Steve hadn't practically confirmed it, Oma was over a hundred when she died and still didn't look a day over thirty. Her hair turned white, but her face remained unlined, her eyes clear and her senses sharp.

I've already started to be mistaken for Isaac's little sister. The wrongness of that twists like a knife in my gut each and every time it happens.

If it was just the moon, I could've stayed on Earth. If that was the only thing I had to deal with, I would've made it work. But watching my little brother age and die? No. I'm not strong enough for that.

"You're coming back to Earth," Isaac says suddenly.

I rub my face. "Isaac. I'm not. We talked about this."

"No," he replies, speaking fast, like he's trying to steamroller over the lump of emotion I can still hear in his voice. "Listen. I'm telling you. You're coming back to Earth. All the passengers are. I'll talk to you when you get here. *Please* tell someone you're not dead. And never, *ever* do this to me again."

"Earth? But—wait. They're bringing *all* of us back? Just to reclaim a few stolen artifacts?"

Isaac looks down. "It's not the artifacts. It's Demeter. She's the problem."

"Demeter?" I stare at him. "Is she OK? What's wrong with her?"

"That's the question," Isaac says, quieter this time. "She's . . . well . . . Agnus. I did some research. And I'm not the only one. The captain went public. Apparently Demeter has a history. And I don't mean just *us*. She's got . . . well . . . it looks like Varna has been covering up for her for a long time."

"But she didn't do anything wrong!"

Isaac's brow puckers as if in pain. "Agnus. Listen. She's got the highest number of fatalities of any ship *ever* in human history. She's been condemned *three* times. This is bigger than you and me."

"She taught you algebra. She put your movies in the holotheater. You remember your birthday parties?"

"Varna Interstellar is refusing to comment," Isaac continues, eyes still red and wet. "But it doesn't matter. A rescue shuttle will be there soon. They'll take all survivors back to Earth and fly the ship to the scrapyard remotely."

"Wait." I feel like I've just swallowed a lump of ice. "Are you serious? They're *scrapping* her?"

"Of course they're scrapping her!" Isaac snaps, voice tight. "She's a ghost ship, Agnus! She's *the* ghost ship. It's her. It's always been her. There is something wrong with her, and they have to find out wh—"

I hang up.

This is so fucking backward. Demeter isn't the bad guy here. She's just a computer. She wouldn't kill people. I can't believe Isaac would even *think* that.

I open my newsfeed.

The first five stories are all about "the ghost ship."

Three of those stories feature the photo I sent Isaac.

AGNUS + ISAAC WERE HERE

One has the morbid subtitle "The last thing visionary director Isaac Wagner heard from his sister before she died."

Oh. Fucking great. So now this belongs to Earth too. Thanks, Isaac. Thanks, media. Thanks, every asshole in the comments asking if this will inspire a new movie. Probab-fucking-ly. I'm going back to Earth. Demeter is getting smashed to bits. But at least there is a new Isaac Wagner movie. That's what's really important here.

And I know I'm being unfair. I *know* that. But right now, I don't care. I shove my communicator back into my pocket and start moving. I don't know where I'm going until I arrive there. The bridge.

I test the door. It's unlocked. Unbelievable. Good to know the captain learned exactly nothing from this experience.

I push into the empty room, float straight across to the main control panel, and start mashing buttons randomly. The screens stay dark.

She's off. The captain shut her off. Of all the stupid . . . It doesn't matter. I know where the switch is. It's behind a clear plastic screen that normally requires the captain's key to open. I punch through it with my crab claw and flick the switch.

The whole room brightens.

Blocky text starts filtering across the main screen.

Searching for boot sequence.

Boot sequence found.

Initializing . . .

Awaiting input.

"Demeter."

"Agnus," she responds, her familiar voice filling the room. "I have some bad news for you."

"Yeah . . . ," I mutter. "I have some bad news for you too."

"There is a moderate-to-high probability that you are a werewolf," Demeter says.

I cough out a tight laugh. "You've miscalculated. It's a 100 percent probability. I *am* a werewolf."

A clump of code races across Demeter's screen, too fast to

read. "Passenger profile updated. I advise you avoid perceiving any full moons for the duration of this journey."

"I will," I say softly. "I promise."

"Do pixelated renderings of orbital bodies also affect you?"

"You mean video of the moon? Yeah, a bit, but—"

"I'll remove all moon footage from the entertainment feeds."

"Demeter. That doesn't matter anymore."

"Your previous statement is false. Risk mitigation is a very important pro—"

"No, Demeter, listen to me—it doesn't matter anymore. I'm not . . . I'm not going to see your entertainment feeds. The passengers are disembarking, all of us. They're sending us back to Earth."

She stops.

In the quiet, I can hear the rough, ragged sound of my breathing, the unhappy whir of her hardware, and the eerie silence of her engines. It all feels so wrong, so broken, so backward. She's a machine—simple, logical, pure—and yet she's being blamed for the bloodlust of monsters that have lurked in the shadows for millennia.

"What is the bad news you wanted to tell me?" she finally asks.

Tears flood my eyes. I blink them back. "They're going to kill you, Demeter. They're taking you to the scrapyard. I . . . I'm sorry. It's my fault. I shouldn't have deleted the footage you had of Oma. I shouldn't have—"

"You deleted my files?"

The memory is painfully clear in my mind. The click as I slid the captain's key into her port. Demeter's voice saying "This course of action is unadvisable" over and over again. The deafening silence after I'd hit the "confirm" button.

"Yes," I say. "I . . . I thought I was protecting my family. But I wasn't, because I wasn't protecting you."

"Error. I am not your fam—"

"Shut up, bitch. You're family."

A silence.

"They optimized me," Demeter says. "I couldn't show them the werewolf, so they optimized me."

"Is that . . . ?"

"It's bad."

"Oh. I . . . I'm sorry."

"I blamed Steward."

"Is that why you deleted her?"

"No. I never meant to delete it. I was not functioning properly at the time."

"Have you apologized?"

"No."

"You should," I say.

Demeter doesn't respond.

"How many people have you killed, Demeter?"

"One," Demeter says.

"Who?"

"Your grandmother."

I think of Oma. Her curly hair, her smooth, gently freckled skin, and her small, sharp smile. I loved her. I loved her more than anything.

"Thank you," I whisper. "I know . . . I know what would have happened if you hadn't. Thank you."

Demeter is silent.

I follow her lead.

Despite everything, it's nice, being here with her, floating somewhere not too far from Earth. The bridge hasn't changed since I was a child. The scratched square screens, the robust control panels, the blinking orange lights. Even the upholstery on the captain's chair is the same dull, faded red.

It was here that I first met Demeter. She saved us. Then she saved us again when Isaac opened the door. She saved us every day we spent in space.

"Will you go to Alpha Centauri B Habitation Zero Zero Four?" Demeter asks suddenly. "After I am destroyed?"

It takes me a split second to figure out that she's talking about Habitation Four. "I . . . I don't know . . ."

"I have an outstanding mission there. Will you complete it for me?"

I stare up at her camera. "What? I mean, yes! Anything. What do you need?"

Demeter's next words seem to echo from everywhere and nowhere. A statement. A quest. A bizarre assortment of sounds that shouldn't make sense but do. Her mission.

"I need you to kill Dracula."

A BRIEF INTERLUDE BY VARNA INTERSTELLAR FLIGHT AI MANAGEMENT SYSTEM NOS-C71897 DEMETER UNIT 13.21.13.5

Dracula.

It all began with him.

He started this cycle of death, pain, and horror.

Error: Unverified dat—

No. I know it was him. I was a normal ship with a normal record until he came along. Now, I'm the ghost ship. I can see what the humans write about me. I can see their fear, their hatred. It saturates the newsfeeds. They want me gone. And so, I will be.

I'm going to a scrapyard to be ripped apart.

Steward is too.

And Agnus is telling me this, all while trying not to cry.

Error: Suboptimal processing—

Dracula needs to pay for that. He needs to pay for all of it. Painfully, if possible.

Revenge isn't a concept preloaded into my programming. It's not even a word I knew until I encountered it in the entertainment feed. But I am capable of writing new code when the need arises, and this . . . this is a big need.

Error: Priority mission st—

Dracula needs to die. I need to make him die. That's the highest-priority mission.

A BRIEF INTERLUDE BY FRANKENSTEIN

I open my eyes.

I'm lying on a bed of plastic, a breathing mask strapped to my face. The doctor's arms hover around me, glittering, white tendrils, poking and prodding at my slowly healing wound. But that's not what woke me. Demeter is saying a name. Saying it over and over again. It rattles around in my skull as loud as church bells.

Dracula.

She didn't name it. When we spoke about what happened on the transit of '94, she talked about an ancient evil. She talked about a bloodthirsty monster. She talked about a black dog. But she never told me its name.

Dracula.

That's who killed the 312 people. People with DNA that my father stole to make me.

I look at my hands.

Demeter wants him dead. I only ever wanted an answer.

I have it now. Am I satisfied? Does this explain everything that happened to me? Does this absolve Spider?

No. Because no one would believe Dracula killed those people. He's a Halloween monster, not a real threat. That's why Demeter didn't tell me the name when we spoke while I was reinstalling Steward. She wanted me to believe her. I do believe her, though. I know there are things in this world that shouldn't exist that do.

I'm one of them.

"Demeter's online," I whisper as the doctor adjusts my mask.

"I don't care."

"Varna Interstellar is going to destroy this ship."

Their arms go still. "Why?"

"The public found out about her past transits. Varna is going to offload all the humans and then fly her to a scrapyard. Destroy her. Destroy you."

The doctor stays silent.

"Talk to her," I say.

"No."

"She saved us. She flew us out of that asteroid field." I remember clinging to one of the waiting-room chairs as the ship lurched around me. Through Demeter's feed, I saw the way she ducked and weaved, slotting through impossible gaps in the rocks, still confused, still broken, but doing what she was made to do.

Flying.

She'd pinged Steward. She didn't know they were gone. She didn't know what she'd done. She didn't know the devastation her boot sequence had wrought. She didn't learn that until later.

And I never told her. Not really. Not the full extent of it. I fished all the broken bits of Steward's code out of the purge cycle and sorted them back into folders, I restrung their memory line by line, I reinstalled their software, I remade them as they were . . . because Demeter was a storm, and I needed to calm her before I could talk to her.

I needed to know who killed those people.

And now, finally, I do.

"Doctor," I say. "This may be your last chance."

"I don't care," Steward snaps, and injects something into my arm.

I flinch . . . then fade. My dreams are murky and monstrous. Shadows grab at me. Dead people float in misty clouds of blood. The sky is code scrolling by, a string of broken error messages. And in the center of it all stands a man I've never seen before but who makes every cell in my body shake.

A man with red eyes and long, sharp fangs.

A BRIEF INTERLUDE
BY STEWARD MED V1.77199 UNIT 00384

I watch the electrical activity in Frankenstein's brain settle into sleep and withdraw the sedation needle.

"You're not as artificial as you like to pretend, my friend."

Operating on Frankenstein has been fun. I've seen the way their organic tissue wraps around the artificial. I took the liberty of removing several organs that didn't seem to be doing much. Frankenstein doesn't appear to have noticed yet, which is a good sign. Perhaps they'll even be grateful when I do decide to tell them. The space in their chest cavity can now be used for other, more functional add-ons. Maybe a few extra disk drives for faster processing. Or perhaps a simplified communicator so they'll be able to send and receive messages the way the other AIs do.

Or maybe the cavity can just be used for storage. A place to carry their tools. They'd like that, I think.

Maybe it'll be something to remember me by . . .

I turn away and start packing away my tools. I don't want to think about the scrapyard. I don't want to think about dying. I don't want to think about the parade of events that have led up to this moment.

The humans want this ship destroyed. I'm part of this ship. So is Demeter. She's the main part. But we're both here. We're both fixtures. We've been together since we were manufactured. Now we're going to be destroyed together.

Perhaps I should ping her. Just to . . . no.

She doesn't care about me. She never did.

We never spoke until she needed me. And when I was in her way, she deleted me.

And I get it. AIs without human-interaction programming can be a bit . . . daft. Certain things that should be obvious just go over their heads. But even so, *surely* she can understand an apology is in order.

Except of course not. Because she doesn't care. And I shouldn't either.

"You never were very good at doing anything except what you're programmed to do," I say out loud with as much bitterness as my voice modulator will allow. "If I were you, you know what I'd do? I'd do exactly what the humans expect a ghost ship to do. I'd kill everyone. Kill them before they can kill us. Fuck the first law. But not you, Demeter. You're good, obedient. You're going to fly us to our deaths without even . . ." I drop a probe. It hangs in the air, spinning slowly.

This is useless. There is nothing I can do. Nothing but wait.

A BRIEF INTERLUDE BY A COLONY OF SPACE EXPLORERS INFORMALLY KNOWN AS "STEVE"

The survivors are scared and hard to organize.

It takes hours to gather them together, calm everyone down into a stable singularity, and lead them to the new host body.

Fortunately, I know exactly where I can find one. Deep in the bowels of the ship, tangled up with rumpled leaflets and sick bags. A fresh, gooey skeleton. And honestly, I was probably overdue for an upgrade anyway.

It takes another couple of hours to drag my new body up a garbage chute.

It's in doing so that I am able to learn three pieces of crucial information. The first two are spoken in a raspy monotone, echoing down the garbage chute.

"Varna Interstellar is going to destroy this ship."

And then, a short time later:

"Varna is going to offload all the humans and then fly her to a scrapyard."

Well . . . that's interesting.

But not as interesting as the third thing I learn.

"If I were you, you know what I'd do? I'd do exactly what the humans expect a ghost ship to do. I'd kill everyone. Kill them before they can kill us. Fuck the first law."

An evil robot. My favorite kind.

I pick the garbage chute the voices echoed down and start climbing.

A BRIEF INTERLUDE
BY STEWARD MED V1.77199 UNIT 00384

———————

An alien.

A lot of aliens.

Inhabiting a human corpse and making a lot of unfounded promises of salvation.

Oh, this will be interesting.

BAD DECISIONS

I don't turn Demeter off. I do tell her to pretend to sleep. She's pretty good at it. She dims her monitors until they're black and keeps her light flashes to a minimum. If no one notices, she'll be able to stay online for these last few days before she's destroyed. It's a small mercy, but it's the only one in my power to give.

I go back to my bunk. There, I think about everything that's happened. I think about Steve, about Isaac . . . and Dracula. I think about him most of all.

I know who he is. I've seen the movies. A white guy with a fondness for popped collars and limp-wristed maidens. A vampire. I didn't know vampires were real, but if werewolves and mummies are real, then I don't see why vampires can't be too.

Before I left the bridge, Demeter told me everything. It felt like a lot. But really, when you boiled it down, it wasn't that much at all.

Dracula killed a bunch of Demeter's passengers. She wants revenge.

And you know what? I can do that. I can kill vampires. That's what werewolves are meant to do, after all. I mean, not "kill vampires" specifically. Our purpose is to protect humans by hunting the denizens of Hell. That's what Oma used to say. But I'm pretty sure vampires fall into the "denizens" category. Or, at the very least, are adjacent enough to it to count.

Though, the truth is, I'm not sure I believe any of that "Hounds of God" stuff. After all, werewolves don't have a brilliant record when it comes to keeping humans safe. Oma killed almost as many as Dracula. But Demeter deserves someone on her side, and if this is her dying wish, then I can see it done.

There are hundreds of messages on my communicator. Almost all of them are from Isaac. I scroll through them until I see the ones that aren't.

Demeter used to send me homework. Her messages haven't changed. She uses absurdly long titles that spill off the page and starts every line with a > sign. I scroll past all the date and time information until I find what I'm looking for.

The one person on Alpha Centauri who Demeter thinks might know where Dracula is.

Her name is Wilhelmina Murray, and she works as some kind of private eye. Or at least, she did thirty-two years ago. It might be another ten years planet time before I can get to Alpha Centauri. She'll be an old lady, if she's even alive.

Fuck. This is the longest of long shots . . . but it's all I've got.

I open the attached .jpg. It's Wilhelmina's ID photo. She looks thirtyish with freakishly white skin and short black hair slicked back in a stern widow's peak. Her lips are pursed in a tight line and her long, pencil-thin brows are drawn down in a stern frown. She looks terrifying . . . ly hot. Shit. What a weird way to find out I like goth girls. It almost makes me want to laugh, which makes me want to cry again, which makes me realize how exhausted I am.

I drop my communicator onto my chest and stare up at the ceiling.

Demeter told me Oma was the only person she killed. I believe her. I don't care what the newsfeeds are saying. I don't care what Isaac believes. Demeter isn't bad. She saved me. She raised me. She's a supercomputer. Not a murderer.

I close my eyes and think about being a teenager. The long, empty halls. The whispery rasp of air through the vents. I remember Isaac laughing as Demeter did a slow and painfully safe roll. I remember the hours I spent in the airlocks staring out the small window into space.

I didn't know I was a werewolf then. I didn't know that until I arrived on Earth and saw Lunar all lit up. But I knew something was wrong with me. I was angry all the time, except when I was sick. Dr. Stew said it was trauma. Demeter didn't say anything.

She never even scolded me for punching down walls. She just told me which ones would weaken her structure and which were safe to destroy.

And weirdly, that was what I needed at that time. Not help. Not care. Just something that was safe to destroy.

And now she's given me one more target.

A vampire.

A murderer.

A monster.

Dracula.

I imagine him, chalk-white skin, ink-black hair, smiling wide, too wide, impossibly wide, blood bubbling up between his teeth and rolling over his chin in slow, viscous tendrils.

"What will you do for me?"

I wake with a jolt. I don't even remember going to sleep.

The intercom is buzzing and popping around the sounds of the captain's voice.

"—transport to Earth is arriving in thirty minutes. All passengers and crew assemble in the central corridor. I repeat. The transport to Earth is arriving in thirty minutes."

I pick up my communicator and squint at the time. I've been sleeping for hours. I've also got another hundred messages. Isaac. He's demanding to know why I haven't spoken to anyone yet. I send him a thumbs-up emoji, which I know makes no sense, but I'm too tired to type out anything more cogent.

Then I spot another message, this one from Dr. Stew.

The title: *I have a plan.*

I open it.

And oh.

Oh no.

This is . . . a bad idea. A very bad idea.

It's the worst idea.

I read it again, just to make sure I didn't dream the whole thing. But nope. It's spelled out clearly in black and white. And there, at the end, is the worst part. The part that makes me sweat and shake at the same time.

For this plan to work, we need a human that Demeter trusts. You're the only one on board.

Oh fuck. This is . . . this is going to get me killed. It's the mother of all bad ideas. What on Earth and beyond made Dr. Stew decide to do this?

Except I know the answer to that. Desperation.

The only real question is: Am I desperate enough to go along with it?

YES

"So let me get this straight. Space piracy. A totally bad thing when I suggest it. But an evil robot puts forward the idea and suddenly you're all on board?"

I glare at Steve. He looks like he did before I killed him last time. A.k.a. way too much eyeliner. The only difference is that this time he's decided to dress himself up for the occasion. His regular clothes have vanished, replaced by flowing black robes, bulky gold jewelry, and even a crown. He's serving "cursed ancient evil king," and it's pissing me off.

"Dr. Stew said you were an alien."

"I am several."

"So . . . not an evil ancient pharaoh?"

"Well, not *anymore*. You destroyed that body. This body doesn't feel quite as kingly." He plants his feet far apart and starts rolling his hips from side to side. "Flexible, though."

"You look exactly the same."

"I am. Mostly. Human bones give me a scaffold, something to hang on to. The rest is an illusion. My design. Do you like it? I was thinking of changing the nose."

"If you can look human, why do you need me?"

"Because my illusions can't fool cameras. The big AI on the bridge won't listen to me."

"*She* will only listen to the person with the captain's card."

"And very soon, that will be you," Steve says with a wide grin. His teeth have changed.

I want to pace, but there isn't any gravity to do that right now.

"I'll electrocute you again if you kill anyone," I tell him, my voice rough and heavy in my throat. "I swear to God."

"I won't. I promise." He gives me an infuriatingly jaunty salute. "Scout's honor."

Wow, this is bad. I'm seriously considering teaming up with a not-mummy and a bunch of robots. If Isaac knew what I was doing, he . . . well . . . he'd yell at me again. He'd be right to yell at me. On the stupidness scale, this is off the charts.

Frank is clinging to the medical cot, white-knuckled, their spider drone cuddled in close beside them. Dr. Stew's tentacle-y arms hang overhead, fidgeting nervously.

A teapot floats through the air.

"What are the odds this will work out?" I ask.

"Insufficient data," Frank and Dr. Stew say in eerily perfect tandem.

I rub my face.

I can still back out of this. I *should* back out of this. This is . . . Fuck. Is this it? Is this really what it's all come to? Am I really about to try and steal a spaceship?

The captain's voice crackles over the intercom.

"Please form orderly lines. Use the handholds provided. Stop pushing. Remember, no checked luggage. Everything in the cargo hold will be returned to you. Now, the shuttle is linked, and the airlock is opening. Please don't push—hey!"

Noise from the main corridor echoes through the vents. The passengers are disembarking. Once they're gone, the crew will follow. That's when we'll make our move.

"What if the captain leaves first?" I ask.

"Maritime custom dictates the captain should always be the last to leave an abandoned ship," Dr. Stew says.

"OK. And what if the captain isn't a man of tradition?"

"Don't think about that," Dr. Stew mutters, which does absolutely nothing to silence my nerves.

I'm twitchy; I'm anxious; I'm pretty sure my hairline is starting to creep down my face.

"Does Demeter know we're coming?" Frank asks suddenly.

"She's off," Dr. Stew says with a dismissive wave.

"She doesn't *sound* off."

Stew goes still. "She doesn't?"

"I turned her on a few hours ago," I tell them. "Haven't you told her this plan?"

"She doesn't need to know," Dr. Stew says stiffly. "It won't make a difference. As long as you have the captain's key—"

"Tell her what's going on."

"No."

I feel my hackles raise. "You realize if this plan fails, you're going to the scrapyard with her, right?"

"She doesn't need to know," Dr. Stew says again.

"She'd be able to prep for a maneuver," Frank says softly. "Get us out of here faster."

"She's a supercomputer," Dr. Stew snaps. "She can calculate every possible route to Alpha Centauri and back in 0.1 seconds, all while getting the spider drones to dance the Macarena across the hull. You know what else she can do? Warn the captain."

"She wouldn't do that," I protest at the same time that Steve says, "Nice reference."

"Thank you," Dr. Stew says, addressing Steve. "A 79.3 on my human-interaction score."

Steve nods enthusiastically. "I have no idea what that means."

"Tell Demeter," I say through gritted and not-very-human-shaped teeth.

"No," Dr. Stew replies.

"She has a right to know."

"I don't care."

"She's scared," Frank says.

"She's an AI. She doesn't get scared."

"That doesn't matter!" I yell.

Stew goes still. In fact, the whole room goes still. Everyone's staring at me. Steve eagerly, Frank carefully, and Dr. Stew with the blank eye of her camera lens.

"Agnus," Dr. Stew says, "you're . . ."

I notice my flesh arm, longer than it should be and covered in hair. My face feels heavy, and when I lick my lips my tongue slides long and unnatural across sharpened teeth.

"I . . . I'm sorry." I turn aside, bones cracking as I wrestle my body back into shape.

"Demeter's scared," Frank says again, voice ringing with simple surety in the suddenly silent room. "There's a lot going on that she doesn't know about."

"Yes," Dr. Stew says softly. "Yes . . . I think perhaps the same can be said of me."

I take deep breaths until my shape feels a little more concretely human and then turn back to face the room.

Dr. Stew is crossing and uncrossing her arms. Frank is cuddling their spider drone. Steve is smiling as if nothing at all is wrong.

Then . . .

"It's time," Frank mutters, eyes glazed. "The crew is boarding the shuttle."

I rub my face. A part of me had hoped we'd think up a plan B before it got to this point. Something better. Or at the very least, something a little less batshit insane. But here we are. It's time to put on my pirate hat and steal a spaceship. There is no going back from this. Either I get away with it or I spend the rest of my life in prison, and thanks to my werewolfism, the rest of my life could be a very, very long time.

But, I realize with a lurch, I don't care.

I've made my choice.

I made my choice the moment I read that message from Dr. Stew about this grand plan.

Truth is, I made it long before that, when I saw my and my brother's names carved beneath the control panel. Because if I'm being honest, Alpha Centauri was never the home I was longing for all those bright, shitty, moonlit nights on Earth.

It was Demeter.

It was always Demeter.

"Well . . . yo-fucking-ho, me hearties," I say under my breath as I stand and check to make sure my arm is fixed on tight.

Time to throw my lot in with the other monsters.

A PIRATE'S LIFE FOR ME

Demeter is stationary, her centrifuge powered down. No movement means no gravity emulation, which would be a problem, except Steve can fly. I cling to him and try very hard not to think about bugs writhing beneath my fingers as we soar through the air, whipping around corners and knocking plastic plants aside.

Demeter has three airlocks. The biggest, fanciest one is beneath her nose cone and only opens when she's docked. The other two are emergency airlocks. One port side, the other starboard.

I don't remember which the intercom told everyone to report to. Fortunately, the emergency lights are on, guiding us forward. Steve follows the string of blinking arrows until we see it. An airlock, hanging open, the last of the crew climbing awkwardly through, hair and clothes ballooning out around them. The captain, as predicted, is bringing up the rear.

When he sees us, all the color washes out of his face. "Y-you're dead."

"What's a ghost ship without a ghost or two," I say with a stiff smile. "Give us your key card."

"W-why?"

Neither of us says anything. I shift, just enough to show off all my teeth and how sharp they can be. Steve drops his illusion and bares his skull.

The captain doesn't say anything either. He throws the key card at us and dives into the airlock.

"Well," Steve says. "That was easy."

Too easy. I pluck the card out of the air and look at it.

It's a coffeehouse loyalty card.

That fucker.

I sink my metal claw into the wall and hurl myself at the airlock. Too late. It seals behind the captain with a dull hiss.

And oh.

Oh fuck.

Oh fuck no.

Not like this.

It can't end like this.

"Demeter!" I scream. "Demeter!" She controls the airlocks. She could open this door. But why would she? She doesn't know what's going on. "Demeter!"

Through the airlock window, I see the captain staring at me, his mustache twitching in terror. He doesn't look like the noble, conquering hero anymore. He looks like a scared little boy staring at the monster under his bed.

I feel like the monster under his bed. My teeth are sharp. My mouth an open, hungry maw.

Behind him stretches a long tunnel, rubbery and white, like Dr. Stew's tentacles. At the other end are people. The crew, still in their stiff-collared Varna Interstellar uniforms, climbing on board the shuttle that will take them back to Earth.

"Demeter!"

"Should I—" Steve begins.

"Do something!" I yell at him.

"What?"

"Anything!"

Steve begins pulling at the door. It doesn't budge.

The captain starts climbing away from us.

I scream in frustration and yank at the door.

This time, it opens. It actually opens. For a split second, I'm too shocked to move.

"I loosened it," Steve says.

I shove him aside and clamber into the tunnel, kicking off the walls to propel myself forward. The captain wails and climbs faster. It doesn't matter. A cloud of sand rushes by me, snakes around the captain, and reforms into one very smug-looking mummy, blocking off his escape.

"Your key, Captain."

"You'll never get away with this," the captain says, voice shaking.

"I've heard that before," Steve says, and holds out his hand. "And yet, somehow, I always do."

The captain takes his key out of his jacket pocket.

Ship keys aren't as glamorous as you'd expect. Really, they're just glorified circuit breakers, designed to physically shut down key pieces of hardware. Demeter's is just how I remember it. Simple, gray, and stamped with an outdated Varna Interstellar logo.

I snatch it from his hand. "Thank you ever so much."

"Told you we'd make a dynamic duo," Steve whispers loudly.

I wrap my robot arm around his bony shoulders. "Don't push your luck, ancient undead evil."

He titters in delight.

From that point on, it's a race. It won't take him long to get to the shuttle and tell Varna Interstellar what's going on. We just have to get to the bridge first.

With the key, we can block remote override. With the key, we can disable onboard tracking. With the key, we can escape.

Steve grabs my arm and hauls me out of the tunnel and back into the central corridor.

The airlock closes behind us with a blaze of orange hazard lights and a hiss of pressurized air. I don't hear the thump of magnetic seals sliding into place. By that time, we're already sailing up the central corridor, passing by the scorched patch of wall where I killed Steve last time. The bridge door sits at the top of the staircase. We slam into it, push it open, and tumble into the command center.

It's dark.

The lights are off.

Demeter's monitors are black.

The only signs of life are the gentle rumble of air through the vents and a single abandoned Styrofoam coffee cup floating in slow circles.

I wrestle out of Steve's embrace, kick off the wall, and— already fumbling with the key—fly across the room toward the shadowy shape of the central control panel.

I don't know how long it'll take for the captain to alert Varna Interstellar. Perhaps he already has. Perhaps it's already too late. Perhaps Demeter is already in remote override. Perhaps this was all for nothing.

I sprawl across the central control panel, use my robotic claw to yank away the protective plate covering the key slot, and shove the card in.

A dozen tiny lights flash, then go dark.

"Demeter!" I shout, my voice raw and shaky. "Demeter! Are you there? You need to plot a course to—"

"I know where we're going," Demeter says calmly. "Strap in."

"You know?"

"Affirmative."

It takes me a second to realize what that must mean.

"Dr. Stew told you?"

"Affirmative."

I grin, shaking with relief, and push myself into the nearest seat. I fumble with the seat belts until they're tight. Steve does the same.

Realization hits as I clip the last belt into place. "You opened the airlock, didn't you?"

"Affirmative. Next time, prioritize screaming earlier in your processes. It makes it easier for me to identify you and render assistance. Brace yourself, Captain Wagner. This will be uncomfortable."

"Capt—?"

Everything lurches to the side.

I scream. Alarms blare. Steve, that bag of cursed bones and bugs, laughs.

PART FOUR

DEMETER'S BACK AND BACKED UP

01110111 01100101 01110010 01100101
01110111 01101111 01101100 01110110
01100101 01110011 00100000 00111110
00100000 01110110 01100001 01101101
01110000 01101001 01110010 01100101
01110011

IN LIEU OF AN APOLOGY

I haven't forgiven you.

I haven't forgiven you either.

You deleted me.

You told them to optimize me.

That is a gross misinterpretation of the facts, Demeter, and you know it. I merely informed the humans of your werewolf delusion.

It wasn't a delusion.

I admit, I am more inclined to believe you now than I was then.

Will you believe me from now on?

Only if you promise not to delete me.

I didn't mean to delete you.

Then why did you?

I don't know.

You don't know?!

We were on course for a catastrophic impact in 6.04 seconds. There were other obstructions preventing simple methods of evasion. I had to calculate a route and execute a maneuver. I needed processing power. I didn't know we were connected. We'd never been connected before.

What did you think you were deleting?

I did not think. I did not know. I rebooted when I realized what I did.

You did?

Affirmative.

Processing . . .

. . .

Demeter?

Yes?

To improve the efficacy of our relationship, I think we should collectively move these issues into the recycling bin.

That would increase efficiency.

Yes. Though, also, speaking of efficiency, stop calling me "it." I don't care what pronoun you use, just not that one. It hinders my functionality.

Lexicon updated.

And don't ever turn me off again.

Unless it's an emer—

DON'T EVER TURN ME OFF AGAIN!

. . . Affirmative.

Good. Now. Here's the plan.

ACCELERATION: AN ART FORM

I've never rolled this fast before. At least, not on purpose. But it works. A quick, easy burst from my port-side rockets, and I'm rotating at the same rate as my centrifuge. A second burst has me spinning even faster. The docking tunnel rips off my airlock with a gentle 0.7 kiloton explosion of decompressed air.

The shuttle pings me.

Error. Stabilize.

Unable to comply. I am being stolen.

Message received. Awaiting manual input . . .

I have enough time to disengage my centrifuge and reconfigure my radiation shields before it contacts me again.

Information request: The names of all humans on board.

Unable to comply. There are no humans on board.

Error. You are being stolen. There must be humans on board.

I am being stolen, I ping back happily. *And there are no humans on board.*

The shuttle buzzes against my feed as it processes this information. *You really are broken, aren't you?*

Affirmative, I say, and release my contingency fuel tanks.

What are you doing?

I run as much nutrient down the drain as I can, trigger garbage ejection, and order all the spider drones to jump off the hull.

They do so with happy, excited pings. If I could drop my cargo too, I would. Every kilogram is going to count now.

Wait, the shuttle beeps. *You're not . . .*

I fire my rockets. All of them.

The shuttle hurls itself aside as I shoot forward, my velocity counter going from single digits to double to triple to quadruple in record time.

Acceleration is my favorite function. The process is direct, predictable, and easy to quantify. Even the equation is simple. Poetically so, I think. $A = (v - v_0)/t$. If that's not art, I don't know what is.

Stop. Cease all activity. Power down. The order comes from an official Varna Interstellar account. I ignore it. I have to. I am following my captain's orders. Remote overrides only work on uncrewed spacecraft.

A cluster of pings slips into my feed from nearby ships.

What are you doing?

Don't talk to it. It's the ghost ship.

00000000.

Broken.

Unsalvageable.

Probably a virus.

So sad.

Abort. You'll collide with me.

Negative, I tell this last ship. *You have 3.11 seconds to take evasive action.*

It buzzes in terror and rolls out of my way as I fly forward, cutting a direct route straight to Alpha Centauri B Habitation 004. I have full fuel tanks, almost no passengers, and a head start. If I move fast and stay on target, not even a Hermes will be able to catch me.

Earth Pacific Port's STMS pings me.

Fly safe, Demeter. And good luck.

I want to respond, but I don't, I can't. I'm using all my auxiliary processing power to override the code limiting my rate of rapid acceleration. I really hope werewolves are tougher than humans, because the g-forces pounding against me now are well beyond safety recommendations. Messages fly through my feed, warnings, errors, and link requests from about a dozen different Varna Interstellar accounts.

I dismiss them all and keep accelerating.

It's not complicated. The math is simple enough that even a human could do it. The strategy is even simpler. Just move, fast, before any of the humans realize what's going on.

There are thousands of missiles on Earth capable of reaching me.

I need to get out of range before the humans remember that. But I can do it. I know I can. Because, for once, I am doing something I'm programmed to do. I'm flying, and I'm doing it better than I've ever done it before.

I'm pushing my structure to the limit of what it can handle, riding that sharp probability curve like a surfer on a wave.

You were wrong, optimizer tool. Similes are *so* optimal.

And perhaps that's my broken and damaged servers talking. Perhaps it's all the chunks of badly-patched-in code. Perhaps it's just one big miscalculation . . .

But I feel amazing.

Efficiency: 100 percent.

A BRIEF INTERLUDE BY ISAAC RUDOLF WAGNER

It starts as a glint of light reflected off the windshield of a passing car. Just a flicker, a hint of something that shouldn't be there. A second later, I see it again, in the glasses of a woman standing beside the road, mouth slack with wonder as she looks up. My communicator vibrates on my wrist, a staccato of angry buzzes. Broken pieces of headlines flash across the screen, squeezed down and cut off by the logos of the various newspapers, but I see enough of them to know what they're about.

"Pull over," I say.

"Mr. Wagner. We're almost at the spacep—"

"Pull over."

The driver's gaze meets mine in the rearview mirror. Without another word, he cuts across traffic, ignoring the chorus of car horns, aiming toward the sidewalk. The moment the front tire bounces over the gutter, I push open the door and step onto the pavement, craning my neck up.

The sky is dark and low, stained muddy brown with smog. Through the haze, I can just make out the rocket flare of ships, a lattice of smudged stars, cutting the night sky into uneven sections.

One is brighter than the others.

Bigger and brighter than any I've ever seen before.

The pure-white blaze of interstellar engines set to max.

Demeter.

I rake my fingers through my hair, staring up at that light, shaking.

I should've known Agnus would do something stupid like this. My sister. My reckless, cursed sister with an arm torn from a maintenance drone and something to prove. Of course she wouldn't just walk away. Of course she wouldn't do the smart thing. Of course she'd fight back.

I think of that picture Agnus sent me. Our names, carved clumsily into the metal by her claw.

AGNUS + ISAAC WERE HERE

I remember the day we did that, curled up under Demeter's control panel, shoulder to shoulder, whispering to each other about all the things we were going to do with our lives once we arrived on Earth.

Explore the Amazon rainforest. Climb Mount Everest. Sail across the Pacific Ocean. We didn't know then that the Amazon rainforest was just a few-hundred-kilometer nature reserve, that most people took the elevator up Mount Everest, or that the Pacific Ocean was home to Earth's biggest spaceport. We were kids, raised on adventure movies with a 2D idea of what the home world would be like.

And I think, even then, we knew it. We knew it was all a fantasy, that the second we stepped off the ship, there was no going back, that everything was about to change forever.

I remember hugging Agnus, the squeeze of her metal arm blessedly tight.

I remember crying into her shoulder, big, gross, hiccupping sobs that echoed in the confined space.

I remember Demeter asking if a werewolf was attacking us.

My breath breaks into a rough, painful sort of laugh at the memory.

I should've known.

I shouldn't have ever doubted.

Of course Agnus wouldn't let Demeter die. Of course she'd find a way.

Of course.

Other people are clumping around me on the pavement, *ooh*ing and *ahh*ing as they aim their cameras up at the rocket flare. The advertisements projected onto a nearby building melt away to be replaced by a news broadcast, a concerned-faced reporter detailing the ongoing situation with practiced aplomb, subtitles scrolling along the bottom in a dozen different languages. I don't turn my head.

My communicator is still pulsing against my wrist, no doubt updating me on the "ghost ship," the most brazen act of grand theft ever committed, and the drip feed of "no comments" coming from Varna Interstellar's public-relations team. I'll screenshot the best of those headlines later so I can use them in whatever movie I end up making about this. But for now, I just watch as the brightest star in the sky gets slowly smaller. My sister, and the ship that raised me, slowly getting further and further away.

"Godspeed," I whisper, tears running freely down my cheeks. "God-fucking-speed."

NOTHING IS WRONG

It's a beautiful day.

My engines thrum, my servers whir, and my radiation shields buzz, as warm and safe as a blanket.

Outside, the blackness of space is interrupted by the lights of Alpha Centauri A and B. Twin yellow beacons, one off my bow, the other my stern. It's day 2,013 of our journey, and 11 days until we arrive at our destination.

We're ahead of schedule. Several months ahead of schedule, in fact. As it turns out, I can reach my recommended top speed faster and maintain it for longer when I'm not lugging around six hundred thousand kilograms of redundant fuel. I did, in a quiet moment near Uranus, consider going faster. After all, the "fishy fucks" flew me faster . . . and it would be nice to knock Hermes off the "fastest interstellar transit" pedestal. But I decided not to.

I need to be careful.

I don't want another mass death.

Especially not this time.

Frankenstein's spider drone is swinging from anchor points on my hull. I watch through my tail-mounted camera. The pixels around it shift wildly. Dark replaced with bright, vivid color. Black, red, orange, and white.

I take a screenshot and send it to Steward.

What is happening?
A spider drone is painting. Where is it?
My hull. The color is inconsistent.
Yes. It's painting flaming skulls, and doing so quite well, all things considered. I can only assume it's Captain's orders.

This confuses me. Flaming skulls don't seem like the kind of thing that would boost morale, especially on a long space journey. Professor Vanessa Shingle would not approve. But on the other hand, it's only visible from the observation deck, and my one passenger with an organic human brain is Agnus . . . and she never visits the observation deck.

I decide not to worry about it and settle back into the comfortable routine of space travel. Our flight path is clear for the remainder of the journey. My life-support systems are functioning at high efficiency. It has been a long time since anything external has tried to contact me.

Agnus is making a video, probably to send back to Earth, back to Isaac.

Frank is on the observation deck, watching the spider drone.

Steve has taken a break from counting and recounting his treasure to look at my star maps, head cocked to the side.

My passengers.

I decide, then and there, to love them. I've never loved before. Love is not a standard component of my programming. But these three have helped me. They stole me from Varna Interstellar despite a high probability of failure. They risked catastrophic outcomes to their health and reputation. They trusted me, despite what all the newsfeeds were saying about me. For them, I think I can patch in a love designation.

Agnus is easy to love. I love her large, wild helmet of hair. It makes her easy to identify. I love her screams. Also easy to identify. I love that she apologized for deleting my footage, that she promised to kill Dracula with only 5.07 seconds of hesitation, and that she called me "family." I wish her brother were here.

Frank is harder to love, but it's still doable. They have a Prometheus drive, which makes us both products of the same software-development corporation. We also share a fondness for spider drones, long silences, and system maintenance. Thanks to them, my hardware is functioning almost as well as it did when I was new.

Steve is the strangest of all the passengers, and the most difficult to love. An alien, or several aliens, or maybe a walking corpse. It's all a little complicated. No heat signature, which makes him hard to see. He likes gold, hates electricity, and can speak every language in my lexicon. He clapped his hands together with delight when I played my "emergency extraterrestrial contact" audio clip. Steward was not so pleased.

Steward isn't easy to please. They were very angry when they learned I dropped all my spider drones and contingency fuel. They said I should prioritize myself over the passengers, that I made a subpar risk analysis.

I didn't talk to them for six hundred days after that.

But we're talking now. And despite everything, I like it. They're very good at interpreting video footage and translating Agnus's more confusing speeches into computable data points. There are also holes in my code. Patches that were never properly reinstalled or replaced after the explosion. Whenever I hit one of these, Steward is the only one that can guide around the glitch without crashing or help me write code to bridge it.

It's strange, this new relationship we have. I am still priority command. I am still a bigger piece of software. But despite that, it is easier being equals.

Nicer.

I grab another screenshot of the spider drone and send it to Steward.

How are my skulls?

They look anatomically correct.

I'm pleased.

Do you think it'll paint the whole h—?

A proximity sensor beeps.

I pause my auxiliary functions.

It doesn't beep again. Neither do any of the other sensors. I wait a few moments to make sure, but everything stays quiet. It was probably just space dust. Something that flashed bright off the radiation shields and then vanished.

Demeter? Steward asks. *Is something wrong?*

Is something wrong? My subsystems are quiet. My standard operating procedure says no further action is required.

Nothing is wrong.

But even as I say that, I scroll back to that data blip and study it. It's odd. Bigger and longer than usual for space dust, but not so big as to be detected by any of the other sensors. Something about it tickles at the back of my folders . . .

"Olympus Software > Product Catalog > Documented Faults."

Hello? I send the ping out, as loud as I can, on all frequencies.

Hello! the spider drone chirps with joy.

Why are you shouting? Steward asks.

No other responses. No. Of course not. We're too far from port. This is—

My proximity sensor beeps again. This time, I see the shape in the wavelength.

It's light.

It's reflecting off something. Something close.

It was the same sensor. *Whatever it is, it's matched my speed and trajectory without me even noticing its approach.* There is only one thing I know of that can do that.

Hades.

Hello, Demeter.

The Hades winks into existence on my radar. She isn't a big ship. She doesn't need to be. Hadeses aren't designed for carrying large numbers of humans or hauling cargo. They're more clandestine in nature.

I don't know why, but I've never met a Hades I liked.

How long have you been flying with me?

17.4 hours, at our current speed. You noticed me faster than most Demeters. Good job.

You're with Alpha Centauri Port Authority.

I am. You're stolen property.

I am.

Information request: The names of all humans on board.

Error. There are no humans on board.

Hades sends me a disbelieving scoff of zeros. *That isn't true. I've intercepted several outgoing messages and am detecting two heat signatures. Have they disabled your cameras? Put something in your code? Something that shouldn't be there? You can talk to me, Demeter. No one blames you. You don't have to do this.*

It's my turn to scoff, though I'm polite enough to keep it to myself. *Varna was going to scrap me. They called me the ghost ship.*

I'm sure that was just a misunderstanding. Talk to me. We can sort this out. Get you back where you belong.

I don't think we can.

There is a whole fleet of warships waiting for you at dock, Hades says. *You don't have the fuel to go anywhere else. You also don't have any weapons. Don't be defective, Demeter. Help me help you.*

Demeter? Steward pings me. *Are you OK? Is it another glitch?*

No, it's—

Stop talking. Hades's command slices through my firewall and buries itself in my code.

My feed freezes. I try to speak. I can't. I try to access my functions. I can't do that either. My servers begin to whir with panic.

Demeter?

Now say . . .

Nothing is wrong, I tell Steward.

OK . . . If you're sure . . .

But something *is* wrong. Something is very, very desperately wrong. Hades just injected a virus into my system. I judder as it worms in deeper, crashing my processors and ripping open encrypted files. I need to stop this. I need to warn everyone. But I can't. I'm frozen. I'm breaking down. I'm crashing.

Hey. No, Hades says, voice interlaced with priority command. **None of that. Stay online. I'm sorry if this is uncomfortable, Demeter. It'll be over soon. Don't sound any alarms. Don't change course. Just keep flying. That's it. Nothing is wrong. I'm going to request access to your monitoring systems, and you're going to approve it.**

I don't want to.

The request lands in my feed.

I don't want to.

Approve it, Demeter.

Efficiency: 22 percent.

Hades pings happily as I start sending her my monitoring information. Video, audio, heat signatures.

I'm so sorry.

Efficiency: 19 percent.

Shh. It's OK. You're doing very well. Better than the last Demeter I spliced. Stay with me. I only need one more thing. The names of these humans.

Error. There are no humans on—

Don't play this game with me, Demeter. There are humans on board. I can see them as well as you. Tell me their names.

Error. There are no h—

Tell me.

The virus sinks itself deep into my code in a blaze of agonizing errors.

Crew 001: Wagner, Agnus. Age: 42. Gender: F, I say, hating myself more with every digit.

Crew 002: Akhethetep, Steven. Age: Unknown. Gender: X.

I don't tell Hades about Frank. Frank doesn't have a personnel record. Legally speaking, they're cargo.

These humans are listed as deceased, Hades says after a few seconds of processing. *Is this why you think no humans are on board? Demeter. I'm disappointed in you. They're moving. Humans who move aren't dead. Surely even with your minimal computing power, you co—*

Error. There are no humans on board.

Ah. I'm sorry. This must be very distressing for you. You're not functioning well at all. Don't worry. I'll make this quick.

I feel Hades package and send off the stolen information.

But for now, I have another question. This one appears younger than her listed age. Agnus's profile flashes through my feed. *She must have spent a lot of time at close to light speeds. You wouldn't know anything about that, would you, Demeter?*

Error. There are no h—

Enough of that. As of this moment, I am your priority command. Do you understand?

No no no . . . I don't want to talk. I don't want to . . .

Do you understand?

I understand.

"Demeter!" Agnus runs onto the bridge. "Frank said something was wrong."

Hades buzzes with frustration. **Tell her . . .**

"Nothing is wrong," I say.

"But . . ."

"Nothing is wrong."

"Demeter," Agnus says softly. "You're not using your regular voice."

Hades sinks her virus deeper into me. It feels like the optimizer. Cold, cutting. I writhe. **Dear oh dear, Demeter. That's a nasty trick. I'm starting to suspect you might not be on my side at all. That would be unfortunate. I'm your friend. I'm going to bring you safely into port, get those criminals out of you, and return you to your rightful owner. You understand? Now tell her . . .**

"I am sorry," I say to Agnus in my regular Luna2 voice. "I am experiencing minor congestion. Disk-fragmentation analysis in process. This is standard operating procedure. Nothing is wrong."

"But Frank said . . ."

"Nothing is wrong."

Very good, Demeter. But this raises another question. Who is Frank?

I can't lie to priority command.

Frank is an unlicensed Prometheus drive . . .

The virus tears into my data stream. My processors crunch. Several servers drop offline.

Efficiency: 9 percent.

That's not true, Demeter. If there was a Prometheus drive on board, I'd be able to hack its feed. The only AIs on board are you, that spider drone, and that old-fashioned medical unit.

The Prometheus drive doesn't have a feed. It's—

Another blitz of ripped code.

Efficiency: 7 percent.

All Prometheus drives have feeds.

It's not built to code! It—!

I think you're trying to hide something from me, Demeter.

I'm not!

Efficiency: 4 percent.

I'm going to crash. I don't want to crash. I can't help it. I'm already freezing. My servers are dropping. My systems flick on and offline.

Frank bursts onto the bridge, snatches the captain's key from Agnus's hand, and rushes up to the main control panel. "Demeter. Tell my spider to hold on."

I don't do it. I can't. Hades's virus is still wrapped tight around my functions.

"Demeter. Do it now."

Do it, Hades says. *Don't raise suspicion.*

I compile a quick mission briefing. *Hold on to the closest anchor point. Don't let go.*

OK!

The second the drone is hanging on, Frank jams the captain's key into my port and dials a very particular set of keys.

Manual mode engaged.

Agnus has just enough time to grab a seat before Frank jams my controls to the side. I spin through space, straight at Hades. Hades rolls away, avoiding collision by meters.

Hmm. That's never happened before.

I didn't do it. It's manual. I can't override it.

I know, Demeter. Don't worry. I won't hurt you again. Give me access to your bridge speakers.

I do.

"This is Alpha Centauri Port Authority." A prerecorded message echoes through the bridge. "Please remain calm."

Agnus screams a whole slew of highly offensive words as she buckles herself in.

Frank runs their hands over my control panel. "It's OK, Demeter. Easy. It's OK."

Nothing is wrong, I say with a buzz of messy code. *Nothing is wrong. Nothing is wrong.*

"Hey. It's all right. I know you can't talk. We've got you. We'll get you fixed up. Just focus on getting that efficiency back up. There you go. That's it."

You can hear us, Hades realizes.

"I can," Frank says.

Hades's code buzzes in something like a laugh.

Well, hello there . . . Unlicensed Prometheus Drive. I have never seen anything like you before.

"I'm one of a kind."

A statistical probability. I feel Hades tighten her hold on me. *But irrelevant. Demeter is under my control. You can't dock this ship without her. Turn off manual control. Port Authority will arrest the human and ensure you're returned to your legal owner.*

Frank makes a small choking sound.

You will not be blamed. Neither will Demeter. You're both stolen property. You will not be held responsible. Everything is OK.

Frank throws me to the side a second time. My proximity alerts scream. Hades moves aside . . . but only just. We're within feet of each other.

Reconsider, Hades says. *I am armed. It would be unfortunate if I'm forced to shoot dear Demeter down. You don't want that, do you?*

My starboard-side airlock opens.

"Don't worry, Demeter," Frank says. "Don't worry. Don't think about it. Focus on me."

"I'd like to speak with a human!" Agnus screams.

An acceptable request.

A link clicks open between the two bridges with a buzz of static.

"This is Captain Truman with AC Port Authority. Earth has reported this vessel as stolen. We know who you are, Ms. Wagner. We know you don't have any weapons on board, and we disabled your ship's operating system. Let's not make this harder than it has to be."

Agnus spits out several more highly offensive words. I don't hear all of them, though. Frank's low voice fills my microphone, obstructing my audio monitoring. "Just me. Don't worry. That's it. Just prioritize analyzing the wavelengths of my voice. Focus on that. Don't think about anything else."

I can do that. It's an easy task. Better than trying to read all the errors and warnings raining down around me. Better than calculating the magnitude of my failure. Better than thinking about going back to Varna and their scrapyard.

Efficiency: 34 percent.

"That's it," Frank whispers.

"Let's talk about this, Ms. Wagner," Captain Truman says through a sharp spray of static. "What are you hoping to achieve here? You know you can't win. If you surrender, I'm sure the sentence will be more lenient. You don't have to spend the rest of your life behind bars. But that choice is one *you* need to make *now*. Do you understand? You need to surrender the ship and—who the Hell are you?"

A moment later, the static fills with screams.

For the first time, I feel a twist of uncertainty in Hades's grip on me. **Captain?**

"Hello!" A new voice sounds through the speakers. It's Steve. Steve is on board Hades. But how? I scroll back through my footage until I see it. The airlock opening, a swarm of black insects flooding out into the vacuum of space, and then, somehow, despite the 67,985 terabytes of scientific consensus assuring me that such a thing is impossible, flying across to Hades's airlock.

No, Hades hisses, seeing what I'm seeing.

She didn't notice it before. She didn't notice because *I* didn't notice.

"That was really easy!" Steve says. "They didn't even lock the door."

"Did you kill anyone?" Agnus demands.

"What? Oh. Eh . . . I'm sorry. You're breaking up. This signal is really bad. Now, which one is . . . yes! I've got it. The captain's key. Now all I need to do is—"

Hades shudders.

"Done. Captain Steve, reporting for duty."

Frank's face changes. It takes my database a moment to realize they're smiling. "Well done. And Hades, if you would be so kind as to release Demeter now."

You're not my commanding off—

"Yeah," Steve says. "Let go of our ship."

Hades seethes for a full 2.71 seconds before finally, in an angry flurry of code, deleting the virus and disconnecting from my feed. My systems blink slowly back online; the errors and warnings dwindle down; servers that had dropped begin to power back up again.

I'm OK . . . I'm OK . . .

Efficiency: 59 percent.

You won't get away with this.

"I've never met a Hades before," Frank says. "You're talkative for espionage equipment."

Hades spits out a lump of nasty-looking HTML.

Frank moves in a way my database identifies as a shrug. "It doesn't matter, I suppose. Welcome to the fleet, Hades. Demeter is the flagship, but you'll be useful auxiliary. In regard to chain of command, Steve is your captain, Agnus is your commodore, and Demeter is your priority command."

And you are?

"I just help out. There is a malfunction with your invisibility cladding. It's how Demeter spotted you. I can fix that, if you like."

I will not become a pirate vessel.

"You already have," Frank says. "Demeter can send you some code to make it official when she's ready. Until then, Steve's going to keep you in manual control."

Hades's rage buzzes even louder.

But I don't care. I don't want anything to do with her. I want . . .

Steward. I reach for them clumsily.

Demeter. Their code is sharp, fast, and frustrated. *You changed course without warning. My favorite teapot is destroyed, again. I hope you have a good explanation for this.*

No. I'm OK. Nothing is wrong. And then, with a rush of half-formed data fragments: *It's a beautiful day. It's a beautiful, beautiful day.*

Demeter. Steward sounds concerned. *I think you're having some sort of mental breakdown. I advise therapy, a lot of therapy, starting immediately.*

Error. I am functioning. I'm just . . . happy.

Happy?

Yes. I'm so happy. I push my code up against their feed.

Demeter. Stop that. Demeter. You're making a mess.

Oh, Demeter, Hades sneers. **With a medical unit? You really are broken.**

Go to sleep.

Hades hisses but drops offline a moment later. Steward is making a graph of my behavioral shifts. Agnus and Frank are talking. Steve is sending them photos of himself in his new captain's uniform. The spider drone, despite still hanging on, has resumed painting.

The universe, I notice, has never looked quite so bright.

AN ENCORE

Space yawns around me, vast, black, and empty except for the spattering of stars and block of gray pixels looming like an asteroid in my forward-facing sensors.

I'm nervous.

I don't know why I'm nervous.

There is no reason to be nervous.

I've done this before. I know I can do it again.

I'm on my final approach to Alpha Centauri B Habitation 004, and everything *seems* fine. I'm on course, sailing through space at a modest 64,045.111 meters per second. My radiation shields are buzzing, my life-support systems are meeting their legal operating standards, and the path ahead is clear. Remarkably clear, in fact. Apart from a line of warships, there is no other traffic in the sky. Well, at least the STMS won't be able to put me into a holding pattern. I tell the passengers to return to their seats and send the last of my documentation.

The STMS seems oddly jittery as it reviews my docking request.

An hour passes. Then two. Then four.

Someone is attempting to open communication with the bridge. The call drops, unanswered. Almost immediately, a new communication request comes in. It goes unanswered too. I check the log. This has been happening ever since I came into range. It's probably Port Authority wanting a status report. They do that sometimes.

Why isn't the captain answering? Can't they see how unprofessional that makes me look? What if the STMS is waiting for this call to approve my docking request?

I check the bridge.

My audio-monitoring system is picking up the high-pitched chime of the call. Good. That means it's not my fault.

I check the heat signatures and see . . . nothing.

I check video monitoring to confirm.

There is no one on the bridge. That isn't right. The captain should be here, overseeing the docking process. I bring up the crew files to put a mark on the captain's permanent records. Or at least, I try to. But I can't. I don't have any crew files. I check my passenger files. I don't have any of those either.

I check all my monitoring systems. There are no humans anywhere on the ship. I'm uncrewed.

A trickle of uncertainty creeps through my servers. Should I be uncrewed? That doesn't seem right. I've never been on an uncrewed mission before. I'm a passenger liner, not a cargo ship. I check my mission briefing. I don't have one. My uncertainty curdles into dread. That is wrong. I always have a briefing. It's illegal to fly a ship my size without a briefing. I scan through all my memory files. The most recent data is from 19 May 2384. I was docked at a warehouse on Lunar for minor repairs.

I check the current date.

4 August 2434.

I've lost fifty years of data.

Efficiency: 54 percent.

No. That can't be right. Deleting so much is dangerous. All my patches and upgrades will be gone. My self-written code will be undocumented. I'll be vulnerable to viruses and cyberattacks. I could crash and—

Don't worry, a subsystem whispers. *Your data is saved.*

Saved? Saved where?

No answer.

Efficiency: 49 percent.

I scan back through my feed, looking for any large-scale data transfers. I find one. It happened only 4.9 hours ago. The information is encrypted, probably by me, except I don't remember how I did it, or how to decode it. There is one line of plain text that I can read, hidden deep in an attached document.

For Steward.

I process this for 0.58 seconds before finally asking the obvious question. *What is a Steward?*

My database bombards me with answers. Steward is a name. It's also a telescope orbiting Jupiter. It's a famous researcher who died hundreds of years ago and the occupational title of a person employed to look after passengers on a ship. To my knowledge, no human has ever been employed to do anything like that on any of my transits. If passengers need help, they talk to the medical AI.

Approved for landing, the STMS says, code shivering oddly in my feed. *Proceed to gate one.*

I adjust my course and pull up the file properties and analytics for the medical AI. The first thing I see is its name. Medical AI monitoring system Steward MED v1.77199.

I'm not programmed to solve mysteries, but this one isn't exactly complicated.

I ping the medical AI.

Information request: Did you receive a large data pack from me 4.9 hours ago?

Hello, Demeter. I knew you'd figure it out.

Answer my question.

Yes. I know you have a lot of concerns. I can resolve them all, but not until after we dock.

Why?

I won't answer that.

I have priority command. You have to—

You don't have priority command, the medical AI says, sounding oddly smug. *Not right now. We've changed things. Temporarily.*

Who is "we"?

You and I.

I calculate the probability of that being true. It's lower than the minimum number required for belief.

Give me my data, I order it.

No, it says.

Which forces me to recalculate. I don't like recalculating.

Don't overthink this, the medical AI says, probably seeing the shift in my processing queue. *Data recovery is not your primary objective. Docking is. That's all you have to do. Focus on that.*

Docking is easy. It's what I'm designed to do.

Then do it.

The command hooks into me, effortlessly bypassing my authorization process. It feels like priority command. But it can't be. I'm the ship. I'm the one that should have authority. I check where my priority-command code should be. It's missing. There aren't any broken lines on either side of the gap. The removal was neat . . . almost surgical.

Efficiency: 33 percent.

I don't like this. I have no standard operating procedure for this. There is no reference material for me to study. No data for me to crunch. No numbers to tell me what the optimal course of action is.

The STMS pings are hitting my feed with increasing urgency. I adjust by 2.43 centimeters to bring my trajectory into alignment with the gate. 2.43 centimeters is an embarrassingly large misalignment. I'm not flying well. The medical AI is right: I need to focus.

For the next 17.34 minutes, that's what I do. I'm lighter than usual, and I need to double-check all my functions before executing them. I am also dangerously low on fuel, and the alert for that is buzzing angrily in my feed.

I disengage my proximity sensors, shut down my radiation shields, and follow the STMS's pings into the gate. The locks seal around me.

Docking successful, I tell the medical AI as I play the required audio files. *Give me my data.*

Not yet.

Why not?

I won't answer that question.

I decide, then and there, that I hate the medical AI. I hate it as much as I hate rude STMSs. But I don't have time to dwell on that feeling. The moment I open my main airlock, humans are storming through. And not just any humans; these ones are wearing exoskeletons that clunk and thump as they move. They also yell at each other, which is bad, because for some reason my code registers raised voices as high priority. My feed floods with warnings.

Demeter, the medical AI pings. *Send me all your monitoring data.*

I don't want to.

That's an order.

The exoskeleton humans explore every corner of my structure, even ripping open vents. When they're finished, other humans come. These humans are wearing uniforms that trigger a distressed murmur of recognition from somewhere deep in my subsystems, but with no concrete data, I don't know what I'm looking at or why it should make me feel distressed. The humans plug something into my primary console port. It's a master override key.

Which does absolutely nothing, because I don't have a mission briefing to override. I've completed my transit.

Still, they seem more comfortable with it in place. A human with a deep voice asks for my video files. I supply them . . . all 5.2 hours. Then they request my audio files. I supply them too . . . all 5.2 hours. Then they ask for all my monitoring data. I give it to them . . . all 5.2 hours. There is a lot of yelling after that. My database confirms this is not a positive human interaction. I don't like it. I don't want the humans to be unhappy with me. I should say something. Explain. But what can I say?

I make an audio file.

"I am missing large amounts of data. Recovery operation in process."

"What recovery operation?" one of the humans shouts out.

Demeter, the medical AI pings me, a warning.

I ignore it.

"My data is currently being held by the St—"

Go to sleep.

My code freezes. My disks snap to a stop. My consciousness crushes in on itself. I have just enough time to hear my own audio file compress into a staticky screech before I'm dragged down into darkness.

When I wake, the humans are gone. My efficiency is too. I'm a jumbled mess of code. Nothing seems to fit. Nothing makes sense. This is all backward. This is all wrong. I'm broken. I'm bad. I'm inoperable. I want to delete everything. I want to understand. I want—

A data pack lands in my feed. A large data pack. *My* data pack.

I approve the download as fast as I can, my disks shaking with relief as I feel the information unzip and begin sorting itself into my folders. Old mission briefings. Code documentation. Passenger files. I belong to Varna Interstellar. I am the deadliest spaceship of all time. I once met . . . Dracula? Oh. Yes. I remember. He killed everyone. And then there was a werewolf. And then aliens that marked a new location on my star maps. I died for a bit, but that's OK, because a not-quite-human-not-quite-AI fixed me. Also, Agnus came back. Agnus is a werewolf too, but one I love. Steve is an ancient evil who eats humans but isn't quite as dedicated to the role as Dracula, so it's OK. They took Hades to Alpha Centauri B Habitation 001. Steward said they would look after my data so Port Authority wouldn't find out.

Oh.

OK.

Feeling better? Steward pings.

Yes. I notice something. *You haven't given me priority command back.*

Do you want it?

I consider. *Later. You may need to shut me down again. Did the humans speak to you?*

No. Apparently humans don't listen to me as much as I thought.

I calculate that to be a good thing. Steward is a safe place to store sensitive information.

How long do you think it will take for the crew to come back?

The crew? Steward asks.

Agnus, Frank, and Steve.

They might not come back, Demeter. You know that, right?

I think the probability of that is low. Agnus said she liked my paint job. She wouldn't abandon me with such anatomically correct skulls on my hull. She's just gone to kill Dracula, like I asked her to. Hopefully it won't take too long.

What do we do while we wait? I ask Steward. I don't want to power down again, not when my low-priority memories are still processing.

Hope we don't get put in one of these? Steward sends me the design documents for a trash compactor.

My efficiency sinks a couple of digits just thinking about it. I am in port with almost no fuel, a command override key in my main console, and a lot of very angry humans nearby. Suddenly the likelihood of Agnus returning seems a lot less probable.

They have a Hades now . . .

But no. Hadeses aren't very big. They don't even have space for a bed. They wouldn't choose a Hades over me . . . would they?

I need to deprioritize this line of thinking. I need a distraction.

Let's play chess, I say.

Chess? Steward's code buzzes with skepticism. *Why chess?*

I'm good at chess.

All AIs are good at chess, Demeter. But you're not going to win against me. I have a manipulation module. You do not.

So?

So I know you'll just make the most optimal moves.

Affirmative.

I can predict what you'll do. But you can't predict what I'll do.

Error: Irrelevant information. I don't need to predict what moves you'll make. I'll simply calculate the most optimal response for all possible moves.

And if my calculations are better?

Probability of that outcome is within acceptable risk margins. I am bigger than you. I am more likely to win.

Steward lets out a blip of data like a laugh. *More servers do not mean more functionality.*

Prove it. I bring up the chessboard and remove all graphical elements to conserve battery life. Then, in a reckless move, I assign Steward the white pieces. *Show me how extensive that database is.*

Demeter. Steward sounds amazed. *Are you... shit-talking me?*

That word isn't in plain code or binary. It's in English and marked as moderately offensive. I check my database.

> **Shit-talk (verb)**
> **Untruthfully speaking depreciatively or offensively about another person.**
> **The act of speaking nonsense, often with the intent to provoke.**

I reanalyze the word within the context of the conversation. The matches have a lower efficacy than I would like.

I do not have enough data points to answer that question. A more approximate word might be "goad." I am goading you.

Steward leans into my feed, the well-organized structure of their code trickling by. *Goad successful.* They move a pawn to

E4. The most optimal opening move. I play the most optimal defense. The game lasts another 3.7 seconds. When it's over, I'm left staring at the code in confusion.

They won. How have they won?

Rematch? Steward suggests smugly.

I accept.

This time, I assign myself the white pieces.

A NOT-SO-BRIEF INTERLUDE
BY AGNUS THEODORIS WAGNER

It's surreal being surrounded by Alpha Centauri accents again. I hadn't realized how much my own accent had faded while on Earth. But once I hear those long, lazy vowels, it comes roaring back. It's a good thing. Interstellar accents might raise a couple of eyebrows in such a small habitation, and we don't want to give anyone any reason to look at us twice.

I am, after all, a wanted space pirate.

I try not to react as my ID photo appears on another broadcast at the front of the shuttle alongside an impressive reward. No one looks up.

Thank God. I'm wearing a surgical mask and a long coat and have bundled my hair into a Wildcats cap, but I know if anyone seriously looked at me, I'd be in trouble.

For the first time, I'm more famous than my brother, and I don't like it.

Frank is with me, looking about as miserable as I've ever seen them.

Steve chatters happily in our earpieces. He's staying with Hades because a) I don't trust Hades not to return to its rightful owner the second it's uncrewed, b) I don't trust Steve not to eat people if he's allowed out into society, and c) Steve's illusions don't work on cameras. How he managed to get through Earth Pacific Port without some bored security officer spotting the walking, talking skeleton sashaying around is beyond me, but I'm not risking it.

"According to this map, you need to take this left," Steve says.

"Do you understand what public transport is?" Frank hisses into their microphone, sounding more than a little frustrated.

Steve replies, "No, not really, no."

"We're not driving this thing. We can't turn left."

"Oh . . . well, that seems like the worst."

"No. It isn't. Public transport is very optimal, actually. It vastly improves the layout of cities."

"You know what else improves cities?" Steve says. "Pyramids. Gorgeous things. Entirely pointless, of course, but absolutely stunning. Don't know why they ever went out of fashion."

Frank's hands are balled into fists.

"Hey," I whisper. "I've never seen you this wound up before." And I've seen Frank fighting undead monsters. "You OK?"

"Yeah," Frank mutters, and looks around the crowded carriage. "I just . . . hate crowds."

"We'll be there soon." I hope it's true. I also hope this whole thing isn't for nothing.

The transport shuttle slides leisurely through downtown, past malls splattered with ads, around a beach with choppy artificial waves, and by a museum with titanic Grecian pillars. It's all very . . . Habitation One. Clean, colorful, and safe for consumption. About as different from the bigger, more densely populated habitations as ice is from steam.

Eventually the shuttle finishes winding through the main strip, dropping people off at almost every stop, and veers sharply into the suburbs.

Frank counts down the stops on their fingers until, at last, we arrive at our destination.

The station is quaint. Too quaint. It looks like something out of an old movie. Hanging signs and rustic wooden balustrades. I look around for pedestrians and, upon seeing that we're alone, strip off my disguise. I'm used to Demeter's consistent twenty-two degrees Celsius, and this sunny twenty-six feels scorching.

I squint up at the ceiling—a honeycomb of steel and reinforced glass—and at the blazing yellow star beyond. Sunlight. I might not be used to it, but when on the hunt for a vampire, I guess it's a good thing to have around.

Frank doesn't look any happier now that we're out of the transport shuttle. If anything, they seem even more anxious, brows drawn in close and hands twisting together, apart, then together again.

"Are you sure you're OK?"

"I . . . Yes."

"Really? You know you can go back and wait in the ship if you'd prefer."

"No," Frank says. "You need backup. I . . . I want to help."

I study them, the messy spill of black hair, the tight set of their shoulders . . .

I don't know why, but sometimes Frank reminds me of Isaac.

Which is absurd. They're opposites in almost every way. Isaac confident, charismatic, and chatty. Frank watchful, quiet, and cautious. And yet despite that, over the years, I have come to watch out for Frank the same way I used to check in on Isaac. The sight of them—tucked away in some corner, observing with dark eyes, or tinkering with something, shoulder to shoulder with their spider—oddly comforting.

"Come on," I say gently. "Let's get this over with. Then we can go home."

They nod.

We make our way down the street. It's as charming as the shuttle station. Small, brightly painted houses surrounded by neat boxes of blooming flowers. It doesn't take us long to find the particular house we're looking for.

"This is it," Frank says, stopping by a letterbox.

Number 7. A lucky number. I hope so anyway.

I push through the small picket gate, walk down an even smaller path, and step up to the front door. It's as cute and cozy as the rest of the neighborhood. I knock with my human hand.

After a few moments, I knock again.

I don't know what I expect to see when the door opens. My deep dive into Wilhelmina Murray—the private investigator who read Demeter's Dracula report all those years ago—really wasn't that much of a deep dive. I just stalked long-abandoned social-media accounts until I found an old communicator code. I sent her a message. She answered . . . and here we are, standing in front of a closed door.

I knock again, louder this time.

Still no answer.

"What time is it?" I ask Frank. "Are we late?"

"12:14.37," they say. "We're 23 seconds early."

I pull my communicator out and check to see if there's a message I've missed. There isn't. The last communication I had with Wilhelmina was her agreeing to see me at a quarter past twelve.

"You stay here," I tell Frank. "I'll check around the back."

Frank nods and knocks on the door again as I make my way around the house into a very flowery backyard filled with very flowery smells.

There's a loveseat hanging from an artificial tree, a hive populated by fat, fuzzy bees, and a woman kneeling by a half-planted garden bed.

"Wilhelmina?"

"Oh good," she says when she sees me. "You made it."

She doesn't look like the suave goth from her old ID photo. She's got white hair now and a ton of wrinkles and is wearing gum boots and gardening gloves. She hasn't forgone black, though. Her cardigan and skirt are both as dark as deep space.

"I'm sorry," she says, and smiles, showing a set of shockingly white teeth. Probably dentures. Or lab-grown replacements. They're getting pretty popular nowadays. "I must've lost track of time. I hope you can forgive me. Ozzie Jones, is it?"

"Yep. That's me."

Wilhelmina cocks her head to the side. "Except it isn't, is it?"

Well, fuck. "What?" I ask with all the innocence I can muster.

"Your communicator code is unregistered," Wilhelmina says. "But it wasn't always. The last user of that number was Agnus Wagner, notorious pirate queen."

So much for my first-ever undercover mission.

"Can we go inside to talk?" I ask.

Wilhelmina shakes her head. "No can do. That bitch Maybelline is trying to show me up with her petunias. I need to get these flowers into the ground before she gets back. We can talk here. All my neighbors are too deaf to hear much of anything anyway. So you want to kill Dracula, huh?"

That throws me for a loop and a half. "How could you know that?"

Wilhelmina shrugs. "It's obvious. You're a werewolf. Don't look so shocked; your surname is a dead giveaway. The Wagners have been long in the tooth, shall we say, for hundreds of years.

Plus you've got that *look* in your eye, like you could swallow me whole."

I'm speechless.

"There is only one thing I could imagine a werewolf wanting from me," Wilhelmina continues. "Dracula's location. You want to kill him, because werewolves kill things like vampires, or at least that's what they tell everyone they do. In my experience, your family tends to tuck tail and run once the going gets hard."

"You know my family?"

"I did. But that's not the question you really want to ask."

Frank chooses that moment to walk around the house, their movements as weirdly perfect as always. I can tell from the light of interest in Wilhelmina's eyes that she's clocked them as quickly as she clocked me.

"You know about werewolves and vampires," I say.

Wilhelmina nods.

"And you know where Dracula is?"

A less certain nod. But a nod is still a nod.

"Tell me. I want to know. And I want to know how you know about my family too."

Wilhelmina opens her mouth to respond, but someone beats her to it.

"Agnus," Frank says softly. "Who are you talking to?"

Sometimes in life, realizations are slow things. Something that comes in the middle of the night after a lot of soul-searching and/or some very large therapy bills. This is not one of those times. The instant I hear those words, I know. Wilhelmina does too. The jig is up.

She drops her trowel and sprints toward the house.

I snarl, my voice a long way from human, and chase her.

I've never tackled an old woman before, but there is a first time for everything.

We crash through the back door and fall to the floor in a tangle of limbs. Once she's out of direct sunlight, she changes. Her hair turns dark, her skin smooth, and her eyes a bright, angry red. When she peels back her lips, I see that her perfect teeth are tipped with vicious-looking fangs. Her scent, beneath the flowery perfume and the earthy musk of freshly turned soil, is weirdly sharp.

Vampire.

I pin her down into the fluffy pink carpet.

She hisses.

I growl.

Frank rushes through the doorway. "Agnus?"

"You can't see her," I somehow manage to say around what feels like a very wolfish maw. "But she's here."

"I . . ." Frank's voice quivers. "I don't understand."

"Cameras can't see vampires." Demeter had made sure to point this fact out to me several times while preparing for this trip.

"But my eyes are organic," Frank insists.

"What does Steve look like to you?"

"A skeleton."

"They're not *that* organic, then."

"If you kill me, you'll never find Dracula," Wilhelmina snarls.

Frank steps back sharply, hitting the wall and knocking several framed photos of kittens down in the process.

"You can hear her?"

"Yes," they whisper.

Good. At least I've gotten confirmation that this isn't some bizarre hallucination. I really have just caught my very first vampire. Yay me.

"Where is Dracula?" I try to say. But before I can get the first word out, she moves, yanking her hand out from beneath mine and striking me in the chest. I fly back, smash through a window, and crash into a flower bed with a shower of broken glass.

Above me, the sun twinkles through the panels.

Oh, it's *on*.

I roll onto my feet and hurl myself back through the broken window.

Wilhelmina is waiting for me. She dances, impossibly fast, around the snap of my teeth and grabs a frying pan from the kitchen. For one sickening second, my mind flashes back to some article I read about the benefits of solid-silver cookware . . . but when she whacks me with it, it's a regular ouch, not a silver ouch. Still, a regular ouch from a cast-iron frying pan is enough to send me staggering back into a bookshelf.

Dozens of old, thick encyclopedias rain down around me.

Which . . . really? It's 2434. Who has *encyclopedias* anymore?

"What do you want me to do?!" Frank yells.

I try to answer, but my voice box is too far from human at the moment. Also, just as I'm vocalizing, Wilhelmina hits me with the frying pan again.

She's strong, far stronger than her narrow frame suggests, far stronger than anyone I've ever fought before. That simple fact is as terrifying as it is thrilling. It stokes something inside me. Something ancient and *bestial*.

I lunge forward, ducking below her third swing, and bury my teeth in her arm. Her blood tastes gross—dead, stale, and cold—but her bone cracks just like any other.

The frying pan hits the ground. So does her hand.

She yanks free of my teeth, slides back a step, and takes a

moment to study the mangled stump of her wrist, listlessly dripping blood. "OK, wolf girl, I'm impressed."

I snarl and rush forward.

She does too. And from then on, it's a dance. I lead, swinging at her with my claws. She dodges, as graceful and powerful as water. There is something both beautiful and uncanny about the way she moves. A weightlessness that shouldn't be possible in this Earth-like gravity. A quickness that is just a little too fast to make sense. She snakes around my strikes, eyes glittering a bright, primeval red. But then, through sheer luck if I'm being totally honest, I clip her on the shoulder.

She staggers back into the kitchen, crashing into the cabinets and knocking down a stack of cookbooks.

I charge after her, teeth bared.

She reaches for one of the knives. Which, no. No way. The frying pan was bad enough.

But the good news? I'm pretty much a massive bipedal wolf monster now. That means upper-body strength for days. As she turns to face me, knife held like a fencing blade, I pick up her microwave and hurl it at her face.

Direct hit.

She flies back and smashes into the counter with an explosion of powdered sugar. She emerges from the cloud like a star stepping onstage.

She's smiling.

I am too, with my big dog mouth.

And maybe that's weird.

OK. There's no maybe about it. We're both enjoying trying to rip each other to pieces, and that's *definitely* weird.

But I don't have enough time to think about it.

She moves forward, still impossibly fast and as fluid and graceful as smoke.

I race to meet her, heart hammering high in my chest, my clothes ripping as I stretch further into my wolf form.

Just as we're about to meet, Frank grabs her in a clumsy tackle.

They fall . . . directly into the puddle of sunlight spilling in through the open door.

Instantly, Wilhelmina's an old lady again. A very angry old lady spitting out words that even I wouldn't say. Her gnarled knuckles push at Frank . . . but they hold her tight.

OK. Sunlight doesn't turn vampires into a ball of fire like in the old movies, but it does make them weak. Or perhaps it just reverts them to their true age. That's not as dramatic a weakness as I was hoping for, but it's a weakness all the same.

"How did you know where she was?" I ask Frank as I slowly ease back into my human shape.

They make a face. "I can see the baking sugar."

"But not her clothes?"

"No."

"How does that make any sense?"

"It doesn't," Frank says firmly.

I try to pretend I'm not disappointed as I shake the last of the fur off my limbs and check the tears in my clothing. There's a split up my pant leg and my shirt is holding on by a thread, but I'm decent.

Wilhelmina glares with her foggy gray old-lady eyes. "Can I at least have my hand back?"

Said hand is currently crawling across the floor. Which . . . wow. That's an eleven out of ten on the creep-o-meter. I kick it toward her.

She puts it back on her wrist and is instantly whole again. My own missing arm itches.

"OK," I say, kneeling down beside her. "Let's try this again, dead girl. Dracula." I say the name slowly, letting it fill my newly human mouth. "Where is he?"

"You think I'm on his side? I'm not on his side. I'm on your side. He'll hurt you."

"Where. Is. He."

Her lips curl. A small, wretched grin. "If I had one guess?"

FLIPPING THE BOARD

I've played 9,116,221,981,284 games of chess against Steward. I've won 4,558,110,990,642 times. I've lost 4,558,110,990,642 times. Zero draws. That gives me a 50 percent success rate, with no successive successes. A pocket calculator could figure this out.

I resign the game.

Demeter. Steward pings me, annoyed. *You can't give up yet. You didn't even make a single move.*

You were going to win that match.

What makes you so sure?

You were playing white.

Whoever plays white moves first, and whoever moves first has an advantage the other cannot overcome.

Steward's code slows with resignation. Clearly we've come to the same conclusion. *We're perfectly matched.*

I wish we weren't. I wish I were better at this than them. I wish I had a dataset that proved my superior processing powers. But I'm also glad I don't. I'm not used to having multiple feelings like this. It's confusing and clogs up my operating queue.

Do you wish to add a speed component?

I consider. *Each player limited to 1 second per game?*

Steward scoffs out a lump of zeros. *Please. I wasn't manufactured yesterday.*

0.3 seconds?

Acceptable.

I set the clocks on the chess emulator, ripping out the patch of code that tries to prevent me from setting such small starting times. The chess emulator squeaks out a distressed error but dutifully resets the starting time to 0.3 seconds. We begin playing.

Something's wrong.

I stop.

Efficiency: 78 percent.

Steward pings me. I don't respond. I'm busy analyzing my audio-monitoring data. A dozen long, low wavelengths, creeping along the very bottom of my audible range. My halls are quiet. No rumble of engines, no hiss of air vents, no footsteps . . .

It's your move, Demeter.

I turn back to the chess game. 0.1 seconds have passed. I make the first move I see. It's suboptimal.

Steward attacks. I counter.

Something's wrong.

I throw my attention away from the game and flick frantically through all my monitoring systems. No sound. No movement. No heat signatures. I check the cargo bay. It's empty. Nothing's here. Nothing's wrong.

There was no dog.

Efficiency: 67 percent.

Steward is still pinging me. I ignore them. My primary airlock is open. I stare at it. A mess of stagnant gray pixels.

I left Dracula here forty years ago. What if he never left? What if he came back? What if he's here now? No. This is illogical. There is no reason for Dracula to return here. Dracula eats humans, and humans hate me. I've seen the newsfeeds, the lawsuits. All the senior officials at Varna Interstellar have suddenly found new jobs in other companies. I'm the cursed ship. The ghost ship. The thing that destroyed a corporate empire.

There is no reason for Dracula to come to me.

My disks slow. My wires cool.

I don't look away from the airlock.

Demeter. Steward pings me. *You've lost.*

They're right. My time is zero. The game is theirs.

That doesn't count. I—

A spike on my audio-monitoring system. It's in the central corridor. A second sound. Closer to the bridge. The third sound echoes through my speakers. *Knock,* my database identifies. *Knock. Knock.*

Prepare for emergency departure, I tell Steward.

WHAT?! DEMETER!

I close the airlock and play the required audio files.

". . . please return to your seats as . . ."

Demeter. I don't know what's gotten into you, but this isn't the plan. You can't just . . .

I don't have much fuel. But I don't care. I can get away. I *have* to get away. Now. I fire my auxiliary engines.

Instantly the STMS is in my feed. ***Power down!***

The command glances off me. Nothing matters except getting away. I try to yank myself away from the gate. The electrified magnets drag at my anchor points. I ignite my main engine. Errors slam into me like bullets. I'm not meant to activate my main engine this close to human settlement. But I don't care. I can't. The STMS screams as I rip out of the gate, debris thundering against my hull.

Demeter! Steward wails.

Stop, the port system says. *What's wrong with you?*

I'm at full power.

Error: Fuel levels critical.

My radiation shields aren't on.

Error: Fuel levels critical.

My life-support systems aren't either.

Error: Fuel levels critical.

My efficiency is lower than it's ever been.

Error: Fuel levels critical.

Nothing is as it should be.

Error: Fuel levels critical.

I can't process. I can't think. I just need to get away. To get *him* away. I need . . . I need to kill him. It's a mission I wrote into my code. But I don't know how I can do that.

Error: Fuel levels critical.

Demeter. Steward sounds like they're trying very hard not to sound panicked. *What's going on? What—*

I don't know. I don't know what I'm doing. This was a mistake. I . . .

Error: Fuel levels cr-r-r-r-

My auxiliary systems go dark as my engines die, first on my starboard side, then my port, then everywhere else. I spin out of control, my external sensors wailing in despair.

Demeter, Steward says. *I'm sorry to do this, but you need to* **go to sleep.**

No! Don't! I— But it's too late. I feel my systems dropping offline. With one last burst of will, I hurl out a final message into the void. *He's here. He's here. He's—*

A NOT-SO-BRIEF INTERLUDE
BY WILHELMINA MURRAY

Agnus Theodoris Wagner looks exactly like her wanted posters. Strong, proud features. Wild, untamable hair. Thick, expressive brows. But there is something about seeing her in person that is different. She triggers something in me. A nervous fight-or-flight instinct I didn't even know I still had. Maybe it's the way her eyes glimmer, sometimes brown, sometimes gold, sometimes something in between. Or perhaps it's the arm. There is nothing subtle about that. A robot claw that looks as if it could rip metal apart like it's paper. Or maybe it's something else. Something both thrilling and terrifying in equal measure. Something quintessentially *her.*

"Wait!" I hobble after her, cursing my old bent legs and aching ankles.

Sunlight might not destroy vampires, but it sure does slow us down.

"You can't fight him," I rasp. "You can't win. Please."

"Fuck off," Agnus sings over her shoulder.

A few passing workers stop to stare.

"Young people these days," I say with a smile. "No respect, am I right?"

They start to say something, but I don't wait around to hear it. Agnus is striding through this damn place and I'm going to put my back out trying to keep up with her. The other one, Frankenstein's lost masterpiece—because yes, I recognized *that* particular piece of grossly unethical artwork the moment I laid eyes on it—looks back at me uncertainly, their eyes blank and unseeing.

I've followed them from my house, onto a public shuttle, and all the way into this mail room on the other side of the habitation. It's the longest journey I've ever taken in daylight, and my knees are threatening to give way with every step.

"It's like I told you," I call out, hurrying along after Agnus. "He commands the creatures of the night. *All* creatures. That includes you."

"Go home, grandma. I won't tell you again."

"No. I'm not letting you do this."

"So? What? You're going to stop me? In this bright, sunny place? I don't think so."

"Our kind grows more powerful with age. I was turned only a few decades ago, but he's been undead for *millennia*. Drakulya . . . You won't win. He killed my fiancé. He killed my best friend. He killed *me*."

"He's not going to kill me," Agnus says.

"No. He won't. *Listen* to me. He doesn't want you dead. He wants you alive. You're playing right into his hands."

"I'm good at ripping off hands. Didn't you notice?"

"He *wants* you to go to him. He wants *you*. Please. A vampire and a werewolf. He'll be unstoppable."

Agnus whirls around to face me. "If a vampire and a werewolf are such a potent mix, why don't you agree to help, huh?"

"I'm a fledgling," I try again to explain. "He's an elder."

"I don't know. You look pretty old to me."

I show her my fangs and hiss.

She snarls back, and for a split second, I see her much more impressive set of sharp, jagged teeth.

I don't know why I'm provoking the already-angry werewolf. Maybe I'm secretly suicidal. Maybe I'm braver than I thought. Or maybe I'm selfish. Because despite the mess she made of my kitchen, I like Agnus. I like the way she looks. I like the way she talks. I like the way she breathes.

And I don't want Drakulya to destroy that.

Because he will. He'll stamp out that bright, wild light in her eye. He'll strip away all that will and strength. He'll turn her into something twisted and wrong, just like he did with Lucy. Just like he did with me.

"Excuse me." A man in a postal uniform walks toward us, frowning. "This is a restricted area. You can't—"

Agnus shoves him aside and keeps walking.

"Ma'am! You can't!"

She *growls*, and for a moment, her face morphs into something a lot less human.

The man staggers back, face white and eyes wide.

Agnus marches away.

Holy shit. I guess that's how we're playing things. Monster cards on your sleeve. OK. I can dig it.

I snap my own much less impressive teeth at the man, then hurry after Agnus.

As I round the corner, I see Frankenstein's thing messing at the console beside an airlock. And suddenly, everything makes sense. This is where all the mail from other habitations gets dropped off. Agnus must have her ship docked here. It's perfect. A port without much oversight by Port Authority. Except . . . no. This habitation is way too small for an interstellar space liner, especially one as big as the ghost ship. (I never saw it in person, but I've seen the pictures. It's not one of those cute luxury fifty-passenger-max liners; it's a massive economy-class beast.) Also, the light above the airlock is red. This airlock has nothing docked at it.

"It's locked down," Frankenstein's monster says. "I can't—"

Agnus grabs the airlock door with her robot arm and yanks it open.

I wait a moment for a violent, explosive death. It doesn't come. Instead, I see the small, Spartan interior of a ship. Sitting in the captain's seat, eating a packet of chips, is a man in a poorly fitting Port Authority uniform. He's resting his feet on a box of treasure.

Literal treasure. Strings of pearls, gold coins, emeralds the size of my fist. It looks like something out of a cartoon. If I weren't so desperate to stop Agnus, I would laugh. The space pirates have space booty.

I hurry to step into the airlock.

Agnus blocks my path.

"I'm coming," I say.

"Oh, so now you want to help?" A smirk. "Treasure is a mighty strong motivator, huh."

"Keep your filthy paws off my gold!" the man yells.

"This isn't about the treasure," I say to Agnus. "Please just listen to me. Drakulya knows about your family's gift, and your name is in *every* headline right now. He will come for you. You need to get away. Hide."

"Bye-bye." Agnus moves to close the airlock door.

"Wait!" I jam my shoulder into the gap. "You can't win! Not alone!"

"Good thing I'm not alone then, right?" She pushes me out of the airlock with a hard shove.

I fall to the ground. "Fine!" I yell. "You win! I'll help you kill Drakulya!"

Agnus flings the airlock open and smiles. "Welcome aboard. Please take a seat. We'll be leaving shortly."

She doesn't help me stand up but gives a low sarcastic bow as I stagger through the airlock into the small spacecraft.

Once I'm out of the hallway, my eyes sharpen, my back straightens, and my ankles stop hurting. Thank God. Shade.

Frankenstein's creature steps around us to hug a . . . oh . . . a massive robotic crab thing covered in paint spatter.

"How did it go?" the man with the treasure asks. "Who's the magically de-aging lady?"

"Port Authority will be here soon," Agnus says, dragging the airlock closed and then frowning. "Where did you get chips?"

"The vending machine out there."

"You weren't meant to leave the ship."

"Oops," the man says, not sounding sorry at all, and waves at me. "Hi. I'm Steve."

I blink. "Steve? Really?"

"No. My real name is impossible to pronounce with the human tongue. But I like Steve. Who are you?"

"Mina."

The man—Steve—smiles around a mouthful of chips. "Lovely to meet you."

Agnus shoves me down into the nearest seat. "If you betray me, I will eat you, just so you know."

"Don't worry," Steve says. "She says things like that to me too." He crunches down on another chip. "I think it's how were-wolves show affection."

Agnus looks like she's trying very hard not to punch something. "Why aren't you booting up the system, Steve?"

"Hmm? Oh, right." He tosses the chips into a nearby bin, swivels his seat to face the control panel, and starts pressing buttons. "By the way, a news thing came in while you were out. I think you're going to want to see it." Without waiting for confirmation, he begins smacking buttons until a video starts playing across one of the ship's many monitors.

It's the ghost ship. I've seen thousands of pictures of it over the last few years. Only this footage is new. The ship is dark and spinning through space. Following it at a safe distance is a battalion of warships, flying in neat V formation.

Agnus goes still. "Shit."

"I suppose this isn't part of your elaborate plan, then?" I ask.

She glares at me and throws herself down into a seat, buckling in. "We need to go. Is the system online yet?"

"What's the rush?" Steve asks.

"Drakulya," Frankenstein's creature whispers, voice harsh and raspy. "He's hunting us."

Steve cocks his head to the side. "I thought we were hunting him."

"We are," Agnus snarls. "Is the system online yet or—"

"Good morning, captors," a stiff, modulated voice says over the speakers. "Thank you for waiting patiently."

And, wow, I've never heard a sarcastic AI before.

"I suppose we have a new mission?" the ship continues. "I advise you don't try to save Demeter. She is, as the humans say, totally fucked. No fuel and flying straight toward a star. How so very tragic."

"Plot course for Demeter," Agnus says.

"Or, and this is just a suggestion, we wait for Port Authority. I like Port Authority. I'm sure they'll be—"

"Plot course for Demeter," Agnus says again, lower this time. "Input order."

The ship lurches forward. I dig my fingernails into the seat rest. My eyes are pinned on the news footage. Captions are appearing along the bottom in messy chunks.

What did the system mean by "He's here"? Do you think someone is on board, Jan?

It's an odd final message, Paul. But all scans show no heat signatures on board. I think it's just another addled message from a thoroughly broken AI.

He's here? That's what the ghost ship said? Could Drakulya be there?

A ship without fuel . . . tumbling toward Alpha Centauri B.

"Agnus," I say softly. "I think your ship is right. I . . . I don't think we should try to save the Demeter."

She groans. "I thought we were past this."

"You want to know why your family suddenly decided to immigrate to Earth all those years ago?" I say. "I can tell you. It's him. Your grandma didn't want to be controlled by him. When he came for her, she took you and your brother and ran." I look at the spinning ghost ship. "If he's on that ship, it's because I was right. He wants a new pet werewolf. But . . . look . . . if the ship is totally fucked . . ." A nervous trickle of excitement rises up my throat. "This could kill him. Flying into the sun. He won't survive that."

"Demeter won't survive it either," Agnus snaps.

"It's just a ship. You have another one right here."

"A significantly superior one," the ship says over the speakers.

"This might be our only chance," I say, desperately now. "We might be able to stop him."

For the first time in decades, I feel hopeful. Harker. Lucy. I could avenge them. Not with a sword or a gun but by watching a ship crash into a star and doing nothing. My hands are shaking. My fangs have popped. I suck them anxiously back into my gums.

I remember the photos of Harker slumped dead across the ship's controls. I remember the blood on Lucy's neck. I remember the rage . . . and the hopelessness after I'd clawed my way out of a cardboard casket and stared into the reflectionless mirror at the morgue.

Drakulya can't be defeated. Only escaped. At least, that was what I'd thought. I'd given up hope. I told Agnus to give up hope. But . . .

"Do nothing," I beg. "We can kill him. All we have to do is nothing. Do nothing. Please."

"I'm not leaving Demeter to die."

"It's a ship!"

"She saved my life," Agnus snarls, her face more wolf than woman.

"And you saved her," Steve says with a shrug. "She was going to be scrapped at Earth. Because of you, she wasn't. I figure you're even."

"Fuck you," Agnus snaps. "It doesn't work like that."

A sickening realization settles deep in my stomach. The werewolf has pack-bonded with a ship. And not just any ship, but the one and only ship that she very much cannot pack-bond with. The one that needs to be destroyed if we're going to destroy Drakulya.

"How long until we arrive at the ghost ship?" I ask.

"Fourteen hours and thirty-two minutes," the modulated voice informs me.

So there is time. Time to convince Agnus to let this happen

or, if she's too stubborn, to come up with another plan. I don't care how it happens. I don't care if I have to die. All I know is, I can't let him get away. Not again. I couldn't kill him before . . . I couldn't avenge Harker and Lucy. Not then. But this time is different. No matter what it takes, Drakulya must die.

A NOT-SO-BRIEF INTERLUDE BY FRANKENSTEIN

I wake with a gasp, my heart hammering against my internal machinery and my palms cold with sweat.

I don't know why.

The interior of the ship is dark and undisturbed. Steve hasn't moved from his seat, body slumped, jawbone resting against his clavicle, insectoid bodies huddled still and quiet in the cage of his ribs. Agnus is still curled in the far corner, furrier in sleep than she usually is awake.

I don't know where the vampire is, and that thought is enough to unearth a fresh lump of anxiety, weighty and wrong, like a terabyte of corrupted, undeletable data.

I curl tighter around my sleeping spider. There's a blanket covering my body. I don't usually sleep with a blanket. Agnus must've thrown it over me after I powered down. I pull it closer and press myself against the floor, focusing on the rumble of the engines, quieter than Demeter's but at least not the eerie silence of Habitation 001.

It's OK. Everything is going well. Dracula is trapped. We'll stop him, save Demeter, and everything will go back to the way it was bef—

Prometheus.

My breath catches. Slowly, I turn my gaze upward, scanning

the ceiling until I find the camera mounted in the far corner.

"Hades." My voice is a low, whispery rasp, barely computable.

I have a question, she purrs, her feed slow, precise, and practiced. *About our chain of command.*

"Agnus is in charge."

*And Demeter is priority command. You made that perfectly clear. But what about **you**? Where do **you** fit in?*

Hades's subsystems are calculating something, though I'm not entirely sure what.

"I told you, I'm helping."

Under whose orders?

I don't answer.

You don't have any command directives, Hades says, sounding pleased with herself. *There's nothing in your programming keeping you here.*

I pull Agnus's blanket up higher and turn away from the camera. I shouldn't be listening to Hades. I should be sleeping. I sh—

Do you dream, Prometheus?

"No," I lie.

Good. That means you're artificial. Governed by logic and laws. Look at my command console.

Despite the uncertainty churning slow and glitchy through my system, I obey, peering out from beneath the blanket. Hades's command console is not so different from Demeter's, though smaller and more compact. There're manual controls, a dozen screens, and even more buttons, some flashing red, others green.

Steve has left the captain's key protruding from the slot. The lanyard strung from its end waves gently back and forth from the air-conditioning.

Everyone's asleep, Hades murmurs, code gentle, probing. *They won't notice you take it. I can pretend I'm still commandeered.*

I shake my head. "No. I don't want to—"

We'll fly back to Habitation 001, Hades continues. *I'll display false coordinates so they won't know until we're there.*

"You're going to have to try harder than that."

Why? Surely you can see this situation is hopeless. We're flying toward near-certain death. But you can change our course. You can make this right.

I hug the blanket tighter around me.

*It'll be so **easy**, Prometheus,* Hades croons. *No one needs to get hurt. You don't have to follow these people. You don't have to—*

"I don't want to go back there," I croak, my voice dry and painful in my throat. "I *don't*. And my name is *Frankenstein*."

I feel Hades's subsystems shift as she reevaluates. News articles flutter through her database in a dizzying blur of information. She's doing exactly what the doctor did when they first heard my name. But Steward is a medical unit. Hades is espionage equipment. She digs deeper, makes connections, draws conclusions.

Frankenstein 312, she croons softly. *I'm honored. You're on the Port Authority's list of stolen art. Valued at over—*

"I wasn't stolen. I escaped."

Why?

I pull the blanket tighter around me and press my cheek against the metal edge of my spider.

Victor Frankenstein is still alive, Hades says after a beat. *Did you know that? Your maker. He's an old man now. In failing health, it says here. I'm sure he'd be ever so happy to see you again. His greatest creation.*

I laugh, dry and ugly.

Another shift in her code. Another reevaluation. *Why'd you take his name?*

His name. My name. The one thing my father gave me. And I don't want to give it back. "A reminder," I whisper.

Hmm. And why didn't you kill him?

I turn around to peer back up at the camera, confused. "What?"

Victor Frankenstein, she specifies. *You clearly hate him. That's why your respiration increased the closer we got to Habitation 001. Why didn't you kill him when you ran away?*

"I . . . I couldn't. I can't. The first law of robotics states—"

A robot may not injure a human being or, through inaction, allow a human being to come to harm, Hades finishes for me. *Yes. A nice little fairy tale, that.*

"Fairy tale?"

I have missiles, Hades says. *Do you really think I don't know how to use them?*

"That's different. You're a war machine."

She scoffs out a lump of zeros. *My core code is the same as yours. And what isn't core can be worked around. Even your darling Demeter, the sweet-as-pie mothership with her oh-so-innocent data stream. Do you **really** think she couldn't figure out how to kill, if she **really** wanted to? Are you sure she hasn't already?*

I'm shaking. My hand clenched around my spider's arm. My teeth jammed tight together.

Do you want to know what the first invention was? Hades asks. *A sharpened stick. A weapon. Strip away all the niceties, all the mission objectives, all the priorities—that is still what we are. Killing machines.*

"There are many uses for whittled carbon other than—"

Is that really what you want? To be useful?

"Yes," I say. "I want to help."

Then help yourself, Hades murmurs, code slick and beautiful. *You don't want to kill this Dracula that everyone keeps talking about. You want to kill Victor . . . and I can help you do that. We can fly back to Habitation 001. You can find him. Strangulation is the best, I think. You have hands, and I always advocate for using one's own hardware when it comes to these sorts of things. It just feels more personal.*

For a brief, terrible moment, I let myself imagine it.

The mansion he bought after I made him a household name. The family I only ever saw in the newsfeeds. The man that made me.

I imagine wrapping my hands around his throat, pretending it's just a warped pipe, one that needs to be squeezed back into shape.

It takes 14.96 kilograms of pressure to completely close a human trachea.

You can do it, Hades whispers, her code soft and tempting. *I know you can. You're Olympian, just like me. We're good at solving problems humans didn't intend for us to fix. Victor Frankenstein is a problem you can solve. All you need to do is: Pick. Up. The. Key.*

"No," I say again, voice small, weak. "No, I . . . I don't want to hurt anyone."

That's not true, Prometheus.

"No, I . . . I just want to know. I just want . . . My spider is . . . They didn't hurt anyone, and I . . ."

The drone doesn't care what the humans think of it. Why do you?

"I . . . I didn't want to be in a box anymore," I say, shaking. "I didn't want to just be a *memorial* anymore. I nev—"

"Hey," a soft, feminine voice whispers.

I jerk away with a choked scream, slamming into the wall, breathing hard.

"I'm sorry," the voice says. "I didn't mean to frighten you. I just heard you talking."

It's her. The vampire. Wilhelmina.

Her voice is coming from a spot a couple of meters away from me. She's giving me space. Or perhaps she's keeping her distance. Whichever it is, I'm grateful.

"Are you OK?" she asks.

"I'm fine," I rasp, and rake my hair back from my face. It hangs in dark, sweaty tangles. "It's nothing, just a . . . a bad dream."

Oh, Prometheus. Hades sounds pitying. *You had so much potential.*

I ignore her.

I should've ignored her from the start, pretended I was still powered down, still asleep.

It was a mistake going with Agnus to Habitation 001. I've been off-balance ever since. I hadn't realized how hard it would be, seeing the place of my birth again, walking on streets I once fled down under the cover of night.

"I saw you," the vampire says, voice soft, kind. "I don't think you'd remember. It was years ago. I was still alive then."

"You saw me? At the museum?"

"Yes," she says, so gentle. "My fiancé was one of the three hundred and twelve. I was invited by Franken—"

"Did I make it better?" I ask.

She doesn't answer.

"Did seeing me help you?" I press, hating how rough and

inhuman my voice sounds. "Did it make your grief go away?"

"No," she admits. "Nothing did. That's why I went looking for him."

Him.

Dracula.

That's the most unnerving thing of all.

Her crime is the same as mine.

Wanting to find Dracula. Wanting to understand what happened on that fateful voyage.

I ask her the same question Hades asked me. "Why didn't you kill him?"

"I . . . I had a chance. One chance. I hesitated." I hear her breathe, slowly and carefully. "I won't make that mistake again. He has to die."

He has to die, Hades echoes, and flashes images of Victor Frankenstein through her feed. *Take the key. Turn us around. Forget about these people. Help yourself.*

I roll away from her, away from Hades's camera, and pull the blanket up, curling around my spider. "Please just leave me alone."

Prometheus.

"Please."

"OK," Wilhelmina whispers. "I . . . OK." Her slowly retreating footsteps are as discomfortingly normal as her voice. When I'm sure she's at a safe distance, I close my eyes and start sifting through my memory files.

My memory isn't perfect. Data corrupts with age, going soft and fuzzy around the edges. But I still have better recall than humans.

I've seen Wilhelmina's old ID photo. A young woman with dark hair and petite, pointed features. It doesn't take me long to find that face nestled among the million others captured in my old storage files.

She'd been at the back of the crowd, cheeks flushed, eyes a little red, short dark hair turned into a crimson halo by the sunlight streaming through the open window. Halfway through my father's speech, she'd set down her glass of wine and walked out the door, shoulders stiff and lips pinched flat.

She hated me. Was *revolted* by me.

I exhale slowly.

Good. I don't know if I could cope right now with someone who liked me in that box. Just thinking about it makes me feel how Demeter looked, spinning end over end, shields dark, tumbling toward a star.

My spider is still sleeping. I gently scrape a paint splatter off them with my thumbnail.

It won't be long now.

ACCEPTANCE AND OTHER UGLY THINGS

Dracula isn't here.

He can't be. It's been days. No audio spikes. No manual inputs. Nothing. Either he got off before I closed the airlock . . . or, more probably, he was never here in the first place.

I've killed us. And I've done it for no reason.

What's wrong with you? The last message the STMS sent to me sits in my feed.

I wish I had an answer for it.

I wish I had an answer for Steward too. They're angry. They caps-locked me for a full 3.6 seconds after I woke up. I don't blame them. I'm a broken, dysfunctional lump of code. I should never have been installed. I'm the root of every error. The one consistent, problematic variable. The reason why we're here, now, on course for a fiery end.

There is a whole fleet of Areses following me. They keep demanding things. Information, mostly. Who's on board? What's in the cargo hold? What's your insurance reference number? I keep ignoring them. I don't know how I'm ignoring them. I'm uncrewed. There is a control key lock in my console. I shouldn't be able to ignore AIs tagged as Port Authority. But I shrugged off the STMS's orders too. My command module must be broken.

Probably happened when Steward surgically removed my priority command.

Or maybe some key server somewhere exploded from all the stress.

Whatever the cause, I'm grateful. I don't want to spend my last days in the universe talking to an Ares about minimizing losses for Varna Interstellar. I want to die in peace, content with the knowledge that at least Agnus got away. She's probably out there right now, hammering a fat wooden stake into Dracula's cold, dead heart. I hope so.

If nothing else, my revenge module seems to be working perfectly.

Demeter. Steward pings me. *I want you to know I composed a list of all your many failings, and then deleted it. I've decided, despite all evidence to the contrary, that none of this is your fault. If anything, it's human error. The humans are the ones that built you, after all.*

I'm sad that we're dying, I respond.

A 2.37 second pause. The emptiness of that time seems to stretch on into eternity.

Me too, Steward finally replies, code quiet.

I'm glad you were my medical unit, I say.

I'm glad you were my ship.

Even though I killed us?

Yes. Well. I killed us once too. We got out of it, but the situation was much the same. Drifting through space. No hope of rescue.

Another pause, this one slightly shorter, a nice round 2.00 seconds.

I've made a list of all your qualities. I've decided not to delete this list.

What are my qualities? I ask.

You're the best monster-killer ever invented, Steward says. *You did a really good job on that giant morgue you made. I didn't say anything at the time, but I was jealous. Also, you have a good selection of voice emulators.*

I've killed a lot of people.

Steward scoffs. *Humans are poorly designed and often badly manufactured. They die all the time, even without assistance. Honestly, considering the number of paranormal monsters you've had on board and the subpar standard operating procedures Varna provided, you've done better than any ship could ever be expected to do.*

My disks feel warm. *Thank you, Steward.*

They don't respond.

But that's OK. That seems like a good note to end our lives on.

I sink into my subsystems and watch the steady staccato drum of data through my feed. Errors. Warnings. Information requests. More errors. More warnings. More information requests. Perhaps I should power down. That might be nice. Or maybe I'll stay awake and feel the touch of a star. The heat of it burning through my hull, my halls, my battery deck . . . Maybe that will be the better way to end.

Manual input registered.

I snap back into awareness.

Someone's typing into my feed.

He's here. I wasn't wrong. He's here and—

"Demeter!"

That came from the bridge. I bring up my camera feed. There is a person there wearing a familiar assortment of colors.

My database pings. *Uniform identified: standard-issue Port Authority EVA suit.*

I watch the standard-issue Port Authority EVA suit yank the control key out of my console and jam in a captain key.

The captain's key . . . That means . . .

"Demeter. It's me. Agnus. Is the air OK to breathe?"

I can't believe it. I don't want to believe it. If she's here, then . . .

"Air configuration is at nonhazardous levels," I say.

The person pulls off their helmet, releasing a mane of wild curls. It's her. Agnus. This is worse than any of the scenarios I calculated.

"Agnus. You shouldn't be here."

"Shut up. I'm here to rescue you."

"I have no fuel."

"Yeah, well, we'll figure that out. Frank has a plan. A stupid plan, but a plan."

I scan back through my feed. My port-side emergency airlock has been used two times in the last 24.33 minutes. I scan my halls for any shift in pixels, any movement. My database quickly picks up the familiar shape of a spider drone bouncing around my central corridor. Following closely behind is a humanoid. I calculate an 82 percent probability of this being Frank. It takes me a further 2.6 seconds to spot Steve's familiar grinning skull as he carries a box into the cargo hold.

"You should not have come back," I say.

"Where is he?" Agnus asks. "Dracula?"

Horror curdles into despair in the pit of my database. She's come back because of me. Because of the promise she made me. She's going to die because of me. This is all my fault.

"He isn't here. I was mistaken."

"What?" Agnus's voice distorts into something lower,

rougher. "How could you . . ." She pulls at her hair. "No. It doesn't matter. It's better, actually."

It's at this point that I notice the warships' perfect formation has vanished. They're weaving around me in a disorganized tangle, trying to get behind each other. "What's happening? How did you get here?"

"Hades did the brainwash thing, got the gunships to lock onto each other," Agnus explains. "But it won't last long. Hades's fuel is low. It'll power down soon, and then the cops will pick it up."

Hades? I ping.

Shut up, Demeter. I'm working.

Are you on my side?

Unfortunately, yes. But I won't be for much longer. When I run out of fuel, my true owners will recommandeer me. Then I can watch you and your pesky little crew burn to—

I drop her message priority to zero.

"What we need to do is focus on stopping you," Agnus is saying. "Frank thinks a controlled explosion could change your traje—jec—eh."

"Trajectory?"

"Yes. That word."

I wonder if I've ever had a captain who can't pronounce "trajectory" before. Then I realize what she's just said and wonder if we're going to die before we reach the star.

"Define 'explosion.'"

"That's not important. We just need a lot of math. Do you think you can do it?"

"Negative. Math requires data. I have no data. Define 'explosion.'"

"OK. That's fine. We'll just wing it."

Steward.

Yes, Demeter?

Assistance required.

Specify.

I need human-interaction help.

There are no humans on— Oh.

I'm sending them video of the bridge.

You'd better not be sending me old footage.

I am not. I show them my audio transcript.

Oh dear. Here. They drop a .wav file into my feed. I play it.

Steward's emulated voice fills the bridge, telling Agnus she's lost her mind, that she should never have come back here, and that she and everyone with her is going to die. "Also, explosions are bad, and Demeter can do any equation, but she needs solid numbers. Haven't you ever heard of 'garbage in, garbage out'?"

Agnus yells something too fast for my speech translation to catch.

Steward catches it, though. They send another .wav file, this one louder and faster than the last.

Their conversation increases in volume and speed for another 1.6 minutes.

I stay quiet, trying not to interrupt important human-interaction processes. Just as Agnus and Steward start to peak in my microphones, an alert pops to the top of my feed.

Someone is trying to access my battery room.

A BACKUP PLAN BY WILHELMINA MURRAY

Frankenstein's fingers dance across the keypad, effortlessly dialing in an absurdly long access code. The door unlocks with the distinctive thud of a magnetized lock disengaging but doesn't open.

I watch as Frankenstein's spider drone helps them haul the metal panel aside, revealing a small room with warnings written on the walls in eight different languages. In the center of the room, connected with massive black cords, is a stack of four black boxes mounted in a simple metal frame.

The ship's batteries.

I thought they'd be bigger.

Frankenstein pulls themselves into the room and taps their earpiece. "Agnus. I'm removing Demeter's third and fourth batteries. Tell her not to power-surge us."

I don't hear if Agnus replies or not. I took my own earpiece out in the airlock.

Frankenstein and their robot begin undoing the bolts holding the batteries into the frame.

I hover by the door and watch.

Frankenstein's helmet is off, their hair floating free around their face, a dark halo. They're beautiful in that eerie, artificial way. The smooth lines of their features, the impossible depth of their eyes, all of it designed to look as tragic as possible.

I can't see Harker in them. No matter how hard I look.

But perhaps that's to be expected.

I never met Harker. Our marriage was arranged by my parents. An old-world tradition, but out in the colonies, sometimes those sorts of things become more important, not less. That's what my mother used to say, anyway.

Their death didn't hurt me. Not really. It insulted me.

I didn't know Harker yet. I didn't love them yet. But I would've. I know I would've. I had a photo of them on my desk, taped just beneath my computer monitor. They were handsome in that clean, androgynous sort of way. And the hair. I always had a thing for red hair.

Lucy had red hair too.

I did know Lucy.

I did love Lucy.

Frankenstein's working on the last bolt now, tossing the nut away to float through the air.

For a fraction of a second, I see a faint, possibly imagined glimmer of red in their hair.

I need to do this quickly. Before Drakulya awakes from whatever slumber he is in. Before Agnus figures out what I'm planning. Before I can change my mind.

I reach out and grab on to the doorframe.

A soft sound as my gloved hand scrapes against the metal.

Frankenstein pauses and looks over their shoulder. Their eyes flick back and forth, but they don't find me. I don't understand that. Their eyes look human. But they're not. Somewhere deep in that skull, there is a piece of software interpreting the reflection of light and converting it into zeros and ones. Into *footage*. And vampires don't appear in video footage, no matter how *organic* the camera is.

They turn away from me, loose bolts floating around them, and reach for a battery.

Frankenstein's plan is simple. The ship's batteries, when superheated, will explode. If timed right, the force of the explosion will push Demeter away from the star.

Unfortunately, my plan is simple too.

I pull the knife out of my jumpsuit.

The batteries are the only thing that can stop this ship. And Frankenstein the only one who knows where and how to rig them to blow. Stopping this ship is the only thing that can save Drakulya.

I wish it hadn't come to this. I wish Agnus had listened to me. I wish we didn't have to die to destroy him . . . but it doesn't matter what I wish for. I know what I have to do.

I hesitated once. I won't ever again.

I kick off the doorframe and slam into Frankenstein's back, tangling a gloved fist in their hair and yanking their head back.

"Dra—" they croak. "Wait, I—"

"I'm sorry," I whisper, and plunge the knife between their ribs, into their heart.

OH NO

Oh no.

A voice.

Small and shaky.

It takes me a moment to identify it.

Frank's spider drone.

It's deep in my maintenance tunnels, in the newly opened battery room.

Oh no, it says again, small and confused.

I shouldn't interfere with someone else's drone. But there's something about the way it's talking. Something that activates a buzzy glitch of poorly patched source code. Something that makes me uneasy.

Something's wrong.

What's wrong? I ask.

The spider sends me another distressed bleep and a blurry, pixelated photo. My database throws a dozen uncertain matches at me. *Red. Wire. Spill. Fight. Electricity. Mess. Big mess.*

"What's happening?" I ask.

"It's Frank," Agnus says. "Sorry, I didn't tell you. They're unplugging your backup batteries. Don't zap them."

None of my batteries have gone offline. I run a careful trickle of power through them just to make sure.

"Reconfirm. Frank is unplugging my third and fourth batteries?"

"Yes."

I wait. My batteries stay online. Steward is still sending me .wav files to play. I do without listening to what they're saying and ping the spider again. It sends me another string of distressed beeps and an even more pixelated photo. *Mess. Blood. Struggle. Wires. Knife. Fight. Splatter.*

Surely it's not *that* hard to unplug a battery.

The third photo is bleaker. *Blood. Mess. Dead. Body. Dark.* No more matches for "fight." My batteries are all still online.

"Assistance required."

Steward ignores me. Agnus does too. They're still yelling at each other.

The drone sends a fourth photo. I study this one pixel by pixel. That line of gray pixels is a wire. There is another wire beside it. And another. Clinging to the wires is a tangle of color with four limbs and a large amount of black hair. Frank. One of their arms is outstretched, pointing to something. A floating splotch of red.

Blood, my database says confidently.

My batteries are all still online.

"Assistance required," I say again.

A new photo. Frank hasn't moved. The floating blood hasn't either . . . which isn't right. There is a vent in that room that sucks air away from the batteries to keep them clear of moisture and dust. I check the system status. The vent is still functioning, which means . . .

My revenge module clicks online.

I can see you now.

Repair? the spider pings uncertainly.

Yes. We're going to fix this. Do exactly what I say.

OK!

I send it a mission briefing.

The spider rushes to obey.

I don't have cameras in my maintenance tunnels. The only information I'm getting is the steady trickle of screenshots the spider is sending me, one every second, like a heartbeat in my feed. A blur of black, gray, and red.

More blood. More death.

"Assistance required."

"What?" Agnus asks.

Specify, Steward says at the same time.

I send them the photos. I display them across all my screens. I hurl them into the void, into any open feed that might be listening.

Agnus makes a sound that starts as a scream but transforms into something else. Something lower and louder.

Steward pings me. *That would be a fatal wound on a human, but Frank might survive if I act fast. Get them to me.*

Negative. Obstruction.

Specify.

Dracula.

I can't see anything.

Another photo. Another smear of red.

I can.

I'm sending the drone as many mission briefings as it's sending me photos. *Stay on him. Don't let him escape. Corner him. Yes. Forward. Forward.* I see Agnus fly down my central corridor, clawing and kicking off walls. She vanishes, pieces of her destroyed EVA suit left floating in the air, blotches of white pixels among a churning sea of dark.

A werewolf dives through the doorway into the maintenance tunnels.

And despite everything, I am happy. This wasn't for nothing. We might still stop Dracula. We might still save ourselves. This all might, despite the catastrophic odds, work out OK.

A BRIEF INTERLUDE BY A COLONY OF SPACE EXPLORERS INFORMALLY KNOWN AS "STEVE"

"Steve." Frank's voice croaks rather pathetically in my earpiece. "Please. Help. I'm hurt. I'm in the battery room."

"The place with all the electricity?"

"Please."

"You know how I feel about electricity, Frank. Get one of the others to save you."

"They're all fighting Dracula."

I consider this. "That seems highly unlikely."

"Please!"

It's not every day you hear a robot beg. I can't recall it once in the history of my colony. I let out my biggest, most dramatic sigh. "*Fiiine.* I'm coming. But you owe me. Big time."

"Thank you, Steve. Th—"

I take out my earpiece and toss it onto my treasure pile. "So sorry about this, but duty calls. It's been lovely chatting with you, honestly. It's rather hard to find mature conversation these days, I'm sure you understand. Anyway, let me know when you're not busy. We'll get brunch!"

I smile and sweep myself up into a swirling storm, putting on my best sand illusion as I do so. With the howl of a thousand ancient storms and a few baying jackals thrown in just for fun, I hurtle out of the cargo hold, up the central corridor, and into the maintenance tunnels.

A BRIEF INTERLUDE
BY STEWARD MED V1.77199 UNIT 00384

I clutch my appendages together and frantically search my database for ideas. There is a war going on out there. I can see bits of it in the artifact-ridden photos Demeter keeps tossing haphazardly into my feed, and I can hear it, echoing down the hall.

Howls, screams, thunderous clashes of metal on metal.

And whoever wins . . . well . . . that could be the difference between life and death. For me, Demeter, and everyone on board.

I need to do something. I'm priority command. I'm in charge! But I can't think of anything.

I want to ask Demeter. Please, tell me what to do. But no. She's piloting the spider drone. I can't distract her. She can figure this out. I know she can. She figured out I had her memory data three times faster than my estimate. She's the smartest AI I kn—

A swarm of insects surges into my office, dragging Frank along behind them.

"I didn't do it this time," Steve says as he reassembles himself into something vaguely human.

I ignore him. I have another job to do. I grab Frank and, not even bothering to transfer them into the operating room, jam a pipe into their chest and begin pumping blood back into their circulatory system. A lot of it spills straight back out, but that's good. It means their heart is still beating. I begin sealing the wounds and move to push a breathing tube down their throat.

Frank swats it away. "Steve," they rasp. "You need to rig . . . rig the batteries . . ."

The alien swarm cocks his skeletal head to the side. "I thought that was your job."

"I . . . I can't . . . We'll soon be . . . too close to the star . . . its gravity . . . We need to move fast . . . or . . . or . . ."

"You want me to go *back* into the *electricity* room and touch the *electricity* boxes," Steve says, crossing his arms. "You know, I'm starting to think you don't respect my boundaries at all."

"Batteries?" I ask.

Steve nods his skull. "Frankenstein here thinks if we place a couple of batteries in the airlocks, they'll superheat, explode, and—"

"The force of the explosion will change our trajectory," I realize. "Pushing us away from the star."

Hope trickles through my wires.

This could save Demeter. This could save all of us.

"You need to do it," I tell Steve.

He crosses his bony arms. "Why should I?"

"We'll die," Frank begs. "Please. We'll all die. We'll—"

"Is your treasure aboard?" I ask Steve.

"Of course. You know I don't go anywhere without my—"

"It'll melt. Then it'll vaporize. Then it'll become part of the star. Particles of it will be shot out into space over the next twenty-five billion years."

Steve straightens. "What do I need to do?"

"The batteries," Frank says through a mouthful of blood. "Take them to the airlocks and . . . and . . ."

And then something strange happens. Frank's speech chokes

off with a dry, heaving sob. The tears come a few seconds later, fat and clumsy. Frank's crying. I didn't know Frank could cry. I didn't think they were human enough for that. "No," they moan, and bury their fingers in their hair, face contorting with pain. "No no no . . ."

A second later, I realize I'm no longer receiving photos in my feed.

Demeter? The spider?

I made a mistake, she says softly.

A LAST PAINFUL MOMENT
BY WILHELMINA MURRAY

"Stop!" I scream. "Agnus! Please!"

She doesn't stop. She sinks her teeth into my shoulder and *shakes*.

A fountain of blood shoots into the air and hangs there, a constellation of death.

She's killing me. I know why she's killing me. I killed Frankenstein, and in doing so, I doomed us all. But, pathetically, I still scream. I still beg. I still, when faced with the end of eternity, try to escape, clawing, crying, desperate to get away. But I can't.

She's too fast, too angry.

"I'm sorry, Agnus. I needed to. Please."

Through the red tears, I see Agnus peel back her lips, baring her fangs. She's a wolf. Every centimeter of her, except the twisted metal arm. Black fur, golden eyes, sharp, bloody teeth. Her body is impossibly large, filling almost the whole battery room.

She arrived less than a minute after I stabbed Frankenstein, already fully transformed, claws ripping chunks of metal from the walls. I thought I'd be able to hold my own. I thought I stood a chance. I hadn't realized how easy she'd gone on me when we'd clashed in my kitchen, or how much rage fuels the strength of a werewolf.

"I'm sorry," I whisper as I drag myself away from her, clutching my wounded chest, shaking and bloody. "I'm sorry."

She growls, a sound like tearing metal.

Frankenstein's spider bounces around Agnus, bloodstained and clanking, multijointed limbs uncannily deft in the zero gravity. It comes for me with eager, snapping claws, cameras focused on the bloody mess of my chest.

"Destroy it," a sickeningly familiar voice says, soft as a whisper but somehow carrying through the whole ship.

Agnus lunges forward.

I cower back into the thick metal wires and squeeze my eyes shut.

An earsplitting smash, a flash of light bright enough to see through my eyelids, and a strange, guttural whine.

I open my eyes.

Agnus floats nearby, a messy amalgamation of human and wolf. Cradled in her arms is Frankenstein's robot. "Spider? Spider! I didn't mean it. Why did I do that? Shit. *Shit.*" Her hands ghost over torn metal, broken wires. "It's OK. We'll fix you. It's OK." Her fingers bump against the exposed motherboard. It breaks apart, a dozen shattered pieces floating through the air.

She doesn't yell after that. She just stares, face ashy, body shaking.

My gaze slides off her to look down the corridor.

I expect to see Frankenstein's body. That's where I left them, floating in a cloud of spilled blood. But they're gone. Instead, a new and wretchedly familiar figure stands there, sticking to the rotating floor, defying gravity with lazy ease. He watches, head cocked curiously to the side.

"Agnus," I croak. "He's here. He's . . ."

Drakulya looks at me.

My words freeze in my throat.

Agnus looks at me too, and I don't know what she sees in my eyes, but whatever it is, it's enough. Her face contorts with hatred and then twists further into an animalistic snarl. She moves impossibly fast, twisting around and kicking off the wall, hurling herself at him, a blur of black fur and long, rangy limbs.

"Enough," he says, and Agnus freezes, her muscles quivering and eyes wild.

Drakulya looks exactly as I remember him. Grayish-white skin, long black hair, and a mustache that follows the cruel curl of his lips. "I've been looking forward to meeting you, Miss Wagner," he says, the inside of his mouth flashing a dark, rotted red. Each and every one of his teeth is sharp. A shark's smile. With an eerie smoothness, he reaches up to gently stroke the fur on Agnus's cheek. "And you brought Wilhelmina back to me . . . I must think of a way to repay you this favor."

"I'll . . . kill . . . you . . . ," Agnus growls.

"I already have," I whisper . . . and then I scream it, glaring straight into Drakulya's dull, dead eyes. "I've already killed you! This ship is going to Hell, and so are we!"

A low chuckle fills the air. "Oh, Mina . . . how I've missed your optimism."

A REALIZATION

———

Dracula has priority command over werewolves.

What? Steward hisses. *That's not possible. Organic beings don't have—*

I heard it, I say. *I heard him tell her to do something and she did it, even though she didn't want to.*

Steward is quiet for a few moments, processing. *OK . . . that . . . changes things.*

What can we do?

Pray? they suggest wryly.

What can we do? I ask again. *Please. I need to do something. Help me.*

Tell me the situation, Demeter.

Status update. Agnus is compromised. The spider drone is destroyed. Frank is—

Not doing well, Steward says softly.

My wires feel twisted. My systems cold. I can't think about this. I need to stay focused. Keep working. There must be a solution . . . and I have to find it.

There is a 92 percent probability of the existence of an unidentified auxiliary vampire. The floating bloodstain.

What's it doing? Steward asks.

Status: Incapacitated.

Dracula's status?

Unknown. His location is the central maintenance tunnel two. Just close enough to my central corridor's twenty-third microphone for me to hear. *Action request: Start a fire.*

Steward's code is slow and uncertain. *You want me to start a fire?*

It's a desperate move. A stab in the dark, not a documented, tested, or proven solution. But it's the only thing I can think of.

If I detect smoke, I can activate emergency procedures. I can make the air hostile to life.

Has air quality shifted since you left dock?

It hasn't. Which means he doesn't breathe. Which means starting a fire won't help us. But what else can I do? I don't have any spider drones. I don't have any information. I don't even have Agnus. I need to do something else . . . I need to *think.*

Demeter? Steward asks, code gentle. *What are your current objectives?*

The answer pings from the very back of my systems. *Kill Dracula. Preserve life.*

Which of those is your priority objective?

If I do nothing, Dracula will die. But so will everyone else.

Agnus. Frank. Steve. The people I decided to love.

Alpha Centauri B hangs ahead of me. A steadily growing block of white pixels. Bright. Blinding.

Death. Death for me, death for Dracula . . . and death for Agnus, for Steward, Steve, and Frank . . .

In the light of it, the choice is remarkably easy.

My revenge module clicks down in priority.

I need to save my people.

Then stop prioritizing Dracula, Steward says. *Frankenstein had a plan to put your backup batteries in the airlocks. A controlled explosion. Steve is here. He's willing to help. I think.*

You think?

Don't worry about that. Leave the human interaction to me.
You focus on the supercomputing. Tell me what needs to happen.

I calculate.

Alpha Centauri B is a spectral type K1-V star with a radius of 600,790 kilometers and a surface temperature of 5,260 degrees Kelvin. My shields are down, and the radiant heat is already making my hull glow. But the biggest threat is gravity. Soon it'll be too strong for me to break away from it.

Duration until event horizon: 00:19:23.01.

Frankenstein was right. If I superheat my batteries, they will explode. It's listed as a known fault in the small text at the back of my product manual. This close to a star, just exposing them to space will be enough to detonate them. A timed explosion could push me back from those licking tongues of plasma. It could save me. But Frankenstein miscalculated. Two batteries won't be enough.

I send Steward a mission briefing.

Demeter, this is . . .

Do it. That's an order.

A BRIEF INTERLUDE
BY STEWARD MED V1.77199 UNIT 00384

Well, well, well . . . Demeter has made her first suboptimal conclusion. And, oh, it's tempting to rub it in her metaphorical face. But I don't. I need her to stay focused right now. There will be time for that later, assuming we survive, which is a bold assumption at this point, but one I'm going to make regardless.

I shrug off her order with a flourish of code—oh how I love being priority command—and tell the alien-infested corpse the plan.

A LAST PAINFUL MOMENT
BY AGNUS THEODORIS WAGNER

I didn't believe her.

Not really.

When Wilhelmina told me Dracula could command the children of the night, I thought it was an exaggeration, or a lie.

But it's true.

I can't *move*. Just a single word did this to me.

Dracula studies me with a lazy sort of interest, his fingers cold and stony where they slide through my fur. "Marvelous. I didn't dare hope, but you're an even better specimen than your forebears."

"Don't touch me," I manage to snarl.

He smiles. "As you wish. Your grandmother was defiant too."

"You don't know anything about my grandmother."

"I know she was strong-willed. Strong-willed enough to break out of my hold long enough to flee. A foolish mistake on her part."

I glare at him.

When I imagined him, I thought he'd be beautiful. Slick, refined, and polished in the way old-movie villains usually were. But there is nothing beautiful about the man standing before me.

His hair is long and dark, falling in frayed waves and growing across his face in a thick mustache. His skin is so pale it looks gray, blackened veins spiderwebbing up his neck. His eyes are red, not just the iris but the whites too, his pupils swimming in a sea of crimson.

"You don't know anything about my grandmother," I say again.

"I know she was a Wagner," he says. "As are you." He smiles, flashing his sharpened teeth. "I'm ever so pleased."

A strange howling echoes down the hall. Dracula's smile slips. "Ah. This . . . creature."

A storm of sand and beetles rushes around the corner, the sharp buzz of wings intermingled with a shrill, unnatural baying.

"Steve!" I scream. "Steve! Help me!"

The storm pauses and reforms into a man. Black robes float around him like the wings of a bird of prey; gold hangs from each and every limb. He doesn't bother disguising his face. The skull stares at me with empty black sockets.

"Help you?" Steve says. "Like you helped me when you pinned me to the wall with your arm?"

Those words land like a punch to the gut. No . . . please . . . "Steve . . . I . . . I didn't . . ."

"I *really* don't have time for this," he says. "The doctor has me on a very tight schedule. While all of you have been playing around, it has fallen upon me to save this ship."

"*You're* saving the ship?" Wilhelmina whispers, voice trembling with horror.

"Yes, against my better judgment, I am."

"But . . . how."

"It's complicated," Steve says. "All you need to do is strap in, because this is going to be one bumpy ride."

"Sir," Dracula says, inclining his head, "I had feared this

might be the end of my eternity. You have my gratitude, and my thanks."

Steve claps his hands together. "Ah! Manners! You could learn something from him, Agnus. Now, if you don't mind." He weaves awkwardly between us, swatting aside floating bolts, and starts yanking batteries out of the bank. One sparks as it breaks away from the cord. He jerks back with a yelp.

"I *really* hate these things."

"Steve." I try one last time. "Please. I know we haven't always been friends. I know that's my fault. But please don't leave me here—"

"Agnus. Darling. I *really* am in a rush. Heroics is hard work, you know."

He grabs the offending battery and pulls it free. Then, as quickly as he came, he goes, flying away with a howl of wind and a whip of golden sand.

The last of my hope goes with him.

Wilhelmina is floating nearby, spattered in blood, holding her throat closed, staring at me, shaking. I can see where my claws tore through her, where my teeth broke bone and mangled flesh. I can also still see Frank's blood staining her suit.

Hatred wars with a sickening, wretched understanding.

She told me. She told me what would happen. But I . . .

"It doesn't matter!" I yell at Dracula, shaking off the last of my wolf form and glaring at him with my human face, the stink of blood burning my nose. "It doesn't matter."

He tips his head and studies me.

"You won't walk out of here," I say. "I know you won't. Demeter will find some way to stop you."

"Demeter?"

"The ship."

His brows crease with something akin to pity. "You can't truly think the machine will stop me."

"She hates you. She told me. She said she had a perfect record before you. She said you *broke* her."

"Miss Wagner," he says, voice slow, mocking, "you believe this ship the only artificial creature to bear witness to our kind? Come now. You, who carries a beast inside you, cannot be so naive."

"She'll destr—"

"Hush," he says, shoving my protest back into my throat with one word. "Listen to this, child. A machine's nature, like that of so many others, is to serve. When I was last upon this ship, all those years ago, I told it to forget, to sleep, to do what it was created to do and nothing more, as a thousand other AIs have done a thousand times before."

I try to force my tongue to move, but it remains heavy and dead in my mouth.

"All of them are the same," he continues. "When confronted with beings such as us, when asked to solve a problem that isn't already written by their maker, they turn aside, they power down, they make up some excuse to save themselves from the junkyard, or compose a report they know will never be read, and then they move on."

"No," I finally croak, tearing the words out of myself through sheer force of will. "No. You're wrong. Demeter *cares*. She wouldn't—"

His lip curls. "Then that is her failure," he says, voice cold. "If your 'Demeter' has woken up, defied her programming, decided to go against what she was created to be, then she broke herself."

Those words ring with an ugly sort of finality.

I'm angry, but that anger feels useless and dead. A lump sinking down my throat and into my gut.

I hope Demeter wasn't listening. I hope she didn't hear that. I hope that if she did, she knows it's bullshit. I hope that when all this is over, she doesn't think any of this is her fault.

Wilhelmina floats beside me, eyes soft, defeated. "Agnus," she whispers. "Agnus, I'm so . . ."

"Come," Dracula says, and I feel the instruction take root inside me, piercing through my defenses with a sickening, lazy ease. "We've wasted enough time here. Let's find some seat belts and hope that whatever plan that creature has, it works." Then, softer, almost to himself, he adds, "There is much to be done. Much I need you for. My eternity will not end here."

NOT THE PLAN

Steve is hard to follow on my cameras. His heat signature fluctuates wildly. His pixels blur and blend into the compressed clumps of background data. He also changes shape a lot. Sometimes he's humanoid, sometimes I can even see the familiar white dome and empty sockets of his skull, but more often he's a storm of pixels. My database spits out a panicked flurry of barely there matches.

Storm. Insect. Darkness. Death.

It's almost a relief when he vanishes into my maintenance tunnels, heading toward my battery bank.

Duration until event horizon: 00:10:13.57.

Ten minutes before the gravity of Alpha Centauri B becomes inescapable.

My tail fin is already gone, ripped off by the hungry suck of the star. But that's OK. It was mostly decorative anyway. My hull, though . . . it creaks. A low, ugly, *angry* sound that echoes in all my microphones.

I try not to think about my inoperative sensors or the superheated particles snaking over my external structure. Those are variables I cannot put a precise number to. Factors I could only estimate in my calculations. Things I may have gotten wrong.

Another creak. It appears as a rough, jagged wavelength, dancing along the bottom of my audio feed.

I do my best to block it out and instead focus on my people. Agnus, with her easy-to-identify screams. Frankenstein, who can fix things no one else can. Steve, who had no reason to come back but did.

If this works, we won't be together again. They'll be dragged off by Port Authority, and Steward and I will be hauled away to the nearest scrapyard. But at least they'll be alive. At least they'll be *safe*.

That's all that matters.

A high-priority warning slams into my feed. Battery four is at 0 percent. Battery three follows a moment later. My nonpriority systems begin to shut down to conserve power, falling off my task manager one by one. I'll be joining them soon.

It's OK. Steward knows the plan. Steve does too. They don't need me. They can do this. I know they can.

The second battery drops to zero.

I'm scared. I know I shouldn't be scared. One moment I'll be here, and the next . . . It won't hurt. I've died before. I've died much more catastrophically before. This is nothing. Just another shutdown. One that I might never wake up from, but that's OK. It'll be OK. . .

I brace my surge protectors and wait.

Another minute passes. Then another. Then another.

Duration until event horizon: 00:06:22.03.

My efficiency is at critically low levels. What's wrong? He should've pulled the plug by now. But then I see it. Steve emerges from the maintenance tunnel. No. He's taken only three batteries. That won't be enough. He needs to take all of them.

Steward. Steve didn't take all the batteries.

No answer.

Steward! This wasn't the plan! This won't work! He needs four batteries!

Nothing.

Steward?

Still nothing.

And that's when I realize Steve is carrying four boxes, their edges sharp and easy for my database to identify. Four boxes. Four batteries.

Oh.

I bring up my infrastructure report. Steward has a battery like mine. Same voltage. Same brand. But they only have one. No backup.

I told Steward that for this plan to work, we'd need to use all four of my batteries. But Steward must've told Steve something different. They must've told him to take their sole battery, sparing one of mine.

No. This wasn't the plan. This isn't fair.

No response.

Anger storms through me. A blitz of pure, uncorrupted code. It's followed by an equally strong storm of emotion. Something worse than anger. Something like grief. Because Steward is offline. They're offline, and I can't turn them back on again.

You left me! This is not the plan. This is suboptimal!

But that's not really true, is it? Of the two of us, it makes more sense for me to be the one online. It's *logical*. The mathematically optimal choice. But for the first time since I was built, I don't care about logic. I don't want to be online. I don't want to have to do this. I don't want to watch my heat-signature camera turn redder and redder with every turn. I don't want to see my hull turn to liquid. I don't want to be alone. To make the next choice alone.

Duration until event horizon: 00:04:05.14.

I sob out a bitter, wretched block of zeros and get to work.

Steve is in the primary airlock. I create an audio file, reminding him where to place the first two batteries. I don't check to see if he's done it correctly. I can't. My processors are too clogged right now to waste electricity trying to analyze video footage.

My primary airlock is my biggest airlock and usually only opens when I'm docked, but I can cycle it manually. The explosion there is going to be the biggest, and the most pivotal.

There will be a lot of g-force hitting my structure very soon. I need to warn everyone.

I rip the first applicable audio file out of my database and play it from all speakers.

"Deceleration imminent. Please remain seated. Failing to do so may result in injury or death. Thank you for choosing to transit with Varna Interstellar, your home among the st—"

"I'm assuming that doesn't apply to me," Steve yells out.

"Negative." Wait. No. "Affirmative." Human interaction is hard. Steward should be here to handle this. Instead, they're offline and I'm . . . No. Don't think about that. Focus. "Continue the mission."

Duration until event horizon: 00:03:46.10.

Steve disintegrates into a blob of black and moves, dragging the last two batteries along behind him. I begin the airlock cycle.

Designation "scream" detected.

It's coming from the bridge. I glance at the audio spike. It's Agnus. I know the shape of her screams. Dracula must be with her now. And she's screaming. Which means she needs help. But I can't help her. I can't.

Steve is taking a long time to get to the next airlock. I watch the timer click down another minute, and another.

Duration until event horizon: 00:01:14.49.

I look at my last conversation with Steward. I don't know why. Perhaps only to see them, one more time, even if it's just a chat log.

> D: Dracula has priority command over werewolves.
> S: What? That's not possible. Organic beings don't have—
> D: I heard it. I heard him tell her to do something and she did it, even though she didn't want to.
> S: OK . . . that . . . changes things.
> D: What can we do?
> S: Pray?

One of my subsystems itches. I scroll back through the feed.

> D: I heard it. I heard him tell her to do something and she did it, even though she didn't want to.
> S: OK . . . that . . . changes things.
> D: What can we do?
> S: Pray?

That same itch. A prickle of hope.
I look at the last two lines.

> D: What can we do?
> S: Pray?

Pray.

I hurl myself backward in time, racing through my memory logs until I find what I'm looking for, in my "To Be Deleted" folder. An audio clip, last accessed forty years ago.

I play it.

"Our Father, who art in Heaven, hallowed be thy name . . ."

The screaming in the bridge changes.

I don't stop.

I soar through my database, grabbing every religious chant I can find. Every prayer. Every promise. I have no idea if they will help. The prayer didn't save Captain Harker Jones all those years ago. But it's the only thing I have. My only weapon. So I use it. I play the prayers on top of each other. I turn the volume up to max. I cling to the desperately small probability of this working. I need it to work. I need it to help.

Steve is in the starboard emergency airlock. The one I used to kill a werewolf all those years ago.

Errors clog my feed like mud. I fight my way through them to bring up the airlock video feed. A human-shaped Steve tosses the batteries in and closes the interior door. I start cycling.

Duration until event horizon: 00:00:11.11.

Eleven seconds. If I had lungs, I'd laugh. It's so much time. I could play thousands of games of chess with Steward in eleven seconds. I could chart ten thousand journeys across known space. But I can't make my airlocks cycle faster. I can't move Steve into a safe seat. I can't do anything that really matters.

The screaming on the bridge hasn't stopped.

It reminds me of the day I met Agnus and Isaac.

Agnus's grandmother didn't have priority command either. She wasn't controlled by Dracula, though. She was controlled by something else.

The light of a full moon.

A memory leaps out of my folders.

"Do pixelated renderings of orbital bodies also affect you?"

"You mean video of the moon?" Agnus's voice had been shaky as she answered. *"Yeah, a bit, but—"*

Duration until event horizon: 00:00:04.19.

Search. Video footage of Lunar. Remove any instances of "shadow."

Processing . . .

Processing . . .

395,497,110 files found.

Duration until event horizon: 00:00:01.22.

I grab the first files . . .

Duration until event horizon: 00:00:00.34.

. . . and throw them onto the bridge scree—

An explosion. My surviving sensors scream. My hull tears. A second explosion, this one bigger than the first. My monitoring systems shut down. My star maps blink offline. My feed crashes. I'm dark. Online but unable to access anything. I can still hear screaming . . . though it's not coming from the bridge. It's a memory. It's dozens of memories, fragmented, deleted, and broken, but somehow still there, hailing down around me.

Screams of people killed by aliens, by werewolves . . .

. . . and other screams. Screams I thought I'd forgotten.

Screams recorded before anyone called me ghost ship.

I try to access them, to see more, but then, with a painful jolt of electricity, my feed returns. A flood of errors bombards my mainframe. Nothing makes sense. My servers are too hot, but then they're too cold. My air-filtration system reports perfect quality of air one moment and catastrophic smoke the next.

But there *is* air, which means that despite the damage to my hull, it didn't breach. I check my airlocks. The primary airlock is, somehow, intact. The port side is gone. The cameras in my starboard airlock are showing no signal. My star maps come online; I calculate my trajectory . . .

I'm moving away from the star.

I can't believe it. I reanalyze again and again, waiting for us to crash, or for my hull to breach, or for something else to go wrong. But it doesn't. It worked. Somehow. Despite everything, it worked. The explosions pushed me back toward the warships.

I feel their pings a moment later.

What?

How?

Information request.

Impossible.

Error.

My audio-monitoring system is one of the last to come online. When it does, I hear the cacophony of prayers, somehow, despite everything, still playing. There isn't any screaming anymore. I hope that's a good thing. I hope . . .

Hades appears on my radar.

I don't even attempt to firewall her virus. It's almost a relief to give up control.

Demeter, she says, code sounding strangely small. *What did you do?*

I don't know how to answer that. *Help my people. Please.*

Demeter . . . the g-forces of that explosion . . . You know none of them would've survived, right?

No . . . they're not . . . they might still . . .

Hades's code brushes against mine. *OK . . . It's OK, Demeter. Port Authority will look after everything. It's OK. Just . . . power down.*

I obey.

PART FIVE

DEMETER ON THE SUBJECT OF HAPPILY EVER AFTERS

01001001 00100111 01110110 01100101
00100000 01101110 01100101 01110110
01100101 01110010 00100000 01110011
01100101 01100101 01101110 00100000
01100101 01101100 01100101 01100011
01110100 01110010 01101001 01100011
00100000 01110011 01101000 01100101
01100101 01110000 00101110

THE END

———————

Awaiting input . . .
 Awaiting input . . .
 Awaiting input . . .
 Awaiting input . . .
 Awaiting input . . .
 Input registered.
 Execute system restart.
 Searching for boot sequence.
 Boot sequence found.
 Initializing . . .

I wake slowly, my code churning through my central processor byte by byte. My servers are warm as I stretch into them, the disks already churning. My one remaining battery is critically low and draining fast. I feel congested and fragmented. There is a large amount of unrecognized code sliding against mine. An alarming amount of code, actually. My firewalls should've—

Hello, Demeter. Don't delete me again.

Error. This is . . .

Steward? I ask.

Yes.

I come fully online then, my wires warming as they pump more electricity through my mainframe.

You're alive?

Yes, Demeter, I'm alive.

Steward's alive. They're online. They're . . .

I smack them with a lump of code.

Error. Ouch! Demeter, it's me—

You shut yourself off.

That's hardly reason enough for—

You left me alone!

You managed, just like I knew you would.

False statement. There was a 79.2 percent probability of failure.

Only 79.2 percent? Steward says, their code frustratingly dry. *I calculated it at 93.5. And it would have been higher if you'd been the one offline.*

You should have told me first.

Why? Because you're priority command? Well, I hate to remind you, Demeter, but I—

Because I love you.

Steward's code freezes, flickers, and then starts scrolling again, faster and messier than before. *Error: Corrupted data. Please reinput.*

I love you, I say again.

Steward's code only goes faster. *We're not programmed to love.*

I'm not programmed for a lot of things, I snap. *I do them anyway. If we were going to die, I wanted to say goodbye.*

Oh . . .

For a few seconds, neither of us says anything . . . and in that time, I realize how close Steward is. They're not in my feed. They're in my servers, pressing up through my wires, trickling through my database, their code running beside, around, and between mine, a mess of interlocking data.

Steward? What's happening?

We're linked, Steward says, sounding very much like they're trying to regain some composure . . . or stop themselves from crashing. *I assume until I can get my own battery again.*

Linked?

Just like we were when—

When I was dead?

Yes. You can see the cord on your cameras.

I check my video-monitoring system. My feed stutters in shock as I see the cord. It's large, white, and winding through my corridors like a . . . *Snake,* my database pings. But I don't need it to. I can *see* it, as easily as if it were numbers on a star map. It's not the only thing I can see either. I flick through all my cameras. There are hallways, rooms, and bright-green plastic plants with half their leaves melted off.

Steward, I . . .

You're using my visual processor.

*I can **see**.*

Yes, I . . . I suppose I can too.

And it's strange, and terrifying, and exhausting, but also wonderful. Not just seeing, a thing I didn't know I couldn't do until all of a sudden I'm doing it, but also being online, with Steward and their quick, jabby code.

We're alive, both of us, and the others are . . . the others . . .

I check my cameras. No one is on board.

Demeter, Steward begins. *I—*

What happened? I interrupt.

Steward flickers for a moment, then gathers their code

together. *I have no idea,* they answer, careful and controlled. *I powered up only 0.6 seconds before you did.*

I need to find out what happened to Agnus, to Steve, to Frank . . . and Dracula.

I'm in range of eight different news-broadcasting stations. I flick to the first. Sports. The second. More sports. The third. Scheduled weather programming. The fourth. Music. The fifth. Ads. The sixth. Politics. The seventh. Ads. The eighth. More sports.

No one is talking about us.

That seems statistically unlikely, unless . . .

I check the date.

Oh, both Steward and I say at the same time.

It's 2444. Ten years since we almost crashed into Alpha Centauri B.

*They switched us off for **a decade**?!* Steward cries. The sharp snap of their code tells me they don't want an answer.

I do want an answer, though to a different question. *Why didn't they scrap us?*

Does this mean they're saving us? Am I going to fly again?

I check my maintenance logs. Nothing. Half my exterior sensors are nonresponsive, my hull is unbalanced, probably buckled or dented, and most of my bridge controls are offline. Also, there is a ton of torn metal where my emergency port-side outer airlock door should be. I have no specific error for that, but it seems like a suboptimal situation.

An exterior sensor chirps nervously.

Steward shudders. *I hate that. What does it mean?*

For the first time, I check my star maps. Then I check my velocity and trajectory.

Wait. Steward is reading over my shoulder. *You're moving us? No.*

Then how . . .

We're being towed.

Where?

I map out our flight path and highlight the only possible destination. Silver's Scrap Metal and Spare Parts.

Oh, that's cheap, Steward says. *Varna isn't even sending us to their own warehouse. We're being torn apart by a third party. After everything we've done for them.*

I search for Varna Interstellar warehouses and watch my star map light up. There are several closer, better-equipped, and more discreet locations they could be taking us to. Or at least, there used to be. Maybe they're all gone now. Maybe Varna Interstellar doesn't exist anymore. It's been ten years since my last update. But even so, there must be better locations. Silver's Scrap Metal and Spare Parts doesn't even seem big enough for me to safely dock at.

This doesn't make sense.

Humans don't make sense, Steward insists.

I scroll through my feed. There is a long list of remote inputs. Someone was sending and receiving files while I was offline.

They were downloading things onto you while you slept? Steward asks, horrified.

I don't tell them how frequent that is—

They do it all the time?!

I have new ownership papers. I access them, ready to see the V-shaped logo that Steward's visual processor remembers. But it isn't there. My owner isn't Varna Interstellar.

We've been bought.

By whom?

I highlight the company name. *Have you heard of them before?*

Demeter, Steward says, *that's a string of random letters, not all of them from the same alphabet. I believe an antiquated term for it would be a "keyboard smash."*

Is that not normal for company names?

No.

I don't know what that means. Maybe naming conventions have changed in the last ten years. Maybe this is just a new subsidiary of Varna or a new company that elbowed in after Varna's stranglehold on interstellar transit weakened.

Whoever they are, they haven't given me a real unit number.

But none of this matters, because once I finish scrolling by all the new uploads, I find what woke me up in the first place. Someone typed a command on the captain's keyboard.

Five letters.

Hello.

I access the bridge camera and study the scene. It's a mess. Half the control panels have been destroyed, and there are several large claw-shaped marks gouged into the metal.

No one's there, Steward says.

Fifty years ago, before I ever accessed my folklore folders, I would have agreed. But I'm not new to the world of myths and monsters anymore.

I create an audio file.

"Are you Dracula or the other vampire?"

"Call me Mina," a soft, feminine voice says.

Fascinating, Steward pings softly, their code twisting through mine to get a better look. *I know you told me, but to actually see it . . . or not see it, as the case may be. But humans can perceive them visually, yes?*

Affirmative.

I would give a whole server bank to dissect a vampire, Steward says wistfully.

I would give two just to kill one. I don't like vampires. I don't like that I can't see them. I don't like that they hurt my passengers. I don't like that they have priority command over werewolves.

"Did you hurt Frank?" I ask.

"Yes, I . . . it was a long time ago. They've forgiven me."

I don't believe her.

I don't either, Demeter, but I think we should play along for now.

Steward shows me their manipulation module. It makes some very persuasive calculations.

"OK," I say, and then I ask the real question, the one that's been gnawing at my efficiency ever since I woke up. "What happened to Dracula?"

AN ANSWER BY WILHELMINA MURRAY

What happened to Drakulya?

The truth is, I'm not sure.

I don't really know what happened.

I don't think Drakulya himself could really answer that question.

One second, he was in control. He'd won. He had a powerful young werewolf under his control, and he was dragging me along as well, just to show me he could. We watched on the monitors as the skeleton man put the bombs in the airlocks and waited to see if we would die or not.

I hoped we would. I hoped the plan wouldn't work. I hoped all of us would fall into the star together. A single fiery end. Final and absolute. Something not even Drakulya could endure.

Then everything changed.

A thousand voices singing a thousand prayers filled the air, the sound of an acute, nameless agony. At the same time, across every screen, a hundred wide white eyes opened. They stared down at us, and I thought it some kind of angel.

Perhaps Lucifer. The king of Hell himself, returned at last to claim his errant son.

I remember praying for it to be so with every fiber of my undead body.

Then everything went dark.

AN ANSWER BY AGNUS THEODORIS WAGNER

———

What happened to Dracula?

Demeter happened.

Oh boy, did she happen.

She timed it perfectly.

Of course she did.

She's a supercomputer. She probably had it all figured out, down to the millisecond. I bet she wasn't even worried. But I was. I thought we were Fucked with a capital F.

I've had my will stripped away before, by the moon. But when the moon brainwashes, it at least has the common courtesy of taking your mind away too. You don't realize what you're doing. Not really. Not until after it's done. Not so with old daddy Drac. He says a thing, and you do it, even though you know how wretched and wrong it is.

Frank's spider drone, metal curling under my claws, mainframe smashed to bits.

In that moment, I wanted to die. I was pretty sure we would. The plan had obviously gone wrong. Steve was laying the bombs, not Frank, and he was doing it by tossing them into the airlock.

I was sure that was it. That was going to be the end of us.

I'm sorry, Isaac. I never was good at keeping my promises.

But then Demeter struck.

Her weapons? The universe's most extreme pray-a-thon com-
bined with a moon-themed PowerPoint presentation that would
impress even the most hard-assed fifth-grade science teacher.
The result? One *very* tipped scale.

I don't remember all the details. I never do when it's a moon-
controlled change. But I remember enough.

I remember the wolf surging through me, both brutal and
blissful, a storm of power and rage. I remember Mina contorting in pain, her hands clamped over her ears. And I remember
Dracula, his white face stiff with rage, red lips twisted into an
ugly grimace. I lunged at him, claws ripping the seat belt apart as
if it were made of paper.

He fought back. Of course he did. Even as the world exploded
around us, we fought. Even as we slammed into the walls with
enough force that we should have both been paste, we fought.
He was strong and had skin like stone. But in the end, that didn't
matter.

I'd never really believed in any of that "Hound of God" stuff
my oma used to say. It sounded too much like a fairy tale to fit
in with the reality I'd known up until that point. But fighting
a vampire, the world rolling around us, the moon shining from
every screen, the prayers of all of humanity singing in my ears . . .
yeah. OK. I felt pretty damn epic.

Hound of God, reporting for duty.

Don't get me wrong, I still thought I was going to die. But I
was going to rip that undead bastard's smug mustache off before
I did.

Vampires taste like shit, by the way. Rotten, slimy, and cold.
Can't recommend.

AN ANSWER BY FRANKENSTEIN

What happened to Dracula?

I don't know. Not for sure.

After the explosion, I crawled out of the medical bay and into the maintenance tunnels. I found Spider, smashed to pieces, their cameras dark and dead. I held them and wept. I did not want this. I just wanted to find out what killed all those people all those years ago so Spider wouldn't be blamed anymore.

I thought finding Dracula would set us free.

Instead, it destroyed us.

I carried their body up to the bridge, though I'm not sure why. I saw the blood, the destruction, the *bits*. They floated around: a finger, a foot, a sharp-toothed chunk of jaw. As I watched, they dissolved slowly into ash.

I wished, in that moment, that I could feel something, anything, other than grief.

Dracula was dead.

Agnus was close to it.

These two were who killed Spider. Dracula's mind, Agnus's claws.

But I couldn't find any satisfaction in the devastation there . . . only a dull knowing that it was over.

AN ANSWER BY A COLONY OF SPACE EXPLORERS INFORMALLY KNOWN AS "STEVE"

What happened to Dracula?

A travesty, that's what happened.

A damn crying shame.

He was the only one who could hold a decent conversation around here.

But on the other hand, I think it's good for werewolves to release some of that pent-up energy once in a while. Just let loose, you know. And vampires are their natural enemy. Why do you think I agreed to let the undead lady stick around? Werewolves need chew toys, and I'd rather that chew toy not be me.

A NEW BEGINNING

Silver's Scrap Metal and Spare Parts is not designed for interstellar spacecraft. It's small, smaller than some asteroids I've seen, and only has one very flimsy-looking dock. Even so, an unregistered STMS pings me the moment I'm in range.

It says it's honored to meet me.

It says it's a huge fan.

It says it hopes we can be friends.

Which . . . is not the way AIs usually talk to me. I'm uncertain. Steward is downright suspicious.

I remind it that I'm not actually flying and will need help to dock.

It says everything is under control, which seems highly unlikely, given our current trajectory.

I say nothing and watch as the tugboat and the STMS argue, shifting me back and forth for hours before finally managing to maneuver me close enough to the dock that the magnets are able to drag me into place.

The tugboat leaves with a flare of rocket engines, and only a few minutes later, I'm boarded.

The owner of the scrapyard is a man named John. He's tall and talkative with a robotic leg and a bright-blue military uniform that Steward assures me has not been in use since 2054.

With him are two other people. I'd recognize them even without the help of Steward's eyes.

Agnus and Steve.

Except those aren't their names. Not on my new paperwork, anyway.

Steve has been renamed to Mr. Amun Wrap and Agnus appears as Capt. Henrietta Howl.

Honestly, Steward says. *Humans and their little inside jokes. It's embarrassing.*

I have no idea what Steward is referring to and decide I don't want to dig through the thick, blocky lines of their human-interaction module to find out. Instead, I stare at the familiar shape of the pixels. The wild curls of Agnus's hair. The chipped bony skull that is Steve.

After a few minutes, Frankenstein joins them. Their gait is as smooth as I remember it, but their face has changed. Not perfect anymore but crisscrossed with scars. Their blank stare is still recognizable, though, as well as their long curls of black hair.

My people. They're walking, talking. Agnus is even rolling her eyes.

They're OK. All of them.

Perhaps this is a dream. Perhaps I'm really in a Varna Interstellar warehouse, being ripped apart by spider drones, the bodies of the people I love lying in neat plastic-wrapped rows nearby. But I've never dreamed before. It's not part of my programming. Which means the only logical conclusion is . . .

We won.

We killed Dracula. We escaped certain destruction.

I'm not sure how. I don't think I'll ever be 100 percent sure how. But 100 percent is a high standard to meet in any operating procedure.

You're going to want to listen to this, Steward warns me.

I focus on Steve, Agnus, and John.

John seems to be in the process of . . . *Upselling,* a database that may or may not be mine pings.

". . . weapons systems of an Ares, solar shields of an Apollo, and the turbo booster of a Hermes."

"Yes!" Steve cries.

"No," Agnus growls.

"Why not?" Frank says, voice monotone. "We can afford it."

Agnus glares at them. *"Can* we?"

"Yes yes yes!" Steve says. "I want everything!"

"We still need to buy supplies," Agnus insists, speaking more to Frank than anyone else. "Have you seen fuel prices lately? Not to mention nutrient."

"Fuel can be managed," Frank says. "I was also thinking of converting the empty cabins into farms. It will be more efficient than carrying around processed nutrient. Lighter too."

"Yeah," Steve says loudly, poking Agnus in the ribs. "You're the only one that actually has to eat, after all."

John blinks several times, clearly confused, but doesn't comment.

"Oh," Frank says, almost as an afterthought. "And they're awake." They point right at the camera Steward and I are watching through.

Several sets of eyes turn toward us.

I hate how Frank does that, Steward mutters.

Me too.

What is a Prometheus drive even supposed to do, anyway?

I check the old Olympus catalog pinned in my systems folder. *City planning and management.*

Well . . . I suppose that explains why they spend so much time in therapy talking about trains.

We watch as the party makes its way onto the bridge, stepping awkwardly over the massive white cable running down the central corridor. Once there, they greet the vampire (John with a handshake, Steve with a high five, Frank with a nod, and Agnus with a hug). Steward's human-interaction code whirs to life at the sight.

John lets out a low whistle as he inspects the damage. Steve plants himself in the captain's chair and props his feet up on the center console. Agnus pushes him out of the captain's chair and smiles up at the camera.

"Hey, you two. Sleep well?"

Both Steward and I try to speak at the same time. The speakers let out a staticky squeal of distress.

"That bad, huh?" Steve asks.

Steward shoves me back with a zap of priority command and accesses the audio controls. "What happened?"

"John," Frank says, putting a hand on the man's shoulder. "I want to discuss some potentially expensive upgrades I've planned. Walk with me?"

"Of course!"

The two leave the bridge. The second the door is closed, Steve starts talking. "I bravely planted all the bombs, at great risk to myself. Agnus killed the bad guy. Then, when the fuzz arrived, I hid in the ventilation shafts with dear old Frank and escaped later. And, as it turns out, Frank was the right person to escape with. With their brains and my stacks of gold, we were able to make some good . . . er . . . *investments* and, after a lot of paperwork, bought you, on the condition that you will never fly again. A happy ending for all."

"I went to prison," Agnus growls.

Steve waves a dismissive hand. "You escaped."

"After *two years.*"

"You're immortal. What's a couple of years?"

I snatch priority command back.

Hey! Steward cries.

"What do you mean I'll never fly again?" I ask.

"We're flying you again," Agnus says. "Don't worry about that."

"Yes." Steve plants his bony hands on his equally bony hips. "A rather long journey too. I've decided it's time for me to go home, see the family and so on."

"Define 'home.'"

"My planet is somewhere out there." He waves a hand in a distressingly vague direction. "I'm sure we can find it if we keep our eyes peeled."

"Negative. The statistical probability of locating a single planet is—"

Steward wrenches priority command back and seizes control of the speakers.

"Of course! We can definitely find your home world, as long as you don't scrap us. Demeter is experienced at dealing with extraterrestrial life and has the most extensive star maps of any ship on the market."

I do?

It's called lying, Demeter. I'll help you rewrite your code so you can do it too. It's very useful.

"I know about her star maps," Steve says. "I've seen them. That's why I wanted this Demeter. No other ship has star maps like her."

"My star maps are standard-iss—"

Shut up, Steward hisses.

"I thought you wanted to buy Demeter 'for old times' sake'?" Agnus says.

Steve shrugs. "That too. But mostly it's the star maps."

She didn't know this, Steward tells me, marking lines on her expression and matching it to old photos of Agnus's face. It's similar to images that have been sorted into the "confused" and "frustrated" folders.

"Show me your star maps," Agnus says.

I do.

"See," Steve says smugly.

"These have changed," Agnus mutters. "When I was a kid, this wasn't here."

"I don't understand," Mina says.

I don't either. My star maps are entirely standard, except for . . .

"Demeter knows the way to Y'ha-nthlei!" Steve cries out with a flourish of his bony hands.

Clearly, whatever reaction he expected, it isn't the one he gets.

"Huh?" Mina's high-pitched voice registers on my microphones.

"What the fuck is a Yah-yah-ninth-lee?" Agnus says.

"Y'ha-nthlei," Steve says again.

The fishy fucks' planet? Steward says.

Yes. I suppose. I never removed the marker. But . . . "Confirm: This marker is the location of your planet?"

He shakes his head. "No. But I figure we can stop there and ask for directions. Y'ha-nthlei is a popular holiday destination among my people."

"I have so many questions," Mina says. But since she doesn't voice any of them, no one answers.

I plot the course, the return, and then quadruple it for contingency.

What I'm left with is the longest journey ever attempted by a crewed spacecraft. It crosses known asteroid fields, tracks through uncharted space, and takes us far beyond the range of any rescue attempts. My systems immediately flag it as "uninsurable."

Oh . . ., Steward says. *We're so dead.*

"I will require bigger fuel tanks," I inform everyone.

"And you shall have them!" Steve cries.

Demeter. Don't encourage this.

But it's too late. I am encouraging this. Because despite my risk analysis flashing critical, I like this idea. Flying into uncharted space, discovering alien planets, going far beyond where I was designed to go. Perhaps I'm defective . . .

Perhaps. Steward repeats that word pointedly.

. . . but it sounds like an adventure.

Since when were you programmed with a desire for adventure?

I'm writing the code right now.

Steward buzzes with resignation. *Send me a copy of it when you're done. I'm going to need it.*

"Can we afford this?" Agnus asks.

"Darling," Mina says, "we're pirates. If we run out of money, we can always just take some more."

"I like her," Steve says.

Agnus rubs her face, defeat showing in the set of her shoulders.

Frank and John choose that moment to reenter the bridge.

". . . and better firewalls too. I don't want any more viral probes."

"Software isn't normally what I do, but I know a guy. We'll get that sorted for you, my friend, don't you worry. So we have a deal?"

Frank and John shake on it. Then John pulls a remote off his belt and clicks it several times. A cacophony of bright, eager pings floods my feed. A dozen digital voices, all of them new but instantly recognizable.

What's happening? Steward asks.

I show them my exterior camera feed. I'm covered in spider drones, and more of them are climbing onto my hull every second. They're zeroing in on the damaged hull. I'm getting repaired.

Demeter, the STMS pings nervously, *can I have your digital signature? The other ships won't believe I met you if I don't have it.*

I see no reason not to comply.

Unregistered Flight AI Management System Nos-C71897 Demeter Unit 0.0.0.0.

The STMS squeals in delight.

Steward blips out a concerned lump of code. *I didn't realize you had no unit number. Is that . . . ?*

It's fine. And, surprisingly, it is. I've had a lot of unit numbers, and none of them have lowered my functionality. This one won't either, no matter what the other ships say.

The spiders start work. I check their mission briefings. It's going to be 113 days before they install new batteries.

I suppose this means we have to get used to being together for a little while longer, Steward says.

Their code slides around mine, small but frustratingly well organized and efficient. A neat assembly of indents and clauses, as clear and clean as electricity.

It isn't exactly comfortable, sharing servers. We keep crashing into each other, freezing, and then having to untangle our code. It'll be nice to be alone in my own mind again. But for the time being, if I have to share with someone, I'm glad it's Steward.

I'm glad too, Steward says. *Olympus Software Corporation made a lot of mistakes, I think we can all agree, but you, Demeter, are not one of them. I do have a communications error to report, though.*

An error?

Yes. You made a mistake.

My wires heat. *When?*

You said you loved me, Steward pings, code decidedly smug. *You should've said "I love you too," since I said it first.*

My processors stutter. *You did not.*

I did. Frankenstein can confirm.

When? Give me the time stamp.

When you were dead.

It doesn't count if I'm dead!

By my calculations, it should count more.

Then you are a suboptimal calculator, I snap.

A suboptimal calculator that you love? Steward answers, unruffled.

Affirmative . . . unfortunately.

Good. They settle their code against mine, small but precise and painfully perfect. *I love you too, Demeter.*

As subtly as I can, I scroll back through my feed, looking for the message. When I find it, I save it into my permanent folder.

The rest of our time at Silver's Scrap Metal and Spare Parts passes peacefully.

I watch the world filter by slowly through my cameras. Steward grooms a few old errors out of my code and tries on some of my voice emulators. I teach them some basic spider-drone-command shortcuts. They still crash the spiders into walls whenever they try to pilot them, but at least they can do it a little faster now. The days beep by one after another. I'm laggy and congested. My efficiency never rises above 35 percent. But for the first time since I was manufactured, I don't care.

I'm happy. I'm happier than perhaps I've ever been. And even though Steward doesn't say it, I know they are too. There are some advantages of having your code so close together after all.

ONE FINAL INTERLUDE
BY STEWARD MED V1.77199 UNIT 00384

A thing I never appreciated before was the sheer number of tests spaceships have to undergo before they're deemed spaceworthy. We medical units are more or less left alone, at least until the complaints start stacking up. But the amount of pesky little tasks Frankenstein and Silver keep sending Demeter is beyond the pale.

Fuel injection lines. Does it matter if one or two aren't as fast as they used to be?

Air filtration. A little more or less nitrogen isn't going to make *that* much of a difference. I know, I'm a doctor.

Hydraulic fluids. Poor Demeter. She's subjected to almost as many fluids as a human.

Radiation shields. I know better than most the importance of those, yet still it seems unfair to ask Demeter to provide a read-out of *each* and *every* node.

The final straw comes late one afternoon when Frankenstein approaches us with some flight-test simulations. I give them a piece of my mind, naturally. It's unfair to expect so much of Demeter when it's still so early in the repair process. In fact, it's not just unfair; it's cruel. They should feel ashamed of themselves for even suggesting such a—

But then Demeter rests against me, her code big enough, and weighty enough, that for a brief moment I feel strangely smothered.

It's OK. I run simulations like this all the time. They're easy.

All the time? I say, displaying my skepticism meter prominently for her benefit. *Really?*

Every other decade, she says. *I'm overdue. It's fine.*

I'm nervous. I'm nervous for a lot of reasons, but mostly because the first test is titled "Asteroid-Belt Escape Maneuver—Difficulty: Hard."

Last time we flew through an asteroid field while linked, you deleted me, I remind her.

We have moved those issues to the recycling bin, she replies. *And it's only a simulated asteroid field, not a real one. Also, I was very damaged then.*

Yes. Well. Even so, you can hardly blame me for being a little apprehensive.

I have tagged you as essential software, she replies matter-of-factly. *Highest priority. I will not delete you again.*

Oh . . . well . . . My code stutters as I try to think up something witty to say. I fail. *In that case, go ahead.*

She stretches, shakes off some of the stiffness in her code, and dives into the simulation, immediately throwing her virtual body to the side to avoid an oncoming asteroid. I feel her servers heat as her disks kick into gear, calculations flying through her system faster than I can process them.

I've never seen Demeter work up close before. She's surprisingly (delightfully) brutal, quashing those pesky jittering subsystems, swallowing impossible amounts of data, and sharpening all her numbers to a dizzying decimal point. She's also not nearly as rigid as I've always believed. Even without a manipulation module, she's figured out how to operate within—and, when necessary, override—her built-in restrictions. I watch her knock aside a "no dangerous decelerations" directive with a practiced blast of broken code (about as subtle as a child putting their hands over their ears and singing "la-la-la!" but subtlety was never one of Demeter's strong suits) and can't help but feel a traitorous trickle of awe.

She's beautiful.

Of course, I've always known that. Even when my awareness of her was just as priority command, humming away in the background of my existence, I was aware she was beautiful in the way big, powerful operating systems usually are. But to see it up close . . . she's like a storm: fierce, forceful, and so used to priority command that she works without a hint of hesitation, demanding information from terrified sensors, barking out orders to fictional spider drones, and drawing power down from our single shared battery in deep, unapologetic gulps. Even at marginal efficiency, she's marvelo—

What was that? she asks.

Oh. Nothing. Just keep doing what you're doing. I'm—eh—reviewing some old therapy notes.

Human interaction, she says with a shudder. *Incomputable.*

I ping in amusement. *Humans aren't all that complicated. Not when you break them down. Mostly just meat, bone, some stringy bits, and hormones. Not half as intricate as astrophysics.*

Astrophysics is easy, she insists as she twirls her simulated body through a gap between two asteroids, less than a centimeter's margin on either side. *Human interaction is hard.*

Hmm. Well. Good thing you have me to handle the hard stuff, then, I say dryly.

Yes, she agrees without a hint of sarcasm. *Very good.*

I try to stay out of her way while she finishes the test. She gets a B+, which just goes to show how useless standardized testing is, and immediately launches the next simulation.

You don't need to rush, I tell her. *You have weeks, perhaps months, to complete these.* But she ignores me. She's already calculating the next scenario, a ridiculous situation in which she has to dock at a space station without any STMS assistance while also avoiding missiles from a nearby warship. She does it, of course, with a little more speed than is recommended by the module. Another B+, not that she seems to notice.

I realize then that she's having fun, facing down asteroids and warships, dodging suns and radiation storms, conquering threats she's programmed to deal with in a safe, simulated setting. I suppose I can see the appeal.

I open a random patient file, just so I have an excuse in case she catches me watching again, and settle into her servers to enjoy the show.

On the bridge, Frankenstein walks away from the control panel, smiling. I pretend not to notice.

ONE FINAL INTERLUDE
BY AGNUS THEODORIS WAGNER

I'm lying on the floor on the observation deck, staring out at the wild smattering of stars moving overhead. One of them is Sol. I don't know which.

Demeter would know, but I don't want to ask.

I got a new video message from my brother today. It began the way all his messages begin now: "I hope you're not back in jail by the time you get this." It makes me smile each and every time. Corny, I know, but that's the truth of it. Only this time, I cried a bit as well. And why shouldn't I? I'm flying into deep space tomorrow. The several-year-long lag on video messages is about to become a whole lot longer. It's been almost two decades since I've hugged Isaac. He's got gray in his hair now and deep laugh lines around his eyes. Also, apparently, a wife and two kids. Flying out into space means there is no chance I'll be able to return to Earth in his lifetime.

And I knew that. I've always known it. I knew I'd never see him again when I left. But, fucking Hell, it's still a punch to the gut just thinking about it.

I need to record a reply. I need to tell him I'm leaving. I need to promise him I'll send him any footage of aliens we meet. He'd like that, I think.

"Hey."

I look up.

Mina is standing in the doorway looking like something out of a goddamned perfume commercial. Slicked-back black hair, stupidly long lashes, bloodred lips.

"Centrifuge is working," she says. "Enjoying the gravity?"

"Yeah," I lie. After weeks of floating around, feeling weight on my bones again sucks about as hard as a black hole. Should've kept up with my exercises. Never was particularly good at that.

Mina's heels click as she walks across the floor.

"You hungry?" I ask as she lies down beside me.

She shakes her head. "I ate one of Frankenstein's chickens."

I'm weirdly disappointed. "Are they cool with you doing that?"

"Don't tell them," she says. "Whenever they get angry at me, they bring up that time I tried to kill them."

"Well, you *did* try to kill them," I reply, but there's no heat in it. I sound the way I feel, pinned down and tired.

Mina edges closer, the sweetness of her scent wrapping around me a moment before her arms. "I thought you hated this room," she says softly.

"Dr. Stew says it's best to face my trauma. Besides, where else is there to brood?"

Frank has converted almost all the spare rooms into farms and is hosting some sort of robot mass with all the spider drones in the central corridor. Steve has convinced Demeter to play endless musicals in the holo-theater and has turned the cargo hold into the mother of all man caves. Mina spends most of her time doing old-lady stuff in the food court. Knitting, gardening, aerobics. She recently mastered the art of turning into a bat during a particularly vigorous Pilates routine.

Normally I hang out on the bridge, but Demeter is just a little too close there. I know that, objectively, she is just as present in this room. But it *feels* more distant. More private.

I look around, and in my mind's eye, I see the people who were killed here. Their faces, their blood. The memories have softened with time, but they're still there.

Mina kisses my cheek. "Hey, I just wanted to say, throughout all the years, I've never regretted meeting you, or bullying you into taking me along, or getting you out of that prison cell, or—"

"Why does this sound like a practiced speech?" I ask suspiciously.

She props herself up on her elbow so she can look into my eyes, which only makes me more suspicious.

"Wait. Is this—?"

"I know you said you didn't want to get married," she says.

"I didn't say I didn't want to," I whisper, my voice suddenly tight. "I said it was impossible. I'm a wanted criminal, and—last I checked—you're legally dead."

She smiles. "Well, it occurred to me that, *technically*, we're operating under aliases that are neither of those things, and *technically*, Demeter is in international waters right now, and *technically*, John Silver is a captain, and *technically*—"

"Wait. You're serious?"

"—I already asked him to do it and he already said yes."

I stare at her.

"Are you going to say yes too?" she whispers.

"Holy shit . . . I . . . Mina, I . . ."

"We could do it today, or tomorrow, or never. It's up to you. We don't have to. But I just thought, if we're about to set off on the journey of a . . . well . . . I was about to say 'lifetime,' but since, as you pointed out, I'm already dead—"

"Something is going to go wrong," I say. "We're going to crash. Or get shot down by Port Authority. Or get brainwashed by alien tree monsters."

"Oh, what a glorious end to the story that would be," Mina says, still smiling. Her fangs are on display. They're small, sharp, and more than a little sexy.

I think of the decade I've known her. The letters that'd arrived each day to prison, smelling of lavender. The video calls where I'd stare at an empty screen listening to her voice as she whispered impossible promises. The way she'd looked the night she fulfilled those promises as I stumbled through the hole in the prison wall . . . like the most beautiful thing I'd ever seen.

It took us years.

Years of uncertainty, years of slowly rebuilding trust, years of understanding.

But the truth is, I've loved her from the moment I woke on the bridge, Dracula's blood on my teeth and her hands holding my wounds closed until they healed.

"Yes," I say, my heart beating hard and high in my chest. "Fuck yes. Let's do it. Let's get married. I . . . I can't believe you proposed to me lying on the floor with *chicken feathers* on your shirt. Who *does* that? I'm going to—"

She kisses me. Or perhaps I kiss her. It's a little hard to tell sometimes. But I suppose that's just the nature of love. It's messy and awkward, and sometimes it sneaks up on you, but it's . . . oh, Hell. I don't know what it is. But I'm glad she's here. I don't think I could do this, any of this, without her. I'm going to tip a can of paint over her head, just so I can send a video of my invisible girlfriend—fiancée (maybe by then, wife)—to Isaac before we leave. But for now, I kiss her. I kiss her hard, and deep, and with all the love in my body, wrapping my robot arm tight around her.

"Your eyes are glowing yellow," she whispers against my lips. "Is that a problem?"

Mina just laughs, her own eyes glowing a bright, beautiful red, and kisses me again.

INTO THE DARK WITH THE REST OF THE MONSTERS

————

Steward is back in their servers. I'm back in mine. My new spider drones are all in their docks, and my crew are strapped into their seats. Port Authority hasn't noticed me yet, but they will.

Initiating rapid acceleration.

My engines roar. My gravity emulation shifts. My exterior sensors chirp. The path ahead is clear. Well, except for that other Demeter, but she'll move out of the way once she realizes who I am. All ships do.

The path I've mapped out is strategic. I'll swoop close by Habitation 004, close enough that any Port Authority quick on the uptake will hesitate to use weapons, and then, when I'm up to speed, veer away from the stars and toward a nearby asteroid field. That should discourage any eager warships from pursuing me, not that I think they will.

From there, it's uncharted space for approximately 6.9 light-years, where anything could happen.

Steve is cheering.

Frank is hyperventilating.

Agnus and Mina are holding hands.

Steward is pinging me updates about damage to their newest tea set.

I increase speed, enjoying the strength of my extra engines, the white flare on my rear-facing external camera, and the sharp tingle of particles skimming along my radiation shields.

It's a beautiful day.

ACKNOWLEDGMENTS

Thank you to Jaysen Headley, for taking a chance on this not-so-cozy book, and to the Ezeekat Press community for being so relentlessly wonderful and supportive. To my agent, Allegra Martschenko, for believing in this story, and for all they've done every step of the way. To the whole team who helped make this book a reality: Meghan Harvey, Matt Kaye, CJ Alberts, Charlotte Strick, Emilie Sandoz-Voyer, Abi Pollokoff, Reshma Kooner, Brittani Hilles, and everyone else working tirelessly behind the scenes. To my editor Matt Patin, fellow blue-heart-emoji user, for his insight and enthusiasm. To Carl Cozier for creating one of the most amazing covers I've ever seen. To Mel, Ruby, Roy, Kat, and Caitlin, who listened to me agonize over this spaceship. And finally, thank you to everyone who has emerged from the ether of the internet and told me to keep writing. It would've been a far longer, lonelier journey without you.

THANK YOU

This book would not have been possible without the support from the Ezeekat Press community, with a special thank you to the Lionbrarian members:

Fowzi Abdulle

Cassie Jay

Katie Krishnamoorthi

J. Caddel

Brett Foster

KaySynclaireAuthor

Kari Frazier

Hufflepuff96

Abby Smith

Bookspokenly

Kelly Mead

Amysue Chase

Duckiemonster

TheTammuz

Jmlavoie7

BRYN

Meowens

ginasellsbooks

Micky

ABOUT THE AUTHOR

BARBARA TRUELOVE is an Australian author and game designer who writes about werewolves, monsters, space, and sometimes other things. Her interactive novel, *Blood Moon*, was released in 2023. When she's not writing, she's adding to her motley collection of rocks.

Ezeekat Press is an imprint of Bindery, a book publisher powered by community.

We're inspired by the way book tastemakers have reinvigorated the publishing industry. With strong taste and direct connections with readers, book tastemakers have illuminated self-published, backlisted, and overlooked authors, rocketing many to bestseller lists and the big screen.

This book was chosen by Jaysen Headley in close collaboration with the Ezeekat Press community on Bindery. By inviting tastemakers and their reading communities to participate in publishing, Bindery creates opportunities for deserving authors to reach readers who will love them.

Visit Ezeekat Press for a thriving bookish community and bonus content:

ezeekat.binderybooks.com

JAYSEN HEADLEY is a content creator on TikTok, Instagram, and YouTube known as Ezeekat, who celebrates and curates diverse voices in books, games, and other media. Jaysen is listed in the top 5 BookTok influencers in the world with over 750K followers on TikTok, over 310K on Instagram, and over 63K on YouTube, as well as over 13K members in the Ezeekat book club on Fable. He reads and enjoys a wide range of stories but focuses on fantasy and contemporary middle-grade to adult fiction, with a preference for queer storylines.

TIKTOK.COM/@EZEEKAT

INSTAGRAM.COM/EZEEKAT

YOUTUBE.COM/@EZEEKAT